Love in Reverse

NONA DAY

NATAVIA PRESENTS

 This book is a work of fiction. Names, characters, places, and incidents either are the product of the author's imagination or are used fictitiously and are not to be construed as real. Any resemblance to actual persons, living or dead, business establishments, events, or locales or, is entirely coincidental.

NATAVIA PRESENTS

NATAVIA
PRESENTS
Is now accepting submissions!
Genres accepted range from Urban Fiction, African American Romance, Interracial Romance, Street Lit, Paranormal Fiction, and more...
Please send:
1. First Five Chapters
2. Synopsis
3. Contact information
to Natavia.stewart@yahoo.com

May 2012

Jetta

"Jetta, hurry up! Why do you always have to be late?" Miriam said as I continued to get dressed.

Me and Miriam were only seventeen years old and living life to the fullest. We are on every party scene. It's our senior year and I'm going to make sure we enjoy it. I'm the reason behind most of the punishments from our parents. I always get Miriam caught up in my shenanigans.

"Girl, you know I have to make sure I'm on point. You know these bitches waiting to see me off my shit," I said.

I slipped on my black Louboutin six-inch heels. I decided to wear a short, backless, off the shoulder Prada dress. I brushed through my long Brazilian weave and gave myself one last look in the mirror. I wasn't a thick girl, but I wasn't skinny. I had excess fat in my waist area. My thighs were thick and my breast were more than I needed.

"Girl, I can't believe you spent all that money on that dress. I thought your father told you to watch your spending," Miriam said.

"You know he says that every time I go shopping. He can't expect me to do that when he spoils me rotten," I said smiling.

"True, my parents make me work for everything. Whenever I ask them for something, they remind me of how my older siblings worked hard for what they have," she said rolling her eyes.

I laughed, "I'm glad I'm the only child."

"I can't believe I'm letting you drag me to this ratchet ass party. You know how ghetto that club is," Miriam said.

I loved my best friend, but she is so bourgeois and judgmental. We met when I came to live with my father. He had begged my mother to let me live with him after they broke up. I was four years old when we moved to Paris. She wanted to pursue her dreams of being a model. She eventually married a rich white man. She decided to let me come live with my dad when I was eleven years old. I was so happy. I loved coming back home during the summers. I loved partying with the older kids. I grabbed our fake IDs and Gucci clutch bag off my dresser.

"Damn, these look real," Miriam said looking at the fake ID.

We didn't like going to our high school parties. We attended private school. Most of the students were white. Their parties were either too wild or boring. I had us IDs made to get us in the clubs. The way we dress and carry ourselves you would think we were older than seventeen.

"You know I only get the best," I said winking at her.

"Whose party is this?" She asked.

"I don't know. Some guy gave me VIP passes when I was in the mall," I told her.

She looked at me as if she wasn't sure about going to the party. I was always having to pressure her into going out to certain clubs. She didn't like hanging around thugs, drug dealers and gang bangers. I didn't care whose party it was, as long as I was on the scene. Everyone knew not to disrespect me. My father would kill anyone that did without giving an explanation.

"Relax, we're going to have fun," I said smiling at her.

"My parents would kill me if they knew where I was going," she said with worry in her eyes.

"That's why they won't find out. As far as they know, we are having a girl's night. They don't know dad is out of town. I can't wait to get behind the wheel of his all black Spyder," I said winking at her.

"Bitch, are you crazy! That car is worth more than my life. Shit, it's worth more than both our lives!" She said staring at me like I had lost my mind.

I laughed, "I guess we better not wreck it then."

I pulled her by the hand leading her out the room and down the long, wide stairway. I loved my father's house. It was enormous with a beautiful landscaped yard. We lived in a ten-bedroom, twelve-bathroom mansion with a family room, den, library, study room, elegant dining area, huge kitchen that I never use, theatre, weight and game room. I spent most of my time outside by the pool. There was one thing I hated about living in the city, there were no beaches. I loved the water. I miss going on trips with my mother to different countries. We visited so many beaches, I can't count them all.

We made our way to the garage. Miriam stood there staring at the car. "What?" I asked looking at her.

"I got a bad feeling about this. Maybe we should just take your Benz. The Benz is brand new. Your father just bought it a couple of months ago for an early graduation gift," she said.

“No, this is an A-list party. We are going to roll up like we are on the A-list,” I said unlocking the doors.

I hopped into the driver’s seat as she slid in the passenger’s seat. “Wow, this shit is nice!’ She said looking around in the car.

*****

I turned up the music as we drove toward the club. Miriam was finally relaxing bopping her head to the music. I stopped at a liquor store to get some gum and a bottle. I figured we could drink before we arrived at the club. We hurried inside to purchase what we wanted. Miriam was looking down at her phone as we made our way to the door. She walked into a tall, heavy set guy knocking her back. She fell against me nearly causing me to fall.

“Damn, my bad Shawty,” the big guy said looking at Miriam.

“Don’t be sorry. Watch where the fuck you are going next time,” I said. I knew it was Miriam’s fault, but I didn’t care.

“Yo friend walked into me. How is that my fault?” He asked.

“You saw me coming. You should’ve said something,” Miriam said with an attitude.

"Man, fuck them. We don't have time to stand here arguing with irrelevant bitches," the guy behind him said. He was tall, dark skinned and so damn handsome. Too bad he was an asshole.

"Watch who you calling bitches," I said stepping in his face.

"I call'em like I see'em," he said staring down at me.

"Listen, my bad Shawty. Why don't you give me your number? I can take you out and make it up to you. My name Titan. This my boy, Shaka." the big guy said to Miriam.

I laughed. "What kind of name is that?"

"The kind that will fuck yo lil ass up," Shaka said staring at me.

I smacked my lips and waved him off. "Fool, you better learn who I am before coming at me sideways. I can end your existence with one call."

He chuckled. I tried not to look at him too hard. He had a sex appeal that he didn't flaunt. His clothes were worn and dingy, but he didn't smell. I couldn't help but notice the muscles in his upper arms. He was just a boy with more muscles than half the men I know. A fresh cut, new clothes he could be somebody worth giving the time of day. I wasn't a hoe, but definitely wasn't a virgin. I lost that innocence on my sixteenth birthday.

"No thank you," Miriam said grabbing me by the arm and walking pass them.

I laughed. "He was big, but handsome. He smelled good too."

"Whatever Jetta. That big nigga will smoosh my little ass," she said.

They were still standing outside the store when we walked out. "See you around, Beautiful," Titan said as we walked past them.

"You know they say fat boys have little dicks," Miriam said loud enough for him to hear.

I giggled. She was right. Miriam was short, petite with a big country booty. She was beautiful with a short, pixie cut. She cut all her hair off just to piss her parents off. I always tell her she reminds me of a young Jada Pinkett, but thicker. We were already turned up when we got to the club. I pulled in front for valet parking. We were getting ready to have the time of our lives.

Shaka

It was Friday night and we didn't have anything to do. We didn't have money to buy weed or liquor. We were posted in front of the liquor store scoping out our next victim when the big mouth girl and her friend walked out the store. She didn't know how close she came to being our mark. I had to admit she was sexy as hell. Titan didn't want to rob them because of the chick with her. The big nigga was a sucka for a pretty woman. I watched them step into the expensive ass black car and regretted not robbing them. I wouldn't have hurt them, but I damn sure would've loved to see fear in her eyes, with her smart mouth ass. They hopped in the car and sped off. After not being able to come up with any money, we headed back to his house

******

"Man, come on. This a quick lick. We ain't got shit to lose," Titan said as we sat on his mother's porch.

We lived in the rough streets of Atlanta. The houses we lived in were called "shotgun houses" because of the everyday shootouts that occurred on the streets. We jacked whoever we had to, to eat. Sometimes I didn't know where I was going to get my next meal. I was a seventeen-year old man struggling to find a place in the world. I've been living on the streets for the past year and a half. I refused to go into the system. After my mom got sent up for killing some bitch about stealing her crack, I didn't have anywhere to go. Titan would let me stay at his house whenever he could. Most of the time his mother was tripping. I would sleep in one of the old, abandoned houses on the street when I didn't' have anywhere to go.

"Man, that's like committing suicide. Do you know who them niggas work for?" I asked him.

"If we do shit right, they won't know who the fuck hit them. We can get that crazy ass nigga, Rhino to help us," Titan said trying to get me to go on a suicide mission with him.

Rhino was our other friend. He didn't live in our neighborhood but went to school with us. He has a crazy ass temper. He's been kicked out of numerous schools for fighting teachers and students. I sat in deep thought for a minute. I felt like I was living a life of struggle just to die. I didn't see a way out of the hell I was living. I had nothing and saw no way of having a better life. Life with my Ma was no better. Every dime she got she used it on drugs. She never told me who my old man was, and I never cared to ask. If I mattered to him, I wouldn't be living on the streets. The system didn't give a damn about me. I was fifteen years old when she got locked up. They never came looking for me. I stayed in our house until an eviction notice was put on the front door. As far as the system was concerned, I was grown enough to fend for myself now. I tried robbing niggas to come up with the money, but niggas around here were just as broke as me. We were robbing niggas for pennies.

"When you trying to do this?" I asked.

I couldn't turn down the chance to come up on some real money. I figured with what we got from them I could cop some work and sell at school. Hard as life was, I was determined to graduate. A homeless man named George looked out for me on the streets. He died in an abandoned house a few months ago from pneumonia. I didn't know if he had any family to contact. I had no money to give him a proper burial. We stole a car to bury his body in the woods. I promised myself when I got some money I was going to give him a proper grave. I kept the hole we dug marked, so I'll always know where to find his remains.

"Shit tonight. I've been scoping the drops. They so careless they don't have anyone guarding the outside," Titan said excitedly.

I realized what he said. We had robbed many times. I've even shot at a couple of niggas, but never killed anyone. As far as I knew Titan hadn't killed anyone.

I stared at him, "You ready to kill a nigga?"

"Man, I'm so damn hungry right now I'll kill my bitch ass Mama for a come up," he said smiling at me.

"Let me hit Rhino up and see if he's down," I informed him.

"Hell yea, we bout to damn start eating," Titan said with a crazed look in his eyes.

"Get yo fat ass up and go to the store for me," his mama said walking outside on the porch.

Titan was tall and big as hell. He was only sixteen years old. His weight was never a problem for him. He was fast as hell for a big dude. No one could wire jack a car faster than him. He would bet skinny niggas in the neighborhood he could run faster than them. They lost a lot of money betting against him.

"Go to the store for yo damn self," he said glancing up at her.

"I bet if I do, yo fat ass won't eat here tonight. You know yo big ass can't go an hour without putting something in yo damn mouth," she said bopping her head.

She glanced at me. "And don't even think about inviting anyone to stay and eat. I don't have food to feed the neighborhood."

I wouldn't eat anything her ass cook anyway, I thought to myself. I chuckled. His mama was cool sometimes. Other times, she was a straight bitch. Titan always say she bipolar as hell. I think she was just ghetto as hell.

"Man, I'll holla at you later," I said standing up.

"Fuck her. You can stay here tonight fam. I paid the mothafuckin' rent in this bitch this month. That's why I'm broke. She used all her money for that long ass horse hair in her head," Titan said standing up.

"Nigga this ain't come from no damn horse. This hair comes from China," she stated.

"Yea, now yo ass broke," he said shaking his head.

"You think cause you got that lil fast food job you big money. Nigga, you just as broke as me."

Titan always kept a job. I didn't have the mindset to punch a clock. I was to busy trying to survive in the streets and graduate. I wanted to prove to myself the system was wrong about boys like me. They saw us as only a statistic. I was going to make it out of these streets or die trying.

I decided to stop the bickering, “Nah, I’m good fam. I gotta spot for tonight.”

“She get on my damn nerves ,” he said rolling his eyes at his Mama.

I don’t know why their relationship was so dysfunctional. They had a love hate kind of thing. She talked to and treated him like shit but would body anybody for fucking with her only son. I know he loves his mom. I think he hates that she won’t grow up. She runs the streets like she’s a teenage girl. She loves fucking young niggas and clubbing. She was only fourteen when she had Titan. I guess she was making up for the years she spent raising him. I didn’t like the way she talked to him, but I respected her for choosing to raise her son. That’s the fucked up world we live in. I shouldn’t have had to respect her for doing something any mother or father should do. Being a parent should be something that doesn’t need to receive merit, but with the life we live, it was an honor to have just one parent in your life.

Rhino

"Where Titan's fat ass? He the one set this shit up and he late," I said to Shaka.

We were standing a few blocks from the trap house we were going to hit. It was surrounded by abandoned houses. I knew the neighborhood because I had occupied a few of the houses some nights.

"He'll be here. He went in to do a couple of hours," he said.

I laughed, "His fat ass just went there to eat." Shaka laughed with him, because he knew I was right.

"You got the Glock?" I asked him. He raised his shirt to show it to me.

"Here he comes," I said spotting Titan walking toward us.

"Don't start talking shit, Rhino. I already see it in yo crazy ass eyes," Titan said to me.

"You didn't bring us no damn food? Shit, we been waiting on yo ass for an hour," I told him.

"Man, we didn't have anything left over. I didn't have time to cook nothing, because I was trying to get here."

"Shit, that's cool. Once we get this money, we can eat whatever we want," I said.

"Nigga, you damn near stay in the suburbs. I don't know why you be hanging in the hood like you broke and shit," Shaka said.

He was right. I lived with both my parents. They weren't wealthy, but we never went without. They made sure I had a warm home and hot meal every day. I loved the thrill of robbing niggas. I enjoyed living life on the edge. I also knew my old man couldn't stand the life I was living. My parents hated the school I attended. They wanted me to go to another school to play basketball. I loved the sport, but not enough to dedicate my life to it. My father chose not to believe in my passion, so I chose to rebel against his dreams of me playing basketball.

"It makes my dick hard," I said grabbing my crotch and smiling.

Shaka shook his head, "I bet you wouldn't feel that way if you didn't have a home to go to."

"That's why we doing this shit. So, we can get you and fat boy here out of this shit hole," I reminded him.

I met Shaka and Titan when I started high school with them. We immediately clicked. I look at them both like family. I hated seeing the struggle they were having living in the hood. I was going to do whatever I could to get them out the situation they were in. Mine wasn't great, but at least I didn't worry about food and a roof over my head.

"Let's go do this," Titan said.

We made our way down the dark street. We ducked off behind abandoned houses as we got closer to our target. Shaka crept away, so he can hit them from the opposite side of me and Titan. We were going to hit the suppliers before they made it in the house. We kneeled quietly waiting for the car to pull up like Titan said it does every first Friday of the month. Just like he said, the car came. I gave Titan a look to see was he ready. He read my eyes and nodded his head.

"Kill them before they kill us," I reminded him. We waited until they exited the car. One of them walked to the trunk and retrieved a bag. I know it was the product. We pulled our ski masks over our faces. The moment he closed the trunk we rushed them.

"Put the mothafuckin' bag down nigga," Titan said as we pointed our guns at both men.

"Nigga, y'all done lost y'all damn minds. You must don't know who work this is," the taller one said staring at us.

"We don't give a fuck. Drop the money and the guns," I demanded.

The other one chuckled. "You gone have to kill my ass. I'm not going back without his money." I wasn't playing games with these fools. We were on a mission and they were wasting my time. I didn't kill him but shot him in the kneecap. He went down to his knees.

"Fuck!" he yelled and dropped the bag as he fell to the ground.

They both laid their weapons on the ground. Titan scooped the bag off the ground. He opened the bag to see how much work was in it. I could see the smile on his face without him looking up. I knew we had hit a major lick. The moment I looked down I heard a gun go off. I looked up to see one of the nigga's brains leaking on the ground. There was another gun on the ground beside the dead bodies. We forgot to check their body for additional weapons. Shaka was standing there daring the other nigga to move.

"Damn, good looking," I said to Shaka. He nodded his head. I didn't know Shaka had it in him to kill a man. I've only killed once. It was him or me, so he had to go. We knew the gunfire alerted the two waiting inside. We had to move fast.

"Stay with him!" I told Titan. Me and Shaka ran toward the house.

Shaka went to the back while I covered the front. I shot the lock off the front door and rushed inside. I heard gunshots in the back of the house. I rushed through the house praying Shaka was okay. He stood there staring down at both bodies with a bag in his hand.

"Niggas never saw what hit them," he said looking at me.

"Damn, I thought you never killed before," I said.

"I haven't. When you hungry enough, you'll eat anything," he said.

"You mean do anything," I said.

"Nah, I said it right. I just ate their souls, so I can feed my flesh," he said staring down at the dead bodies.

"There you go with that philosophical bullshit," I said laughing. "Let's get the fuck outta here."

We ran around the building. Titan stood there leaning against the car eating a got damn hamburger. "Nigga, where you get food from?"

He shrugged his shoulders. "I had it in my pocket." I shook my head as Shaka laughed.

"Where the other nigga?" Shaka asked.

"In the trunk. The car already hotwired. Let's get the fuck outta here," he replied.

"We ain't taking that nigga with us. Let his ass out," I said.

The trunk popped open. Shaka pulled him out the trunk. He walked him around the house and we heard a shot go off. He came back and we all entered the car. I thought I was a crazy mothafucka. Tonight turned Shaka into a fucking beast. We ditched the car, halfway to Titan's house. After hiding the money in his room, we walked to the corner store to get some blunts. We were going to smoke, count and divide the money and work we just scored.

Belle

"Belle, why are you sitting at home studying on a Friday night? You should be out having fun with your friends," Granny asked laying in her bed.

I smiled at her. "I'm fine right here at home. I got a big test Monday I need to prepare for anyway."

"You so smart. You don't have to study," she said smiling back at me.

My grandmother was my heart. She was all I had in this world. My mother died giving birth to me. My father was in and out of my life, mostly out. The past couple of years have been rough for us. Her health was failing, and medicine was taking what little money she had remaining from her disability check. She was diagnosed with Lupus years ago. Lately, the disease has taken a toll on her. Some days she was too weak to get out of bed. After school, I would come home and care for her. I didn't want her to know I was a misfit at school. I didn't have friends. The only time other kids would talk to me was to cheat off my test or do their homework. I didn't mind, because I made money that way. I sat in the big recliner in the corner of her bedroom studying for a chemistry test. I wanted to go to college to become a doctor. The only way that was possible was if I could get a scholarship. I had to make sure my grades were on point.

After she fell asleep, I went into the kitchen to find something to snack on. She owned the home, but she borrowed money against it to pay medical bills when she first got sick. Now, we were struggling to make the monthly payments. The little check she receives is barely enough to cover monthly bills. Our house was old and small, but it was ours. It was all she had to call her own for all the hard work she did for years. She worked in the medical field as a certified nursing assistant. She took care of so many people, now it was her time to be taken care of. I rummaged through the empty cabinets looking for something to eat. After coming up with nothing, I checked the time. It was almost two o'clock in the morning. I decided to walk to the twenty-four-hour corner store to get some snacks. I wasn't sleepy, so I knew I was going to be woke for a while. I put on my worn-out sneakers and headed out the door.

*****

It was May, so the weather was nice with a nightly breeze. The store was only a block away from our house. I got nervous when I saw the group of boys standing in front of the store. I started to turn around, but my stomach growled. Whatever they were discussing, they were all hyped. They were three of the most popular guys at our school. All the girls had crushes on them. My eyes were always focused on one of them, but I was too shy and scary to say anything to him. A guy like him would never be interested in someone like me.

"Excuse me," I said to Rhino.

He didn't move. I knew all three guys, because they went to the same school as me. He always scared me. He was mean and crazy as hell. I saw him beat a boy's face in with a lunch room tray. Blood was splattering everywhere. The funny thing is no one stopped him, not even the teachers. Everyone knew not to touch his crazy ass.

"You that smart ass nerd girl, ain't you?" He asked not moving from in front of the door.

My heart started beating fast. Those were the first words he ever spoke to me. I was elated and nervous at the same time. I knew I should've turned around. I pushed my glasses up on the bridge of my nose. I looked up making sure not to look him in the eyes. I heard he hated for people to stare at him.

"Yea," I said nervously. I gulped down the saliva in my mouth to sooth my dry throat.

“What you doing in this neighborhood?” He asked arching his brow.

“Man, leave that girl alone. She stays right down the street,” Titan said.

Titan knew me, because he stayed a few blocks from Granny’s house. We weren’t friends but he’s always nice to me. Granny knew his mama. She would call her a midnight woman. That was her way of calling her a whore.

“Shut yo fat ass up. I’m just wondering what the fuck she doing out here in these streets by herself this time of night,” Rhino said to Titan.

“Nigga, just move and let the girl in the store,” Titan said.

Shaka never said anything. He was leaning against the wall just looking at us. I had a few classes with him. He was a street boy, but a fucking genius. It was funny to me. One would think they never attended school, but they were there consistently. Rhino was tall and slender. He was light brown with long dreads in his hair. He wore a pair of loose fitting jeans, oversized black tee shirt and Timberland boots.

“What you come to get from the store. You must be smoking?” He asked with a smirk on his face.

Shaka laughed, “Man, leave her alone. You know damn well she don’t smoke.”

He finally stepped to the side and let me in the store. I breathed a sigh of relief reminding myself never to walk to the store this time of night again. I grabbed as much junk food as I could with the ten dollars I had. They were still standing outside talking and laughing when I walked outside the door. I prayed Rhino didn’t bother me again. He glanced at me but didn’t say anything. I dropped my head and started walking fast. They started walking behind me. I could hear them talking about dividing the money they had. I wondered where they got money from. I knew the only one worked was Titan. It wasn’t enough to divide between the three of them I’m sure. I put my headphones on and turned on my music to drown them out. I stepped off the curb to cross the street. I was immediately snatched back by my arm and slung to the pavement. I immediately started screaming with my eyes closed. I prayed they weren’t going to rape or kill me.

“Shut the fuck up!” He barked snatching my headphones from ears .

I immediately stopped crying. I laid on the pavement in a fetal position sobbing quietly with my eyes closed. I waited until one of them put their hands on me.

There was no way I could get away from them. I only hoped I came out of this alive. I didn't want to leave my Granny in this world alone.

"That car almost hit yo blind ass!" Rhino said angrily.

I slowly opened my eyes. A beautiful, black car was rammed into a pole across the street. Shaka and Titan were crossing the street. I was praying whoever was inside was okay. I never saw or heard the car coming. I was surprised when he helped me stand up. I mistakenly stared into his eyes. Just for a brief moment, they seemed soft and caring.

"You straight?" He asked. I nodded my head.

He walked across the street to the car. I stood on the sidewalk still discombobulated at how fast everything happened. I watched as a girl jumped out the car disoriented. It was obvious she was drunk. She looked around and then focused on the car. She covered her mouth in shock as she examined the damage to the expensive car. The front of the car was damaged with smoke coming from under the hood. I saw Titan pulling a girl from the passenger side of the car. I prayed she was okay. I immediately rushed across the street. I was relieved to see she was able to stand. Titan held on to her, because her balance was off. Blood was dripping from a small gash on her forehead.

"You stupid bitch! You made me wreck my Daddy's car!" the other girl screamed at me as she walked up on me.

I stood there shocked that she was blaming me for this accident. All I wanted was some snacks to eat while I study. Now, I was almost killed and blamed for wrecking a car I wasn't driving. The girl looked like she wanted to snatch my head off. I don't know why my eyes immediately went to Rhino. He stared at the girl with those crazy eyes that I fear so much.

Titan

"You wrecked yo own shit! You shouldn't have been driving so damn fast!" Shaka said to the girl that yelled at Maribelle.

I knew Maribelle from the neighborhood and school. People in the neighborhood called her Belle, students at school referred to her as "Nerd Girl" because she was so smart. She was shy and didn't have any friends.

"You shut the fuck up! I'm not talking to you," she screamed at Shaka. Shaka chuckled and shook his head.

"Oh my God, are you okay?" She asked her friend who was standing beside me.

"Yea, my head just hurts. I think I need stitches," she said wobbling. They were both drunk as hell.

"Nah, you good. It ain't that bad. You just need to clean it up," I said.

She looked up at me. "Thank you." I nodded my head.

She was beautiful even though she was wasted. She smelled like peppermint and cocoa butter. I held on to her slim waist as she struggled to keep her balance. I know if she was sober she wouldn't dare let me touch her.

"I have so many questions about the scene. Why the fuck you driving drunk? Why you in the neighborhood with a car like that? And why the fuck you driving so damn fast, Shawty?" "Who the fuck is y'all? Man, this shit suspect. We need to get the hell out of here," Rhino ranted.

"We took the wrong exit driving home. We were driving to find our way back to the interstate," said the short beauty standing beside me.

"What's y'all names?" I asked.

The beauty standing beside me answered, "I'm Miriam and this my best friend, Jetta. We have to get her father's car home before the cops come. They will arrest her."

"Shit, I don't know what you looking at us for. We didn't wreck it," Shaka said. Miriam starting puking everywhere.

"Damn," I said as I looked down to see vomit covering my shoes.

"I need to lay down," she said bending over.

"Please, just help us get home. We both are in no condition to drive," Jetta pleaded.

Rhino laughed. "Shit, you knew that before you got in the car." Me and Shaka laughed with him.

"Here, drink this water. She needs to sit down," Belle said handing Miriam a bottle of water. She gulped the water down never stopping until it was empty.

Rhino looked at Jetta, "You need to apologize to her before we do anything for you."

"Man, we ain't helping her rude ass! Fuck her! We got shit to do," Shaka said walking up to him.

"Please! I can pay you. I have plenty of money. Just help me now, and I'll pay you Monday morning," she pleaded with us.

"Shit, why Monday?" I asked.

"Because I can't get my hands-on cash to pay you tonight. I have to go the bank," she explained. I looked at Shaka and Rhino.

"Nah, we need the money now," Shaka said.

"Fine! These earrings are worth over ten thousand dollars. You can pawn them," she said taking them out her ear. She shoved them in Shaka's hands. He put them in his pocket.

"Jetta, your grandmother gave you them," Miriam said to her.

"I don't have a choice," she said sadly.

"Now, apologize to "Nerd Girl," Rhino said mean mugging at her.

She exhaled in frustration. She reluctantly apologized to Belle. Shaka sat in the car. It surprisingly started. He backed the car away from the pole.

"This car is a two-seater. How you plan on getting the car, you and your friend home if I'm driving?" Shaka asked Jetta.

"Don't one of you have a car?" Jetta asked.

"Nah, we walk where the fuck we need to go," I said.

"Just sad," Jetta said shaking her head.

"Bitch, you can drive yo damn self. We ain't gotta do this bullshit," Shaka said getting out the car.

"I'm sorry. Please," Jetta pleaded again.

I looked at Miriam. She looked like she was going to pass out. I opened the car door and sat her in the passenger seat of the Spyder. She sat in the car resting her head on the headrest.

"I'll be back in a few minutes," I said before jogging off.

I saw a car parked on the side of the road and hotwired it. I drove back to the spot. Jetta stood there debating rather to get in the car or not. After Rhino threatened to leave her standing on the curb, she hopped in the car.

"Gone in the house and forget this shit happened tonight," Rhino said to Belle. She didn't waste any time getting away from all of us.

*****

Shaka trailed us as he drove the Spyder with Miriam in the passenger seat. Rhino sat in the front seat with me while Jetta sat in the back seat of the stolen car. We drove in silence. It was too dark, but I knew the area we were in. I dreamed of living in an area like this. We pulled up to a huge mansion with a locked fence. Jetta jumped out the car and walked up to the gate. She put the security code in and the gate opened. She got back in the car and we drove up the driveway. Shaka pulled the car into the garage once she opened the garage door. I don't know who her dad was, but it was obvious he had plenty of money. I didn't know what she planned on telling her dad about his car and didn't care. My only concern was getting Miriam somewhere she could rest. I'm sure I'll never see the beauty again. I just wanted to make sure she was okay. I got out the car and helped her out.

"I don't know you. I don't want you going into my house," Jetta said to me. I chuckled.

"Stop being so damn rude, Jetta. Thank you, I'm okay to walk," she said giving me an angelic smile.

"Stay woke for a few hours. You might have a concussion. If you do, the worse thing you can do is go to sleep," I advised her. She nodded her head.

"Come on, we did what we had to do," Shaka said. "You have one week to find me, or I will pawn the earrings."

"How am I supposed to find you? Just give me yo phone number," she said with an attitude.

"Nah, you'll find away," he said walking away.

"Asshole," she uttered under her breath.

This was one crazy night. We drove back to my house discussing ways of spending the money. When we got to my crib, we split the money and work. We knew there was going to be hell in the streets about the hit. We decided to wait a while before selling the work. It was funny to me. It was like the incident with the girls never happened to us. At least that's what we thought.

Three weeks later

Shaka

"You mean to tell me this lil mothafucka stole my shit?" said the man sitting behind the desk.

No one spoke.

"Where your friends?" He asked staring at me.

"I was solo. What friends?" I asked with a smirk.

He chuckled. "Do you know who I am?" He asked.

I didn't respond. Everyone in ATL knew who he was. He ran these streets. No one ever fucked with him. I was shocked when we pulled up to this house. This was Jetta's father. We robbed the nigga of the girl we helped.

"My name is Omega. I've been running these streets since I was fourteen years old. Not once have I had a nigga try me. What's your name?" He asked.

"Shaka," I said.

He laughed, "Shaka Zulu, the tribe leader. I can see that. I'm not going to even ask you to give me the name of your friends. I know that's not going to happen."

"Daddy, I need to talk to you," Jetta said barging into the room.

"I'm handling business, Jetta. What is it?" He said agitated.

She looked at me and stopped in her tracks. "What is he doing here?" She asked him.

"You know him?" He asked.

"No," she said nervously.

He smirked, "Do you know my daughter?"

He stared at me. I knew if I said yes. I was a dead man. I could see rage building in his eyes. I glanced at her and she pleaded with me through her eyes to say no. I almost got caught up staring at her. Her deep chocolate skin looked as if it was poured on her body. She was wearing a pair of short jean shorts that showed her thick, brown thighs.

"Nah," I said.

"What do you want, Jetta?" He asked.

"I know I'm on punishment, but this my last year in school. Miriam is having a big party. Can I please go?" She asked.

"No," he replied.

"Please Daddy. It's at the country club. You know her parents are strict, so I'll behave. You can take me and pick me up," she pleaded.

He sat in silence for a few minutes, "Give a few minutes and I'll discuss this with you later."

She cut her eyes at me and hurried out the room. She was a spoiled brat that I wanted to stay away from. I never heard from her after that night we helped her. I was surprised she never returned to get her earrings. I guess they weren't as important as she claimed.

"What do you supposed we do about you stealing my shit?" He asked.

I knew I was a dead man. There was no way he was going to let me live. We had stolen over fifty thousand dollars of his product. With the money we took from the customers, we came up big. We were smart enough not to start spending the money. We were pushing the drugs through the school. I didn't reply to his question, because I already knew my fate.

"I don't usually do this, but I'm going to honor Los' request. He told me you could've killed him. He knows you from the streets. He thinks you would be a bigger asset alive," he said.

I glanced at Los. He never looked at me. I didn't know if him speaking on my behalf was a good or bad thing. I knew I made a mistake letting that nigga go. I knew him from the streets. He was homeless just like me. I had sympathy for him, because I knew he had a daughter. I'm not surprised he snitched on me. He had to save his own life. I was willing to pay the price for trying to come up.

"You are going to work the money off that you owe me. I would advise you to get with yo boys and make that happen. You will run errands for me when necessary. You know, like my lil errand boy," he said with a smirk.

I hated the thought of a man owning me. I didn't have a choice in this matter. I knew if I didn't do as he requested, he would find Titan and Rhino. I put us in this situation by letting Los live, so I had to get us out.

"Your first errand is taking my daughter to this party. See, not only did I honor Los' request, I also know you know my daughter. She drove my car from the house, you drove it back. I know what happened to my car. I owe you for bringing my car and daughter home safely. Since, she seems to be in good hands with you around I trust you to take her to the party," he instructed.

"Hell nah, I'm not a got damn babysitter," I barked.

He laughed, "You don't have a choice. Kill will give you work to sell. You will bring him the money the end of each month. I expect all of it to be sold, so you can reup. I expect you to be here Saturday night to pick Jetta up for the party. Leave your phone number with Kill."

Kill looked like a grimy nigga that I knew to stay the fuck away from. Omega left the room leaving me sitting there furious. I hopped back in the car for them to take me back to the hood.

“I would’ve killed yo punk ass,” Kill said looking through the rearview mirror at me.

“Nigga, fuck you,” I said mean mugging him. Los sat in the passenger seat quietly.

*****

The remainder of the ride was quiet until we pulled up to a corner in Titan’s neighborhood. I was glad Titan and Rhino wasn’t posted on any of the corners. I know if Los spotted them he would tell Omega. Everyone on the corners started whispering when I stepped out the back seat. I guess they figured I was running with Omega’s team. I wish that was the case. I was about to become Omega’s do-boy.

“What’s yo damn number?” Kill asked. I hopped out the car without responding.

“Yo Shaka, you don’t wanna do this,” Los said getting out the car.

“Nigga, I didn’t ask for your help,” I said walking up to him.

"I know you didn't. I owed you. You could've killed me," he said.

"I wish I would've now. Got me babysitting some spoiled ass bitch," I said.

"My bad, man. That was some cruel and unusual punishment," he said smiling. I shook my head.

"You ain't gotta deal with that nigga. Just give me yo number. I'll hit you up with some work in a day or two," he said.

I gave him my number and he stored it in his phone. He called my phone, so I could save his number. I didn't know how, but I knew something was going to change in my life. I just didn't know if it was for the good or bad.

Five years later

Rhino

"How we gone get that nigga to the club. You know he hates being around a crowd of people," Titan asked sitting in my passenger seat as I drove.

"I told him we got some new customers that wanted to cop. He thinks they only want to meet at the club. He wasn't with that shit, but you know that nigga ain't turning down money," I said smiling.

Life had changed for us over the last five years. Shaka didn't tell us about Los snitching him out to Omega. Los stepped to us calling us out for leaving Shaka holding the bag. Of course, we had no idea what he was talking about. Los filled us in on everything. We wondered why Shaka wasn't hanging on the blocks with us much. We just thought he was studying hard for his last year of school. All of us was graduating the same year. Me and Titan had satisfactory grades, but Shaka was smart as fuck. People thought we were just dumb niggas hanging in the streets. We confronted Shaka about working to pay off our debt. We didn't fault him for letting Los live. Shaka could be a mean ass nigga, but he had a soft heart for things that mattered to him. Los was once out there with him in the streets . He respected Los for getting on his feet. He didn't want to end his life when he was finally getting on his feet. We went to work with him to pay back our debt. Omega was so shocked at how fast we paid the debt back, he hired us permanently. Now, we are money making niggas with our own cars and homes.

"Yo Titan, ain't that yo damn uncle," I said laughing as we pulled into KFC parking lot.

"Where?" He asked looking around.

"You see that nigga on his scooter at the drive thru."

His uncle was a diabetic. His legs were amputated after an infection set in. He was Titan's only uncle. His mother and uncle shared a house Titan purchased for them. He was always in the streets caking crack heads.

"Man, look at this shit! Yea, that's that nigga," he said jumping out the car when I parked.

"Unc, what the hell you doing riding yo scooter through the drive though?" Titan asked as we walked toward him.

"Boy, I ain't got no damn legs to walk my ass in there. Your mama was supposed to drop me off something to eat, but you know how that goes."

"You should've called me. I would've gotten it," Titan said.

"I didn't want to tempt you to get fat again. You done got all in shape and shit. You don't need to be eating this unhealthy food," he said seriously.

I burst into laughter. Titan loss hell of weight when he got locked up for stealing a car. He did almost two years. It happened right after we graduated. He worked out while locked up and came out looking like a different person.

"Man, I work out every damn day. I can afford to eat. You a damn diabetic. You shouldn't be eaten this shit," Titan said laughing.

"Shit, I'm a dying man. I'm gone eat what the fuck I want while I can," his Uncle said laughing.

"Get out these streets on that thing. You know how wild these fools get," I told him.

"Here, pay for your food," Titan said giving him a fifty-dollar bill.

"Shit, I got enough to get my dick sucked by crack head Glenda now. Look at God," Unc said smiling. We burst out laughing.

I was shocked to see who was working behind the register when I walked into the restaurant. Nerd Girl was standing at the register waiting to take my order. She looked at me like she wanted to run for the hills. I hadn't seen her since that night she was almost hit by the car. I could see the nervousness in her eyes when I stepped up to the register.

"Damn relax. I'm just here to get some damn chicken," I said.

"I am relaxed. What can I get you?" She asked trying to relax.

"You can tell me why yo smart ass working at KFC," I said.

She giggled, "I just graduated from Spelman. I start medical school in the fall. I'm working here to save some money."

"Oh ok, I was going to whoop yo ass if you flunked out. Congrats on the graduation," I said. She smiled.

She pushed her glasses up with her index finger and looked at me, "Thank you."

She looked different. I don't know what it was, but she didn't seem as nerdy as she was in high school. I thought about her a lot after that night. It was something about her I couldn't shake. She just disappeared. I thought she moved to another state.

"What you do to celebrate?" I asked her.

She shrugged her shoulders. “Nothing.”

“That’s sad. Look, we having a party for Shaka. He graduated from UGA. You should come through and celebrate your own accomplishment.” I placed a couple of VIP passes on the counter.

“Thank you, but I can’t. I truly appreciate the offer though,” she said smiling.

“She’ll be there,” some thirsty ass chick said grabbing the tickets off the counter.

“You better come. If I see her there without you, I’m throwing her out,” I said. She looked at me to see if I was serious. I didn’t crack a smile.

“Man, is you gone damn order or what? I got shit to do,” Titan said.

“Nigga, chill out. Mena nagging ass gone be there when you get there,” I said glancing over my shoulder at him.

“Titan?” She said trying to figure out if it was him.

I laughed. “Yea, that nigga lost a whole damn person.”

“Wow, you look great. I mean not that anything was wrong with you before,” she said anxiously.

“Thanks Belle, how you been? How’s your grandma?” Titan asked.

"I'm doing good. She still has her good and bad days, but she's a fighter," she said smiling at him in a way that I didn't' like.

"Let's fucking order since you got places to damn be," I said. He chuckled.

We sat down at a booth and started eating. "What nigga?" I asked when I looked up to see Titan smiling at me.

"You got a thing for Belle," he said smiling.

"Nigga, I will break Nerd Girl's back. I don't fuck inexperienced girls," I said.

"That's doesn't mean you don't have a thing for her. And how you know she's inexperienced?" He asked.

"Nigga, shut up and eat yo damn food. You always trying to give me a damn female. You need to get rid of that ignorant, aggravating one you got." He laughed and shook his head.

My eyes widened when I saw Belle wiping the table of one of the booths. Her damn ass had spread. She was fine as hell. She turned and caught me staring. She blushed and dropped her head. My dick jumped watching her walk back behind the counter. I didn't like the thought of her being experienced at giving her body to anybody.

Miriam

"Damn baby, slow down," Lyle said as I rode him trying to relieve my built up stress. I ignored him, and I kept riding his dick like my life depended on it.

"Fuck me Lyle!" I demanded. I wanted him to ram his big dick deep inside me.

He had a big, thick dick and no clue how to use it. I rested the palm of my hands on his chest. I twerked my ass allowing his hard dick to slide in and out of my wet pussy. Harder and faster I went as I felt the head of his dick hitting my spot. Sweat dripped from my body as I continued to bring myself to an orgasm. I was doing all the work. This fine ass specimen had no clue what to do with a woman. He tried lifting his torso, but I slammed him down. I needed to bust this nut and go on about my business.

"Oooohhh shit! Hold still! I'm almost there," I screamed. I bounced faster until I felt my orgasm rip through my body.

"Aaaaahhhh yyyeeeeess!" I moaned as my body stiffened and quivered.

After the sensations left my body, I hopped off his soft rod. I went into the bathroom to shower. I came out to find him sitting up in the bed waiting for me to come out.

“I’m sorry, but I’m in a hurry. I have to pick Jetta up from the airport,” I said as I started to get dressed.

“Every time you come over here you in a damn rush. It’s like all you want from me is to fuck you,” he said.

“Baby, you know that’s not it. We are going to have the rest of our lives to spend together,” I said smiling at him.

Lyle and I were due to marry in six months. I always wanted a winter wedding. We had our lives and careers planned. He has his own accounting firm. I’m starting a new job as a vice president of a Fortune 500 company. I’m going back to school to get my masters degree in the fall. I’m planning to be CEO of a huge, successful company in five to ten years. I loved that Lyle and I were on the same page as far as our goals. The only problem was I didn’t love Lyle the way he loved me. Lyle was boring. When we first met, he was romantic and sweet. Once we got engaged it all changed. I was starting to treat him like he was treating me. He couldn’t stand it. I loved him as a friend and business partner. That’s what I felt like I was doing with him, agreeing to a contract by marrying him. I didn’t mind, because my career and goals came before love. Hopefully, that will happen between us. My parents introduced us. I wasn't initially attracted to him, but I liked where his head was at. We've been dating for two years.

"How long Jetta staying?" he asked.

"She didn't say," I replied.

I was surprised when she told me she was coming home. After graduation, she convinced her father to let her travel for a year. When she failed to enroll in college after the year was over, he cut her off. She moved back to France with her mother. She still hasn't enrolled into college as far as I know. Her mother spoils her more than her father. I hope she will eventually grow up and decide what she wants to do with her life. Lyle only met Jetta once when we visited her in France. He didn't care for her. He thought she was a bad influence on me. I laughed to myself remembering all the crazy stunts she would convince me to do. I gave Lyle a kiss and rushed out the door. I was running late.

*****

When I arrived at the airport, Jetta was standing outside looking like the diva she is. I smiled as I hopped out the car to help her with her bags. She rolled her eyes at me. I missed my best friend. I was happy to have her home. I needed a distraction from my life. She was the perfect person to give me that.

"Sorry, I'm late," I said pouting.

She couldn't help but smile and gave me a hug, "You better be glad I missed the hell out of you."

"I'm so happy you are here," I said squeezing her tight.

"Me too, I actually miss this place," she said breaking our embrace to put her luggage in the car.

"Damn, you brought enough stuff to move back home," I said once we were inside the car.

She glanced at me, "I'm home to stay."

I was shocked but happy, "Are you serious?"

"Yea, I'm going to start school for fashion. It sounds crazy to leave France if I wanted to go for fashion, but my daddy is here. He's sick Mir. He's been sick for over a year, and I'm just finding out," she said as water filled her eyes.

"I'm so sorry Jetta. What's wrong with him?" I asked.

"He has prostate cancer," she said as she started to sob.

"I wasted so much time with him being childish. Now, I'm going to lose him forever," she said wiping her tears.

"Don't think like that Jetta. Your father is a fighter. You are here now," I said trying to console her.

"He doesn't know I'm coming. That ignorant ass Shaka called me cussing me out for not coming to see him. He was the one who told me he was sick. I can't stand his black ass," she said angrily.

I laughed, "Because he doesn't let you throw tantrums to get your way."

"I hated Daddy made him go everywhere with me. I couldn't get away with doing shit with him," she said.

"I know. He had your ass on a leash like you was his woman," I said.

"I wouldn't fuck him if my life depended on it," she said rolling her eyes.

I believe her. She truly disliked Shaka. They would argue like they were a couple. He wouldn't let Jetta date anyone. Guys were scared to deal with her, because of him. I remember he broke a guy's arm for being in Jetta's room. Jetta could never pull the tricks on him like she did her father.

Titan

"Nigga, I know you got some money. You slinging more dope than anybody round here," Ma said as she followed me inside my house.

I turned around and stared her in the face. "Lower your damn voice. This ain't the hood."

"You giving all yo money to that lazy bitch. All she gotta do is suck yo dick and you like a jackpot machine, just pouring out money. I'm telling you that hoe is grimy," she spewed.

I ignored her and continued in the house. I dropped the bags I had in my hand when I walked into the kitchen. Mena was spread out on the kitchen table butt ass naked. Mena was my current girlfriend. We have been rocking for a minute.

"Told you," Ma said standing behind me.

Mena jumped of the table, "What the fuck is she doing here?"

"Bitch, this my son. I should be asking your stank ass why you here, but I already know the answer," Ma said stepping from behind me.

"Man, y'all chill out. I told you I was coming by yo spot. How the fuck you get in here?" I asked Mena.

"I made a spare key. I've been waiting all mone...I meant morning for you," she said seductively .

Ma burst out laughing, "Nah, you meant money. You've been waiting on his money."

"You act like that's not why you here," Mena snapped back with an attitude.

"Man, have some respect for my Moms. Go put on some damn clothes," I said staring at her.

She stormed out the kitchen. I met Mena at a kickback when we started hustling for Omega. She gave me the attention a female on her level never did. They always said I was cute, but too damn fat. That shit never fucked with me though. It was their loss.

Ma sat beside me. "I know our relationship is dysfunctional as hell, but I got love for you. It's been me and you since day one. I know I wasn't the best Mama. I'm trying to change that now. It's not because you have money, now. Seeing you grow into the man you are makes me want to do better. I'm a work in progress, but that girl ain't shit."

She actually had sincerity in her eyes, "Well, you can start by making sure Unc is good. Nigga was at KFC on his wheelchair scooter."

She laughed, “My bad. I forgot. I had a job interview.”

I looked at her like she was crazy, “A what?”

Ma hasn’t worked since I was sixteen. She was dealing with a small-time hustler until he got locked up. She always caking old men to give her money. She even had young niggas giving her money. I made her stop all that when I started making money. She still was hitting the clubs. I didn’t mind her having fun. I just didn’t want her out there in the streets fucking different men.

“You heard me. I had a job interview. It’s working at the front desk of a hotel,” she said smiling.

“Wow!” was all I could say.

“I’m trying, boy,” she said with an attitude.

“I appreciate that, but you know you ain’t gotta work. I got you. Yea, we dysfunctional as hell but you still Ma Dukes,” I said laughing. She laughed with me.

“I’m doing this for myself,” she said.

“I respect that. As far as Mena goes, she’s been with me since day one. She was feeling a nigga when I was the size of two damn people,” I reminded her.

“Yea, because she saw the money and not you,” she said.

"I'm not asking your approval. Just lay off her," I told her.

"How the interview go?" I asked.

She smiled. "They offered me the job."

I reached in my pocket and handed her a wad of money. "Go treat yourself and check in on Unc. I'm going to be tied up for the rest of the evening. It's Shaka's surprise graduation party."

"Oh shit, I'm in there!" She said excited jumping out her seat and twerking.

"Oh hell no , you will not be there," I told her.

"Boy, y'all couldn't hang with me anyway. Y'all go to the club to stand around. I turns the fuck up when I walk in," she said propping her hand on her hip.

I laughed and shook my head. She gave me a hug before walking out. I sat shocked. Ma never showed me physical affection. It was something different, but strangely comforting. I grabbed my bags and headed upstairs. I knew Mena was going to be bitching about Ma. I wasn't in the mood. I wanted to take a long nap before the party tonight. When I walked in the room, she was sitting on the bed flipping through channels. I stripped down to my boxers and laid down on the opposite side.

"So, you just gone let her disrespect me like that?" She asked shoving my shoulder.

"Man, you know how she is. I'm not with that shit right now," I said closing my eyes.

"But I'm horny," she said straddling my lap.

I decided to let her be my sleeping pill. Mena is beautiful. She's tall, caramel skin, slim and thick in all the right places. I slid my fingers between her wet pussy lips. She reached down and pulled my hard dick from my boxers. I flipped her over on her back. I slid my dick inside her as I massaged and sucked on her hard nipples. She wrapped her legs around my waist.

"Yes baby, just like that," she moaned as I drilled inside her. I unwrapped her legs and pushed them over her head.

"Shit, this pussy wet," I groaned as her juices spilled on my dick. I rammed inside her deep and hard.

"Ffffuuuck!" she screamed as she exploded.

Her body trembled as I continued to pound inside her. I pulled out and flipped her over on all fours . I shoved deep inside her smacking her ass.

"That's it Daddy! Fuck this pussy!" She moaned.

I pushed her head down into the pillow and slammed my dick in and out until I felt my nut coming. I pulled out and jacked off on her ass letting out a loud groan. I went into the bathroom to take a shower. She followed me to the shower blessing me with one of her Superhead blowjobs. After I finished showering, I laid down to take a nap.

"Baby, I need to get an outfit for tonight," she said softly as she dressed.

"Wear what you got. I just gave you money to go shopping the other day," I reminded her.

"That was for my trip with the girls next week," she said.

I shrugged my shoulders, "Not my problem."

"Really Titan?" She asked shocked. I ignored her trying to fall asleep.

"Fuck you nigga," she said walking to the bedroom door.

"You just did, baby girl," I said.

She slammed the door behind her. I wasn't stupid, I didn't have proof she was cheating. I just know she's been moving funny lately. I'm just letting her dig her own grave. I didn't want Ma to know I was suspicious of Mena cheating. Ma would've started a full-blown investigation to prove she was.

Shaka

"You made those pickups?" I asked Kill without looking up at him.

"Yea," he said dryly.

"Make sure Los get that. He needs to count it," I told him.

"Nigga, you telling me to do shit I've been doing longer than you," he said angrily.

It's been years since our first encounter and I still can't stand the nigga. I don't trust him even with him in eyesight. He couldn't stand that Omega gave me a position he claimed he's been working years for. The problem with him was he thought tenure guaranteed him the position. He felt like he didn't need to get out there and put in work. He let inexperienced block boys do his work. Numerous times we had to come through and make up for what they didn't do, because he wasn't checking his workers. He was too busy showing off in the streets as the next nigga in charge. We came to blows when Omega called us in for a meeting when he found out he had prostate cancer. He gave me the highest position and made Kill my right hand. I didn't like the thought of having him knowing my every move. I would've felt better with Titan or Rhino beside me. Hell, I would've taken Los. He was still hungry. He knew what starving felt like. Kill was just a nigga wanting to make money to shine. We wanted money for livelihood, success and power.

I chuckled. “Yet, here I am.”

I leaned back in the huge, executive desk Omega once sat. Most of his time was spent in his bedroom, now. He declined to continue chemo treatments. He didn’t see the point in prolonging the inevitable. I hated it, but I understood his logic.

“I need you to be there for the pick up tonight,” I instructed.

“Hell nah, let Los do that shit,” he stated angrily.

“Los hanging with me tonight,” I told him.

I didn’t want to celebrate my graduation, but Titan and Rhino insisted. I let them talk me into going to Magic City tonight. Plus, we were meeting a new customer. I figured I’ll relax and watch them enjoy my graduation while I discussed business. They been with me since the beginning of the come up. Not once have I had to question their loyalty or trust.

“Whatever nigga,” he said walking out the study.

I chuckled as I stood up. I went to the east wing of the mansion to check on Omega. He had a twenty-four-hour nursing staff along with a chef to care for him. I checked on him often to make sure he's being properly cared for. I was happy to see him sitting up in the bed watching television when I walked in.

"Man, Victor Newman a bad ass nigga," he said looking at the television.

"You up for a walk today?" I asked.

He nodded his head yes never taking his eyes off the television. I had to laugh at his gangsta ass watching soap operas. I tried to take him outside once a day. We usually would walk around in the backyard. I remodeled the already beautifully landscaped yard. It was something I loved doing. I was obsessed with looking at yards when I would pass a nice house. The neighborhood I grew up in people barely had grass. I was surprised at the strength he was showing. He got up and dressed himself. He had lost a tremendous amount of weight. Since he was such a big man, he still looked fit.

"I'm not as tired since I stopped taking the treatments. I know it's only short lived, but I'm going to enjoy it as long as I can," he said as we walked out the sliding backdoors.

"You looking good," I told him.

"I'm thinking we all should take a vacation. Everyone has worked hard to secure my place. Your team stepped up numerous times when niggas tried moving me out the way. They thought my sickness was my weakness. They didn't know about a lil hungry ass nigga that stole from me and became my predecessor," he said.

I laughed, "You made us work our ass off for that shit too. Where you wanna go. I'll make it happen."

"Shit, surprise me. As long as; I can get a fat ass to sit on my face by the beach, I'm good," he said.

I burst into laughter. I could see the old Omega coming through. When I started working with him, he was a true player. He said he never been in love and didn't want it. I felt him on that. I didn't know anything about loving a woman and wasn't trying to find out. He married Jetta's mother when she got pregnant. He still believes she trapped him.

"I'm sending Kill to pick up that shipment tonight," I told him.

"Make sure a team is with him. I've noticed Kill doesn't hustle as hard as he once did. "I've been sick not dead, Young Shaka. I see a lot of shit. I just don't speak on it. You handling everything as I would," he said.

I looked at him surprised without speaking on his statement. I wasn't never the one to be the teacher's pet. I never ran to Omega when anyone on the team was slipping.

I handled things myself. I enjoyed talking with him to get knowledge of moving in the streets. He stayed off twelve's radar and made his money. Those were the footsteps I wanted to follow.

"It's already covered. He has a team going with him and a ghost team he knows nothing about," I assured him.

He nodded his head. "You came in and reconstructed my entire organization. I never realized how sloppy our shit was until three lil knuckleheads robbed us. You got shit locked down and bringing in twice as much money. You know, I won't be here too much longer. I don't know what your plans are when I'm gone. I know I want you to consider your future. Secure the bag and walk out while you can. I know you didn't go to college to be a kingpin. Follow those dreams you have once you've made the money you want."

I didn't like talking about death. It made me think of Homeless George. I nodded my head assuring him I would. We walked until he got tired and hungry. I was happy to hear him say he wanted a big steak. His appetite was coming back since stopping chemo treatments. He ordered the chef to cook a Porterhouse steak, steak fries and a chef salad. I declined the offer to join him. We were going to dinner before hitting up the strip club. I went upstairs to take a shower while he ate. Just as I finished getting dressed, someone knocked on my room door. I had my own place but moved in with Omega when his sickness got worse. I wanted to be close to monitor his health.

"Sorry to interrupt you Sir. Mr. Omega would like for you to come to the main kitchen," Betty, the nurse said when I opened the door.

"Okay, but will you please stop being so formal with me. You are my elder. You have no business referring to me as sir," I told her.

She smiled, "Okay, I'll try."

She was a short, nice looking middle-aged woman. I had to be picky about who was working in the house. Niggas use bitches every day to set up a lick. I've been through a few nurses because some were more focused on the men coming in and out the house than Omega. I didn't like that so many knew where we rested our heads.

Jetta

"I wanna go out tonight," I told Miriam as we pulled up in front of my father's house.

"We can do that. I'll be back to scoop you up at eleven," she said.

"You aren't going to see Daddy?" I asked.

"No, I wanna give you some time with your dad. I'll see him tomorrow. I know he's going to be happy to see you," she said smiling.

I hope that is true. We haven't spoken in some time. I regret the time I wasted being angry with him. She helped me carry my bags inside the house.

"Ok, I'll see you later then," I said giving her a hug before she left.

"Ms. Murphy?" Clara, the housekeeper said walking up to me.

"Hi Ms. Clara, it's me," I said smiling at her.

She looked shocked to see me. She has worked for Daddy for as long as I can remember. She pulled me into her arms and hugged me tight. I missed her. She always treated me like I was her daughter. She was an elderly woman with no family. We were her family. I realized I abandoned her as well as my father when I left.

"I miss these hugs," I said hugging her tighter.

"Your father is going to be so happy to see you," she said breaking our embrace with a big smile on her face.

"I hope so," I said nervously.

"He's in the kitchen. Come on," she said pulling me by the arm.

"I have to take my bags upstairs first," I told her.

"Child please, I'll get Shaka or one of his friends to take them upstairs later," she said as she kept pulling me.

When we walked into the kitchen, Daddy had his head down. I didn't have to look hard to see he had lost a lot of weight. My father was a tall man with nothing but muscles. He still had his muscles. He just wasn't as thick as he once was. His low fade was now bald. I guess it was from the chemo treatments. He looked up when he heard us come in. He dropped his fork on his lap. He stared at me as if he was trying to figure out if it was really me.

"Hi Daddy," I said softly. I was scared and ashamed.

He stood up. I wanted to run and hug him tight, but I didn't know if I could. He had to be angry at me for staying away so long. He walked over and stood in front of me. I slowly lifted my head looking up into his eyes. I could tell he wasn't the same strong man he was before I walked away. His eyes were weak. Water started to fill up in my eyes. He immediately wrapped his arms around me and held me tight. My body relaxed as I sighed heavily. This was home. This is what has been missing in my life. The entire time I was away I never felt complete . Knowing I still had my father's love completed me.

"Boopsy," he said softly calling me by my pet nickname he gave me.

"I'm sorry Daddy. I've missed you so much," I sobbed as I rested my head on his chest.

"Come, sit down and talk to me. Why didn't you let me know you were coming? I could've sent the car service to pick you up," he asked.

"Miriam picked me up. I wanted to surprise you," I said smiling at him.

"Well, you did a very good job. I didn't think you could get any more beautiful, but you have. You are absolutely gorgeous."

I blushed, "Thank you, Daddy. Why didn't you call and tell me? I would've came sooner. I had no idea you were sick."

"I didn't want you to worry about me. I thought I could beat it. All I can do is prolong it," he said sadly.

"Well, that's better than nothing," I said trying to sound optimistic. He gave me a half smile.

"How long are you going to be here?" He asked changing the subject.

"For as long as you will have me here," I said.

He laughed. He called Clara back into the kitchen. He instructed her to prepare my old room. She smiled and winked at me before walking out. He sat back down to finish his meal.

"So, what have you been doing with yourself?" He asked.

I shrugged. "Just traveling. I've decided to enroll in a fashion school here. I want to be a stylist and designer."

I held my breath waiting for him to tell me he doesn't like my career choice. I knew he was going to give me a long speech about applying my full potential. He felt like I wanted things in life without working for them. I can't say he wasn't right. I didn't know how to work hard for anything. Everything was always giving to me by him.

"That sounds like something you would be great at doing. Make sure you reach for the top. Don't settle for mediocre shit," he said.

"I won't. I'll be styling for the biggest celebrities when I make it," I said smiling.

He nodded his head. I was surprised by his response. He looked past me. I turned around to see what caught his attention. I hated the sight of him, but God the man was built by gods . I'm not talking regular gods . I'm talking some alien Ancient gods . He was dressed in distressed, dark denim Balmain jeans, a long sleeved Versace button down shirt, and a pair of Tom Ford loafers.

His dark chocolate skin looked edible. He wore his hair in a low fade. His beard and mustache were cut low and neatly trimmed.

"Look who decided to bless us with her presence," Daddy said.

He stared at me, "I see."

Daddy laughed, "You two still hate each other."

"He's a parasite," I said waving him off.

"Takes a leech to know what a parasite is," he said. Daddy chuckled.

"Whatever. Daddy, I'm going up to my room. You can bring my bags up," I said staring at Shaka.

"Wait on it," he said.

"Shaka, I would appreciate if you would take them upstairs for her," Daddy said.

He simply nodded his head. He walked out the kitchen as I rolled my eyes and licked my tongue at him. I don't care how sexy he was, I still didn't like him. I was going to make sure he knows it too.

"Boopsy, I'm staying in the east wing. Come say goodnight before going out tonight," Daddy said.

"What makes you think I'm going out?" I asked.

He laughed. I couldn't help but smile. He knew me too well. I kissed him on the cheek before dismissing myself. I couldn't help but inhale the alluring cologne he was wearing. His muscular back was designed like a cobra snake getting ready to strike its prey. He stood at my door waiting for me. I could see how impatient he was. It only made me walk slower.

"I swear I'll drop them here," he said.

I smacked my lips and opened the door. My room looked the same. The only difference was it was neater. My room was always messy, because I would throw clothes everywhere . It felt like I had stepped back into my teenage years walking into my bedroom. I jumped when I heard a thud behind me. I turned around to see Shaka had slung my expensive Louis Vuitton luggage in the corner of the room.

"That luggage is worth more than your life. Don't throw it," I scolded him.

"Label hoe," he uttered before turning to walk out the room.

I ran to him and pushed him in the back. "Don't call me a hoe again."

He turned around and grabbed a handful of my weave. He slammed me on the bed. He stared down at me with cold eyes. I just knew he was going to hit me he was so mad. I didn't care. He irked my last nerve.

"Don't ever put your hands on me again. I'm not your damn babysitter anymore. Stay the fuck out of my way," he said.

"You still a homeless bum . If it wasn't for my daddy, you still wouldn't be shit. You'll always be my do boy," I screamed as he walked out the door.

Belle

"Girl, you would be a fool not to go to this party. Those niggas are making major moves in the ATL and surrounding states. How do you know them?" Quita, my coworker asked as we rode home from work.

I didn't consider her a friend, but she was cool. I often gave her a ride home from work. I was still that same nerd that didn't have friends. The only friend I had was a girl I took college classes with named Tiera.

"I went to school with them," I said.

"Well, we going to this party. What time you picking me up?" She asked.

I didn't plan on going to the party. If I was, I would take Tiera with me. I didn't know Quita well enough to hang out with her. We only conversed during work.

"I'm not going. They only gave me two tickets. I can't go without my friend," I told her.

"Shit, just hit the nigga up and get another ticket," she suggested.

I probably would've done that, but I had no way of contacting any of them. After the night Rhino saved me from being hit by a car, I never talked to any of them again. I didn't want to remember that night. That night changed my life forever. I was surprised Rhino remembered who I was. He still had the same crazy, but sexy look in his eyes. I remember I would catch him looking at me sometimes in high school, but he never said anything to me. I often wondered what happened to him when I moved from the neighborhood. It's good to see them doing good for themselves.

"I think dude was feeling you. You need to hook me up with his friend," Quita said smiling at me.

"Rhino?" I asked her.

"No, the one with the low cut. That nigga was smiling at you like he was feeling you," she replied.

I laughed, "Titan is just friendly. We lived in the same neighborhood until I moved. He used to be fat. He looks like a different person now."

"Well, which one you want? I'll take either one of those fine ass niggas," she said.

"Neither one, they are not my type. Pick which ever one you want. I didn't really want her to pick Rhino. I had a crush on him that I knew could never go anywhere. I could tell he didn't look at me that way. I was also sure she wasn't his type," I told her.

“Shit, fuck around with a bitch like me, I’ll have them both,” she said smiling. I don’t know if she was joking or serious.

After dropping Quita off, I headed to my next destination. I pulled in front of the blue and pink building. I had my life planned. Never in a million years did I think this would be a part of my life so soon. Regardless, I love the unexpected detour that changed my life forever. I took a deep breath and walked inside the building. I made my way to the room her laughter was coming from. I stood at the door smiling as she played with a little girl. She looked up and saw me.

“Mama!” She screamed as her little fat legs came toward me as she tried to run.

I scooped her up in my arms and hugged her chubby body tightly. She was the most beautiful baby girl in the world to me. I’m sure every mother felt that way about their child. I placed kisses all over her chubby face as she laughed. Hannah wiggled to get out my arms. I placed her down on the floor.

“Hi, Ms. Wiles,” Claudia, her daycare provider said walking up to me.

“How was she today?” I asked Claudia.

"A blessing like always. She's so smart and attentive. I think you are going to have a little genius on your hands," she answered.

I smiled with pride. Hannah was an unexpected gift in my life. When I found out I was pregnant, I didn't know what I was going to do. I cried until I realized it wasn't going to solve my problem. I couldn't imagine aborting my child. I felt as if God gave her to me for a reason. I just didn't know how I was going to raise a child. I hid my pregnancy for Granny until I couldn't anymore. She knew before I could tell her. Against my wishes, she sold her house. We moved into a small two-bedroom apartment in a different neighborhood. I enrolled into a different school as a pregnant teenager. I was embarrassed and ashamed. Pregnant teenagers were the norm in my generation, but not for me. I wasn't supposed to be one of those stupid girls that let some no good boy get her pregnant. After I had my daughter, I was able to get assistance for her. It truly helped a lot. I used the money to pay for daycare and help Granny with bills. I eventually got a job while attending college. I know things are going to get a lot harder once school starts again. I will be raising an active daughter, caring for Granny, and attending med school. I had decided I was going to enjoy this summer as much as possible. I know I won't have time for anything else once classes start. I chatted with Claudia for a while before heading home to Granny.

"There goes my little butterball," Granny said when we walked into the house.

"You look well today," I said flopping on the sofa.

"I feel good today. This disease is bipolar as hell," she said shaking her head.

She was right. One day she'll be feeling fine, the next she can barely get out of bed. I love seeing days like this. She's happy and energetic.

"How was your day?" She asked.

I shrugged my shoulders, "Same old. I did get invited to a party by an old classmate from our old neighborhood."

"Belle, have some fun. You know Pam will be happy to babysit for you," she said.

Pam was our next-door neighbor. She was in her early fifties. She would check in on Granny while I was at work. She always offered to babysit for me. She didn't have any kids and her family lived in California.

"I'll think about it. If Tiera agrees to go with me, I'll go," I said.

"Good," Granny said smiling.

NATAVIA PRESENTS

Rhino

"Y'all made sure everything set up for the drop?" I asked Titan and Shaka as we sat in the strip club. A thick tall stallion with long blonde hair bounced her ass in my face. Her fat, round ass bounced up and down.

"Yea, we straight. Everybody in place. We'll meet up in the morning," Shaka replied. A short, thick, big breasted stripper was giving him a lap dance. He was mad that the customer he thought we were meeting never showed up. We convinced him to just enjoy his night.

"Y'all bout ready to head to the private party?" Titan asked. Shaka thought we had booked a suite for a private party with some strippers.

"Only if she allowed to come," I said smacking the stripper on the ass. She winked and smiled at me.

"Yea, let's get up out of here," Shaka said tapping the stripper on the ass.

After giving the stallion a couple of VIP passes we headed out the door. Titan had a stretch limo waiting outside . I already had three workers to follow us, so our vehicles would be at the club when we left. I didn't know who, but some female was going to be blessed with this dick tonight. I was already feeling the Hennessy and weed. We popped a bottle of white Hennessy as we drove to the club. Shaka rolled a blunt and started passing it around.

"Yo, guess who we ran into today?" I asked Shaka.

"Nigga, it's over seven billion people in the world. How the hell am I supposed to guess that shit?" He asked. Titan laughed.

"Man, fuck you. You supposed to just play along and try to guess," I said.

"Shit, Barack and Michelle?" He asked with a serious face.

"You know got damn well they don't know me," I said laughing.

"You didn't say you knew the person. You just said you ran into someone," Shaka said laughing.

"We saw Belle, today," Titan said still laughing.

"Who?" Shaka asked with a confused look on his face.

"You know Nerd Girl. The one that almost got ran over that night," I explained. I don't know why she kept popping up in my damn head. I was definitely not the type of nigga for her.

"Oh shit, what happened to her? She just disappeared from school. I'm glad she did. She was the only one giving me competition for valedictorian," Shaka asked.

"She graduated from Spelman. She's working at KFC until school starts back in fall," Rhino said.

"What she going to school for?" Titan asked.

"Med school," I replied.

He smiled, "He stood up there damn near drooling out the mouth."

"You feeling Nerd Girl?" Shaka asked with a smile on his face.

"Man, fuck y'all. I saved her life. I feel like her protector now. Kind of like when you were babysitting that high maintenance, spoiled chick," I said smiling at Shaka.

His face frowned up. "She showed up today. I already had to check her disrespectful ass."

"But you was always cock blocking niggas from getting that," Titan said smiling.

"I was doing my damn job," Shaka replied.

Shaka didn't want to admit it, but he had something for the boss's daughter. He hated her and cared for her at the same time.

"You always trying to match some damn body. You need to be concerned about that sneaky ass female of yours," I told Titan.

"Let me handle that," Titan said before hitting the blunt.

*****

The line was wrapped around the building. Everyone had come out to show Shaka love for his accomplishments. He hated crowded places, so we knew he was going to trip.

"Man, what is this shit?" Shaka asked angrily.

"Come on Shaka. You deserve this shit. Celebrate your accomplishment. Man, you was fucking homeless not knowing where your next meal was coming from. You never let that shit deter you from your education. You could've said fuck that shit, but you didn't. Not only did you graduate, you are the got damn valedictorian. We proud of you, man. This your party," Titan said.

He looked at us both. "Y'all still ain't shit, but thanks."

"When I accomplish something great, I'm getting you to introduce me for my speech," said Titan.

We all laughed as we exited the car. We made our way to the VIP entrance. I stopped when I heard my name being called. There were several females calling my name, but one voice made me stop in my tracks. I turned around to see her. She made my dick jump. She wore a fitted black dress with a low cut in front and cleavage out. Her big breasts was damn near about to pop out the dress. Her thick thighs left no room for air between them. She was short as hell, but the heels gave her at least five more inches. I stared at her as she sashayed toward me.

"Hi," she said smiling nervously.

I cleared my dry throat, "Nerd Girl, I'm glad you decided to celebrate. What up?"

"I need a favor," she said looking over her shoulder at two girls.

"What up?" I asked.

"I need an extra pass for my friend Tiera," she said.

"Damn, you were acting like you were about to ask me for a kidney or something. Yea, I gotcha. Come on."

"Thank you," she said smiling at me.

"Yes, we really appreciate this," the thirst bucket said.

"You need anything let me know," I said to Nerd Girl.

She smiled before I walked away. I didn't like the feeling I was having being around her. She needed to stay the fuck away from me. I was going to keep my eye on her tonight. She wasn't leaving here with some lame ass fuck boy.

Miriam

"I told you I was going out tonight. I don't know why you tripping," I said to Lyle.

I stood in the bathroom applying my makeup. He was standing in the middle of the bedroom furious. We didn't live together, but we were always at each other's place. I wanted to wait until we were married before moving in together.

"Tripping? Every time you start hanging with her you start using that ghetto slang," he replied.

I snickered, "Jetta is so not ghetto, and you know it. We're just going out for a little while to celebrate her coming home. I promise I won't be out very long."

"Where are you going?" He asked.

I didn't like the way he was treating me. I am a grown woman that doesn't feel the need to answer to anyone. He was treating me like a child. I hated the way Father controlled Mother. I vowed I would never allow a man to have that much power over me.

"To some club, I'm not sure. When I get there, I'll text and give you the name of the spot," I said walking up to him. I tiptoed and kissed his lips softly.

"We need to discuss some things tomorrow," he said.

"We can go out to dinner tomorrow evening. Now, let me get out of here. When I get home, I'm sitting on your face" I said walking toward the bedroom door.

"Make sure you shower first," he said.

I stopped and started to speak on his comment but didn't. The sad part about his comment was he meant it. Sex with him was always planned. It had to be clean sex. He had no clue how mind blowing nasty sex could be. I'm not even going to think about his pussy eating skills. I shook my head as I thought about how unskilled he was. Spontaneity was a foreign word to him. His dick was the perfect size, but his sex was boring. I always had to do extra to make myself come. I pushed thoughts of him to the back of my head. I was going to hang with my best friend and enjoy the night.

*****

Once I made it to Jetta's house, I called her to let her know I was outside. She must be eager to go out. She hurried out the door and hopped in the car. She was flawless and beautiful as always. Jetta's skin complexion was a rich dark chocolate. Her grandparents on her father's side were Jamaican. They moved to the states before he was born. They moved back years ago. She never talked about her mother's family much. She only mentioned an aunt she never knew.

"We cannot turn up listening to slow music," she said unplugging my aux cord.

I laughed. I loved 80's and 90's R&B . They can keep this new shit they listen to now. Kodak Black blasted as we drove. I wasn't into rap but loved the beats. Jetta danced in her seat as she rapped along with the song. I turned the music down as I drove.

"How's your dad?" I asked.

"That lying dog. I know Daddy is sick, but he called me like he was on his death bed," she said referring to Shaka.

"So, he's doing well?" I asked.

"He's lost a lot of weight, but he's still fit. He wants to see you tomorrow. He's throwing me a pool party tomorrow," she said.

"You know I'll be there," I said. Then I remembered I had plans. I informed her I couldn't make it.

"Just bring him here. I know we don't click, but Daddy wants to see you," she said.

"I'll see if I can change his mind," I said.

I asked her had she seen Shaka since she returned. They didn't realize how cute they were when they argued with each other. He was the only one who could handle Jetta's tantrums.

"That fool nearly pulled my damn weave out," she said with a scowl on her face.

"What? Why?" I asked shocked.

"He called me a label hoe and I pushed him," she said.

I laughed, "You are a label hoe. You know he got a short circuit. You always loved pushing his buttons."

"He makes me sick. You know he lives at my father's house?" She asked.

"No, why? I'm sure he has money to buy his own house."

"He supposedly helps take care of Daddy. I'm going to speak with his accountant Monday. That nigga probably has been stealing Daddy's money ," she said.

"Well, if you find some shady shit, I'll get Lyle to look into it," I told her.

"Thanks Mir," she said smiling.

I had no idea where we were going. I had put the address into the GPS. I looked at the club when it announced we had arrived at our location. There was no way we were getting inside that club. It was almost midnight and the line was wrapped around the building. There had to be celebrities inside. I thought the name of the club was different and catchy. It was called La-Di-Da.

"We are never getting in there," I told Jetta.

She smiled, "Yes, we are. We're even going in VIP style."

"How?" I asked.

"This is Shaka's celebration party. He left a few VIP passes laying on Daddy's desk in the study. I helped myself to a couple of them," she said smiling.

"He's going to kill you, yet," I said laughing.

"Or die trying," she said laughing.

I pulled up to valet. I was relieved to know we weren't going to have to stand in the long line. We showed our passes and was let in. The people on the outside might as well go home. There was no room for any more people. I'm surprised we were let in. The club was packed from wall to wall. Everyone was dressed in their finest clothes. The club was designed with class and style. It was definitely a classy establishment. It wasn't a place I figured a thugged out guy like Shaka would be celebrating. The walls were layered with mirrors. The black marble floors and walls made the cream colored chairs and tables stand out. There were two bars on each side of the club. A spiral stairway led up to the VIP floor. We made our way upstairs. I breathed a sigh of relief when I realized how relaxed and chill it was in VIP. There were huge lounging sofas with tables. Each table had hookahs on them. We searched until we found an empty table. We had a great view of everyone coming up to VIP.

"Damn, this place is nice," Jetta said looking around. I agreed with a head nod. I followed behind her to the railing to look at the bottom floor. It was a sight to see. The people looked like ants on the crowded floor.

The music was interrupted by the DJ, "The guest of honor has arrived. Let's all show Shaka love tonight and celebrate his graduation from UGA with no bullshit. Congrats Shaka!"

Everyone yelled congratulations at the same time. I was completely floored. I had no idea he attended college. I spotted him making his way through the crowd . My attention was immediately taken by the fine specimen walking beside him. The brother was handsome, sexy and stylish. I had to give myself a quick reminder that I was an engaged woman.

Titan

"They came out for yo black ass tonight," I said to Shaka.

We walked up the spiral stairs to the VIP floor. Our table was filled with bottles of Hennessy . The moment we sat down people started congratulating him on his graduation. Shaka didn't like attention. He was humble about his accomplishments.

"What that nigga looking at?" He asked looking at Rhino looking over the rail. I walked over and looked down to see what had his attention.

I laughed, "Damn, she came."

"You invited her. Why you mad?" I asked.

"Ain't no damn body mad. Shut the fuck up," he said walking away. I laughed as I followed him.

"What's wrong with this fool?" Shaka asked.

"He gave Belle VIP passes, now he mad because she actually came," I told Shaka.

He looked at Rhino smiling. "Why she downstairs if she got passes to come up?"

"Nigga, I don't know and don't care. Where the fuck the big booty bitches at. Y'all acting like some, but ain't none," he said looking around. We laughed.

"Yo Shaka, I bet I can make you stop laughing. Jetta spoiled ass in here," Rhino said with his head turned.

We both looked over his shoulder. "How the fuck she get in here?" Shaka said jumping up.

"Yo chill man. That's her friend, Miriam with her. Damn, she finer than she was in high school," I said staring at her as I stood up.

She wore a short, haltered silver dress with deep slits up the side. I couldn't help but admire her thick, toned honey brown thighs as I approached her. Her jet-black hair was shorter than she wore it in school. She crossed her legs and laughed at whatever Jetta was saying. My mouth watered as my eyes zoned in on the huge tattoo on her upper thigh and hip. They both looked up at me when I approached their table.

"Finally found your way back home, I see," I said looking at Jetta. I could tell neither one of them knew who I was. They hadn't seen me since I lost all the weight.

"I think you have the wrong person," Jetta said with an attitude.

"Nah, your name is Jetta and your friend's name is Miriam. I have the right person," I said winking at Miriam.

"Well, whoever you are we aren't looking for company. So, you can excuse yourself," Jetta said. Miriam giggled.

"Still the same. Rude as fuck," I said laughing.

"Who are you?" Miriam asked.

I leaned forward and stared her in the eyes. "I'm glad you asked beautiful. My name is Titan." Her mouth was slightly opened as she stared into my eyes.

Jetta burst into laughter. "No fuckin' way!"

I broke the gaze Miriam and I had. "Yea, it's me."

"Oh my God, you look great. I mean you were always cute, but you got your grown man on now," Jetta said still looking at me with wide eyes.

I laughed, "Thanks. It's good to see you. And you too beautiful." Miriam didn't reply. She took a big gulp of her drink.

Jetta smiled. "This is a nice club. Who owns it?"

"Me," I answered.

"Such a cliché," she said.

"What you mean?" Jetta asked.

"Drug dealer turned club owner. I bet he owns a franchise of car washes too," Miriam stated cutting her eyes at me.

I chuckled. "Why so mean?"

"Right Mir. He was always the nice one. He was the one that made sure you got home the night you were throwing up your insides," Jetta said winking at me.

She shrugged her shoulders. "Sorry, but the truth hurts."

I leaned forward and whispered in her ear, "Nah, but the things I want to do to you might hurt." I heard her gasp for breath.

"It was good seeing you Jetta. I'm sure I'll be seeing more of you," I said glancing at Miriam.

It was something about her. She seemed hard, but there was a softness about her. I was the man to break through the tough girl persona.

"Tell the asshole thanks for the passes I stole," Jetta said smiling.

"Yea, you might wanna stay out his way. Order whatever you want," I told them before walking away.

Mena stopped me as I walked back to our table, "Who are those bitches?"

"Gone with that bullshit Mena," I said stepping around her. I could feel her presence behind me.

"Man, she ain't sitting her ass with us," Rhino said rubbing on some big booty girl.

"Nigga, fuck you. I can't stand you anyway," Mena said.

"Yo, don't bring that shit to my table Mena," Shaka said staring at her.

"This nigga always in some female's face. He gone make me fuck a bitch up in here tonight," she ranted.

"The man owns the club. It's his job to mingle with customers. You would know that, if you gave a damn about his hustle," Rhino said.

She rolled her eyes at him, "Anyway, can you send a bottle to our table?"

She gave me her puppy dog eyes. I looked over her shoulder to see her ratchet sister and friend sitting at her table. I sent a bottle over just to get her out my face. She kissed me on the lips and walked away. I looked over to see Miriam staring at me.

Belle

"Come on, let's go upstairs. That's where all the money getting niggas at," Quita shouted over the music.

"She's right Belle. It's too crowded down here anyway," Tiera said.

I didn't really want to go upstairs, but I followed behind them. It was something in my gut telling me to stay downstairs. I instantly became nervous when we made it upstairs. I felt as if I didn't belong amongst this crowd. We walked around unable to find an empty table. I spotted Jetta and Miriam sitting at a table. I remembered their names, because that was a crazy night for me. I immediately turned to walk back downstairs. I didn't want any interactions with them. I ran into a hard body spilling my drink on whoever it was.

I looked up into the crazy eyes of Rhino. "I'm so sorry."

"Where the hell you running to?" He asked.

"I need to go to the bathroom," I lied.

He wiped the strawberry daiquiri off his cream colored Polo button down shirt. The shirt was ruined. He wore a pair of distressed, black jeans and Timbs. His long dreads hung loose on his shoulders. His full mustache and beard were neatly trimmed and tapered.

"It's that way," he pointed toward the back of the club.

"Can we sit with y'all? There's nowhere to sit up here," Quita asked.

"Quita! We're just going to go back downstairs." I yelled embarrassed that she would ask him that.

"Nah, come to our table after you done in the bathroom," he said staring at me.

"Where you sitting?" Tiera asked.

He nodded his head at the table where Titan, Shaka and a few females were sitting. I don't know why being in his presence intimidated me. I hurried and used a bathroom. I could hear Quita and Tiera discussing how fine him, and his friends are.

I walked out the stall and washed my hands. "We're not going to their table. We're going back downstairs."

"Oh hell no, we not. He invited us," Quita demanded.

"No, you invited us. You put him on the spot," I told her.

"Belle, he don't seem like the type of nigga to be forced into doing anything he doesn't want to do. I think he wants us to sit with him. Besides, it's some fine men he's sitting with. Help a best friend out," Tiera said smiling at me.

I smiled and shook my head. I was relieved to see the other women had left when we made it to their table. Rhino slid to the side. Quita hurried and sat next to him.

"Get yo ass up. Belle sit yo ass right here." Rhino said.

Quita rolled her eyes at him and stood up. I sat next to him. Her and Quita sat between Titan and Shaka.

"Congratulations Shaka," I said smiling at him. He was sitting on my left side while Rhino sat on my right.

"Thanks, same to you," he said nodding his head. I gave him a smile.

"You drink Henny?" Rhino asked.

I shook my head no. I wasn't much of a drinker. A mixed drink will give me the buzz I need. I was driving, so I had to keep a level head.

"No, I'm not a heavy drinker. It doesn't take much to give me a buzz," I told him. He waved a waitress over to the table.

"Bring a strawberry daiquiri for her," he said.

He tapped the waitress on the ass when she turned to walk away. I turned my head to see Quita talking

Shaka's ear off while downing a glass of Hennessy . Tiera was drinking also, while flirting with Titan.

"Why weren't we invited to the table?" Jetta said standing in front of our table.

"I figured we were beneath your standards," Titan said looking at her friend shrugging his shoulders. She rolled her eyes at him.

"I know you, don't I?" her friend said staring at me.

"Yea, yo damn friend almost killed her," Rhino said.

"Wow, yo glow up is real! "What the hell in the water in ATL. Shit, Titan lost a whole person, asshole graduated college and you looking like a new person." I smiled at her attempted compliment.

"Maybe Rhino should drink the same water. It might help his rude ass," she said glancing at Rhino who was ignoring her.

"Hi, I'm Miriam. This Jetta. We were never introduced that night," Miriam said smiling at me. She seemed really nice unlike her friend. I guess she was so drunk she didn't remember telling everyone their names.

"Yea, that night was crazy. I'm Belle," I said smiling at her.

"Who are they?" Jetta asked referring to Tiera and Quita.

"Known of yo damn business wit'cha nosey ass," Rhino told her. She waved him off dismissing his comment.

"Congratulations Micah," Jetta said placing her hand on her hip staring down at him. He nodded his head at her. She seemed agitated by the lack of attention he was giving her.

"Congrats Shaka," Miriam said smiling at him.

"Same to you," he said raising his glass to her.

They made a toast to their accomplishments. I noticed Miriam kept cutting her eyes at Titan. I don't think she liked my best friend flirting with him. It was obvious Jetta didn't like Quita talking to Shaka.

"Come on Mir, this table lame as hell anyway," Jetta said rolling her eyes at Shaka. He continued to ignore her.

"How did you change your shirt so fast?" I asked Rhino before taking a sip of the drink.

I grimaced at how strong it was. They were not slacking on the liquor in their drinks. This would be my only drink for the night.

"I keep a change of clothes in Titan's office," he replied.

"I like that one better anyway," He laughed.

He wore a multicolored button down shirt. He didn't talk to me much as we sat there. Numerous girls stopped and flirted with him. He flirted back as if I wasn't sitting there. He would rub on their asses and thighs. I wondered how his hands would feel against my flesh. Half way through my drink I was more relaxed. I wanted to dance. Only alcohol would give me the courage I was feeling.

"Come dance with me," I said swaying my hips in the seat.

He laughed, "Nerd Girl, I don't dance."

I smacked my lips and stood up, "Well, this is a club. I came to dance and have some fun."

Shaka

I don't know what the female sitting beside me was talking about. Everything she was saying was going in one ear and out the other. I was only entertaining her to avoid conversation with Jetta. I don't know what it was about her that got under my skin so bad. She is a beautiful girl, but her spoiled and better than thou attitude ruined all her beauty. I couldn't deny the way the short, sequined dress was hugging her body. She wasn't curvy the way I loved to see women, but she had enough ass to make me look as she walked away. Her long, chocolate bowed legs seemed a mile long. She looked back over her shoulder to catch me staring at her. She shot me a bird before walking downstairs. I chuckled and shook my head.

"Yo, can you stop talking for five minutes?" I said to the girl who said her name was Quita.

She giggled, "I'm sorry. You just make me nervous. You so damn fine and sexy." Now, I see why Rhino called her a thirst bucket. She was ratchet as hell, but cute. If she learned how to carry herself, she might be taken seriously by some nigga. That nigga just ain't me.

"Who the fuck is this?" Dayzee asked standing in front of our table with her hand on her hips.

I have been fucking around with Dayzee for the past three years. It was nothing serious between us. We were once a couple until I found out she was fucking a big time drug dealer from Florida. Whatever feelings I had for her were irrelevant after that. We still hooked up whenever I needed my dick wet.

"Who the fuck are you?" Quita asked standing up to face her. I couldn't help but laugh. Quita was ghetto as hell. She seemed to be Dayzee's match.

"Bitch, you don't know me," Dayzee said getting in Quita's face. I stood up and stepped between them.

"Cut that shit, Dayzee. I don't know why you always playing yourself like this. We ain't a damn couple and you know it," I told her.

"Whatever Shaka! You don't be saying that shit when you fucking me," she said bopping her head.

"Man, y'all sho know how to pick'em," Rhino said shaking his head at Dayzee.

"What that supposed to mean?" Dayzee said giving Rhino attention.

"You are vitriolic," Rhino said smiling up at her.

I chuckled at his choice of words. I could tell by the look on her face she had no clue what the word meant. He had this thing about learning a new word every week. He made sure to use the words he learned whenever he was getting angry. I guess he was getting agitated by the women coming to the table.

"Shut up, with yo half-baked ass," she said waving him off. He laughed.

"Carry on, little girl," Quita said over my shoulder.

Dayzee tried to reach over me to hit Quita. I grabbed her around the waist and pulled her away from the table. I could hear Quita yelling all kinds of names at Dayzee. I don't know where Belle got her friend from, but she needed to send her back. If I let Dayzee go, she would beat her down. Dayzee was a former gang member. She fought dudes like she was a man.

"Bitch, I'm gone fuck you up the next time I see you!" She yelled as I pulled her toward Titan's office.

"You fucking her?" She asked as I shoved her in the office.

"Who I fuck doesn't concern you. You know how we get down. If not, we can end this shit now. I won't have you bringing that ratchet ass attitude to my boy's place of business," I warned her.

"I'm sorry. You know how I get when it comes to you," she said walking up to me.

I knew the look in her eyes. Whenever she knows I'm mad, she knew how to make me forget about whatever she did. She dropped to her knees and unfastened my jeans. She pulled my soft dick from my boxers.

"I remember you would get hard just being around me. Now, I have to put in work to get it hard," she said looking up at me.

"So, are you going to talk or work?" I asked looking down at her.

She started licking the dome of my dick while her hand massaged my shaft. She didn't waste no time getting my dick brick hard. Slurping sounds echoed over the room as saliva spilled from her mouth. Her full, juicy lips slid up and down my shaft. She moaned as she sucked me in and out of her mouth sending vibrations through my body. She was so caught up in sucking me, she didn't hear the door being opened. I stared at Jetta as she looked down at Dayzee. Her mouth fell open in shock as our eyes met. I gripped a handful of Dayzee's weave and started fucking her mouth never breaking eye contact with Jetta. The more I stared at her the harder my dick became. I rammed my dick farther and deeper inside Dayzee's mouth. I could feel the head of my dick hitting her throat as she gagged uncontrollably . I couldn't stop, nor could I take my eyes off Jetta. She didn't move a muscle as she watched me fuck Dayzee's mouth with no mercy. Jetta's eyes were full of lust as her chest heaved up and down.

"Don't waste my nut," I demanded to Dayzee while staring at Jetta.

She covered her mouth and ran out the room. Dayzee heard the door slam and tried to stop, but I held her head in place until I unloaded inside her mouth.

"Damn, what was that? I almost choked to death," Dayzee said standing up wiping her mouth.

"My bad, you don't know how good that shit be feeling," I lied.

"You coming over tonight, so we can finish?" She asked.

"Yea," I lied again before walking into the bathroom to wash my dick off.

I left Dayzee in the bathroom freshening up. I walked toward our table to see chaos. Mena was trying to get out of Titan's grip. Quita was the fire starter once again. She was talking shit to Mena while Tiera laughed. Rhino and Belle were nowhere in sight. Jetta and Miriam were watching everything go down. It was almost time for the club to close. I walked up to Jetta.

"You need to go home," I said.

“You ain’t my daddy. Remember, your babysitting days are over,” she stated.

“You go voluntarily, or I drag you to the house by that expensive ass weave in yo head,” I said staring at her.

“Ugh, don’t put your disgusting hands on me,” she demanded frowning up her face. I knew she was referring to the scene she watched in Titan’s office. I walked off to help Titan deescalate his situation.

Jetta

"Mmmmm yes, that feels so good. Please, oh God please don't stop!" I moaned as I enjoyed the pleasure of his beautiful, black dick.

His thickness slid in and out of my gushy tunnel as I clawed his back. He had my legs cuffed into his arms driving deeper inside me. His wet mouth licked and sucked all over my neck. I felt like my body was ascending in the air as I felt my orgasm getting ready to explode. I dug my nails deeper into his back as he grinded his hips hitting my g-spot repeatedly.

"Ooooohhh ssshhhhit! I'm coooommming!" I screamed as I erupted like a waterfall.

My body jerked and quivered until the sensations left . I slowly opened my eyes to look at his incredible body. I blinked my eyes rapidly trying to make him appear. He wasn't there. I quickly sat up in my bed and looked down at the sheets. My satin sheet was soaked with my own juices. I looked around for him. I touched myself to make sure I was awake. My skin was clammy from sweating. I closed my eyes with shame and fell back on the bed. I had a wet dream thinking about him. That made me hate him even more. I thought about walking in on that girl sucking him off last night. His dick was massive and beautiful. Thick veins ran through his long, dark chocolate shaft. The head of his dick was like a huge mushroom. Images of him drilling inside me like he was doing her mouth caused my panties to become soaked. I couldn't take my eyes off him until I heard him speak. I ran out the room ashamed for being turned on by watching him.

Bang! Bang! Bang! Someone was banging on my door like the FEDs. My heart immediately dropped. I instantly thought the worst. My father has been in the game a long time and never had the cops to his house. I prayed this wasn't the case now. I grabbed my robe and rushed to the door. I opened the door to see Shaka standing there with a scowl on his face. I couldn't help but lick my lips as I stared at his bare, muscular chest. He pushed me to the side and entered the room.

"What the fuck are you doing?" I asked angrily.

"You better not have a fuckboy in this house," he said checking the room. He looked in the closet, under the bed, and searched the bathroom.

"There's no one in here. I have more respect for Daddy than that," I told him.

"Then what was that noise I heard?" He asked still looking around. He looked out on the balcony.

"What noise?" I asked curiously. I had no idea what he was talking about. I had been asleep the entire time. He walked back over to the bed and looked down at my sheets.

"Either the nigga risked his life by jumping off the balcony or you freaking yourself in here," he said smiling at the wet circle on my bed.

"Get out! Get out my room!" I demanded with rage while stomping my feet. I walked off and started snatching the sheets off my bed.

He laughed as he walked toward the door, "I'm grilling for this irrelevant ass party of yours. We need to go pick up some things. Be downstairs in thirty minutes."

"You can just get the stuff. Why I gotta go?" I asked him.

"Because I'm not your damn do boy. I'm only doing this for Omega," he walked out leaving me standing there more embarrassed than I was last night.

I finished stripping my bed and put my sheets in the dirty clothes hamper. I looked through my closet for something to wear to the grocery store. I pulled a long yellow body dress that had long sleeves. I grabbed a pair of heels. After taking a long hot shower, I dressed. I tied my long Peruvian weave up unto a bun. I beat my face and headed downstairs. He was in the kitchen talking and laughing with Clara. They both looked at me as if I was crazy.

"What?" I asked.

"Where are you going dressed like that?" He asked still staring at me.

"To the store," I answered.

"We are going grocery shopping. Go change. I'm not walking in a store with you dressed like you going to the Academy Awards."

"I care about how I leave the house looking. I'm not changing, so let's go," I told him.

"Well, I guess that cancels the party," he said flopping down on the bar stool.

"You can't cancel my party. Ms. Clara could you please go with him? I can't stand him," I asked her.

"Hell nah, she ain't going for you. You want this party, you come and get your own sh… stuff," I said remembering Ms. Clara was in the room.

We bickered back and forth until Daddy walked into the room, "Daddy, he's trying to make me change clothes just to go grocery shopping."

He laughed, "Boopsy, go change. You are way over dressed."

"Uuuggghhh!" I screamed storming out of the kitchen and back upstairs. I threw on a pair of Versace jeans and low-cut V-neck Gucci blouse. I slipped on a pair of Prada sandals. I checked myself in the mirror and headed downstairs.

"Better," Daddy said winking at me. I walked over and kissed him on the jaw. He instructed me to get him a big T-bone steak. I rolled my eyes at Shaka and walked past him.

"Hurry up, I don't have all day," I said never looking back.

"You live with my father, eat his food, and drive his vehicles," I said shaking my head as we got in my father's Cadillac Escalade. It was an old model that he purchased years ago, but it was his favorite vehicle.

"It's not your father's anymore, freaky girl," he said backing out of the garage.

"What?" I asked.

He smiled. "He gave it to me when I graduated from high school."

I was furious. I begged my daddy to give me the Spyder for a graduation gift. He refused because I had wrecked it once. This nigga stole from him and he gave him his most loved vehicle. He laughed as I sat there pouting all the way to the store.

*****

"What are you trying to have at this cookout?" He asked as we entered the meat market.

"Shrimp, lobster, crab legs, pasta…you know, the typical things," I said walking over to the lobster tanks.

He laughed, "That's not a typical cookout, Ms. Freak Nasty. We getting burgers, hot dogs, and steaks for relevant people."

"You can't tell me how to spend my money," I told him.

"What money you got? Your father paying for this. You can get one lobster for yourself, since it's your party," he said smiling at me.

"I swear I hate you," I said walking away from him.

"Is that why your sheets were wet this morning," he said loud enough that people in the market could hear him. I stood there with my mouth open.

After leaving the grocery store, he went to Smashburger. I hated he came here . I loved their burgers but was trying to cut red meat from my diet. My ass and hips were started to spread. It was hard controlling my weight gain because I hated exercising. He pulled up to the drive thru.

"You want something?" He asked.

"Yes, the Smash Brussels sprouts," I said.

He looked at me like I was crazy, "This a burger joint."

"I know that. I don't eat red meat anymore," I said with an attitude.

He shrugged his shoulders and placed the order. As he drove us home, I ate my sprouts . I loved the Brussels sprouts , but my mouth was watering at the burger he was eating as he drove. I regretted not getting a burger. He caught me staring at the burger he held.

"You wanna bite?" He asked with his mouth full of food.

"It's disgusting to talk with food in your mouth," I said frowning up at him.

He chuckled, "I can't help it. This shit good."

I rolled my eyes at him. He knew what he was doing. He knew I wanted to tear into that damn burger. I crossed my arms over my chest and pouted. He waved the burger in my face. I couldn't take it anymore. I snatched the burger from his hand and took a huge bite. I closed my eyes and savored the delicious taste. He laughed hysterically as he drove. I didn't care. I finished devouring the burger.

"I want a milkshake . Stop at Chick fil a ," I told him.

"Is that an order or request?" He asked glancing at me.

I exhaled in frustration, "It's a request, Micah."

"Why you insist on calling me by my government?" He asked.

I shrugged my shoulders, "No one knows Micah. Everyone only knows Shaka. Who is Micah?"

"The nigga that you owe a damn burger," he said looking straight ahead.

That was typical of him. He never talked about himself . He never opened up to share his inner thoughts with anyone. I could look at him and know when he was in deep thought. This was one of those times as he stared out the windshield.

Rhino

"Oooohhh shhit! That's my spot, baby!" Bria screamed as I dug deep inside her guts.

I hated fucking her, but I need to bust this nut and she was begging for it. She screamed entirely too damn much and loud. You would think I was killing her. I covered her mouth with my hand as I continued to ram inside her from behind. *Bang! Bang! Bang!* Someone was banging on her bedroom door. I hope it wasn't her nigga, because I left my gun in the car. I didn't want to bring it around her kids. Them lil fuckers was bad as hell.

"Momma, what's wrong?" Her little seven-year old yelled through the door. I kept going until I felt my nut coming.

"Catch this nut," I said pulling out of her.

She quickly turned around and swallowed my dick. I poured my nut down her throat. She sucked and gulped until I was empty. I flopped on the bed on my back.

"Man, you need to stop all that hollering. Got Bebe kids thinking I'm trying to kill you in here," I told her.

She laughed, "Don't blame me because you earned your nickname. Damn dick bigger than a Rhino's horn."

“Mama, we hungry!” The little girl yelled banging on the door again. I dressed and walked out the bedroom.

“Nigga, what you doing to my mama,” the lil nappy headed boy asked staring at me.

“Making her happy. Now, tell her to take you and your sister to get something to eat,” I said giving him a twenty-dollar bill.

“I’m still gone tell my daddy you had Mama yelling in the room. He gone beat you up,” the grown ass lil girl said rolling her eyes at me.

I walked out the door laughing. Those two gone cause her to get her ass beat by that nigga. As I was pulling out of the apartment complex, he was pulling in. I gave him a head nod and kept riding. I went home and took a shower. I was supposed to have already been to Omega’s house to help him on the grill. I called his phone to let him know I was on the way.

“Nigga, where you at?” He said answering the phone.

“I’m on the way. Be there in fifteen minutes,” I told him. I grabbed my keys and hurried out the door.

“Swing by and get some more hot dog and hamburger buns.”

“I gotcha,” I said ending the call.

*****

I hurried inside the store and grabbed the buns. The line was long as hell. I didn't have the patience for this shit. I made my way to the front of the line.

"Yo, here's the money for the buns. Keep the change," I said laying a fifty-dollar bill on the counter. I was about to walk away until I saw who had the line held up.

"Nerd Girl," I said looking at her.

I hadn't seen her since the night of the club. The last time I saw her some nigga was too close to her on the dance floor. I made her leave when the commotion broke out between her friends and Mena.

"Will you please stop calling me that?" She asked in a low voice.

I laughed. "Why you got the line held up?"

"I'm couponing," she said. I could tell the cashier was growing impatient with her and me.

"Man, ring her shit up. You got the line damn near to the back of the store. People got shit to do," I said. The cashier laughed and started scanning her items quickly.

"I have shit to do also and it involves saving money," she stated with an attitude.

She stood there with her arms folded until the cashier was finished. She gave me the total and I gave her a hundred-dollar bill. Everyone in line applauded as I pushed her buggy out the store.

"Really?" She asked looking over her shoulder at everyone.

"Man, y'all couponers aggravating as fuck," I said as I pushed her buggy. She was wearing a pair of tights, tee shirt and sneakers. Her hair was pulled back in a ponytail. I noticed she didn't have on glasses.

"Where yo glasses?" I asked.

"I mostly wear them at night now. I have contacts that I wear through the day," she said. She popped her trunk to her old model Camry.

"Thank you," she said after I put the bags in her trunk.

"What you bout to do?" I asked. I don't know what I was thinking, but I wasn't ready for her to go. I didn't know the next time I would see her.

"Go home and relax," she said getting in her car.

"Come to a barbecue with me," I said. I felt like a young nigga asking a girl on a date.

"I mean not as a date or anything. Just to hang out. It's gone be a lot of old classmates there," I restated.

She laughed. "I didn't have any friends in high school. I doubt if anyone will remember me."

"Well, just come eat some good food. You got a bathing suit?" I asked.

"Yea, but I haven't shaved," she said.

"Give me a pen and piece of paper," I said. I jotted down the address and my phone number. I told her to give me a call if she coming through.

She gave me a bewildered look, "Why?"

I chuckled. "Why what?"

"Why do you want me there? We barely know each other. You and your friends think I'm a nerd. I would never fit in with your friends," She asked.

"Man, why you gotta analyze shit. Just come if you want to. If not, forget I fucking invited yo nerdy ass." I said before walking away.

I didn't know how to answer her question. I hated that she made me feel uncomfortable. I never been in a predicament where I didn't know how to react. She did that shit to me. She pulled up beside me in her car as I walked to mine.

"You promise you and your friends are not going to pour pig's blood on me?" She asked seriously.

I burst into laughter, "You tripping. I promise."

"Can I bring a friend?" She asked.

"Not the thirst bucket," I told her.

She laughed, "I'll call you when I'm on the way." I damn near skipped to the car knowing she was coming.

Miriam

"I know what Jetta's father does for a living. We shouldn't be associated with those kind of people, Miriam." Lyle said as he drove.

"Jetta has been my best friend forever. Her father has treated me like I was his very own daughter. What a person does for a living doesn't define their character, Lyle," I told him.

He rolled his eyes and remained quiet the rest of the ride. He didn't want to come to the pool party, but I knew I was going to get my way. All it took was a quick round of sex. Sex with him was like more of a job, now. There was nothing exciting about our sex. I've even tried to talk to him about it. He claims things will get better once we are married. If anything, I think they will get worse. When we arrived, cars were parked along the circular drive way. Valet was in the front to park our car.

"Don't scratch her," Lyle said giving the valet his keys.

I rolled my eyes and shook my head. Omega had a damn Maybach parked in his garage. These guys are not impressed by his Mercedes. He held my hand as we walked to the side entrance of the house. I knew Shaka wasn't going to allow anybody to come through the main doors. The party was lit. People were dancing, talking, drinking, eating and laughing. I knew Jetta was going to throw a banging party. The DJ had everyone turned up. Lyle squeezed my hand without realizing it. I guess he was nervous about being around this kind of crowd.

"You hungry?" I asked.

"I'm not eating food from here," he said frowning up at me.

"Well, I am. "Mingle and meet some people," I said letting his hand go. If I had to deal with his boring friends, he was going to learn to deal with mine.

"Mir! Where's your bathing suit?" I heard Jetta calling my name. I laughed as she made her way toward me. I could tell she was already feeling the alcohol.

"I'm with him. It was hard enough convincing him to come. I wasn't going to push my luck. But what he doesn't know is I have it on under this dress." I said. She laughed.

"That's my bitch! Come on, let's get you a drink," Jetta said giving me a high five as we laughed. I followed her to the bar. The bartender fixed me a Long Island Iced Tea.

I scanned the poolside recognizing old classmates. My eyes stopped when I saw him. He was shirtless with a pair of swimming trunks on. His body was stacked with muscles. He was grinning in the face of one of my old classmates. I spotted Lyle talking to a couple of guys. It was good to see him mingle with people outside of his circle. I became nervous when I spotted Titan headed our way. I didn't stop sucking on the straw until my drink was gone

"Here he comes," Jetta said as we stood watching him approach us.

"What's up beautiful?" He said smiling at me.

"That's not my name," I said.

"It's not your name, but it definitely defines you," he said licking his lips.

I had to get away from him. This man can get me into all kinds of trouble. I turned to the bartender and ordered a double shot of Vodka. Everything about him made my body heat rise. I grabbed the double shot and gulped it down. He smiled at me showing his pearly whites. Something about this man caused a tingle between my legs.

"Yo, you talk to Rhino?" Shaka asked walking up to us.

"Nah," he answered never taking his eyes off me.

“Man, that nigga said he’ll be here in fifteen minutes. It’s been over thirty,” Shaka said.

“Shit, these black folks. Tell them to use damn white bread if they wanna eat the hot dogs and burgers. It ain’t like they ain’t never did the shit before,” Titan told him taking his eyes off me.

“Oh, hell no! We not doing that ghetto shit at my party,” Jetta told him. I laughed at her bougie ass.

“Well, take yo ass to the store and get some,” Shaka told her.

“Wait on it,” she replied.

“There he goes,” I said as Rhino walked through the gates. Shaka cut his eyes at Jetta and walked off.

Titan stepped closer to me. “When I’m going to get a few minutes of your time?”

“That’s not going to happen. I’m an engaged woman,” I said holding up my hand, so he could see my ring.

“What that got to do with us?” He said cocking his head to the side and placing his hand on my waist.

Tingling sensations ran through my body. It felt like the sun was beaming directly on me. I could feel myself beginning to perspire. I glanced to make sure Lyle wasn’t seeing another man touching me.

"Excuse you. Jetta, I'm going to the poolroom to take off these clothes," I said moving his hand.

I hurried to get away from him. The cool air felt good when I walked inside. I sat on the couch and let out a deep breath. I took a few minutes to collect my thoughts. I kept telling myself I was an engaged woman with a plan. I wasn't going to let some fine nigga ruin my future. Lyle wasn't my ideal man, but he was a man with a plan. After cooling off, I removed my dress and rejoined the party. Lyle seemed to be enjoying himself. I decided it would be respectful to check in with him, since he didn't know many people here. I promised myself to avoid Titan at all cost.

Shaka

"Man, bout damn time," I said to Rhino.

"My bad fam. I was deferred by a fortuitous acquaintance," he said smiling.

I laughed. He get on my last nerve with those words, "Man, just go sit the buns on the table, so people can eat."

"Damn, I don't remember all these fine ass women going to school with us," he said looking around.

"That's because most of them are Jetta's friends. They went to private school. And we were focused on the money," I said.

"Shit was, we still is. Oh yea, Los said he needed to holla at us later. I told him we'll meet up with him at our normal spot," he said.

"What's up?" I asked.

Los was always grinding. I never had to check him about his work. He ran a solid team and never came up short. He was making crazy money. Next to Titan and Rhino, he was the nigga I respected most.

"Not sure. He didn't want to discuss it over the phone," he said looking at some thick female that walked by.

"Aight," I said.

I hope nobody was trying to move funny. Money was coming in steady and everybody was eating good.

"Let me check this steak," I said walking over to the grill.

"How he doing?" Rhino asked.

"He's good for now. The doctor said he'll feel good for a while. Eventually, his body will weaken. He wants us all to go on a vacation with him somewhere," I told him.

He nodded his head, "Shit, just let me know. I'm there. I'm 'bout to mingle with some of the big booty bitches."

"Yo, you see Jetta send her this way," I told him.

A few minutes later, Jetta came staggering my way. I shook my head, "What do you want? Don't you see I'm trying to enjoy my party?"

"Never mind, carry on," I said waving her off.

"You know you would be fuckable if you wasn't such an asshole. I mean you got a nice ass body and your dick…oh my God. It's the most beautiful thing I've ever seen ," she said slurring her words.

I couldn't hold the laugh. She was adorable when she was drunk, "Man, no more drinks for you."

"Why?" she asked in a whining voice.

Her eyes were lazy and sexy. I looked at her breast. I licked my lips as I imagined licking and sucking on them.

"You talking out your head, that's why," I said taking the cup from her hand.

She moved in close to me. I could feel my dick growing. She smelled sweet, "I'm drunk, but I know what I saw."

My dick grazed her flat stomach. She looked down at it. I couldn't hide the bulge in my trunks. She looked up at me with a seductive smile. I didn't care for kissing, but her full lips looked tempting to suck on.

"I guess I'm not the only one feeling it," she said with a smile.

"Excuse me," Belle walked up interrupting us.

I had never been happier to see someone in my life. I didn't like what was happening between me and Jetta at that moment.

"Hi Belle," Jetta slurred overly excited.

Belle giggled, "Hi, I'm sorry to interrupt. Rhino invited me. I hope that's okay."

"Girl, yea. Shit, I almost killed you. I'm sorry," Jetta said hugging her.

I laughed at how drunk she was. The sober Jetta would never apologize to anyone but her father. It even took him being furious as hell to get her to apologize. Belle looked at me for answers as Jetta hugged her. I shrugged my shoulders. She finally released her.

"Come on. I'll get you a drink." She pulled Belle by the hand leading her toward the bar.

I called Titan over to watch the grill while I took Omega his steak and sides. I made my way upstairs with the tray. Omega was sitting in his huge lounger watching Scarface on his big screen television. I sat the tray in front of him on his TV tray.

"Everyone having a good time?" He asked.

"Yea, it's thick as hell," I said.

"Sit and rest your feet for a minute. I know Boopsy is working your last nerve," he said laughing.

I chuckled. "Actually, she's quite pleasant when she's drunk."

He laughed, "Thank you for calling her. It took me a minute to figure out how she knew. I didn't suspect you, because I know you two didn't get along. I realized it wasn't about her, it was about me."

"You're welcome. She deserved some time with you," I told him. He nodded his head.

I cleared my throat to speak my mind. I held so much respect for him. It was hard stating my opinion when it went against his. “I know the treatments won’t cure it, but it gives you more time to spend with her.”

“That all sounds good until I realized that time consists of me exhausted and throwing up for hours after every treatment. I’ll die never fully enjoying life again. This way I get to enjoy time with the people that matter in my life. God sent you to me for a reason, Shaka. I need you to promise to look after her. I know she’s a handful, but she needs a strong hand. I never gave her that. I know you will,” he said.

“You know she’ll never listen to anything I say. I’m just a servant to her,” I told him.

“Make her listen. She needs to find her way. You can help her do that. You might not see it, but she respects you. She knows she can’t get over on you like she does me,” he said.

“I’ll do what I can. I just can’t promise you I won’t kill her spoiled ass,” I said. He laughed.

Clara knocked on the door and entered the room, “Shaka, there’s a young lady outside asking for you.”

I wasn’t expecting anyone. No female I fucked with knew I lived here. I stood up and walked over to the entertainment stand and examined the security cameras. Dayzee was standing there with her hand on her hip.

Omega chuckled. I looked over my shoulder at him. He shrugged his shoulders. I headed out the bedroom.

"What the fuck you doing here?" I asked her.

She smirked. "I came to the party I heard you were throwing."

"This ain't yo type of party. I'm gone try to be as respectful as I can. It's best you just leave now," I said.

"My lil cousin told me about the party. That's fucked up I didn't get an invite."

"Man, this ain't my shit. When have you ever known me to invite mothafuckas to a party. You ain't never been here."

"Why is that, Shaka?"

I chuckled, "I'll let you figure that out. Now, get the fuck on."

"I swear, let me find out you fucking another bitch," she threatened me. I slammed the door in her face. She didn't know it, but I felt like her threat was aimed at Jetta. The thought of anybody bringing harm to her infuriated me. I promised Omega I would protect her.

Belle

"What's your poison? I always wanted to say that," Jetta asked before laughing hysterically.

She was so funny when she was drunk. She acted like an entirely different person. "I'll have a strawberry daiquiri."

"You heard the lady. "I always wanted to say that too,"

"I'm sorry for being so mean to you. I'm really not a mean person. I'm just misunderstood. You seem like a sweet person. I need people like you in my life. You would make Rhino a nice girlfriend. You know he's short a few screws, but he's good people. Just don't piss him off," she rambled without taking a breath.

"Oh no, we aren't trying to date or anything. He just figured I needed to enjoy myself more, so he invited me," I informed her.

"Girl, that boy likes you. He's never invited a girl anywhere," she said waving me off.

I blushed. "I don't think I'm his type."

"Why not? You are fucking beautiful. And that body I would kill for. Yea, you are a little timid and nerdy.

Just loosen up and give him some sex appeal. I know you got it," she advised me.

"Sex appeal?" I asked. I've never in my life tried to be sexy. I didn't have a clue as to how to do that.

"You know flirt with him . Say little nasty things that will turn him on. Rhino is crazy, so get crazy with him," she advised me.

I don't know why I was seriously listening to her. Rhino was flirting with every girl that passed by him. I don't even know why he invited me.

"There goes my best friend," Jetta continued slurring her words as Miriam walked up.

"Hi Belle, I see somebody is wasted." she said smiling at me. I smiled and waved at her before taking a sip of my daiquiri.

"She's so cute when she's drunk," I said laughing.

"Shaka Zulu said I can't drink anymore, but I am," she said turning up a shot. We laughed and shook our heads.

"We gotta keep an eye on her. She gets wild when she drinks too much," Miriam told me.

I started to unwind after the first daiquiri. Miriam talked me into taking a couple of shots with her. I was wasted. We all were wasted. No Hands by Waka Flocka blasted through the speakers and Jetta screamed. She started dancing and shaking her ass to the throwback.

"Come on, let's join her," Miriam said grabbing me by my arm.

I know how to dance. I just never danced in public, but I was feeling myself. We started getting everyone's attention when we started grinding our hips and twerking our ass. Guys started throwing money at us. A guy came and stood behind me. He started grinding on my ass. I was so into the music, I didn't stop him. All of a sudden, I was yanked away by my arm.

"That's it! Mothafuckin' party over!" Rhino yelled as he pulled me away.

"Get yo damn girl! She out there wilin'" he said to Shaka as he came out the sliding doors.

"Let me go! Stop pulling on me!" I yelled trying to get out his grip.

"Fuck that! You taking yo hot ass home!" He said as he kept pulling me.

"Get my damn car!" He said to the valet. The guy hurried off.

"You invited me here to have fun. That's what I was doing. What are you mad for?" I asked jerking away from him nearly falling.

"Look at you. You drunk as hell. Out there slanging yo ass for niggas," he said angrily.

"So, what? It's mine to slang. At least they were giving me some kind of attention," I said slurring my words.

He stood there staring at me. My head started to spin as my stomach started doing flips. I needed to lay down. I've only been drunk like this once in my life. I was hanging with Tiera my graduation night. I vomited the entire night. He rushed over and bent me over.

"Shit, you bout to throw up," he said. The moment he said it,I vomited. It felt as if I was throwing up my entire insides.

"Got damn, that shit stinks," he said.

"I think I need to go to the emergency room," I said wiping my mouth.

"Nah, you need to bring that shit up. ER can't help you right now," he said.

I vomited again. The guy pulled up with the car. He opened the passenger door for me to get in.

"I will mess your car up," I told him.

"Man, get yo drunk, nerdy ass in the car," he demanded.

I flopped down in the seat. He hopped in the driver seat and pulled off. He rolled the window down. The cool breeze felt inviting against my face, but it didn't stop the rumble in my stomach. I pleaded with him to pull over. I felt myself getting ready to vomit again. He pulled over but was too late. I leaned forward and vomited on the floor. I looked over at him laying my head against the headrest. He shook his head and pulled off.

*****

When the car stopped, I realized it wasn't at my apartment. I remembered I never told him where I lived. He came over to the passenger side and helped me out of the car. I could barely stand on my own. The red brick two-story house was huge. The yards were beautifully landscaped.

"Where am I?" I asked.

"This my spot" he answered.

"No, I can't be here. This isn't right," I slurred pulling away from him, and falling to the ground.

"Man, you don't have a choice," he said scooping me up off the ground. He threw me over his shoulder. I knew I should've never gone to the party alone. The last thing I remember is him laying me on a bed.

Titan

"Man, tell the DJ to shut this shit down," Shaka said as he stared at Jetta with rage filled eyes.

She was letting some guy grind on her ass. I watched as he stepped to the guy and said something. The guy walked away without saying a word. I laughed and headed toward the DJ. He shut the music off after I told him the party was over. I headed toward the pool house to slip on my jeans and tee shirt. Since no one was inside, I decided to take a quick shower to rinse the chlorine off my body. After showering, I wrapped a towel around my waist. I walked back into the living room. Miriam walked inside with her head down looking at her phone. I couldn't help but smile on the inside.

"You looking for me, Star?" I asked. I knew I startled her.

She jumped and looked at me with wide eyes. She stared at me , before turning to get out the door. She fumbled with the knob until the door opened. I stood behind her closing the door before she could get away. She quickly turned to face me. I don't care what words came from her mouth, her eyes told a different story. Her lust filled eyes stared at me with her mouth slightly gaped open.

She shivered when my fingertips grazed her soft outer thighs. Her breathing became shallow. She bit on the right side of her bottom lip. I would never violate her. I stood waiting for her to make the next move. She closed her eyes and leaned forward pressing her soft lips against mine. I pulled my head away.

"Open your eyes," I said. I wanted her to see me.

I needed to know this is what she wanted as much as I did. She opened her eyes and stared at me. They were full of desire and passion. I pinned her back against the door and buried my tongue deep inside her mouth. Her lips were soft and smooth. Her tongue tasted sweeter than candy. My hands caressed her soft, silky flesh as our tongues explored he each other's mouth. My dick was growing like a balloon being pumped with air. My towel dropped exposing my brick hard dick. Goosebumps covered her skin as my hands massaged her breast and manipulated her hard nipples. She moaned loudly, deepening our kiss and wrapping her arms around my neck. I lifted her and pushed her bikini bottom to the side. She gasped for breath as I slid inside her wet, velvety center. I stared into her sex drunken eyes as I slid in and out her slippery, tight pussy. She wrapped her legs around my waist and started winding her hips. Her walls gripped my shaft as I started driving deeper inside her.

"Oooohhh yyyyess! Deeper!" She moaned as her juices started to pour out of her.

I could feel her liquids spilling on my nut sack. I unwrapped her legs and cuffed them in my arms. My throbbing dick slid deeper inside her. I could feel the head hitting her soft spot. I ground my hips pressing harder against her g-spot. Her eyes rolled to the back of her head. Her body shivered and jerked as she exploded. Her mouth was open but no words came out.

"Shit!" I barked as I felt her warm, wet liquid flooding my dick and sliding down my thighs.

"Ggggrrrr!" I grunted as I started ramming my dick faster and deeper inside her tight, gushing pussy.

"Oh God! Yes! Please don't stop! Sssshhhit!" she cried out as tears poured from her eyes. Sweat poured from our bodies as I continued to enjoy the best pussy I've ever had.

"Damn, this pussy tight and wet," I moaned as my mouth started to water.

Her sweet sex scent circulated in the air making me curious of her taste. Tingling vibrations ran through my spine as my toes knotted up damn near cramping. Her nails dug into my back as she came again spilling her sweet smelling essence. For the first time, I understood what niggas meant with they say, it was too good to pull out.

"Aaaarrrgghhhh! Ggggrrrrr!" I growled as I exploded inside her.

My body trembled and convulsed. I dropped her legs when I felt my knees weakening. We stood there trying to catch our breath. I looked down to see her creamy essence all over me and covering her mound.

"Damn Sunshine," I said smiling at her. My dick was still throbbing and hard as steel. I started slowly gliding in and out of her.

She glanced down at herself, "Oh God, what did I just do? Move!" She pushed me out the way, grabbed her dress from the sofa and stormed into the bathroom. I chuckled and shook my head. I knocked on the bathroom door.

"Please! Just leave!" She screamed through the door. I decided to dress before someone came inside the pool house. I left her to gather her thoughts. I knew this wouldn't be the last time I see her. Rather she knew it or not, we just starting.

"Damn, where the hell you been?" Shaka asked when I walked over by the grill.

There were a few people gathering their things and leaving. I looked around for Miriam's fiancé. He was nowhere to be found.

"Took a shower in the pool house," I said nonchalantly.

His head was down as he cleaned the grill. He lifted his eyes without moving his head and looked at the pool house. I immediately regretted telling him when Miriam came walking out. She kept her head down as she hurried past us and out the gate.

He looked at me and laughed. "No wonder Jetta couldn't find her."

"Man, chill out. Where her drunk ass at anyway ?" I asked looking around.

"I locked her in her room. She needs to sleep the alcohol off," he said. I laughed.

"I'm out. I'll see y'all at the spot tonight," I said dapping him before walking away.

Jetta

"Let me out!" I screamed banging on my bedroom door.

I can't believe he locked me in here. I knew someone had to hear me. No one would open the door. I know he told them not to let me out. I banged until I got tired. The alcohol was starting to wear off , my head was throbbing and I was starving. I soaked in a hot bubble bath until the water got cold. After oiling my body down, I laid across my king size canopy bed. Before I could fall asleep I heard my door being opened. I jumped off the bed. He walked through the door with an evil grin on his face.

"I'm telling my daddy," I said trying to storm out the room.

He laughed, "Who do you think told me to get you under control? You don't need to drink, if you're going to act like a cheap hoe."

I swung to slap him, but he caught my wrist. "What I tell you about yo hands?"

I snatched my arm from him, "I guess it's classy to give blow jobs in someone's office."

He laughed. “Nothing wrong with being a freak in private.” He licked his lips and stared at me. I looked down to see my robe was open .

“Nigga, you wish,” I said closing my silk robe.

“Baby girl, you couldn’t handle what I’m capable of doing to you. You ain’t my type, anyway,” he said. Those words hurt my ego.

“What do you want?” I asked.

“Damn, could this room get anymore girly?” I walked over and sat in the living area of my bedroom. Everything in my bedroom was pink and white like I left it before I left.

“I am a girl,” I said staring down at him.

“You a grown ass woman. You need to start acting like it,” he said.

“If you came in here to insult me, you can leave. My head is hurting and I’m starving,” I told him.

“Sit down,” he said. I flopped down on the light pink Queen Anne love seat.

“Your father wants us to go on a vacation with him. You know what places he like most . Decide where to go and book the flights,” he ordered.

I laughed, “I’m not your damn travel agent.”

He frowned up at me, "Didn't I just say this is for your father. I don't need you doing shit for me." I didn't understand how he could hurt my feelings so easily. I didn't even like him.

"He would want to go to Jamaica," I told him. He nodded his head.

"Who's all going?" I asked. He ran off a list of men. I wasn't going on a trip with nothing but men.

"I'm inviting some women. I'm not going with all dudes," I told him.

"Do whatever you have to do. Just make it happen," he said standing up.

"Are you bringing a date?" The words left my mouth before I could stop them.

He turned and looked at me . "Nah."

He turned and walked toward the door. Even his walk was too sexy to deny. I couldn't stop myself from wondering what it would feel like making love to him.

"Any food left?" I asked.

"There's a plate for you in the kitchen. Make sure you clean up when you are done. I left a bottle of Tylenol on the counter for you," he said.

"Thank you," I said graciously.

He nodded his head and walked out the door. I slipped on a pair of tights and a tank top. I went downstairs and devoured the plate. I took two of the Tylenol from the bottle. I was headed to say good night to Daddy when I was passing the weight room, I couldn't stop myself from stopping to look at him. Shaka was doing pull up exercises . He wore nothing but a pair of basketball shorts. I licked my lips as I admired his sweaty, muscular body. He had me in a trance. I thought of the wet dream I had of him. I wondered was he as good as the dream was. He brought me back to reality by clearing his throat.

"I-I-I was coming to work out," I stuttered through my lie.

He chuckled, "You don't look like the type to work out."

I instantly got an attitude. "What the hell does that mean?"

"Man, stop tripping. All I'm saying is you lazy as hell. Yo body tight," he said looking me up and down.

"I'm not lazy. I decided I wanted to get in better shape," I lied again.

"What kind of exercise you trying to do?" He asked.

I shrugged my shoulders while thinking of a quick lie, "Butt and thigh exercises."

He smiled. "Squats will work on the butt. Not sure about the thighs. Come here," he said staring at my body and making me nervous and hot.

I stared at him to see was he serious. He wasn't cracking a smile. I slowly walked to him. I was ready for whatever he was going to do to me. I could feel the moisture forming in my panties.

"Turn around," he said seductively.

I did as he ordered facing my back to him. Tingling feelings ran through my body as he touched my ass and thighs. I loved the feel of his hands touching me. He leaned in and nibbled on my earlobe. I exhaled. I wanted him. I wanted to feel him inside me. I could feel my heart thumping between my thighs.

"Homeless bums don't fuck spoiled little rich girls," he whispered in my ear.

I pulled away and turned to face him, "You are a fuckin' buffoon!"

I stormed out the room. I could hear him laughing as I made my way to my Daddy's room. Before I could open the door, my phone rang. I immediately hit ignore. I never wanted to speak to him again. That part of my life ended six months ago. I have so many regrets for what I did. It still haunts me.

NATAVIA PRESENTS

Rhino

"Come on, let's make this quick," I said as we sat around the trap.

I had left Belle knocked out in my bed. I didn't want her freaking out if she woke up. She was past wasted. I'm sure she's not going to remember how she ended up in my bed. I had to let her sleep in her bathing suit. She couldn't stand on her own. I didn't want to violate her by removing her clothes without her sober consent. I damn near was drooling as I looked at her thick thighs and succulent breast as she laid passed out in my bed. I studied her face as she slept. She had such an innocent beauty about herself. I wanted to lick my way down to the fat mound between her thighs covered by her bikini.

"What the hell you in a hurry for?" Titan asked.

"Man, I got shit to do," I said.

"Where's Los? What this meeting about?" Shaka asked as we sat around.

Los cleared his throat, "The drop last night. Everything went as planned, but I didn't like what happened afterward."

"What the fuck happened?' Titan asked.

"Kill took some weight to some new workers," he said.

"What got damn new workers?" Shaka asked angrily. No one was put on without Shaka's approval.

Los shrugged his shoulders, "I don't know. He claimed they were some serious hustlers that were going to bring in fast money."

"That mothafucka!" I said shaking my head.

One thing we know fast money ain't always good money. We were smart about our moves in the streets. Allowing the wrong ones to work for you can get you caught up quick.

"You don't know them?" Titan asked.

Los shook his head, "I've worked and lived on those streets for years. I never saw any of them in the neighborhood."

I looked at Shaka. "What you wanna do?"

"Kill gave them our work. He's going to be the one to get them to bring it back," he said. I knew we were taking a trip to Kill's house.

"We got this. You can go home," Shaka said looking at me.

"What?" I asked looking at him like he was growing another head.

He smiled. “Belle’s car is still at the house. Either she’s at your spot or you need to find out where she is. You invited her. She’s your responsibility. She was lit.”

“Man, she good. She’s knocked out,” I said.

“Go check on her. We got this,” Titan said.

I took a deep breath. I can’t believe I was letting a female interfere with my hustle. The thing about her, she didn’t seem like just any female. Something about her was special. Maybe too special for a nigga like me. I decided to let them handle Kill.

*****

I hopped in my car and headed back to the house. I stopped by Waffle House to get her something to eat. She didn’t eat anything at the party. I know she was going to be starving when she woke up. I sat at the counter in Waffle House waiting on my order.

“Hi, Where’s Belle?” Belle’s friend said standing next to me.

“How the fuck I’m supposed to know?” If she didn’t know where her friend was, I wasn’t going to be the one to tell her.

“Dang, you ain’t gotta get an attitude. Don’t you like her?” She asked.

"Man, gone with that bullshit," I said waving her off.

She smacked her lips and walked off. Being a man, I watched her ass as she walked off. She had a nice, fat ass. Too bad she was annoying as hell. After getting my order I headed out to my car. I heard her annoying voice again. I kept walking like I didn't hear her. She caught up with me.

"I'm here with my friend and she's not ready to go. I have to go get my kids. Can you give me a ride?" She asked.

"I'm not going in yo direction," I said.

"Please, I promise I'll make it worth your time," she said smiling at me.

"You gone suck my dick on the way?" I asked.

She giggled. She was pulling my dick from my jeans before I could get out of the parking lot. She licked, slurped and sucked until I exploded in her mouth. I pulled up to her small house.

"You wanna come in?" She asked.

"I thought this was where yo kids was at," I said.

"They is, but I'm gone stay the night since it's so late. My sister stay here. I can put the kids on the couch. We can go in the room." Her crazy ass said.

"Nah, I'm good. I gotta get somewhere," I said.

She looked disappointed, "You want my phone number, so we can hook up again."

"Nah," I replied

"Well, can I have yours?" She asked.

"Man, get the hell out," I said impatiently.

She was getting on my nerves at this point. She smacked her lips and got out the car. She played herself tonight. I pulled off and headed home.

*****

When I got home, there was a car parked in front of my house. I could tell it was a dude sitting in the car. I knew she didn't tell some nigga to come pick her up from my spot. I jumped out the car. She was walking out the front door.

"You brought a nigga to my house?" I asked angrily.

"No, it's an uber. I will send your clothes back," she said referring to my gym shorts and tee shirt she wore.

"I was going to take you home. What the hell you running for?" I asked.

"Did we?" She asked stretching her eyebrows. I knew she was asking did we have sex.

“I ain’t never taken advantage of a drunk female for pussy. Man, what kind of man you think I am?” I asked angrily.

“No, I’m not saying that,” she anxiously.

“Well, what the fuck you saying?” I asked.

“I’m sorry,” she said softly.

“Yea, you gone and get the fuck outta here. I don’t need no damn false ass rape charges being put on me,” I said walking away.

Miriam

"Ms. Halston, you have a visitor," said my receptionist over the intercom.

It was the end of my first week on the job. Everything went great. I was ready to unwind and relax for the weekend. I've been so wrapped up in getting comfortable in my new position, I haven't spent any time with Lyle. What surprises me most is he hasn't complained. I decided I would cook dinner for us tonight to make up for our absence.

"You can send them in," I replied.

I knew it was Jetta. She had called me earlier to say she was stopping by. We were going to get a drink before I went home.

"What's good, Boss lady," she said smiling as she came through the door.

"I'm exhausted. I need this drink," I said gathering my things.

"You just gotta get used to everything. It'll get easier," she said.

"I'm sure it will. Let's get out of here. I'll follow you," I said walking toward the door.

*****

We arrived at the bar and was seated at a table in the corner. After placing our order, we started catching up. We hadn't talked much since her pool party last week. I tried to forget about that night but couldn't. I wanted to regret what I did, but I didn't. I never had a man to touch my soul through sex. Every nerve in my body was awakened by his touch. I couldn't fight my desires for him when I walked in the pool house. His muscular body was dripping wet. I didn't tell Jetta about that night nor did I plan to tell her. Lyle and I got into a huge fight that night. He had been waiting in front of the house while I was fucking a man in my friend's pool house. I don't regret my actions, but I am ashamed for what I did.

"So, have you decided which art school you wanted to attend?" I asked her.

She shook her head, "No, I'm still researching. I'm leaning toward Savannah College Of Art & Design."

"At least submit the app while you're still researching," I told her.

"Ok, I will. First, I gotta find a travel agent to book this vacation for my dad. I want you to come with me," she said.

"Where?" I asked.

"Jamaica. He loves visiting the place where his parents were born. Plus, his grandparents are still there. I would love to see my great grands. I haven't seen them in over three years," she said sadly.

"I can go, but only for the weekend. I can't be taking time off and I just started my job. It'll be a good weekend for me to makeup to Lyle. I haven't given him any time lately," I told her.

"That's cool. I just want you to come. Send me y'all info and I'll book your flights," she directed me. I nodded my head in agreement.

"How's your dad?" I asked.

"He's doing great. I can't believe Shaka. He acted as if Daddy was dying," she said rolling her eyes.

I smiled, "Maybe he was just missing you."

She rolled her eyes, "I seriously doubt that. Can you believe he locked me in my bedroom the night of the party?"

I laughed. I wasn't surprised. Shaka was very protective of Jetta. They were the same age, but he was far more mature than her. They were so different, but their chemistry was undeniable. She would never admit it though.

"Where did you disappear to when Rhino's psycho ass shut everything down?" She asked.

I nervously cleared my throat, "I was inside the pool house washing the chlorine off. Then, I went home."

"Oh okay, I'm trying to hit up Titan's club tonight," she said.

"I have to spend some time with my fiancé. I'm out," I told her.

"Ugh, you know I have no friends," she said pouting.

"You should be friendlier," I said laughing.

"Whatever, can't blame me because bitches envy all this beauty and class," she said referring to herself. I laughed and shook my head.

"What about Belle? She seems nice," I suggested.

"She is. I feel bad for the way I treated her that night I almost killed her," she said sadly.

"You should. You blamed her for you almost killing her," I said laughing.

"I'm going to call and invite her. I can give her a makeover. I mean she is beautiful, but she doesn't know how to punctuate it."

I laughed. Punctuate?"

"Yes bitch, she needs an exclamation point on that ass," she said snapping her fingers and twirling her hips.

*****

After a couple of drinks, we parted ways. When I arrived home, I took a shower and dressed in sexy, red lingerie. I was feeling the Patron drinks I had at the bar. I popped a bottle of Merlot while I cooked his favorite. He loved eggplant lasagna. I didn't have time to make the homemade sauce he loves, so I improvised with store bought sauce. I was taking the lasagna out the oven when he came through the door.

"It smells good in here," he said walking into the kitchen.

"I figured we need a romantic night. We've both been so busy this week," I said wrapping my arms around his waist.

Lyle was tall and handsome. I hated I didn't get the same desires I felt with Titan. I found myself comparing the two. Lyle deserved better than that from me. I was determined to make this relationship work between us. I tiptoed and tried kissing him. He stopped me by unwrapping my hands from his waist.

"I'm going to take a quick shower. You can fix my plate," he said before turning and walking away.

I was speechless. I was standing in front of him damn near naked and he didn't notice. Or maybe he just wasn't turned on by me. I came back down and sat to the dining room table. I had set up a romantic setting with candles. He never acknowledged it. He frowned up as he chewed the lasagna.

"What is this?" He asked.

"It's your favorite, eggplant lasagna," I said.

"No, this isn't the same. Something is different," he said.

I cleared my throat, "I didn't have time to make the homemade sauce. I used store bought, but I seasoned it well."

"Next time, don't bother making it all," he said getting up from the table.

"Lyle, that's mean. I worked hard all week. I wanted us to have a nice evening," I said standing up with him.

"I can't eat that," he said.

I was furious, "Well nigga, how about eating me? Damn, I'm standing here almost naked and you haven't said anything."

“We can have sex later. I have some accounts to look over first,” he said.

“Wait on it,” I said walking out the kitchen.

Shaka

"Got a minute?" I asked Omega. He was having his daily walk around the yard.

"Yea, what's up Zulu?" He said smiling. It was his own nickname for me. I walked beside him.

"I had to let Kill go," I told him.

I knew Kill had worked with him for a while. I didn't know how he would feel about this information. The night me, Titan and Los visited him I cut him loose. He was forced to call the young hustlers back with our product. We found out they were some cousins of his from Tennessee. He told them he was running his own shit and had a connect. He was stealing our product to sell as his own. I explained the situation to Omega.

He shook his head, "I guess he felt I didn't do right by him. He felt like your spot belonged to him. It would have been his had he not let the money go to his head. You did right. Never allow a man to steal from you. Will he retaliate?"

That was his way of asking was he still alive. I stared him in the eyes. He nodded his head. That was the answer to let him know he was dead.

“Have that daughter of mine been behaving?” He asked.

I hadn’t seen much of her since the party. She comes and goes. I always had someone keeping an eye on her to make sure she was safe.

“Yea lately, but it’s the weekend,” I said.

He chuckled, “Shaka, you work entirely too much. You need to enjoy life more. I was you at your age. I regret spending so much time hustling. You’re making big money. Enjoy life. You can do that and still save money for your future family.”

I laughed, “Family?”

“Yea, trust me it’s going to happen one day. I already see it happening,” he said winking his eye .

I had no idea what he was talking about. I wasn’t seriously involved with anyone. A girlfriend, wife or relationship was the farthest thing from my mind. I couldn’t imagine building a life with someone. I don’t know how I would know if I wanted to be with someone the rest of my life. Love was an emotion I didn’t know anything about.

“I’ll enjoy life when I’m not starving anymore,” I said.

“Well, I have a date tonight. I won’t be coming home ,” he said.

"Take security with you," I instructed. He nodded his head.

I went back inside the house. I decided to find a documentary to watch. I made my way to the theatre room with a bottle of Hennessy and a glass. I relaxed in the oversized cushioned lounger. I was watching the documentary *13th* when she came and sat beside me. The lounger was big enough for two people, but it wasn't a place she should be sitting.

"What?" I asked glancing at her.

"This what you do on a Friday night?" She asked.

"Nothing in the clubs for me. I'm good right here," I answered.

Her floral aroma swept across my nostrils. I glanced at her bare thighs that had a slight gap between them. I repositioned myself to control the hardness of my dick. Her hair was styled with long, honey blonde tracks. It made her deep chocolate skin glow.

"I'm going to Titan's club," she said.

"Have fun," I replied bluntly.

"Can I ask you something?" She asked before taking a sip from my glass.

I chuckled, "I don't think I can stop you."

She smiled showing her perfect, white teeth. “Why don’t you like me?”

I laughed, “I can ask you the same thing.”

“Do you like that girl?” She asked.

I gave her a puzzled look, “What girl, Jetta?”

“You know. The one that was in Titan’s office with you,” she said shamefully. I chuckled and shook my head.

“Yes or no?” She asked.

“Mind yo business,” I said turning my head to look at her.

God, she was beautiful. She stared at me with her mouth slightly open. Her full lips looked soft, sexy and inviting. I couldn’t take my eyes off her. I found myself wanting to taste her lips. Against my better judgement, I leaned in and gently sucked on her bottom lip. They were even softer and sweeter than they looked. I looked at her to see her reaction. Her eyes were closed. I knew I should’ve stopped and sent her out the room, but I wanted to taste more of her. I covered her mouth with my lips sucking her tongue into my mouth. She moaned as she allowed her tongue to taste the inside of my mouth. Without thinking, I pulled her into my lap. She had my mind wrapped up in exploring everything about her sweet softness. She straddled my lap as she continued to kiss me passionately.

My hands massaged her smooth, soft thighs. I broke our kiss only to taste her sweet neck. I licked and sucked on her flesh as she moaned in pleasure. My hand pushed up her skirt until my fingers were inside her soaked panties. She started twirling her hips as I slipped a finger inside her wet pussy.

"Oooh, that feels so good," she moaned as she nibbled on my ear.

Everything inside me was telling me to stop, but my dick was overpowering all the warning signs. Her juices were spilling out of her wet tunnel onto my hand. I used my thumb to massage her swollen clit. My other hand was concentrating on her breasts . I pulled one from her low-cut top. My tongue lapped around the dark circles. I softly bit on her nipple causing her to cry out loud. She became wild as she gyrated and grinded on my hand. I slid another finger inside her. I explored her insides until I felt the soft spot. I pressed against it as I caressed her clit. She started bucking like a cow girl. Her body stiffened and quivered.

"Aaaaahhhh! Yyyyeeeesss! I'm commmiiinnnggg!" She screamed.

I felt warm, gooeyness sliding down my hand. She collapsed against my chest still trembling. She started kissing my neck with her soft lips. Her soft kisses were relaxing my body as my dick throbbed. The theatre room door opened causing the light from the hall to shine on us. I knew Omega was going to kill me for violating his baby girl.

"Oh shit, I'm sorry!" I heard Miriam's voice say.

I was relieved it wasn't Omega. Jetta jumped up from my lap. She grabbed her phone and ran hurrying out the door. I didn't stop her. I knew I had fucked up. I looked down to see her sticky, creamy essence covering my hand. I licked one of my fingers to taste her. My dick jumped at the taste of her sweet juices. I had to make sure this never happens again.

Belle

"Are you sure it's okay, Pam?" I asked.

I was surprised when Jetta called and asked me to go out with her. I felt guilty asking Pam to babysit again. I have always been the one to take care of Hannah. School and work was the only thing that kept me from her.

"Chile, go have some fun," Granny said waving me off.

"I don't mind, Belle. You deserve to have some fun. I will keep her overnight. Granny is staying with me also," she said winking at Granny.

"You don't have to. I won't be out long like last time," I said.

"Girl, stop worrying and have fun," Pam said playing with Hannah's chubby cheeks.

I looked at my phone to see the text from Jetta. She wanted to pick me up, but I declined. I didn't want to risk her seeing Hannah. I wasn't ashamed of my baby. I just didn't like people in my personal life. It was some things I chose to keep buried. I texted her to let her know I would meet her at the club. I kissed Hannah and Granny good night. I hopped in my car and headed to the club. I asked

Tiera to go out with me, but she declined. She didn't like Jetta or Miriam. At first, I didn't like Jetta. She's one of those people you have to get to know before judging her. She seems mean, but she's not. Miriam is always nice, so I don't know her reason for disliking. her.

*****

I was lucky enough to arrive at the club just as Jetta and Miriam was walking up to the entrance. I didn't have the money for valet parking, so I parked across the street from the club. I walked across the street to join them. They spotted me and started smiling. I felt under dressed when I observed what they were wearing. I was wearing a pair of black tights and sequined halter top. Miriam wore a short, backless, beige dress. Jetta wore a white, off the shoulder, long sleeved body dress that stopped midway her thighs.

"Hi," Miriam said with her contagious smile.

"I feel so under dressed," I said looking at them.

"You look beautiful," Jetta said smiling at me. I can't believe this is the same girl that almost ran me over.

"Thank you, I didn't know what to do with my hair," I said.

"It's cute," Miriam said looking at my messy bun.

"Don't worry, with that ass men aren't going to be looking at your cute bun. Their eyes will be on your other buns," Jetta said tapping my butt. I giggled.

We made our way inside the club. "Come on, I swiped some more VIP passes from Shaka," Jetta said leading us toward the VIP floor.

We were able to get a good table, "You're sadly mistaken if you think you swiped those passes," Miriam said to her.

"What does that mean?" Jetta said cutting her eyes at her. "Don't mention that shit, Mir. You promised to never bring that up again."

Miriam laughed, "I wasn't going to. I'm just saying. He's leaving those passes for you to find."

"Whatever," Jetta said waving her off.

"Anyway, I'm ready to get wasted," Miriam said waving over a waitress.

"I told you his asshole ways would eventually start showing," Jetta said to her. I assumed she was talking about Miriam's fiancé.

"Fuck him. That's why I left him sitting on the couch mad as hell," she said.

Rhino walked up to the VIP floor with his crazy, sexy swagger. I hadn't seen him since the night I ran from his house. He was thinking the worst about why I was leaving. I was only trying to get home to my child.

"There goes your Bae," Jetta said.

"Is not!" I said looking at her with wide eyes.

"Ewww, you like Rhino?" Miriam asked.

"No," I lied.

Jetta laughed, "Yes, she does. Go talk to him."

I glanced over at the table where he sat. As always, females were flocking around him. I rolled my eyes and gave the waitress my attention. I decided to take it light tonight and ordered a daiquiri.

"Girl, if you like him go stake yo claim. Let them bitches know. Don't pay me no mind. Trust me, I have no room to judge," Miriam said smiling at me.

"Sure don't," Jetta said laughing.

"Bitch, at least I wasn't humping in the theatre room," Miriam said laughing.

Jetta's mouth dropped open with wide eyes. Miriam reached over and lifted her chin to close her mouth. I couldn't help but laugh.

"I can't. He's mad at me," I said sadly. I explained to them what happened.

"Well, go and apologize," Jetta said.

I looked at them to see were they serious. Miriam shrugged her shoulders. I slowly stood up and made my way over to his table. He stared up at me . I didn't know what to say. His crazy looking eyes always looked sexy. My heart started to beat rapidly.

"Are you going to say something or stand there acting preternatural," he asked.

The girl sitting beside him giggled , "What does that mean?"

"It means get the hell on somewhere," he said glancing at her. She smacked her lips and stormed off.

"Well," he said.

"I didn't leave because I was scared of you. I had to get home to my Granny," I said half telling the truth.

"Sit down," he said.

"She cool?" He asked.

"Who?" I asked.

He chuckled and shook his head. "Yo Granny?"

"Oh, yea she's good," I said giggling.

I inhaled his masculine cologne as I sat next to him. He had his dreads up, but they hung loose on his head. It was something about his eyes that pulled me in.

"I'm surprised to see you out again," he said.

I shrugged, “Jetta invited me. I’m trying to learn to live a little.”

“Hanging with her might be too much living for you,” he said.

“She’s not that bad,” I said laughing.

“Don’t let her get you in any trouble. I’ll fuck you up. You got a bright future ahead of you,” he warned me. I nodded my head.

“I ain’t really feeling this club thing tonight. Come on, let’s get out of here,” he said standing up. I looked up at him like he was crazy.

“I can’t just leave. She invited me to hang with them,” I said.

He pulled me up by my hand and walked over to them, “She’s going with me.”

They looked at me and smiled . Jetta told me we were going shopping in the morning. I didn’t have money to shop like them. I shopped at Ross and Forever 21. Before I could reply, I was being taken out the club with my hand in his.

“Where we going?” I asked as we stood outside the club waiting on the valet.

“To eat,” he said.

“My car,” I said remembering I drove.

"Trust me, no one is going to steal it," he said.

"Are you implying my car isn't worth stealing?" I asked propping my hand on my hip.

He laughed and shrugged his shoulders, "You said it, I didn't."

The valet pulled up with a Porsche Macan. I only knew the car, because it was the dream car of a guy I once dated. I fell in love with the vehicle the moment I slid into the seat. I hopped in the passenger side.

"You owe me for throwing up in my shit," he said.

I giggled, "I'm so sorry, but this isn't the car we were in."

"Nah, that was my BMW," he answered.

Titan

"Titan!" I heard my name being called as I made my way inside the club. I turned around to see who was calling me. She looked familiar, but I couldn't remember how I knew her.

"It's me, Tiera. Remember I met you last weekend? I was with Belle."

"Oh yea, what's up?" I asked.

"Can you get me and my friend in? We don't want to wait in this long line," she asked. I glanced at her friend. I didn't have a problem letting pretty women in the club.

I looked at her friend to make sure it wasn't Belle's friend with her. "Yea," I said walking to the entrance. I instructed security to give them a couple of VIP passes. I excused myself and made my way to my office.

After going over paperwork, I turned on the security monitors. I was happy to see how packed the club was. My club had only been open for a little over six months. I wanted to keep my club classy. I didn't allow jeans, sneakers or hats. If niggas looked like they could cause trouble, they weren't allowed inside. If females looked messy, they were denied entrance. I zoomed in on one of the cameras when I spotted her sitting on the couch with her toned legs crossed. The short dress revealed the beautiful tattoo. Memories of the pool house flooded my mind. It hasn't been a day that she hasn't crossed my mind. I turned the camera off and locked up the office. I made my way to the VIP floor. I looked around for Rhino, but he was nowhere in sight. I shook my head at Jetta standing on the table dancing. I wasn't running that kind of club. I walked over to the table.

"Get down Jetta," I said looking up at her.

"Why, I'm having fun," she said swaying her hips.

"Get down or I call Shaka," I threatened her.

She rolled her eyes at me and stopped dancing. I helped her off the table. I looked at Miriam, but she refused to look my way. I know she haven't forgotten what went down between us. I'll wait patiently until she wants more.

"What's up Star?" I asked getting her attention.

She rolled her eyes. "That is not my name. My name is Miriam."

"I know your name. It means star of the sea. I choose to call you a star," I said winking at her.

"Let's go dance," she said to Jetta as she stood up. I smiled as she walked away. I had to get a peek of her round ass jiggling in the short dress. I turned around and looked Mena in her face.

“Why you always in them bitches’ face?” She asked with her hand on her hip.

“Stop fucking tripping,” I said trying to walk pass her.

“Nigga, I haven’t seen you all week. What up Titan? You fucking another bitch?”

“Yea,” I answered bluntly.

“Soon as I find out who she is I’m whooping her ass,” she threatened.

I laughed, “Why? I haven’t tried to whoop Kill ass for fucking you.” I knew she was fucking somebody, but I had no clue it was Kill. The nigga bragged about it before Shaka killed him the night we visited him. No one knew he was dead yet. We just tell everyone he’s MIA.

Her eyes grew big. “What?”

“No need to fake it. Just make sure all yo shit out of my house by the end of the week. You know what, never mind. I’ll pack it all up for you. I’ll even pay for the storage. I’ll send you the address where to find it.” I said walking off.

She grabbed me by my arm. I gave her a look that she knows. I hardly ever lost my temper. Mena knew not to push me to that point. She released my arm and walked away. I walked to the bar to get a drink.

"Everything okay?" Tiera asked sitting on a stool at the bar.

"Yea," I answered.

She started making small talk. She seemed like a level-headed female that had something going for herself. I decided to entertain her conversation. We swapped numbers and I agreed to call her to set up a date. I dismissed myself and made my way downstairs. I tried to block her out of my mind but couldn't. She was swaying her hips to The Weekend by Sza. I walked up behind her and wrapped my arm around her waist.

"Tell me you don't feel this shit," I whispered in her ear.

I could feel her body relaxing in my arms. In seconds, my dick was brick hard pressing against her soft ass. I started kissing her on the neck as my hand slid between her toned thighs. I was surprised when she grabbed my hand and pushed it inside her panties. I looked around to see was anybody watching us. The floor was crowded and dark. We could fuck right here, and no one would notice. I slid two fingers between her wet pussy lips. She started winding her hips against my fingers. I bit and sucked on her neck as she twirled her hips along with the music. I knew she was about to come when she rested her head on my shoulder. I removed my hand and grabbed her. I was going to finish this in my office. Unfortunately, we were stopped by Jetta.

"Bitch, Lyle is here," she said to Miriam with wide eyes.

"What?" She asked looking terrified.

"Yes, he just walked in with his brother," Jetta said looking over his shoulder.

"What the fuck is he doing here?" She asked angrily.

She released my hand and stormed off. Here I was standing in the middle of a crowded dance floor with a dick hard enough to break through cement. Somebody had to help me release this pressure. I walked back upstairs. Tiera was still sitting at the bar.

"Let's get out of here," I whispered in her ear. She wasted no time getting off the stool. I instructed my manager to close up before leaving.

Shaka

I kept checking the time on my phone. It was almost four o'clock in the morning and she still wasn't home. I couldn't sleep. Every time I closed my eyes, her face would appear. I kept seeing her facial expressions when she was coming on my hand. My dick has been hard ever since she left the house. I called Titan to see if she was at the club. He said she was there when he left. I closed my eyes to try and get some sleep. I jumped to answer my phone when it rang. I looked at the screen to see Dayzee calling. I exhaled in frustration but answered.

"What?"

"Damn, who pissed in your cornflakes?" She asked with the same attitude I had.

"Man, it's too early in the morning for bullshit. What you want?" I asked.

"You," she said in her sexy voice.

I was just getting ready to reply when I heard a giggle. I knew it was Jetta and she was wasted. I hung up the phone without replying to her. I opened my room door to see her and Miriam wobbling to her room. I guess they heard my door open. They turned to face me.

"Shaka Zulu! You ready to finish what we started," Jetta said walking toward me nearly falling.

"Man, take your drunk ass to bed," I said staring at her.

"I wanna feel that big, black, beautiful cock inside me," she said barely able to stand. Miriam was standing by Jetta's bedroom door laughing.

"Mir, I thought you had a level fuckin' head," I said looking at her.

She laughed and shrugged her shoulders, "It's the animal inside me. I can't control it."

I shook my head. "Come on Shaka Zulu, take me," Jetta said throwing her arms around my neck.

My dick was hard, and I was furious as hell with her. I threw her over my shoulder and carried her inside the bathroom in her bedroom. I turned on the shower with cold water and placed her inside. She screamed and cussed me out. She called me every name she could think of. I ignored her and walked back into the bedroom.

Miriam was standing there laughing, "That's cruel."

"Don't try to leave this damn house tonight. You too drunk to drive anywhere," I said staring at her.

"Yes Boss," she said almost falling.

I was walking toward the door when Jetta jumped on my back. She started hitting me in the head and telling me she hates me. This would've been hysterical if I wasn't so damn mad. She was wet and drunk, so it didn't take much to flip her off of me. I bent over, and she went flying to the floor. She jumped up and charged into me almost knocking me over. I grabbed her and slammed her on the bed. I straddled her and pinned her hands over her head. God, she was fucking beautiful.

"Calm yo ass down, Jetta," I demanded.

She struggled to get out my grip. She caught me unexpectedly with a knee to my groin. My dick was already hard and aching. The pain I felt brought me to my knees. I let her go and fell over on the bed.

"Oh my God! I'm so sorry Micah," she said sitting up on her hind legs.

I rolled over holding my crotch in pain. Miriam stood there laughing the entire time. She had to pay for this. I gained the strength to stand up. I threw her over my shoulder again. She kicked and screamed for me to put her down. I carried her downstairs and through the house until I reached the pool.

"Shaka, don't throw her in there!" Miriam screamed while she laughed.

"You think shit funny. Yo drunk ass better save her then," I said before throwing her in the pool.

Miriam wasted no time jumping in with her. It was no doubt she was a true friend. I knew Jetta could swim, but she was too drunk to be in a pool. I wasn't going to let her drown. I just wanted to scare her ass sober. Miriam dragged her to the shallow part of the water. They both rested their arms on the side of the pool trying to catch their breath. I stood there smiling at them.

"You fuckin' lunatic! You could've killed me! I'm telling Daddy on you," Jetta screamed.

I laughed as I walked away. I went upstairs and rested peacefully. I didn't wake up until the afternoon. I walked into the kitchen to see Omega sitting there reading the newspaper. It was always funny to see it. He refused to use modern day technology to keep up with the world. He glanced at me and continued reading the paper. I realized he had on the same clothes he had on when he left last night.

"Just getting home?" I asked with an arched brow as I poured a cup of coffee.

"Had a lot of making up to do," he said smiling. I laughed.

"You never slept this late. I guess you had a long night," he said looking at me.

"He sure did! He tried to kill me, Daddy," Jetta said storming into the kitchen. I chuckled and shook my head. She was so damn dramatic.

"What?" Omega asked staring at her.

"He threw me in the pool," Jetta explained.

"So, what? You can swim like a fish," Omega said looking at her.

"I was drunk. I could've drowned," she said staring at me.

Omega looked at me for an explanation. I smiled and shrugged my shoulders. "She kneed me in the groin. He burst into laughter.

"Daddy, it's not funny! He's a buffoon," she said staring at me. I mimicked an ape mocking her.

Omega kept laughing as he stood up. "If cancer doesn't kill me, living here with you two surely will."

"Daddy, do something!" Jetta said stomping her feet like a spoiled brat.

Omega stood up and walked out the kitchen still laughing. I walked over and stood close to her. I could feel the energy between us. I leaned down and licked the side of her face.

“Ewww!” she screeched wiping her face. I tapped her on the ass and walked out the kitchen.

Rhino

I don't remember falling asleep last night. After leaving the club with Belle, we went to eat some breakfast. We came back to my house to watch movies. She wanted to watch some chick flick called *A Walk to Remember*. I couldn't believe how good the movie was. I'll never admit how much I enjoyed the corny love story. I guess I fell asleep when she started watching *The Golden Girls*. I woke up on an empty sofa. I thought she went home until I smelled food cooking. I walked into the kitchen to find her in one of my tee shirts cooking breakfast.

"What you doing?" I asked.

She jumped, "You scared me. I wanted to cook you breakfast before I leave. I hope that's okay."

"Are you scared of me?" I asked walking up to her.

She looked up at me with unsure eyes. "You intimidate me."

I laughed. "Why?"

She shrugged her shoulders. "I don't know. I've never been with anyone like you."

I gave her a puzzled look. I didn't want to cross that line with her. I wanted her, but she deserved more than someone like me. She looked sexy wearing my tee shirt.

“I don’t mean like that. I mean I’ve never been around anyone like you. You so controlling and blunt,” she explained. I stared down at her wanting to taste her lips.

“What you cook?” I asked taking a step back.

“Bacon, cheese grits and toast. You didn’t have any eggs,” she said glancing at the stove.

“I don’t eat them. I’m not eating a damn unborn baby chicken,” I told her.

She giggled, “Sit down. I’ll fix your plate.”

I sat at the kitchen island . She turned her back to me to fix my plate. My dick jumped when she tiptoed for a plate out of the cabinet. The shirt lifted on her ample ass revealing the black bikinis she was wearing.

“Belle, you need to go put on some damn clothes,” I demanded.

“Oh, I’m sorry! I forgot I didn’t have on any pants,” she said pulling down my shirt she wore. She hurried out the room.

I was stuffing my face when she came back downstairs, “I hope you don’t mind, but I slept in your bed last night. You were hogging the couch.”

“Yea, you good,” I said with a mouth full of food.

“I tried to work your surround sound. It’s too complicated. I like to listen to music when I cook,” she said. I got her phone from the kitchen island and hooked it to the surround sound.

"Play your favorite song," I said.

She smiled at me before scrolling through her phone. Some lame ass white folks Pop music blasted through the speakers. It was slow and depressing.

"What the hell is that?" I asked.

She giggled. "*Nothing Compares to You.* I like Pop music." I shook my head at the annoying music.

"Do you kill people?" She asked with a serious face. I nearly choked on the food.

I swallowed the food before speaking. "What?"

"That room that's locked. Is that where you kill people?" She asked. She was dead ass serious. I couldn't stop laughing.

"You need to stop watching Criminal Minds. I ain't no damn pyscho," I said.

She exhaled and sat next to me. "What's in there?"

"Just some personal shit," I stated nonchalantly. That personal shit was wear I poured my heart out. I've never shared that part of my life with anyone. A horn blew.

"Well, that's my uber. I gotta go pick up my car. I hope no one stole it. If they did, you buying me another me," she said smiling.

"What the fuck you call an uber for. I can take you home," I said.

"I know, but I don't want to trouble you. I know you have things to do," she said. I wasn't ready for her to go.

"What you doing later?" I asked.

"Spending the day with my Granny. I've been neglecting her," she said.

"Oh ok," I said disappointed.

She cleared her throat, "My birthday is next weekend if you wanna do something. We could watch a Criminal Mind marathon and eat junk food."

I laughed. "Nah, I'm keeping you away from that shit. Put yo number in here. We'll do something. So, don't make plans." I slid my phone to her and she put her number in.

I looked at my phone. She stored her number under the name *myrmidon* meaning partner in activity. I chuckled. She winked at me and smiled. Her innocence was sexy.

"Next time, clean up yo mess," I hollered as she walked out the kitchen.

"Next time, you might be cooking breakfast for me," she said in a flirtatious manner. She turned to walk away and ran straight into the wall.

I rushed over to make sure she was okay. “I’m fine,” she said hurrying out the kitchen.

I laughed and shook my head at her nerdy ass. After I finished eating and cleaning up the kitchen, I made my way over to Omega’s house. When I pulled up, Shaka was putting some luggage in his Escalade.

*****

“Nigga, where you jetting off to?” I asked hopping out my car.

“Nowhere. I’m just going to stay at my own spot for a while,” he said dapping me up.

I laughed, “Jetta done ran yo ass off.”

“Man, if I don’t leave, I’m going to kill her spoiled ass,” he said seriously.

“She here?” I asked.

“Yea, why?” he asked curiously.

“Calm down fam. That’s all you,” I said backing away from him. He didn’t see the jealousy I saw in his eyes.

“Man fuck you,” he said waving me off.

“Nah, I need her to plan a party for me,” I told him.

He looked at me curiously, "Yo birthday ain't until November."

"Got damn! I ain't trying to fuck Shawty. It's for Belle," I explained as I laughed. This fool don't even realize how gone he is over that girl.

"Oh, her whining ass in there somewhere," he said.

"Alright, we checking traps later?" I asked as he got in his truck.

"Yea, hit me up. I'll be at the crib," he said cranking up.

Jetta

"What the hell you did to my boy?" Rhino asked me snatching my headphones out of my ears . I was lounging by the pool enjoying a beautiful day. His crazy eyes stared at me with a scowl on his face.

"Nothing! He tried to kill me last night," I said sitting up.

He laughed, "I'm sure yo spoiled ass did something to deserve it."

I rolled my eyes, "Whatever. I'm sure he's in the study. As you can see, he's not here."

"I know, he moved out," he told me.

I was shocked but held a poker face. I knew we didn't get along, but I never imagined he would move. He must truly hate me. He would never leave Daddy's side.

"So, what do you want?" I asked not wanting to think about Shaka moving out.

"I need a favor," he said sitting on the lounger beside me.

I just looked at him. I didn't have a problem with Rhino. I just thought he was a little off balance . I don't understand why he uses big words when he's mad. He would get mad so easily. I made sure to stay out his way when he did.

"Well, what is it?" I asked.

"I need you to set up a surprise party for Belle at the skating rink," he said. I smiled. It was obvious he had a crush on her.

"What the hell you smiling for?" He asked.

"You like her," I said still smiling at him.

"Mind yo business," he said.

"Fine, throw the party yourself," I said laying back in the lounger.

"Man, come on. Stop tripping. Set it up for Saturday," I instructed.

"What's in it for me?" I asked.

"I'll keep Shaka from killing yo ass," he said standing up. I didn't want to think about him. I wondered did he tell Daddy he was leaving.

"You better be glad I like Belle," I told him.

He gave me the details of the party. It felt good having something to do. Everyone has lives. All I do is sit around the pool and think of my past. I still grimace at the huge mistake I made. After Rhino left, I dressed in a white Gucci short contoured skirt , Versace low cut, colorful crop top. I wore a pair cream colored, open toed Louboutin boot stilettos. I called to make sure the manager was in and made my way to the skating rink.

*****

When I pulled into a parking space, a car pulled up behind me blocking me in. I immediately jumped out ready to cuss the driver out. I knew it was some nigga that was going to shoot his shot. I was completely wrong. It felt as if my heart was trying to jump out of my chest it was beating so hard. I couldn't move as he approached me with his charming grin.

"Why the look? Aren't you happy to see me?" He asked in his strong British accent. I opened my mouth to respond but nothing came out. He pulled me into his arms and held me tight. My skin crawled at the touch of him.

I pulled away angrily. "How did you find me?"

He laughed, "Come now Jedi, you know I will always know where to find you. We have a lot of unfinished business." I hated when he called me that.

"No! We have no more business together," I stated angrily trying to walk away from him.

He forcefully snatched my arm pulling me into his chest, “Don’t walk away from me. We have business to discuss.”

“Our business is done. You made sure of that. You lied to me,” I said remembering the destruction I caused trusting him.

“Let me show you something.” He pulled his phone from his trouser pants. He played a video on his phone. My chest felt as if it was caving in.

“W-where did you get that?” I asked.

“I always keep insurance,” he said winking his eye at me. I jerked my arm to get out of his grip. I know him too well. I knew he was here to blackmail me.

“What do you want?” I asked feeling defeated. I could never let the video get out. It would destroy me.

“One million sounds fair enough,” he said smiling at me.

My eyes grew big, “You know I don’t have that kind of money!”

“Maybe not, but your father does. You never told me he was a rich, drug dealer.”

He had to have been watching my movements for a while. I became angrier and attacked him. He grabbed my arms and bear hugged me. He laughed as I struggled to get out his grip. I heard Shaka yell, calling my name. I thought I had to be imagining his voice until I turned to see him approaching us. The look on his face was the look of a killer. He immediately released me.

"Play nice," he whispered in my ear wrapping his arm around my waist.

"What the fuck going on?" Shaka asked staring at me.

I didn't know what to say. I couldn't tell him who Cassius was. I met him during a rough time in my life. After I left my father's home, I went to stay with my mother. It didn't take long for her husband to get tired of my spoiled ways. We would get into huge arguments about my spending and disrespect for their home. I was living life without a care in the world. He eventually made my mother cut me off. Being the spoiled brat that I am, I rebelled and chose to move out. It didn't take long before the money I had ran out. I was living in expensive hotels, buying overpriced clothes and shoes with no means of a steady income. I met Cassius in the lobby of the hotel I was staying at. He was sophisticated and charming. He wasn't the type of man I was attracted to, but he was definitely handsome. He is tall with cappuccino colored skin. His body is slim but toned. He always dressed in expensive attire. Today was no different. It didn't take long for us to become friends. We would meet in the bar every evening for a night cap. I enjoyed his company. I especially liked that he never tried to make a move on me. The morning I was checking out of the hotel was when he changed my life for the worse.

"Everything is okay," I said forcing a smile. Shaka stared at me to see if he could read my face. I knew not to look him in the eyes.

"Jedi just a little heated with me for my late arrival," Cassius said hugging me tighter and placing a kiss on my cheek. I wanted to scream at the feel of him touching me.

Shaka ignored him. "What you doing here?" He asked staring at me.

"I-I'm here to see the manager about planning a party for Saturday," I explained.

"Damn Jetta, you just had a party last weekend," he said.

"It's not for me. Rhino is throwing a surprise party for Belle. "What the hell you doing at a skating rink anyway?" I stated with an attitude.

"I own it," he answered.

I was impressed. I had no idea he owned a business. The rink had been around for a while, but it was run down. The owner never re-modeled and business slowly dwindled. Shaka had completely reconstructed the building. It was the middle of a week day and the parking lot was full. I guess summer time is great for business.

"Jedi, aren't you going to introduce me to your friend?" Cassius asked.

"Nah, I'm good. Come on in my office. I'm bout to leave," he said turning and walking away.

"Next time I call you, answer," Cassius said in a low voice. I snatched away from him and ran to catch up with Shaka.

Shaka

I sat behind my desk as she sat on the lounger with her legs crossed. I couldn't get the image of another man's hands all over her. I remembered always running guys away when Omega would send me to check on her. For years I convinced myself I was doing the job Omega hired me to do. I can't tell myself that lie anymore. I can't stand to see another man's hands on her, because I couldn't stop thinking about her. She was like a forbidden fruit. She was my boss man's daughter and she was childish and irresponsible. I couldn't give her my attention. My only focus was never being hungry and homeless again.

"What day you trying to have this party?" I asked.

"Saturday."

"Nah, I got something booked that day," I answered.

"So, you close at eleven. We all grown. Why can't we have it during afterhours? We don't want to be here with a bunch of snotty nose brats anyway," she said. I chuckled. I never considered doing that. That would actually bring in more business.

"You would fit right in with them," I said jokingly. She rolled her eyes but didn't reply.

"Are you doing your own decorations , or you want us to handle it?"

"I'll do everything myself including food and drinks. I just need the building for skating," she replied.

"That'll be fifteen hundred," I said throwing a number out the top of my head.

She looked at me with crazy eyes. "For what? I'm doing everything."

"Lights, water, skates…you know the shit it takes to run this business," I said smiling.

"Fine, it's not my money," she said.

"You really gone charge your best friend?" I shrugged my shoulders.

. I couldn't wait to talk to Rhino. Belle done came through and fucked his head up. She got him out here throwing surprise parties and shit. I just wanted to mess with her head. She sat scrolling through her phone as I kept stealing glances of her. I could tell something was bothering her. I knew it had something to do with the nigga that had his hands on her. It wasn't my place to speak on.

"That's it. We done," I said.

"Why did you move out?" She asked looking up at me.

She caught me off guard with the question, "I never moved in. I come and go between his house and mine."

"I didn't know you had a house. I thought you always lived with Daddy."

"I moved out after you left," I told her.

She stood up and walked over to the desk. The short skirt showed just enough flesh to make my dick hard. "Did you move out because I left?"

"Yea, my job of babysitting was over," I answered knowing it would make her fall back. I didn't need her getting close to me. I don't want to repeat what happened in the theatre room.

"Can I see it?" She asked.

"See what?" I asked shocked by her question.

She giggled, "Your house."

"Yea, one day," I answered.

"Why not now? That girl stay with you?" She asked.

I chuckled. "That girl's name is Dayzee and no she doesn't. Don't you gotta meet yo boyfriend or something?"

Her face became tight, "He's not my boyfriend. He's an ex."

“Well, don’t have that nigga in your father’s house,” I warned her. It was something about him I didn’t like.

“Jealous?” She asked.

“Nah, just careful,” I answered not wanting her to know my true emotions. I was jealous that he was getting what I been dreaming about since she came back home.

“Well, are you going to show me?” She asked again. She looked eager to know. I don’t know why but I wanted her to see it. Only Omega, Titan and Rhino have been to my home.

I shook my head and stood up. “Yea, follow me in your car.”

*****

I pulled into my driveway and waited for her. The neighborhood I lived in wasn’t as nice as Omega’s, but it was definitely better than the streets I once lived on. It was an abandoned house that I purchased cheap and remodeled.

“Must you drive so fast? This neighborhood isn’t bad,” she said looking around.

“You thought I stayed in the hood?” I asked.

“Honestly, yea,” she said shrugging her shoulders.

I ignored her and walked inside the house. “Give yourself the tour,” I said as she stood in the door entrance with her mouth open.

The house was beautifully designed and decorated. Looking on the outside you would never guess it’s inside beauty. The floors were dark brown hardwood. The contemporary style furniture was a light espresso. The walls were a shade lighter than the floors and were decorated with unique artwork. I went inside the game room and flipped on the television while she gave herself the tour. She found me a few minutes later.

“Micah, this is beautiful. Well, everywhere except this room,” she said looking around the entertainment room.

I laughed. This is where I spend most of my time. It had big screens plastered on the walls, pool tables, video games, black plush furniture and two stripper poles. I don’t even know why I had the poles installed. I never allowed females here until her.

“She decorated this for you?” She asked standing in front of me.

“Why you always asking about her?” I asked. She shrugged her shoulders.

"You saw the house. You can leave whenever you want," I said flopping down on the red leather couch.

I needed her out of my sight. The things I wanted to do to her would get me killed. She did the opposite of what my mind wanted her to do. She obeyed the hard bulge in my jeans and straddled my lap.

"Come on Jetta. One minute you hate me and now you trying to fuck me," I said staring at her.

"I only hate you when you hate me. Right now, I know that's not the case," she said reaching down softly grabbing my hard dick through my jeans.

"Yo, you gotta go. I'm not disrespecting your old man by going there with you," I said trying to lift her out of my lap.

She ignored everything I said and sucked my bottom lip into her mouth. All thoughts of her father went out the window. I promised myself this was going to be a one-time thing. I had to get her out my system. Even if it took all day and night, I wasn't going to stop until any sexual thoughts of her were gone. I pulled her halter top over her head causing her breasts to spill out. I wasted no time sucking them into my mouth. I massaged them while my tongue licked and sucked her hard nipples. She caressed my head as she moaned. She placed her hands on both sides of my face and pushed my head back against the sofa. She devoured my mouth with hers as she grinded on my lap. I palmed her soft ass as my dick spread inside my pants. I flipped her over placing her on her back. She lay there staring at me. I removed my shirt and jeans. My dick jumped out in attention. She sat up placing soft, wet kisses on my neck as her hand caressed my shaft. I felt like I was going to explode. I laid her back down pulling her skirt off. Her chocolate skin was glistening. I removed her shoes slanging them across the room. I spread her legs apart with one rested on the back of the sofa and the other on the floor. I laid my body on top of hers licking and sucking her neck and breasts while my fingers explored her clean, dripping wet pussy. I couldn't hold the groans coming from me as I fought the urge to enter her too soon.

"Please Micah," she pleaded gripping my dick.

I placed my throbbing dick at her entrance. I stared down at her. Her eyes were pleading with desire. I wanted her to feel what she has been doing to me since she returned. With one deep stroke I was deep inside her tight, soaked tunnel. My body jerked as the pleasure of her wet, slippery walls gripped my shaft.

"Aaaaahhhhh!" She cried out as her back arched and eyes fluttered.

I hated she felt so damn good. Her pussy was warm and gushy. Her wetness was spilling on my dick as I started gliding in and out of her. Staring down at her only made my dick harder. I became an animal thrusting deeper and harder inside her. She screamed out in pleasure as her walls squeezed me tighter on every stroke. I took her legs and pushed them up to the side of her head. I started drilling inside her until I hit her spot.

"Miiiiicccccaaaahhh!" She screamed out as her body quivered and stiffened. Her sticky, gooey cream poured out of her onto my dick like melted ice cream.

"Fuck!" I groaned as I pulled out of her.

I dipped my face between her cream covered pussy lips. I grunted and groaned as I feasted on her. She screamed for me to stop. The pleasure was too much for her. I licked, sucked and drank from her sweet pussy. I slid my tongue inside her leaking tunnel as I massaged her swollen clit. She tried scooting away from me. I grunted like a caveman and pulled her toward me. I wasn't done tasting her gooey, sugary essence. I could hear soft whimpers and cries coming from her. I didn't care. I was a man possessed by her taste.

"Ooooohhhhhhh sssssshhhhit!" She moaned drowning my mouth with more of her gooeyness.

After licking her clean, I drove my dick deep inside her again. Long, slow, deep strokes had her arching her back and crying out my name. She wrapped her legs around my waist and gyrated her hips. Feelings I never felt before were traveling through my body. It felt like I was on a drug high from the feeling of being inside her. Our eyes connected and all of a sudden shit changed. We weren't two people with built up tension. Something was different. Our animalistic sex turn into slow motion, synchronized sex. I leaned forward sucking her tongue into my mouth as I pressed my dick against her wild spot. Her moans matched my grunts as we felt ourselves getting ready to come.

I couldn't hold it any longer. "Aaaarrrrgggghhhh! Gooootttt dammmnnn!" I roared burying myself deeper inside her as I erupted. Her screams matched mine as she exploded with me. We fucked each other to sleep. Neither one of us could get enough of each other. We christened damn near every room in the house. We finally fell asleep in my California king size bed when the sun was coming up.

Miriam

I found myself slaving away at work again. This is where I wanted to be. I hated going home when I knew he would be there. It's been a week since Lyle and I found each other at the same club. He claimed he was there looking for me, but I know that was a lie. If he was hanging with his brother, I know he was up to no good. Craig was an educated fuck boy. He played on women's vulnerabilities. We argued every time he came over to my house with Lyle. For the past week, Lyle and I haven't spoken to each other. We argued in the club. I accused him of doing the very thing I was doing. I don't know if I was angrier from the thought of him cheating or him interrupting my time with Titan. I tried to fight the feelings Titan gave me. I never had a man control my body the way he did. It felt like every stroke inside me triggered an electric shockwave inside my body. He was demanding and dominate. He was all the things Lyle wasn't. I dreaded going home even more tonight. We were having dinner with my parents. I looked at the time and took a deep breath. I knew it was time for me to leave or we would be late. My father was a stickler for punctuality. Hell, he was a prude about everything. I dropped my briefcase as I stepped off the elevator to the garage. I couldn't believe he was standing there looking absolutely delicious. He walked over and picked up my briefcase. He smiled at me showing his pearly whites. His alluring cologne invaded my nose.

"What are you doing here?" I asked in a low voice looking around.

"I came to see you. You've been ignoring my calls and texts ." He was right.

I was going to kill Jetta when I see her. I haven't heard from her in three days. The last time I talked to her she invited me to Belle's surprise party which is tomorrow night. I declined, because I didn't need to be nowhere near Titan. Here he is…at my job.

"Titan, I'm an engaged woman. What happened between us was a mistake. A mistake that won't happen again," I stated adamantly.

He stared at me cocking his head to the side. "You sure about that."

"Yes," I replied in a low voice.

"You look stressed," he said ignoring my answer.

"Long week. Now, I'm running late for dinner with my parents," I said trying to walk past him. He gently grabbed me around my waist. My entire body relaxed. It felt good being in his strong, masculine arms.

"You can't run from what you feeling," he whispered in my ear.

I pulled away from him. I was almost in tears, because I wanted him desperately. I knew I couldn't have him. My life has been planned out. He didn't fit in it. I could never accept his lifestyle.

"What do you want from me?" I asked.

"A chance to get to know you," he answered.

"For what?" I asked. "We fucked, it's over. Move on."

I quickly walked away. I opened my back door to put my briefcase inside. I turned around to stare him in the face again. Every part of my flesh was screaming for him. Before I knew it, we were tearing each other's clothes off in the backseat of my Audi. Our naked bodies were pouring sweat as I screamed and moaned his name. I rode him until we both exploded together. I collapsed in his arms trying to catch my breath. He ran his fingertips up and down my spine as he placed soft kisses on my shoulders and neck. Goosebumps covered my body from the sensual touches he was giving me.

"I gotta go," I said softly not wanting to leave him.

"Only if you promise the next time I call you to answer," he said smiling at me.

I smiled back at him. “I promise.”

After we dressed, he gave me a long, passionate kiss that left me dizzy. I looked at my phone to see numerous missed calls from Lyle. I broke the speed limit rushing home. He started arguing the moment, I walked through the door. I ignored him and jumped in the shower. An hour later, we were pulling in my parents’ driveway.

“Well, it’s about time,” Mother said opening the door.

“I’m sorry Mother. I got tied up at work,” I said kissing her on the cheek.

“That’s no excuse Princess. You knew of this dinner a month ago,” Father said walking up to me. He leaned down and kissed me on the cheek.

“You’re right Father,” I said like a scorned child.

“How are you Lyle?” He asked shaking his hand .

My father thought Lyle could do no wrong. He treated him more like a son than he treated me like a daughter. He loved the fact that Lyle’s father was a minister.

“Just trying to keep up with the Misses,” Lyle said winking his eye at me.

“Come, dinner is still warm,” Mother said leading us into the dining room.

Lyle and Father talked about work while Mother and I discussed the wedding. She was so excited to see her baby girl get married. After dinner, we made our way to the den. It didn't take long before I knew it was time to go.

"What is this Lyle tells me about you hanging at night clubs?" Father asked. I gave him a look of death. He always running to my father when we have a disagreement.

"It's an upscale club. I was with Jetta," I explained cutting my eyes at Lyle.

"That girl has always been nothing but trouble for you. I know what her father does. Those are not the kind of people you should be associated with. You need to think of your career. Think of how that would look on me and Lyle. No one will take you seriously hanging with hoodlums and gang bangers," Father said.

"Jetta is not a hoodlum or gang banger," I stated angrily.

"We understand that Princess, but her family is," Mother said softly.

"Well, her father has treated me like family for as long as I've known him. I'm not going to walk away from a friend, because of anyone's opinion of her."

"This is what I deal with. She's stubborn," Lyle said shaking his head.

“You will consider your career first. Your sister and brother have great careers and families. You will not let that family ruin this family’s reputation. I have worked and sacrificed my entire life to see my children excel,” Father demanded.

I dropped my head. “Yes sir.”

The ride home was silent. I was fuming. I pulled out my phone as he drove and texted Titan.

Where are you?

I got a reply as we pulled into the driveway of my home.

Where do I need to be?~Titan

Belle

I can't believe he stood me up. I had been excited all week about spending my birthday with him. We've talked all week, but I hadn't seen him. I've been working and spending time with Hannah, Granny and Pam. I've called and texted him numerous times only to get no reply. Here I was looking absolutely stunning for him and he ditched me. I spent the entire day with Jetta. I couldn't believe the money she spent on me. She paid for my expensive hair style. I've worn weave before, but never hair that cost fifteen hundred dollars. She purchased me a pair of expensive jeans, a crop top and J-Lo stilettos. She had my face beat to perfection. I looked like a different person. I admired myself in the mirror one more time before I decided to undress. I grabbed my phone quickly when it rang. I was disappointed when I saw it was Jetta calling.

"Hello," I answered dryly.

"That pyscho stood you up," she stated angrily.

"How do you know?" I asked.

"I just left the house. He's getting ready to hit the club with Shaka and Titan," she informed me. My blood started to boil, and my heart ached. I thought he liked me.

"I can't believe him," I said flopping down on my bed.

Hannah came waddling in the room. I smiled at her cute, chubby face. I picked her up and sat her in my lap. She laughed.

"Is that a child I hear?" Jetta asked. I had forgotten she knew nothing of my child.

"The neighbors. She's visiting my Granny," I lied. I had to hurry and get off the phone before Hannah started calling me Mama.

"Oh ok. Well, forget him. Me and Mir coming to scoop you up. You look too damn pretty and them jeans hugged that ass too nice for you to sit home," she said.

I laughed. I didn't want to sit home and think about him, so I agreed to go with them. "Okay. Just blow when you get to the apartment." I gave her the address to put in her GPS.

The horn blew about forty minutes later. Hannah was fast asleep. I kissed her and Granny good night.

"Bye Mama!" Hannah said as I walked to the door.

"Love you and go back to sleep," I said smiling at her. She closed her eyes and covered her face with her hands. Granny and I laughed.

"Oh shit! Girl, look at you!" Miriam screamed when I got in the back seat of her Audi.

"I told her she was looking hot as fire," Jetta said smiling. I couldn't help but blush.

"Were we going?" I asked as Miriam pulled off.

"Skating. It's girl's night. No fuck boys," Jetta said.

"Agreed," I said laughing. I was hoping we weren't going to the club. I didn't want to see Rhino at all tonight.

*****

"Wow, this place is packed," I said looking at all the cars when we pulled into the parking lot.

"I know. It's an after hours hot spot few people know about," Jetta said getting out the car. We made our way to the entrance. The double doors slung open.

"Surprise!" Everyone screamed scaring me almost to death.

I stood there in shock as everyone started to sing happy birthday to me. I didn't know any of the people here, but it didn't matter. My eyes started tearing up. He walked through the crowd with a gift in his hand. I covered my face as tears fell from my eyes.

He pulled my hands from my face. “What you crying for?”

I looked up at him, “I thought you stood me up.”

“Never that Nerd Girl. Happy Birthday,” he said handing me a beautiful wrapped box.

“Oh, and he paid for all that you wearing. I like you, but girl I’m too selfish to spend that kind of money on somebody else,” Jetta said smiling.

I stared at him in amazement. I tore open the box. I didn’t think he was capable of being this sweet. I remembered telling him I loved to skate. He laughed when I told him someone stole my skates when I was eleven years old. I never imagined him buying me another pair. He had Nerd Girl monogramed on them. I immediately tiptoed and wrapped my arms around his neck.

“Thank you,” I said. He never hugged me back.

“Awwww,” everyone said at the same time.

The night was perfect. I skated and danced until I was exhausted. I laughed until I almost peed on myself at Rhino’s effort to skate. I remembered to watch my limit on the amount of alcohol I drank . I didn’t want a repeat of the last party. I was shocked to see Jetta and Shaka enjoying each other’s company. They looked cute together. It wasn’t my business, but I also noticed Titan and Miriam slipped out the party. It was almost three o'clock when everyone started to leave.

"I don't like coming in this late at my Granny's. Can I stay the night at your place?" I asked Rhino.

"Yea, there's plenty of rooms," he said. I only planned on one bed being occupied tonight.

"Jetta, we're getting ready to go. Thank you for doing all this for me. This was amazing," I said hugging her.

"Remember be seductive, sexy and wild," she whispered in my ear. I giggled but I was going to take her advice .

*****

We talked and laughed as we drove to his house. "Can I ask you something?"

"What?" He asked giving me a side eye.

"Why do you only use those big words when you mad?" I asked.

He chuckled. "I have anger issues. When I get mad I concentrate on words I've learned to calm myself."

I smiled, "I like that. Who taught you to do that?"

"I taught myself," he replied.

We rode in silence for a couple of miles. I burst into laughter. He frowned at me. I guess he thought I was laughing at him.

"I'm laughing at Jetta. Only she would have steak, shrimp and lobster at a skate party," I said laughing.

He laughed, "Only Jetta."

When we arrived at his house, he went into his study. He told me to take whatever bedroom I wanted. After choosing his bedroom, I took a long, hot shower. I wish I had some smell goods to oil my body down. I guess my natural scent will have to do. I gave myself a pep talk before sitting seductively on the bed. I waited patiently for him to come upstairs. I heard him knocking on bedroom doors trying to find me. When he finally opened his bedroom door, I was sitting on my hindlegs completely naked. He stopped and stared at me with his mouth open. I slid my hand between my thighs to massage myself. His eyes grew wide. I licked my lips seductively.

"I want you to dip your banana inside my chocolate pie," I said in a low, sexy voice.

I was trying my best to seduce him. My heart shattered with embarrassment when he keeled over in laughter. I jumped off the bed and locked myself in the bathroom. I can't believe I let Jetta talk me into making a fool of myself. I knew someone like him wasn't interested in me.

Rhino

"Yo, open the door Nerd Girl!" I demanded banging on the bathroom door.

I could hear her sniffling. I knew I hurt her feelings when I laughed, but I couldn't help it. My dick started pounding the moment I opened the door. Her body was flawless. Her full luscious breasts was mouth-watering. Her fat, juicy mound was inviting. Even the small pouch on her belly was sexy as hell. I never imagined words like that coming from her.

"My patience is getting brusque," I stated. I banged on the door again. I stepped away when I heard the door knob turning. I sat on side of the bed as she walked out with her head down. She had a towel wrapped around her body.

"Come here," I said. She walked over to me with her head still down. "Look at me." She looked at me with red eyes. "I'm sorry for laughing. I just didn't expect you to say some corny shit like that."

"I thought it would sound sexy," she said bashfully.

I chuckled, "It probably would, coming from someone else, but not you."

She sighed heavily. She flopped down on the bed sitting next to me, "Why aren't you attracted to me?"

"Man, who said I wasn't attracted to you?" I asked shocked that she would think that.

She shrugged her shoulders, "I want to have sex with you."

"Why?" I asked.

"Because I like you. I've always been attracted to you. Even though, I was kind of scared of you in high school. I still liked you."

I smiled at her. "Yea? You ever had sex?"

"Of course, Rhino. I'm twenty-two years old," she said. I wanted her to say no. I didn't like the thought of another man having sex with her.

I could feel her tensing up, "What is it?" I asked looking at her.

She dropped her head, "I've had sex before, but I've never had an orgasm."

I laughed, "What kind of lame ass niggas you been fucking?" She hit me in the arm and laughed with me.

"So, are we going to have sex?" She asked with a serious face.

She wasn't ready for what I had to offer. I stood up and dropped my pants and boxers. My dick was still hard as steel. Her eyes looked as if they were going to pop out of her head as she scooted back on the bed.

"Oh my God, it's huge. Why is it shaped like that?" She asked.

I laughed loud, "This why I'm called Rhino. Nah, we ain't having sex." I pulled my pants up.

"I think that's best," she said smiling. "Can I get a tee shirt to sleep in?"

"They're in the dresser. I'm going to take a shower," I said walking toward the door.

"Will you sleep in here with me?" She asked nervously.

I took a deep breath, "I swear if you give me blue balls, I'm fucking you up." She laughed.

After taking a cold shower, I slid into bed next to her. The shower didn't work. My dick was still throbbing. We talked about childhood memories and high school until she fell asleep. The sun was coming up when I finally dozed off. I was awakened with her straddling my lap. I opened my eyes to see her naked body again.

"I still want to do it," she said smiling down at me. I only had so much will power. She nodded her head yes. I told her to sit on my face.

She looked at me to see if I was serious, “I’ve had men do that before. I can’t come that way.”

“Man, slide yo ass up here,” I demanded. I didn’t want to hear about some lame ass nigga she’s been with.

She exhaled in frustration as she lifted up. She was taking too long, so I crouched downward positioning her fat pussy lips over my mouth. I lapped my wet tongue over her pussy lips. Her body shivered while my tongue slithered between her slit. Her clean aroma swirled in the air as I stroked my tongue up and town. Her natural juices started dripping from her as she moaned. Her fat mound was juicy and tasty. I grunted as I massaged her plump ass cheeks. She was feathery soft. She started winding her hips as she cried out in ecstasy. Her sweet nectar was smearing over my face as I indulged on her sugary pussy. I licked, slurped and sucked until she was begging me to stop.

I smacked her ass cheek, “That’s it! Feed me that pussy!”

“Oh God! You gotta stop! I have to pee!” She screamed trying to lift off of me.

I wrapped my arms around her soft, thick thighs locking her in place. I sucked and massaged her swollen clit. She bucked like a bronco. She was like a woman possessed as she cried out cuss words. Her body locked up and jerked.

"Oooooohhhhh Ggggooooddd! Aaaaahhhhhh!" She shouted as she exploded drowning my face with sweet nectar.

I became a voracious animal slurping and drinking her soul. I didn't stop until I heard soft whimpers. Her body went limp as she trembled and breathed heavily. I flipped her over on her back. It wasn't my intention to have sex with her, but my dick felt as if it was going to break. My balls were full and needed to be relieved. She covered her face with her hands.

"Man, what you hiding for?" I asked moving her hands. She opened her heavy eye lids staring at me. My heart pounded staring into her eyes.

"I acted a fool," she said shyly.

"Well, get ready to act the fool some more," I said cuffing her legs in my arms. I positioned her to where the head of my dick was at her sweet tunnel. She looked scared. "Just relax. I'm not going to hurt you. She nodded her head.

I slowly started trying to slide inside her. I gave her slow, gentle thrusts as I sucked and nibbled on her swollen breasts . She placed the palm of her hand on the side my face causing me to lock eyes with her. She lifted her head and stroked her tongue across my bottom lip. My heart fluttered when she slid her tongue inside my mouth. We indulged in a deep, sensual kiss as my hands caressed her soft skin. She lifted and twirled her hips causing the head of my dick to slide inside her. A loud groan escaped my throat as we continued our kiss. She was airtight and sloppy wet. Her silky tight walls sucked me deeper inside her. I started sliding in and out of her. She wrapped her arms around my back and buried her face in my neck. Her nails clawed my back as she bit my neck. I tried to hold on as long as I could, but I was fighting a losing battle. I had no control of my body. I've never had sex make me feel this way. I wasn't in control. It was like unbelievable sensations were controlling me. Her tight walls were pulling me deeper inside her. She tensed up when I tried to go deeper. She wasn't ready to take all of me. I started grinding my hips hitting spots that made her tears slide down the side of her face.

"Ooooohhhh! It's cccoooomming!" She screamed holding on to me and digging her nails deeper into my flesh.

Unable to control myself, I started plummeting deeper and harder inside her tight tunnel. Her warm, slippery nectar poured out of her like a running faucet saturating my dick. I buried my face into the crook of her neck lifting her legs higher. I licked and sucked her neck to muffle the loud groans and grunts I couldn't hold in.

"Aaaarrrggghhh! Ffffuuuccckkkk! Ssssshhhhiiitttt!" I roared from the pit of my stomach.

My body jerked and convulsed like it was being shocked with electricity. I rolled over and collapsed on my back pulling her on top of me. We lay there breathless as our sweaty bodies clung to each other. I felt her soft lips kissing mine as I lay there with my eyes closed. She rested her head on my chest as I stroked her back.

Jetta

I couldn't stop thinking about Shaka. Since our first night together, I've stayed with him every night. Our relationship is gradually progressing. We still bicker, but playfully. Daddy still doesn't know anything about our relationship. Shaka wants to keep it that way. I don't understand why we have to keep it a secret. I've learned more about him in the past week than I've known in years. He owns a landscaping company, apartments, and businesses. I sat in the corner of the bar waiting for Cassius. I need him out of my life. I remembered the night he approached me at the hotel about going into business with him.

"Leaving," he asked as he approached me. I was standing by the front desk checking out.

"Yea, on to see more of the world," I lied. The truth was my money was low. I couldn't afford to stay at the expensive five-star hotel another night.

"Let me talk to you before you run off," he said with his charming personality. I followed him to a corner table in the bar area.

"Where are you going?" He asked.

I shrugged my shoulders. "I haven't decided yet." The truth was I had to see where my money would take me.

"You know, I can read people. I can see you are in turmoil," he said scooting closer to me.

"Excuse me?" I said pushing my chair away from him.

He chuckled. "I'm not trying to sleep with you. I'm trying to put money in your pocket." He had my attention.

"How?" I asked eagerly.

"Using your beauty and sex appeal," he said smiling.

I jumped up angrily and stared down at him. "I'm not a whore!"

He laughed. "Please, sit down. Let me explain. This is good money and I think you need it."

I sat down and listened. "I'm going to be honest with you. I'm a criminal, a smooth one. I can use a beautiful woman like you to bait successful rich men. All I need you to do is get me entrance into their homes. I steal jewelry, credit cards , artwork and whatever else is of value."

"No, I'm not a thief," I said adamantly.

"These people are filthy rich. Everything I steal is insured. They will get their money back," he explained.

He stared at me, "I cashed out with over one hundred thousand dollars from my last target. That was small change." I couldn't deny the money made the offer tempting.

"Just try it. I have a target already for you. If you don't like it, you can walk away," he bargained with me.

"How much would I get?" I asked.

"Half of everything," he answered.

I needed the money. Daddy and Mom had cut me off. I couldn't imagine not being able to live the life I was accustomed to living. That day started my career as a thief with a smooth criminal.

I was making more money than I ever imagined. Sometimes I felt bad for some of the victims because they treated me so well. Others, I made sure we took everything we could. They felt as if they could treat me like a common whore. The only rule I had was I never slept with targets unless I wanted to. That was where I drew the line. Things went downhill when I met the sweetest young man named Xavier. Tears filled my eyes as I thought about my part in his death. I was taken from my thoughts when Cassius approached the table. He sat down smiling at me causing a sickness in my stomach.

"I don't have that kind of money, Cass," I said sadly.

"You have two weeks to get me the money. If not, I will make sure your life is ruined," he said with a sinister face.

I know he wasn't bluffing. I regretted the day I agreed to work with him. I had to find a way to get him the money. He had a video of me stealing from Xavier's safe. He threatened to send the video to the UK law enforcement. Xavier's family was powerful and seeking justice for their son. I felt as if they were just as much to blame for his death as I was.

"I'll have your money," I stated angrily standing up. I had no clue how I was going to get a million dollars in two weeks.

"Oh, one other thing. I'll see you in Jamaica," he said winking at me.

"What?" I asked staring at him with crazy, wide eyes.

"I'm your boyfriend. It's only right I accompany you on this trip. I think it's time I meet your father," he said with a wicked smile.

I rushed to the bathroom and screamed. I can't believe I got myself in this mess. I started hyperventilating. I didn't want him anywhere near my friends and family. I couldn't bring him on the trip. I was looking forward to enjoying the time with Daddy and Shaka. Shaka would hate me forever if I brought Cassius on this trip with us.

I drove home in deep thought. I tried to think of ways to get the money. There was no way Daddy was going to give me that kind of money. Even if I sold all the jewels I had, it wouldn't be enough. I started to think maybe I could ask Shaka to help me, but changed my mind. I didn't want him to know about my past. I really liked him and didn't want to mess my chances up with him. I had to figure out a way to get this money.

*****

When I arrived at the house, all my worries went away. Shaka's truck was parked in front of the house. My first stop was to check on Daddy. He's gaining weight and getting stronger every day. I searched the house but couldn't find them. Clara told me they were in the theatre room. I made my way there. I smiled when I walked inside to see my two favorite men watching Daddy's favorite movie, Black Caesar.

"Hi Boopsy," Daddy said when I leaned down and kissed him on the cheek. I glanced at Shaka to catch him staring at me. I wanted to join him in the oversized recliner but chose to sit in the one between him and Daddy.

"I'm going to say good night," Daddy said standing up.

"I just got here, Daddy. Where are you going?" I asked looking up at him.

"I'm the parent. I'll see you in the morning," he said before leaning down kissing me on the cheek. "Love you Boopsy."

"I love you too, Daddy. Tell those freaks my day is tomorrow," I said. He laughed as he walked out the theatre room.

I waited for Shaka to say something, but he never did. "Why so quiet?"

"Where you been?"

I wondered did he know I had met Cassius. I leaned over and whispered in his ear, "I went shopping for some sexy lingerie for our trip."

He stood up. "Come on, I'm hungry."

"I can cook for you," I said excited. He fell back in the chair laughing . "It's not funny. I can."

"You serious?" He asked looking at me. I nodded my head.

“Come on, let’s see what’s in the kitchen,” he said standing up.

“Are you staying here tonight?” I asked.

“If I live through this meal,” he said taking me by the hand pulling me out the chair. I tiptoed and kissed his lips softly. He opened his mouth inviting my tongue inside.

Titan

"Man, where you at?" I asked Unc as I sat at the red light.

"At the Quick Shop. You know the one sell them tough ass pork chop sandwiches," he screamed into the phone.

I laughed. "But you always going there to buy them."

"Shit, they help toughen my damn gums. You know women like tough gums. I be gnawing the hell out them dry cooter heifers," he said. I laughed loud as I pulled off when the light turned green.

I drove until I spotted him sitting in his electric scooter on the corner. He had called me because his battery went dead. He was eating his sandwich when I pulled up. "Boy, you right on time. It's bout to rain cats and dogs outchea."

"Yea, come on. Let me help you in the truck," I said walking up to him. He scarfed down the last of his sandwich. After he finished, I helped him in the truck. I put his scooter in the back of my truck.

"Boy, where you been hiding?" He asked when I pulled off.

"Working Unc, you need something?" I asked. He was a proud man. He never asked me for anything. I always made sure he had food, clothing and a place to lay his head.

"Shit, I'm good. I think something wrong with yo mama though," he said glancing at me. I hadn't talked to her in a few days. She's been working and going to church.

I gave him a concerned look, "Why you say that?"

He shrugged his shoulders. "She's been cooking and cleaning for me every other day. You know damn well that ain't yo mama. I think she's getting ready to die or something."

I laughed. "Nah Unc, she's just trying to change her ways."

"Oh, I thought maybe we needed to perform one of those execution things on her," he said seriously.

I laughed. "You mean an exorcism?"

"Yea, you know what the hell I mean," he said waving me off.

I pulled in front of the house he shared with mama. I hurried and got him and his scooter inside as the rain drops started to fall. I left him sitting in his big recliner watching television. The rain started coming down hard as I drove. I hadn't seen her since the night of Belle's party. We talked and texted every day, but I need to see her. At first, our attraction was physical and sexual . Getting to know more about her caused me to find myself feeling her on a different level. I had to keep reminding myself she was an engaged woman. I decided to stop by her office before heading home.

*****

After parking in front of the building, I rode the elevator to the floor her office was on. Her assistant buzzed her on the intercom informing her she had a visitor. I smiled at her when she opened her office door. She didn't return my smile. She looked angry as she opened the door wider for me to enter. The moment she closed the door, I had her pinned against it . She wrestled to get away, but I pinned her arms over her head with one hand. My other hand was between her thighs as I devoured her mouth. She moaned in pleasure as her body relaxed. I slid my hand inside her damp panties as I kissed my way down to her slim neck.

"Please stop Titan. I can't do this here," she pleaded. I released her arms and stared at her. I was getting ready to back away, but she wrapped her arms around my neck and buried her tongue inside my mouth. I wasn't coming to have sex with her, but just the sight of her made me want to be deep inside her. We were interrupted by her intercom.

"Ms. Halston, your fiancé is here to pick you up," her assistant said. My dick started to soften. I backed away from her.

"You need to dead that bullshit ," I said staring at her.

"Titan, he's my fiancé. I can't just end a relationship I've planned my life around for good sex," she said straightening up her clothes.

I chuckled, "That's what this is?"

I hated that she had me acting like a weak ass man. I wanted her in every way. She belonged to me. Sooner or later, she's going to have to make a choice.

She looked up at me, "You know it's more than that. Please, I can't do this now."

"Yea, you right," I said.

I walked toward the door and she grabbed my hand. She gave me a passionate, deep kiss before releasing my hand. I walked out the office without giving him a look. I was furious he had what belonged to me. I called Tiera to let her know I was coming over. Thirty minutes later, I had Tiera bent over her kitchen counter as I exploded inside the condom. I went to the bathroom to clean up. She was a pretty girl, but was too clingy. She calls my phone nonstop asking me to come see her. She seems too desperate to have a man in her life. I told myself I wasn't going to fuck her anymore after she followed me to my club one night. I had stopped by her house after she kept blowing my phone up. I gave her what she wanted and left. She jumped out her car in front of the club accusing me of cheating on her. I had to yoke her ass up and explain to her we weren't a couple. I hadn't talked to her in over a week until today. I needed to get Miriam off my mind. I thought she would help do it. She only made me think of her more. She was no comparison to my Star.

Belle

"Why you so necromantic about where you live?" Rhino asked over the phone.

He wanted to come over. I still hadn't told him about Hannah. I didn't know how I could break the news to him. I know he would never understand. I constantly made up excuses for him not to come over.

"I'm not being secretive. Granny is very old fashioned. She doesn't think a man should be knocking on a woman's door after dark," I lied.

"You better not have no nigga staying there, Belle. I swear I'll extirpate you and that nigga," he said angrily. I knew he was mad by his use of words.

"I miss you," I said softly.

I really did miss him. I hadn't spent any time with him since my party. I'm always working or spending time with Hannah and Granny through the week. Pam works through some weekends, so her time is limited. I don't have the extra money to leave Hannah in daycare a few extra hours.

"Well, come through," he said.

"Do you miss me?" I asked smiling. Now, I was just being petty and wanted to irritate him.

"Ain't I'm trying to see yo corny ass? I need to slide this horn inside you," he replied.

"Really Rhino? Is that the only reason you want to see me?" I would be hurt if he only saw me in a sexual manner. I really liked him. He was funny, smart and crazy all at the same time.

"Man, stop tripping. I can get pussy anywhere," I replied.

"I'll try and slip out once Granny go to sleep," I said.

"No the fuck you won't! Don't have yo blind ass riding down the road in the middle of the night," he demanded. I laughed at how protective he was of me.

"Well, tomorrow is Friday. I'll come stay the night with you if that's okay," I said.

"Yea, make that happen or Granny just gone have to hear you calling on the Lord," he said laughing.

"Ok, let me run in the grocery store before I go home," I said pulling in front of the daycare.

"Yea, call me to let me know you made it home," he instructed before ending the call.

The rain had finally eased up. It was still coming down, but not as hard. I grabbed my umbrella and hurried inside. Hannah was playing with the same little girl. I laughed when she tried standing up, putting her chubby butt all in the little girl's face. She waddled toward me with excitement. After talking briefly with her daycare provider, I covered her up and rushed to get in the car. I didn't need her getting sick. I tried starting the car, but it wouldn't crank up. I said a silent prayer, but it went unanswered. I got out the car and let the hood up. I had no idea what I was looking at. I didn't know anything about cars. I messed with a few wires and tried to start the car again. It still wouldn't start. Hannah sat in her car seat getting fussy.

"Mama, come on. Let's go see Granny," she whined.

I didn't know how I was going to get home. I didn't have money to waste for an uber. I decided to take Hannah back inside until I figured out what to do. Just as I got her out of her car seat, Titan's black Titan pulled up behind me. I didn't need this, not now. He jumped out his truck and walked over to me.

"You got car trouble?" He asked looking at my hood that was still up.

"Yea, it won't crank," I said pulling the jacket over Hannah's head. The rain had started to come down hard again.

"Go sit in the truck. I'll see if I can get it to crank."

"Thanks, but I called a tow truck and uber," I lied.

"You still need to get the child out of the rain, Belle." The rain started pouring down. I rushed to get in his truck. After a few minutes, Titan got back in his truck.

"Your starter gone," he said.

"Ugh," I said frustrated. I didn't have money for car repairs.

"I'll take you home. I'll have a tow truck bring the car to my shop," he said.

I looked at him, "You work on cars?"

"Nah, I just own an auto repair shop. I have a few people work for me," he informed me.

"Oh ok, thank you." Hannah started to whine. I knew she was getting hungry. She started trying to pull the jacket off her head.

"Who's little chubby girl?" He asked reaching over and pulling her hoodie off her head.

She turned to look at him. My heart pounded in my chest. There was no denying who her daddy was. She was the spitting image of him. He sat there staring at her as she fidgeted in my lap. I eagerly waited for his reaction. He finally broke his trance on Hannah to stare me in the eyes. His eyes asked the question that had already been answered by looking at her. I knew my secret would have to be told one day. I just never wanted him to find out this way.

"Belle," he said in a low voice waiting for me to answer his silent question. He never took his eyes off her.

Tears filled my eyes. "I'm so sorry, Titan. I wanted to tell you."

"Why the fuck didn't you?" He barked angrily. He was so loud he scared Hannah.

"Please, I need to get her home. Her clothes are damp. She's going to catch a cold," I pleaded with him.

He started the truck and pulled off. I gave him my address to put in his GPS. I could see the anger and hurt in his face as he drove. He kept glancing at Hannah. It was no denying her. She was his twin. He pulled into a parking space at the apartment complex.

"How old is she?" He said staring at her.

"I'm four," she said proudly.

He smiled. "She talks."

I laughed. "She's four. Of course, she talks. She's in Headstart . She attends daycare when I work evening shifts. He looked at me in amazement.

"My name is Hannah. What's your name?" She asked smiling at him.

He chuckled. "Titan."

Hannah laughed. “That’s a funny name.”

He tickled her, “Your name is funny too.” She laughed. I felt good seeing them interact with each other. I always wondered what this day would be like.

“Why didn’t you tell me, Belle?”

“Can we please talk about this another time. She’s very observant and inquisitive,” I said glancing at her.

“So when?” he asked impatiently.

“If the weather is better, we can go to a park and talk. That will give you some time with her,” I said.

“How she getting to school and daycare tomorrow?” He asked.

“I’ll get an uber.”

“Nah, I’ll be here to pick y’all up,” he insisted. “Does Rhino know?”

“God no! Please don’t tell him. I’ve been trying to find the right time to tell him. I know he’s going to be furious.”

“Man, that nigga gone need every word in the dictionary to control his anger,” Titan said angrily. “You need to let him know. I’m not disowning my seed, Belle. That’s my boy but I can’t keep this kind of secret from him.”

“I know. I promise I’m going to tell him. Please, just give me some time,” I pleaded.

He nodded his head in agreement. I told him what time to pick us up in the morning. He said goodbye to Hannah. She gave him a big hug. I could see tears in his eyes as we exited the truck.

“Mama, that man nice,” Hannah said as we walked inside the apartment.

“Yes, he is. That’s why we’re going to see him again tomorrow,” I said. She jumped up and down with joy.

Shaka

"Come on, I'm done," Jetta said grabbing me by the hand pulling me from the chair.

I was in the office going over a few accounts Omega left me in charge of. She had cooked fried chicken, rice pilaf, and buttered broccoli. I wanted to help her, but she wanted to do everything by herself. I laughed when she started pulling up YouTube videos before she threw me out the kitchen.

I walked into the kitchen and started coughing. "Damn, it's smoky in here."

"I know. The grease was so hot. When I dropped the chicken in it, some grease spilled out. I had a small grease fire, but I handled it."

"Jetta, you could've burned yourself," I said looking at her hands. "Why didn't you use the deep fryer or air fryer."

"What's that?" she asked. I laughed and shook my head.

"Sit down. I'll fix your plate," she said.

I sat at the kitchen table admiring her physique as she fixed my plate. She wore a pair of black short tights and a fitted cropped tee shirt. Her chocolate skin always glistened. I didn't know what we were doing with our relationship. I wasn't going to spend time analyzing it. I was feeling her in a way I've never considered with any woman. She walked over and sat the plate in front of me.

"Nah, I want you to feed me," I said pulling her in my lap as she tried to walk away. She giggled and sat in my lap.

I laughed when she picked up a knife and fork to cut into the chicken. My laughter became hysterical when blood poured from the beautifully browned chicken breast. She jumped up and stormed out the room. I was laughing so hard I couldn't stop her. I looked at the bloody chicken and thanked God she cut into it first. I searched the house until I found her sitting on the far end of the pool wading her feet in the water. I stripped down to my boxers and swam the length of the pool. I came from under the water with my torso between her legs. She held a solemn look on her face.

"Stop tripping. Thanks for trying," I said lifting her chin.

"You don't understand. I mess everything up. Everything I touch, I destroy," she said wiping the tears from her eyes .

"Damn Jetta, it's just chicken," I said laughing.

She smacked her lips, pouted and rolled her eyes. Those were things I once couldn't stand to see her do. Now, I think they're cute parts of her personality. I started placing soft, wet kisses on her thighs.

"No Micah, all we do is have sex. I wanna do other things with you," she said pushing my head away. I was surprised to hear her say those words. I've never dated a woman. It was always sexual encounters. She was the first one I actually considered dating.

I lifted my body out the pool and sat next to her. "Why?"

She became nervous. "Because I like you. I want to know more about you besides how good your sex is."

"Is it good?" I asked nibbling on her ear.

She gently shoved me, "I'm serious."

"Ok, come on. Go get dressed and meet me downstairs in fifteen minutes," I said standing up.

Of course, she came down the stairs an hour later. "Where are we going?" She asked.

"Nowhere for you to be dressed like that," I said looking her up and down. She was dressed for a night on the town. That was not our destination.

"You wanna tell me why you were tripping about some damn chicken?" I asked glancing at her as I drove.

"I just want to make my daddy proud. I've made a lot of mistakes in my life. Some I can never correct," she stated sadly.

"You know you don't have to do anything for your daddy to love you," I said as I tried lifting her spirits.

"I know he loves me, but I haven't done anything to make him proud. You don't see the way he looks at you. He has so much respect for you. He babies me, because he doesn't think I can stand on my own."

She shocked me with her observation. Her father blamed himself for her lack of ambition, maturity and responsibility. I never knew she noticed the things I witnessed over the years she was here.

"What do you want to do with your life?" I asked.

"I want to be a fashion stylist," she said.

"You enrolled in school, yet?"

"Yes, I start classes in the fall. What do you think about it? You think I'll be successful as a fashion stylist?"

I chuckled. "You dress up to go grocery shopping. I'm sure you will. First thing, stop needing everyone's approval for your dreams. I'm hard on you, because I know you are capable of greatness. Believe in yourself, Jetta. Use the stubbornness you use on me." She giggled, leaned over and kissed my cheek.

*****

She looked at me with frantic eyes. "Micah, why are we at a cemetery?" I ignored her question and exited the car. I walked to her side and opened the door. "Are you going to kill me?"

I laughed, "Jetta, get out the damn car." I helped her out the car and led her through the cemetery.

"Micah, it's getting dark. This is spooky," she said looking around. I stopped when I reached his grave. "Is this your father?"

"Nah, he took care of me when I lived on the streets," I said bending down cleaning his grave off.

"Oh my God, I'm so sorry. I thought those were just rumors. I didn't know you were really homeless," she said with empathy.

"Don't be. It made me the man I am. After my mama got sent up, I ran because I didn't want to go in the system. I met George in an abandoned house I crashed at one night. He made sure I ate when he ate. He would never let me eat out the trash. He told me, we aren't dogs. We are humans down on hard times. He made sure I stayed in school and studied every night."

"What happened to him?" She asked bending down beside me.

"He died from pneumonia. I found him dead in an abandoned house. I didn't have the money to give him a proper burial at the time. Rhino and Titan helped me bury him in the woods. I promised myself I would buy him a grave when I was able. Your father made that possible."

"He would be proud of you," she said softly.

"Yea, I think he would be. Come on, I'm fucking starving, and it's about to start back raining," I said walking away.

I felt myself getting too emotional. She ran to catch up with me. She took my hand and interlaced my fingers with her . She looked up at me with a smile. I felt what was happening between us, and there wasn't a damn thing I could do to stop it.

Where's your mother now?" She asked when we got inside the car.

"Still locked up for killing an inmate. I tried to visit her a few years ago. She declined my visit, so I said fuck it," I told her. I didn't have a connection to my Mama to feel any emotional neglect from her.

We ended up back at my place. I grilled for us. I only allowed her to make the salad. The rest of our evening was spent lounging around my spot watching movies.

Rhino

"Man, let's expedite this! I'm an assiduous nigga! I got shit to do!" I demanded. I was making rounds at the trap houses with Titan.

"What's all the anger about?" Titan asked staring at me.

"Nothing, I'm just not with the jokes today," I said.

Everyone was cutting jokes and getting on my nerves. I hated the feelings I was having. I was feeling like Belle was playing me. She was supposed to come over last night but stood me up. She's had me blowing her phone up for the past two days only to ignore me.

"Aight, we done," Titan said stuffing the money in a bag.

We exited the house and headed to the next trap. "Yo old man in yo shit again?" Titan asked as he drove.

I had a strained relationship with my father. He didn't like the choices I made in life. I didn't see my parents as often as I should. Every time I visited them it ended in an argument.

"Nah," I answered as my mind wandered . We rode in silence for a few minutes. "Yo, let me ask you something. How you know when you the side nigga?"

Titan laughed. “How the fuck I’m supposed to know?”

“Nigga, ain’t you Miriam’s side nigga?” I asked staring at him.

He cut his laugh short. “Damn, that’s fucked up. I am.” It was my turn to laugh. “Why, you think Belle playing you?”

“I’ve called her for two days. She never answers or returns my calls. I know you think she’s all sweet and innocent, but it’s some foul shit going on. I feel it.”

“Belle ain’t fucking around. She probably just busy. You know she takes care of her Granny. You asked her about going to Jamaica next weekend?” I asked.

“That’s why I was trying to holla at her but fuck it. It’s plenty of foreign bitches over there to keep me company,” I said. Titan laughed, but I was serious. I liked her, but I wasn’t the nigga for kissing and chasing ass.

After we finished collecting, we dropped the money off to Shaka. He was just getting home from dinner with Jetta. I would’ve never thought I would see those two enjoying each other’s company. I decided to hit up the club with Titan and Shaka. I was shocked when Shaka said he was going until I found out Jetta was going. I wasn’t the type to sit around pining over a female. We chatted for a few minutes and left. I wanted to take a nap before hitting up the club.

*****

When I woke up, I dressed for the club. I grabbed my Glock and keys. I was shocked when I opened my door. Belle was standing there with an overnight bag.

"Hi, I was trying to build up the courage to knock," she said nervously. I wanted to snatch her ass by her hair and drag her back to her car. "Can I come in?"

"Nah, I'm headed out," I said walking out the house and locking the door.

"I can go with you. Where are you going?" She asked following behind me as I walked to my car. Before I could respond, she was getting in the car.

"I'm going to the club. Get the fuck out," I said staring at her.

"No, I'm going with you," she said crossing her arms.

I hopped out the car and went to the passenger side. I opened the door and tried to pull her out. She turned into a wild woman. She started kicking and swinging her arms. Seeing her wild side made my dick hard as concrete. The next thing I remember, we were tearing each other's clothes off inside the car. Our sweaty bodies clung to each other as I drilled inside her. Her feet were spread over the dashboard as we continued to fog up the windows. I could never go as deep and hard inside her as I wanted. Whenever I tried, she would dig her nails into my back and tense up. Even though I couldn't give her all of me, I gave enough to have her screaming my name. Nothing sounded sweeter.

Later that night, she was stretched out on my bed asleep. I slipped out the room to work on my current project. I slipped out of bed and returned Titan's call. They were worried when I didn't show up to the club. I entered the room and uncovered my work. I put on my Beats by Dre and started working. I was so caught up in my work, I forgot I wasn't alone in the house. I quickly remembered when she tapped me on the shoulder. I closed my eyes remembering I forgot to lock the door.

"Wow," she said softly staring at the painting.

I wanted to be angry with her for coming in the room. I couldn't, because of the expression on her face. She was flabbergasted by my work. I loved painting. It was my true passion that my father disapproved of. He wanted me to pursue a career in basketball. I wanted to become an artist. He didn't support my dreams, so I chose not to follow his choice of career for me.

"Rhino, this is beautiful," she said examining the painting of herself laying in my bed.

"Thanks," I replied graciously.

"These paintings should be in art galleries. Why do you have them hidden in this room?" She asked looking around at the numerous paintings.

"This is just a hobby," I lied.

"No, it's not Rhino. This work was done with passion," she said staring at a painting hanging on the wall.

"I thought I put yo ass to sleep for the night. What you doing woke?" I asked changing the subject.

She smiled. "I'm hungry. You don't have anything in the kitchen to cook."

"We can hit up a spot," I said.

"Ok, are you painting this for me?" She asked with a big smile.

"Nah, this for me. It's going to be a memory of you. Because the next time you ignore my calls, I'm killing yo ass," I warned her. She laughed.

"My phone has been acting crazy." It was obvious she was lying. She had me so wide open. I don't even know if I wanna know if I'm the side nigga.

"Yo, you need to take off next week. We leaving for Jamaica and you coming with me."

"Jetta asked me about going. I can't. I have to work and see about my Granny. It's too short of notice," she said sadly. I couldn't argue with her about her responsibilities. I'll handle shit on my own.

Miriam

I wanted to try and save my relationship with Lyle. I just didn't see how it was possible. I couldn't stand the touch of his hands on my skin. As his dead weight lay on top of me, all I could think about was the way Titan took control of my body. Lyle's kisses felt cold and slimy on my neck. I lay under him stiff as a board. His alcoholic breath made me want to vomit. I closed my eyes trying to imagine he was Titan.

"Here, suck my dick before I give you this good pipe," he said. I opened my eyes to see him on his knees holding his hard dick.

"Are you serious?" I asked.

There was no way I was putting my mouth on his dick. For one, he has no sense of foreplay. I'm his fiancé, not a random hoe he picked up off the streets. Secondly, he always insists I bathe before he goes down on me.

"Yea, why not?" He asked.

"You always insist I bathe . Maybe you should do the same," I said.

"You a woman. Y'all got all kinds of bacteria and shit coming out of y'all. My dick is clean," he said stroking himself.

I was disgusted with him. I noticed the changed in him over the last month. He's not the same guy that wooed me. He's become this chauvinistic, narcissist asshole. I need to get away from him before I tell him how I really feel. I jumped off the bed and went into the bathroom. I ran myself a hot bubble bath and slid inside. I started to wonder was his recent behavior a reflection of my infidelity. Maybe he feels that I don't love him the way he loves me. After I came out the shower, Lyle was gone. I was relieved. I dressed and left my house before he returned.

*****

I tried to stay away from him, but I couldn't. I kept calling his phone. I never got any answer. The only places I knew where to find him was Omega's house or his club. I decided to try Omega's house first. He wasn't there. Shaka and Jetta was walking out the door. They were going to the club. I decided to be a third wheel and join them. I didn't care how desperate I looked. There was an ache in my chest and throbbing sensation between my legs that only he could cure.

After we entered the club, we went to the VIP floor and ordered a bottle of white Hennessy . It was different sitting with Shaka and Jetta. Usually they were at each other's throats. Now, she can barely keep her hands off him. I left them sitting there to go find Titan. After searching for his office, I finally located it. I opened the door causing my heart to drop. He was fucking some random bitch on his office sofa. She moaned as he fucked her from behind. I stormed toward them pushing him off her.

"You mothafucka!" I screamed as I violently swung at him.

"What the fuck?" He barked trying to grab my arms. I was hurt and angry. I could feel tears filling my eyes.

"Bitch, get off him!" The girl yelled grabbing my arm. I turned around and punched her in the face.

She fell on the floor. I felt Titan's arms wrap around my body. "Let me go! You nasty ass nigga!" I struggled until he released me.

"Man, what the fuck is yo problem?" He asked as I turned to face him.

Before I could reply the girl pushed me in the back causing me to fall on the sofa. She jumped on top of me and started hitting me in the face. I was able to kick her causing her to fall on the floor. I felt Titan trying to break us apart. I had too much anger inside me to be controlled. I started stomping and kicking her with my stiletto heels.

"Get her off me!" She screamed in the fetal position. He finally pulled me away from her. She ran out the office crying.

"Yo, have you lost yo damn mind?" He asked staring at me with fire in his eyes.

"You obviously have. In here fucking some bitch!" I yelled at him.

He stared at me with cold eyes. "I can fuck whoever the fuck I want. Ain't you fucking yo fiancé? Don't ever try me like that again."

*****

I had no words. He was right. I had no right to be angry. He didn't belong to me. I was only a fuck like she was. I had to get out of here. I was losing control of my life over a man that only saw me as someone to fuck. I ran out the office. I didn't stop until I arrived home. I knew this night was only going to get worse when I saw Lyle had returned. I opened the door to find candles flickering in the dark living room. Rose petals led down the hall to the bathroom. I opened the door to a romantically decorated bathroom. A bath was filled with rose petals and candles were illuminating the room. I stood there in shock. Lyle had never done anything like this for me. I felt his hands wrap around my waist.

"I'm sorry baby. I love you. I've just been under a lot of stress at work. I promise to do better," he whispered in my ear as he nibbled on my earlobe.

The touches did nothing for me, but I had to make this work. He was my future husband. Titan proved I meant nothing to him tonight. We had sex. It was simple, boring sex. I tried being creative by dancing for him. He told me I was wasting time. I laid down on the bed with him on top of me. He didn't even bother with foreplay. He shoved himself inside me and gave me about seven weak humps. It burned because he couldn't even take the time to get me wet. A simple touch from Titan would open my floodgates. After he was done, I took a long, hot shower. Tears filled my eyes as I thought about the choice I was making. There was no way I could marry him. I couldn't imagine living a life with him when I was falling for a man that has stolen my soul. After seeing Titan with another woman, I wanted to forget him, but I couldn't. I had decided to take the vacation trip. Lyle thought I was going to a business convention in Las Vegas. I knew I was taking a big risk, but I didn't care. I felt like an addict jonesing for a fix. I needed to be near him and to feel his touch.

Belle

I sat at the park watching Hannah and Titan play. They bonded instantly. They were rolling in the grass laughing like two little kids. It was such a happy occasion to see her with her father, but I knew there was a dark cloud over our heads. I was dating his best friend and he was falling for a new friend of mine. I should've stayed away from Rhino knowing I had Titan's child, but I couldn't resist the chance to be closer to him. I started down memory lane the night Titan and I created our beautiful, chubby daughter.

After Jetta wrecked her father's car, I went home like Rhino demanded. I was happy to get away from the craziness. As intimidated as I was in his presence, I couldn't deny my attraction to him. I went inside my room and laid across my bed. I closed my eyes thinking about his tall, slender frame and crazy eyes. I was startled by a tapping on my window pane. I pulled my curtain open to see Titan.

"What are you doing here?" I asked lifting the window.

"I was passing by and wanted to come check on you," he said. Titan was always nice to me.

"I'm okay. I bruised my elbow, but nothing serious," I said showing it to him.

"You smoke?" He asked.

I shook my head no, but I was always curious. "I wanna try though."

"Let me in, so we can smoke this," he said showing me a joint.

"You gotta climb through the window. We might wake my Granny up," I said.

"Shit, how I'm supposed to get my fat ass through this window?" He asked. He was big, but handsome. I giggled and shrugged my shoulders. "Let the window all the way up."

I did as he asked. He lifted his upper body through the opened window. His hands was on the floor as he tried coming through. "Shit, I'm fucking stuck Belle." I couldn't hold my laughter. "Come on man, help me." I laughed as I tried helping him through the window. We were both exhausted after finally pulling him through.

"Is that girl okay?" I asked as we sat on the bed.

"Yea, she just drunk as hell," he replied.

I smiled at him. "You like her, don't you?"

"Yea, but a girl like that would never go for a fat nigga like me." It saddened me that he thought that way of

his self. It was also the way I felt about Rhino liking someone like me. "I mean don't get me wrong. I'm a handsome ass nigga. I just know girls like her don't like fat boys." I laughed relieved to know he didn't carry the low self-esteem like me.

"Rhino is crazy," I said as he lit the joint.

He laughed. "He's good people though. I saw the way you looked at him. You like him." I shook my head no. I didn't want him telling Rhino I like him. The last thing I needed was to have him in my face acting like a crazy man again. He passed me the joint and I looked at it.

"It's clean, Belle. I wouldn't do you dirty like that," he assured me. I slowly put it to my lips and took a puff. I blew the smoke out. He laughed. "Nah, you gotta inhale the smoke for a few seconds."

"Oh," I said taking another puff. I did like he said. It felt as if my chest was caving in. I coughed as he laughed. I walked and hung my head out the window to get some fresh air. I felt the effects of the weed rushing through my body. I felt light headed. All of a sudden, everything was funny. Titan and I laughed about the incident with the two girls until I was crying.

"Titan, can I ask you something?" I asked. He nodded his head. "Why are you nice to me?"

He chuckled. "You good people, Belle. You just don't fit in with people around here. There's nothing wrong with that. The problem is you seclude yourself. That makes people think you are weird. I don't think it's a bad thing you don't deal with these females. They ain't shit."

"I think you good people too," I said smiling at him. Without thinking, I leaned over and kissed his lips. He looked at me with wide eyes. My heart pounded waiting for him to reject me, but he didn't. He leaned over and kissed me with his tongue. It was my first French kiss. I was so caught up in experiencing my first kiss. I didn't realize what was happening. When I finally realized it, Titan's heavy body was on top of my naked lower body. I looked up at him with frightened eyes.

"Shit Belle, I'm sorry," he said as he tried sitting up.

"No, I want to," I said shamefully. He still tried to get up, but I kept asking him to do it. He finally gave in. My twin size bed left no room for us to move around. He had a hard time entering me. He was too big for the small bed. Titan was not only fat, he was tall. We were in the most uncomfortable position, but I didn't want him to stop. He struggled trying to get his dick inside me. He was sweating and breathing heavy. I didn't mind, because he smelled

good. I just couldn't get passed the pain of him trying to get inside me. When he finally got inside me, I started to relax. I mistakenly kept calling him Rhino. All of a sudden, the middle of the bed broke. He didn't stop.

"You gotta hurry and finish," I said softly. He humped a few more times making grunting noises and then stopped.

"You finish?" I asked feeling the soreness between my legs.

"Yea," he said sitting up. "I gotta fucking cramp in my leg."

He jumped up and started leaping around the room. His dick was still hard. I realized the myth that fat boys have small dicks was a lie. If that was what sex felt like, I never wanted to have it again. Before he left, I made him promise to never tell anyone. It never dawned on me I could get pregnant until I skipped my period.

I still don't know why I wanted to have sex with Titan that night. I guess I felt like it was the closest I could ever be to Rhino. I was convinced Rhino would never be interested in me sexually or any other way. He viewed me as a weird, nerd girl and nothing more. I never imagined in a million years, I would be preparing to go on vacation with him.

I hated to end their time together, but it was getting dark. I walked over to them. “Mama, play with us. He’s fun!” She said with a big grin on her face.

“Maybe next time. We have to get you home. It’s getting dark,” I told her.

She pouted and stomped her little feet. He laughed. We gathered our things from the picnic and headed to our cars. He had my car fixed at no charge. I didn’t feel comfortable not paying him, but he insisted.

“Belle, why you never told me,” he asked as we stood outside my car. Hannah was running around the car still full of energy.

“I was ashamed when I got pregnant. I was scared to tell you. That’s one of the reasons I moved away. I thought you would think I tried to trap you. I came to find you when she turned one. I found out you was doing time.”

He shook his head, “I’m her father and I’m here now. I’ll cover daycare and any other expenses she has. I got her on medical, dental, eye insurance. I just need her information to make it happen. Don’t even try to fight me on this Belle. That’s my seed. A fucking blind man can see that.”

I wasn’t going to deny him his child. I’ve done that for too long. “Thank you.”

"I'm getting you another car. I can't have you riding my baby up and down the road in an unreliable car."

"No, that's too much," I insisted. "It just wouldn't look right."

"I'm doing it for my daughter, not for you," I said.

"I know, but I don't think Rhino or Miriam would understand that," I reminded him.

"I don't give a fuck what they understand. You need to tell him," he said angrily. I know I should. I just didn't know how he would take this news. I knew this happened before me and him, but it's still a secret I kept.

"I will. Just give me time," I pleaded.

"You can tell him in Jamaica. Mama will keep Hannah when needed. A nurse will be coming to check on your granny throughout the day."

"What?" I asked confused. I didn't understand how he did all this without my permission. I never gave him permission to tell his mother. He called for Hannah to get in the car. I was starting to get angry.

"Rhino wanted you to come. He was going to visit your granny to see what he could do to make it possible. I had to stop him, so I handled shit for him," he explained

After hearing that, I couldn't be angry, "I still can't go. I have a job."

"I'll let you and him handle that. I did what I had to do to keep our secret until you tell him. You have to tell him before this blows up in my face," he told me.

Jetta

"You gave me two weeks to come up with the money. What do you want?" I asked Cassius entering his hotel suite.

He smiled at me. "Happy to see you also, Jedi." I rolled my eyes at him. "I need twenty thousand dollars to take to Jamaica with me."

My heart ached. Him coming to Jamaica would ruin my chance at winning Shaka's heart. We are getting so close. The only time we are apart is when my father is around. I hated when he would slip out of my bed in the middle of the night. I loved sleeping wrapped up in his strong arms. He was so concerned with Daddy's health, he insisted we stay at the house. I don't understand why he was so concerned. Daddy seemed to be doing fine.

"I'm begging you, Cass. Please don't come to Jamaica. I will give you the money. I promise," I pleaded with tears in my eyes.

"I need the money wired to this account before you leave for Jamaica. If it's not there, I will show up," he said with a stern face.

I breathed a sigh of relief. He gave me a piece of paper with an account number written on it. I didn't have twenty thousand dollars. As much as I hated to do it, I would have to take it from Daddy's safe.

*****

After leaving the hotel, I went home. All I wanted to do was curl up in my bed and sleep. I was disappointed when I didn't see Shaka's truck. I immediately called his phone.

"Yea," he said answering. I heard a woman's laughter in the background.

"Where are you?" I asked with attitude. I needed him here with me. He was the only thing that could get my mind off this mess I'm in.

"Yo, calm the fuck down. I got shit I had to do," he stated angrily.

"You probably fucking that bitch. Nigga, let me find out you trying to play me," I yelled.

"Man, fuck you," he said before hanging up.

I was beyond furious. He didn't know who he was trying to play. I needed to take my frustration out on someone. He made it his business to make his self the target. I waited impatiently for him to come home. I had drunk an entire bottle of wine, and he still wasn't here. I had no idea where he could be. I fell asleep in his bed waiting on him.

"Get the fuck up!" He barked pulling the covers off me.

My head was pounding and the sunlight shining through the windows was too bright. I covered my eyes to block the sunlight. He grabbed my leg by the ankle and pulled me off the bed. I fell on my ass hard.

"Stop it, Micah. I don't feel good," I said in a low voice. The sound of my own voice made my head hurt.

"Ain't nobody tell yo ass to drink a whole bottle of wine," he said as I tried standing up. All I wanted to do was sleep.

"Just let me sleep," I said crawling back in the bed.

"Yo, go sleep in that nigga's bed you met at the hotel," he said snatching me off the bed again. Those words woke me up.

I stood up and stared him in the eyes. They were cold and black as coal. I could see the rage and hurt in them, "It's not what you think. I promise."

"We good. We were just fucking," he said staring at me. He didn't know how he was breaking my heart. I was falling in love with him.

"Don't say that," I said fighting back the tears. He turned to walk away from me, but I snatched his arm. I didn't know what else to do but use reverse psychology on him. I couldn't tell him about Cassius.

"Where were you. I heard the bitch laughing in the background. You have been gone all fucking day. I know you still fucking Dayzee," I spewed angrily.

He shrugged his shoulders. "Guess we even." He walked out his bedroom leaving me standing there shocked and broken hearted.

I refused to chase him after what he just said. I waited a few minutes before going downstairs. I slipped into Daddy's study and took the ten thousand dollars from his safe. I called Cassius to meet me at a local bar. I hadn't realized I had slept so long. It was approximately three o'clock in the afternoon. I hated giving Cassius this money. I only had a couple thousand dollars left from the money I made working with him. I was too ashamed to ask Daddy for money. I didn't want him to think I returned for his money. I promised myself I would return the ten thousand dollars when I'm able. I still had no idea what to do about the million dollars he's asking for. If I didn't come up with it, I would be going to jail. Daddy would never forgive me for what I did.

*****

An hour later, I was sitting in the bar when Cassius came strolling in. The sight of him infuriated me. I had to get him out of my life before he destroyed me. I slid the thick manila envelope to him. He immediately opened it and started flipping through the bills. He looked at me and smiled.

"Now, please stay away from me," I said.

He winked. "I will until it's time to pay up again. I guess you don't have any money in your account. Did Daddy give you this to shop with?"

"No," I answered bluntly. I hated knowing I stole from my father to give him money.

"Well if you need money, we can go back to work. It's plenty to be made," he said smiling. I didn't want to think of my past life with him. I caused enough pain. I would spend the rest of my life regretting what I did.

"I would live on the streets before I work with you again," I said disgusted by the sight of him. He laughed.

*****

I left the restaurant with Shaka on my mind. I had to mend things between us before we left for vacation. I promised myself I wouldn't chase him, but I couldn't help myself. This trip was supposed to be a way for us to get closer. I couldn't make that happen if he was furious with me. Shaka wasn't at the house when I returned. I decided to pop up at his home. I knew he was furious with me, but I had to see him. His Cadillac was parked in the driveway. I took a deep breath and made my way to the front door. I rang the doorbell and waited for him to come open the door. After ringing it again, I decided to leave. Just as I turned to go back to my car, his front door opened. I quickly turned around and nearly drooled at the sight of his sweaty, tattooed, muscular body. I tried to speak, but no words would come out. He stood there staring at me as I lusted over his body.

I finally was able to speak after breaking my stare, "I'm sorry. I only met with him to make sure he knew it was over. I only want you, Micah."

I wanted to tell him how I felt about him but didn't want to scare him away. I just wasn't ready to tell him about Cassius. I had to get him out of my life before he ruined it. Without saying another word, I stepped inside the house praying he didn't reject me. His sweaty musk mixed with his alluring cologne invaded my nose causing a thudding between my thighs. Just the touch of his hand on my flesh set my body on fire. I tiptoed and kissed his lips softly. He lifted me by my waist and wrapped my legs around his body. I licked and kissed his salty flesh as he carried me upstairs. Our tongues danced inside each other's mouth as he removed my clothes. He broke away from me long enough to turn the shower on. The entire bathroom was decorated with black marble floors and walls. He removed his basketball shorts and his dick stood out like a missile ready to launch. He stepped into the shower letting the shower sprayers from the wall and ceiling soak his body. I stepped inside and grabbed a sponge. I bathed his entire dark chocolate body until he was clean. I kissed my way down his broad chest to his chiseled abdomen. His beautiful, thick, long dick jumped when I wrapped my hand around it. I caressed the shaft as my tongue twirled around the huge mushroom head of his dick. I looked up at him as I maneuvered my tongue like a merry- go- round. His eyes were locked on mine filled with lust. I started licking up and down his shaft. The veins in his shaft were thick and long.

"Mmmmmm," I moaned as I slid him inside my mouth. I wasn't a pro at giving blow jobs but I wanted to satisfy him as much as I could.

"Sssshhhit!" He groaned gripping a handful of my long, wet, Peruvian weave.

I sucked his rod in and out while slurping and licking on each stroke. The shower sprayers sprayed us as I continued to lick, slurp and suck him deeper inside my mouth. His dome was hitting my throat causing me to gag but I refused to quit. I continued to go harder and faster as I reached down and fondled his swollen balls.

"Aaaarrrggghh!" He bellowed gripping my hair tighter. He started thrusting his dick in and out of my mouth. I opened my mouth and relaxed my throat allowing him to make love to my mouth. I gripped his shaft and sucked him into my mouth. My hand guided my mouth up and down.

"Got damn!" He barked trying to pull me up. I didn't want to stop. I wanted to feel his sweet thick milk pouring down my throat. I pushed his hand away and continued slurping and sucking his throbbing dick.

"Ffffuuuuccckkkk! Aaaarrrrggghhhh!" He roared as his body stiffened and jerked.

His thick milk poured into my mouth. I sucked and gulped until I drained every drop. He flopped down on the shower bench trying to catch his breath. Our night didn't end until I collapsed. The way his tongue slithered over every inch of my body with beautifully, skilled technique . He made slow, passionate love to me. Tears ran down my face as he slowly and passionately slid his rock hard dick in and out of me. I didn't care if he knew I loved him. The things he did to my body tonight told me he loved me too.

Titan

Mama had a big grin on her face when I showed her the picture of Hannah. I told her about Hannah a few days ago. She was ecstatic at the thought of being a grandmother. It definitely wasn't the reaction I was expecting. I thought she would be one of those grannies that felt she was too young to be a grandmother. She was overjoyed when I asked her about babysitting Hannah sometimes while we were on vacation.

"Boy, you couldn't deny this child if you wanted to. She looks just like you when you were fat as hell," she said laughing. I laughed with her because it was the truth.

"Who's her mother?" She asked still looking at her picture.

"You remember Ms. Burns?" I asked.

"Yea, the lady that was sick with Lupus. She had that geeky ass girl living with her. I always wondered where she got that damn child from. I think she kidnapped that damn girl."

I laughed. Mama was a conspiracist. She was always trying to analyze some shit. "I don't know about all that, but the girl is Hannah's mama."

Her eyes grew wide as she stared at me, "Boy, what the hell you doing mess with that girl? You know damn well she wasn't ready for dick."

I shook my head, "It's something that just happened one night. It was a one-time thing."

"Y'all dating now or something?" She asked.

"Nah, she's dating Rhino. He doesn't know about Hannah yet."

She laughed, "What kind of backward ass shit y'all got going on? Rhino is no more of a fit for that girl than you. Y'all know that boy got anger issues."

I laughed, "He's coping with that a lot better now. Whatever they have going on, it seems to work for them. I'm just trying to give her time to tell him."

"Well, you better keep that child away from him. If he sees her, he's going to know," she warned me.

She was right. If Rhino saw Hannah, he would know she was mine. I never told him or Shaka about what happened between me and Belle. Honestly, I wanted to forget that night. I regretted that night for the longest. I can't say that now after looking at my beautiful daughter. I just know Rhino will flip out when he finds out about me and Belle's true history. A few minutes later, Belle pulled into the drive way. I walked out of my house to get Hannah.

"Hi Mr. T," she said as I opened the car door. It filled my heart with joy that she was happy to see me. At the same time, I hated that she didn't know me as her father.

"Hi pretty girl," I said smiling at her. I helped her out the car.

"We can't stay long. Granny has a doctor's appointment," Belle said getting out the car.

"That's cool. She can stay here with me and Ma until you get back," I said as we walked in the house. I could see the uncertainty in her eyes.

"I don't know about that, Titan. She doesn't know you well," Belle said. I opened the front door and Hannah ran inside. I gently grabbed Belle by the arm to stop her from entering.

"I've lost almost five years of her life. It's not my fault she doesn't know me. Don't fucking act like you can't trust me with her. That's the point of you bringing her over, so you can meet Ma and feel comfortable."

She exhaled heavily. "I know and I'm sorry. I want you to be in her life. I'm just not used to being away from her."

"Ma is a little crazy, but she's good people. She's excited about meeting her granddaughter," I said smiling at her.

She smiled nervously. "Ok."

When we entered the house, Ma and Hannah was sitting at the kitchen table talking like they've know each other for years. I couldn't help but smile at the sight of seeing the two bonding. I could see tears in Ma's eyes when she glanced up at me. She rolled her eyes at Belle. I knew she had animosity toward Belle for keeping Hannah a secret for so many years.

"I see you two have introduced yourselves," I said smiling at them.

"She says she's my grandma too. Mama is that true? I got two Grannies?" Hannah asked excitedly.

Belle looked up at me wanting me to rescue her from answering the question. I couldn't help her on this one. I wanted Hannah to know who I truly was in her life. It was time for Belle to tell the truth. Belle went and sat to the table with Hannah and Ma.

"Yes Hannah, you have two Grannies. I know you've asked me about your daddy before and I told you hopefully you'll get to meet him one day. Well, that day is here. Mr. T is your father. She's his mother which makes her your grandmother."

Hannah looked up at me with a confused look. I assumed she was trying to digest everything Belle just told her. All of a sudden, a big smile appeared on her face. "You tricked me." She ran to me and wrapped her chubby arms around my legs. I breathed a sigh of relief and laughed.

"I sure did," I said picking her up and hugging her tight.

"I'm sorry, I don't know your name," Belle said looking at Ma.

"I don't remember giving it to you," Ma said with an attitude. I gave her a look to let her know I wasn't with her bullshit attitude she gives Mena. "My name is Bernadette. My friends call me Bernie. You can call me Bernadette." I chuckled and shook my head.

"I'm Belle." Belle held her hand out to shake my mother's. Ma reluctantly shook her hand.

"I know who you are. I know your Granny very well. She is the reason I'm not fucking you up right now for keeping my grandbaby away from me."

"Ma!" I barked.

Hannah laughed, "Grandma, you not supposed to say bad words."

Ma stood up, "I'm sorry baby. Come on, let me show you all the stuff we bought for you in your new room." She took Hannah by the arm and led her upstairs.

"New room? She's not staying here," Belle said as soon as they walked out the room.

"She will eventually start sleeping over some nights, Belle. I'm going to spend as much time as I can with her. That's some shit we are going to have to sit down and discuss after this trip."

"She hates me. I'm not letting her keep my child," she said angrily.

"Her feelings toward you has nothing to do with her feelings for Hannah. I advise you to work out a schedule with your Granny and neighbor on when she can come pick Hannah up while we are on vacation. Trust me, you don't want her to think that you trying to keep her away from her granddaughter." She exhaled in frustration. I couldn't feel any sympathy for her. She brought this on herself.

"I wasn't trying to keep you from her," she said with apologetic eyes. I believed her. Honestly, I didn't know how I would've reacted if she would've told me she was pregnant by me. Being the young immature boy I was, I probably would've denied the baby.

"It's okay Belle. I believe you. Now, I just want to be a father to my child."

"What about Miriam. Do you think she will understand?" She asked.

I didn't want to think about her. That girl had a hold on me I never felt before. As much as I tried to stay away and not think about her, I couldn't. I hadn't spoken to her since the night she caught me fucking one of my bartenders. Until she decides what she's going to do about having a fiancé, I couldn't consider her as someone important in my life. If all she wanted me to do was fuck her, that's exactly what she'll get.

"Her opinion doesn't matter when it comes to my child. You know as well as I do, she's engaged," I told her.

"Yea, but I know she likes you and you like her," she explained.

"You just prepare to tell Rhino about Hannah on this trip. If you don't, I will," I warned her.

"What do you think he will do?" She asked nervously.

I honestly didn't know how Rhino would act. I've never known Rhino to take any girl seriously until Belle. I hope it doesn't come between our friendship. I didn't have any romantic feelings toward Belle. She has always been a nice girl that I thought of as a friend. I know it's going to be hard to accept we've had sex. Not only did we have sex, but we had a child together. That would be a hard pill to swallow for any man.

Rhino

"How did you get me off from work?" Belle asked as we rode toward the mall. I had paid just about everyone at her job to take some of her time for the next five days.

"Don't worry about that. Just enjoy this vacation," I said looking ahead.

"Well, where are we going?" She asked.

I glanced at her. It was something about her that I couldn't shake. She was different from any girl I've fucked with. I didn't know what I was doing with her. All I know is I didn't want to stop whatever it was. She was wearing a pair of jean shorts that revealed her thick thighs. I licked my lips as I thought of tasting her sweetness.

"Why you got on them lil ass shorts?" I asked. I didn't like the thought of another man looking at her. As far as I was concerned, she belonged to me.

"It's hot, Rhino," she said staring at me. I didn't reply. I focused on the road as I thought about my intentions with her.

"Rhino, what is your government name?" She asked.

"Brutus," I answered.

She smiled at me. “Were you named after the character from Ides of March?”

“Nah, I was named after my alcoholic grandfather. I’m a third,” I informed her.

“Oh, I’m sorry,” she said.

“Don’t be. The nigga made me the man I am today,” I said reminiscing of the ass whoopings he gave me while my bitch ass daddy stood and watched in silence.

She giggled. “Were you that bad?”

I glanced at her with a solemn face. “Nah, he was just an evil, cold hearted bastard.”

She saw the look in my eyes. She felt the deep resentment inside me. She reached over and held my hand. It felt strange. I’ve never had a female try to get close to me. Most women I dealt with were with me for who I am in the streets. They never tried to get to know the man that held a passion he didn’t feel comfortable sharing with the world.

“We’re going to the mall to do some shopping. I’m sure you need some clothes and shit for the trip,” I told her.

“I don’t have money for new clothes. I’m just taking what I have at home,” she said.

“I didn’t ask you to buy your own clothes. I ain’t that kind of nigga.”

"I just don't want you to think I want you for your money. I'm not that kind of girl," she said nervously.

"I know Nerd Girl. You ain't got that kind of game, Ms. Dip yo banana in my chocolate pie," I said smiling.

She released my hand and punched me in my arm, "You promised to never bring that up again."

I laughed, "My bad."

We hit almost every store in the mall. We argued because she was worried about the price of the clothing she wanted. She finally gave in and started getting the clothes she liked. She thanked me repeatedly as we walked through the mall shopping for clothes and bathing suits . I didn't care for the bathing suits she picked out, so I chose the ones I thought was more suitable. She was trying to show off too much damn skin. After leaving the mall, we went grocery shopping. She wanted to cook dinner for me.

*****

"Daddy, there he goes! That's the man that had Mama crying in the bedroom," Bria's little talking ass daughter said pointing at me. Me and the nigga locked eyes and I knew shit was about to go left.

He walked over to me and stared me in the eyes. I had to give him credit for staring me in the eyes, "You fucking with my baby mama?"

I chuckled, "Nah, I fucked her so good she was crying."

That was all it took for him to throw a punch at me. It landed on my jaw. I stumbled backwards before regaining my composure. I didn't want to fight in the grocery store in front of his kids and Belle.

"Yo, we can handle this botheration another time. This ain't the bailiwick. You got your kids and I got my old lady," I said rubbing my jaw. I wanted to body the nigga. I tried using the big words to calm my anger. If I didn't he would be dead, and I would be locked up for murder.

"Man, what the fuck you just say?" He asked angrily.

I chuckled, and he charged me. I unleashed the anger inside me on him. By the end of the fight, I was bashing his head with a big ass can of Bush's Baked Beans. I could hear his kids screaming and Belle begging me to stop, but I couldn't. I felt arms on me trying to pull me away from him. My rage overpowered them. The only thing stopped me was being tased by twelve. I was handcuffed and put in the patrol car. I glanced at Belle standing outside the store in tears as the police pulled off. If she wasn't scared of me before, I know she is now.

Omega used the connections he had and got me a bond hearing. We were leaving for Jamaica in a few hours. I was released on a bond high enough to pay off the favor given to Omega. Shaka wasted no time bailing me out. Bria's baby daddy was in intensive care but was going to survive the beating I unleashed on him. I tried calling Belle numerous times, but she never answered. I wasn't surprised. I saw the terror in her eyes as I sat in the back of the police car. I only hoped she came to Jamaica, so I could explain things to her. I headed home and packed my bags.

*****

When I arrived at the airport, everyone was there waiting to check in. I looked around to see if Belle was there, but she wasn't. I wasn't going without her. I stood there getting impatient waiting on her.

I walked over to Jetta. "Where's Belle?"

"I don't know. She hasn't answered any of my calls," she answered nervously.

Just as I started to call her she came rushing through the door with her luggage. I walked over to help her with her suitcase. She declined my help with an attitude. I grabbed her by her arm and pulled her in a corner.

"I know you saw me calling you. Stop over exaggerating the bullshit . Yea, I fucked his bitch while his kids sat in the living room. I tried attenuating the situation, but he came for me. I had every right to defend my damn self," I explained.

She looked at me with wide yes. "You didn't defend yourself. You tried to kill him with a damn can of baked beans.

I almost laughed, "I told you I have anger issues. Now, don't piss me off any further. So, let the shit go and let's enjoy this fuckin' vacation."

"I'm going on this vacation for myself and not for you," she said walking past me.

She just didn't know how much she turned me on with that attitude. I watched her ass jiggle as she walked over to Jetta. We all boarded the plane. Belle tried to walk to another seat, but I pulled her by her arm forcing her to sit next to me. She sat there fuming and pouting. She was going to sit her pretty ass beside me rather she liked it or not. Omega looked happy and relaxed as he talked to Jetta sitting in the seat next to him. A few minutes later, we were in the air to what I was hoping was a perfect vacation.

NATAVIA PRESENTS

Shaka

We arrived in Jamaica on time as scheduled. The sun shined bright as we stepped outside the airport. I didn't know how to act being on vacation. The only time I visit another state or country is for business. I would handle what needs to be done and go back home. I was doing this for Omega. I knew how much this meant to him, so I wanted to make sure he enjoys himself. There were three stretch limousines waiting to pick us up.

"Daddy, why do you have three limos?" Jetta asked him.

"I'm riding solo. I got a couple of pit stops to make before arriving at the house," he informed her.

Omega was staying at his vacation home. The rest of us were staying at a resort nearby. I was glad to know he wouldn't be staying at the resort . I just wasn't ready for him to know about us. I wasn't just having sex with Jetta. I was feeling her. I can't lie and say I wasn't in my feelings when Dayzee told me she saw Jetta at a hotel bar with a nigga. I almost fucked Dayzee that same day but didn't. I didn't' want to give her ideas that we were fucking with each other like that anymore. I was surprised when Jetta showed up at my house. She wasn't the apologetic type.

The look in her eyes told me she loved me. I've never told anyone I loved them. I don't know exactly what the word meant. All I know is I wanted to bury myself so deep inside her that she couldn't escape me if she tried. We were running late for our flight this morning because we spent the night fucking each other until she was screaming her love for me. I wanted to say it to her, but I didn't know how to say it. Love is a word that should be shown and not heard. I decided to start doing things to show her how I felt.

Once we arrived at the resort we were staying at, we checked into our rooms. After finding out Omega was staying at his home, I regretted telling her to book us separate rooms. We had made an itinerary for the entire trip. We were scheduled to meet at a fancy restaurant for dinner in a couple of hours. I decided to plan something different for her. After unpacking and getting dressed, I went to her room. She opened the door looking absolutely beautiful. She wore her hair long and straight with a part in the middle. Her soft make up blended perfectly with her complexion. Her low-cut spaghetti strapped mustard colored dress hugged every curve on her. Her ample breasts was spilling out causing me to lick my lips.

"You ready?" I asked not able to take my eyes off her breasts .

She lifted my chin, so I could look her in the eyes, “Yea, let me grab my clutch.”

“Where is everyone?” She asked when we made it to lobby.

“They’ll meet us there,” I said taking her by the hand and leading her outside to the limo I had waiting.

*****

She sipped on a glass of wine as we rode. I massaged her thigh fighting the temptation to taste her. If the limo hadn’t stopped my face would’ve been between her thighs. We exited the limo.

“Where are we?” She asked looking around.

I shrugged my shoulders, “I just thought we could make tonight about us.”

She stared at me with soft eyes and smiled. I took her by the hand and led her out on the beach. I had a tent set up with a waiter to serve us dinner. The moonlight lit up the dark night. The wind gave us a perfect breeze. Candle lights surrounded the tent making the scene romantic for her.

“You did all this for me?” She asked after we were seated.

"Nah, I'm just trying to make sure I get deep in them guts later," I said smiling. She tossed her napkin at me and laughed.

"Thank you," she said smiling at me. I nodded my head at her. We sat quietly and ate while the soft music played.

"I've never thanked you for everything you do for my father. I never imagined you would mean so much in my life the night I met you," she said staring at me.

I chuckled. "Your father is good man. As for you, I couldn't stand yo ass."

She giggled. "You were always so damn mean to me."

I stared at her. "It was something about you that got under my skin. I didn't like you, but I couldn't stop thinking about you."

She blushed. "Is that why you wouldn't let me date?"

"Nah, that was because you were trying to fuck with weak ass niggas," I said with a frown. I couldn't stand when I would see her flirting with other guys. She laughed and shook her head.

I pulled the small box from my jacket pocket. "Don't get too excited. This ain't what you think it is."

I placed the small black box on the table and slid it over to her. She looked at me with wide eyes before picking it up. She slowly opened the box. She stared at her gift for a few seconds before looking up at me. A tear ran down her face as she stared at me.

"I thought you pawned them," she said softly.

"Nah, I kept hoping you would come back for them," I said.

I couldn't bring myself to pawn the diamond earrings she gave me the night she crashed her father's car. She walked over and straddled my lap. She covered my face with kisses before sucking my tongue into her mouth. She started winding her hips causing my dick to rub against her center.

"Yo, you better chill before we be on Pornhub," I said nodding my head at the waiter.

"Well, let's go back to the room," she said getting up from my lap. We didn't make it back to the room. I was buried deep inside her in the limo when we pulled up to the resort.

Miriam

I couldn't believe what I was doing. I was risking my relationship with my parents and Lyle to chase after a man. I tried to get over him, but nothing worked. He made me feel things Lyle never was capable of doing. It wasn't all sexual. He would sit and listen to me talk for hours about my goals and dreams. My thoughts and opinions mattered to him. I didn't have to act like a boring socialite with him. I could be wild and carefree . Lyle and my parents always expected me to act like a refined lady. The world's opinion of me mattered more than my own happiness to them. I was sharing a room with Jetta, so I had no trouble getting inside the room. I told her I wasn't coming, so she wasn't expecting me. She wasn't in the room when I arrived. I saw the itinerary laying on the desk, so I dressed for dinner. I prayed Titan didn't bring another female on the trip. My heart couldn't take it. If he did bring someone, I wasn't going to play fair. I was wearing the sexiest dress I could find to win him back. I wore a nude colored Hermosa bandage dress. The right side of the dress only covered my thigh and leg with a bow. Most of the huge, dragon tattoo on my hip was on display for him. He loved placing soft kisses on it before devouring my womanhood. I gave the maître d the party's name. I followed behind him. My heart was beating rapidly. I didn't know how Titan would feel about seeing me. I saw them before they saw me. I was surprised not to see Jetta and Shaka sitting at the table. Only Titan, Rhino and Belle were at the table.

"Oh my God, Miriam. I'm so glad you came," Belle said getting up and giving me a hug. I returned her hug as I stared into Titan's eyes. I couldn't read them. He was giving me a blank stare.

"I'm sorry I'm late. I had to finish some business before I came," I said taking a seat.

"Shit, you obviously forgot to get that dress finished being made," Rhino said. I shot him a middle finger.

"Where's the rest of the party?" I asked making sure not to look at Titan.

Belle shrugged her shoulders. "Jetta and Shaka stood us up. Mr. O is spending time with his parents tonight."

I took a sip of my water. "Where's your date?" I asked Titan.

"In the bathroom," he replied. My face felt like it hit the floor.

Rhino burst into laughter, "If you could see your face right now. It's on the damn floor."

"That's not funny," Belle said lightly shoving her elbow into Rhino's side. "There's no one in the bathroom." I couldn't hold the sigh of relief.

"Well, we outta here," Rhino said getting up.

"You have eaten already?" I asked Belle.

"Yea, but we can stay until you eat something," she said.

"No, I don't want to hold you guys up. I can order room service at the resort," I said.

"No, you gotta try the red snapper. It was delicious. Besides, I want desert," Belle said looking up at Rhino.

"Shit so do I, so let's go," Rhino said. He didn't give Belle a chance to reply before pulling her up from her seat.

"Her side nigga can stay here with her. We'll send the limo back for you," he said walking away with Belle by his side.

"You can go, too. I'll catch a taxi back to the resort," I said looking at the menu. I couldn't believe he actually stood up to leave. "You really going to leave me here alone?"

"Well, don't say shit you don't mean," he said looking down at me.

I looked up at him, "Will you stay with me? I hate eating alone and I'm starving."

He sat back down. He looked so handsome. He was wearing a pair of Balmain white jeans, a short sleeved button down Gucci shirt and burnt brown Gucci loafers. I placed my order when the waiter came to the table. He sat quietly sipping on his cognac.

"Are you going to talk to me?" I asked wanting to break the silence between us.

"Look, I'm not with the bullshit anymore. If you want this shit, you gotta let it be known. If not, don't ever come at me like you did in my office," he said staring at me to let me know he meant every word.

"What do you want me to do?" I asked.

He chuckled and shook his head, "It's not about what I want. What the fuck do you want?"

"My family expects a certain life for me. My life was planned until you came along," I said.

"That doesn't answer the damn question, Star." I dropped my head. All I could think about was how I would disappoint my parents if I didn't marry Lyle.

"I don't have time for this shit. Go home," he said standing up.

I couldn't let him leave. I immediately stood up and grabbed his hand, "I want you. I want us."

"I-I will end things with him when I return. I just want to enjoy being with you without the thoughts of my life back home. Please, just give me that," I pleaded with him.

He stared at me a few minutes before sitting back down, "No more regretting shit that happens between us." I nodded my head in agreement. I would agree to anything to get my next fix from him.

We talked as I ate. I told him about my family and life with Lyle. He sat and listened to me without judging me. He told me about him and his mother's dysfunctional relationship growing up. Regardless of their past, I could tell he loves her. He told me about his time in prison. I admired his determination to not let his past determine his future. Titan had a big heart. He was a lover, but he wasn't one to let you take his kindness for weakness. After I ate, he had the limo take us to the beach. We walked and enjoyed the moonlight until I got sleepy. We soaked in a bubble bath together before climbing into bed. As much as I wanted him, I was too exhausted. I fell asleep laying on top of him. My life in Atlanta didn't matter at this point.

My only concern was being with him. I fell asleep curled up in his arms.

The next morning, we woke up to banging on the door. He slipped on a pair of boxers and went to answer the door. “Rise and shine, sleepy heads.” I laughed happy to hear Jetta’s energetic voice. She walked into the bedroom as I was sitting up in the bed. She jumped on the bed hugging me. “I’m so glad you came.” I laughed and hugged her back.

“Man, what the hell you want this early?” Titan asked standing in the doorway.

“I have an itinerary. Today is horseback riding at my grandparent’s house and a family barbecue,” she said getting off the bed. Me and Jetta loved to go horseback riding at the country club.

“Well, I need to go to our room and get dressed,” I said getting out the bed.

“No need, your luggage should be here in a couple of minutes,” she said winking at me.

“Be downstairs in an hour,” she said as she walked out the bedroom.

I stared at Titan’s ripped abdomen and perfect V, “I can get dressed in thirty minutes. That leaves thirty minutes to spare.”

I laughed. “Nah, that’s not what this trip is about. Sex is off the table until shit is handled.” He walked out the room leaving me sitting there stunned. There was no way we weren’t having sex in Jamaica.

Rhino

"Hell nah! I'm not riding no damn horse! Fuck that!" I said walking away from the horse. Shaka and Titan laughed but I was dead ass serious.

"Come on Rhino, we are supposed to be having fun," Belle said with a sad face. I hated to disappoint her, but I wasn't getting on that horse.

"We'll find something else to do. I'm not riding that big ass beast," I said walking up to her.

She folded her arms and pouted. I leaned over and whispered in her ear. "You can't handle riding my dick. How you know how to ride a horse?" She elbowed me in the stomach hard and walked away. I was only joking but I could tell I hurt her feelings.

"Don't worry Maribelle. Johnny will take the other horse out with you," Omega said to her as she watched the stable boy saddle up her horse.

I looked around. "Who the hell is Johnny?"

"Johnny!" Omega said as he sat in the lounge chair in the backyard . A tall, dark skinned nigga with more muscles than Arnold Schwarzenegger walked out the back door of the house.

"Yea," he said walking up to Omega.

"Belle needs company on the horseback ride. Take the other horse out with her," Omega said pointing at Belle. He looked at Belle and smiled. I knew he was staring at her ass.

"Nigga, yo Mandingo looking ass must be crazy if you think you riding a damn horse with her," I told him with a scowl on my face. Everyone laughed except Johnny. He was still staring at Belle.

"Saddle Cass' Ole ass up," I demanded to the stable boy. "Big muscle bound nigga will break the horse's back anyway."

"Saddle who?" Jetta asked still laughing.

"Look at y'all black folks. Wanna ride damn horses but don't even know the horse's name in Black Stallion," I said looking around at them. Everyone laughed.

"I swear Omega, I'm killing his ass if he tries to throw me," I said before I climbed on the horse.

"You gotta loosen up. Don't try to ride him all stiff and shit," Titan advised me.

"You taking notes, Nerd Girl," I said winking at Belle.

I knew I was agitating her. I didn't care right now. That's what she gets for making me ride this damn horse. She gently tapped the horse with her leg and she took off.

“Man, when y’all hood asses learn how to ride horses?” I said looking at Shaka.

“At the country club. I don’t know about Belle, though. Maybe she’s a pro at riding other things,” he said with a smile.

“Nigga, fuck you,” I said before tapping the horse with my leg.

He knew I didn’t like the thought of her with somebody else in my head. He laughed out loud as the horse took over. I held on to the reigns as he galloped. I kept trying to hold my balance . I didn’t have a clue what I was doing and it was obvious. I made the mistake of hitting the horse when I almost fell off. He took off fast as hell. To keep from falling off, I leaned forward and held on to him.

“Lean forward and gently pull the reigns. Don’t pull too hard or he will throw you off,” Belle instructed me as she came up behind me. I did as she said, and the horse slowed down. We were deep in the woods, and I was done riding.

“How I stop this beast?” I asked.

“Say woah, and pull the reigns, but not too hard,” she said. The horse stopped when I did as she said. I jumped off the horse.

"Fuck this! I like yo ass, but this ain't the way a nigga gone die," I said. She giggled and got off her horse.

"Where you learn how to ride a horse?" I asked.

"College. This white girl used to invite us to her family's ranch," she informed me.

We walked silently with the horses until we stopped by a small stream. Omega had set his parents up in a beautiful home. There were acres of land with a huge lake in the woods behind the beautiful brick home. I watched her rub the horse as he drank from the stream. She was still mad at me about the fight. She slept with her back to me last night. I guess it was time to talk to her about the incident.

I cleared my throat. "I tried to get the nigga to walk away. My anger is like the fucking Hulk. I can't control that shit when I get too mad. The big words don't help at a point. When he put his hands on me, that was it."

"Other than the big words, what else calms you?" She asked looking at me.

I walked up to her and caressed the side of her face, "You." She looked up and smiled at me.

"What if I'm the one that makes you mad?" She asked.

"Well, you better learn how to ride my dick like you ride that horse," I said smiling.

"Ugh!" She groaned and stepped away from me.

I laughed. "I'm just fucking with you, Belle. You already got a nigga pussy whipped."

"What about the girl?" She asked.

"She was before you and me. Ain't been nobody since you," I told her. I hadn't even thought about fucking another female since her.

"Well, the next time the words don't work. Think about me," she said smiling. I nodded my head.

"I need to talk to you about something. I just hope you will try to understand," she said nervously.

She was getting ready to tell me until we heard noises. We both looked at each other. We walked toward the noise. Belle immediately covered her eyes and walked away. I covered my mouth and laughed. Belle pulled me by the arm. Titan was fucking the shit out of Miriam on a damn horse.

"Now, them some damn freaks," I said laughing as she pulled me.

She smiled, "That made me horny."

"Shit, take off your clothes and I'll climb back up on the damn horse," I said smiling at her.

She pulled me by the hand, “Let’s go do it in the lake.” I started removing my clothes as we walked to the lake. My dick was throbbing as I watched her juicy ass jiggle in front of me.

Jetta

We were having a great time at the family cookout. I always loved visiting my grandparents. They spoiled me more than my father. We were playing volleyball in the huge backyard . It was the women against the men. They were whooping us bad, but it didn't matter. It was all in fun. I would have never imagined Belle being as athletic as she was. She was the only one making the game competitive for the men. The sun was beaming, and I was exhausted. I needed to sit down and cool off.

"Where you going?" Shaka asked as I walked away from the game.

"It's hot. I'm tired and sweaty," I said.

"I like seeing you sweaty," he said winking at me. I blushed and pranced away. I made sure to put an extra twist in my stride, because I knew he was watching. I flopped on the lounger between Daddy and Papa.

"Giving up?" Daddy asked smiling at me.

"Daddy, you know I'm lazy," I said smiling. He laughed. I leaned over and kissed Papa on the cheek. Daddy was the younger version of his father. I loved the relationship they had.

“I hear you getting ready to start school,” Papa said looking at me.

“Yes Papa. I want to study fashion,” I said proudly.

“Well, you’ve invested enough money in it already. Nobody spends more money on clothes than you,” he said jokingly. I laughed.

“I’m proud of you, Boopsy. I knew you had that ambition in you,” he said smiling at me.

“Thanks Papa,” I said graciously.

It meant a lot to have my family’s approval. I want to make them proud of the woman they raised. I’ve been so spoiled that I never considered building anything for myself. After learning about the struggle Shaka has been through, there was no reason I shouldn’t push myself to want more for myself. I sat and admired him playing volleyball . His dark chocolate skin was glistening from the sweat. I started thinking about the sweet love we made last night.

“So, that’s your boyfriend? Is he the reason for the new you?” Papa asked. I was shocked and scared to answer him. My eyes immediately went to Daddy.

“Answer your grandfather,” Daddy said with a stern look on his face.

I didn't want to ruin this trip, so I lied. "No, we're just friends."

Papa laughed. "With a friend like that, you don't need a boyfriend. Papa old, but he ain't blind."

I became nervous. I didn't want Daddy trying to kill Shaka on this vacation. I felt Daddy's eyes on me. I refused to look in his direction. He would know I was lying if I looked him in the eyes.

"Johnny, the barbecue was delicious," I said to my cousin. I was hoping to get off the subject of me and Shaka.

"Thanks cuz, I'm trying to save up this money to open a pit," he said in his strong Jamaican accent.

"I offered to help you," Daddy said looking at him.

"I know Unc, but I wanna do this one on my own," Johnny said. Johnny is Daddy's deceased sister's son. She died from cancer at young age.

"We hitting up a club tonight," Johnny said.

I didn't know if I would be going with them. This was one time I was glad Shaka didn't like clubs. After enjoying the rest of the day with the family we headed back to the hotel. All I wanted was a hot shower and bed. The hot sun literally drained me. I left Shaka downstairs at the bar having a drink with Titan and Rhino. When he came upstairs I was curled up in the bed under the covers.

“Get up, we going out,” he said snatching the covers off me.

“I’m tired. I want to stay in,” I said pulling the covers back over me. I was surprised he wanted to go out.

He sat on the side of the bed. “You and your father told me I should enjoy life more. I’m trying to do that with yo ass.” He knew how to melt my heart . I sat up in the bed resting my back on the headboard.

“Well, why can’t we tell Daddy about us? I hate keeping us a secret,” I asked.

“I’m not the type of nigga yo daddy see you with. I know he respects me, but not enough to be fucking his Boopsy.”

I got behind him and wrapped my arms around his waist. “You are the exact type of man he wants to see me with. You are strong, responsible, and overprotective of me. You don’t baby me like he does. I know he regrets spoiling me. He knows it will take a strong man to make me want to change. That’s what you’ve done. You’ve made me want to be more than a rich daddy’s girl. I love you and I want to be able to tell Daddy that I do,” I whispered in his ear.

He turned his head to look at me. “You get yo ass up and go to this club with me, we’ll tell him tomorrow at dinner.” I hugged him tight and kissed him on the cheek.

“I’m going to hop in the shower,” he said standing up.

“Micah,” I called his name softly. He turned to face me.

“Even though you don’t say it, I know you do,” I said smiling at him.

He stared at me, “I’ve never used the word other than to express my feelings for money. I’ve never had anyone use it to describe their feelings toward me until now. I don’t think the word is sufficient enough to describe a feeling so deep.” I understood what he was saying, but it would be nice to hear him say it.

He walked toward the bathroom door and stopped, “Hey.” I looked up at him.

“I do love you,” he said. All I could do was smile as he walked in the bathroom.

As tired as I was, I didn’t regret going to the club. I got a chance to show Shaka my Jamaican moves. He even danced with me. We laughed and drank with everyone until Rhino got mad. He couldn’t stand to see Belle dancing. She had the figure and moves that made men drool over her. He snatched her off the floor and made her sit next to him for the rest of the evening. As always, Titan and Miriam couldn't keep their eyes off each other. I loved how carefree she was with him. She always acts so reserved when we go out. He brought a side of her out that no one knew about but me. The night ended perfectly until we headed back to the hotel. My phone dinged alerting me of a text message.

Partner in Crime~Cass

I immediately tensed up. Shaka decided it was time for us to leave. He instructed the driver to raise the partition . I watched as he slid down on the floor between my legs, pushing them apart. He placed soft kisses on my thighs until he pulled my panties off. My head fell back, and a loud moan escaped my mouth when he sucked my lower lips into his mouth. He wrapped his arms around my thighs pulling me down lower in the seat. He pushed my legs up to my shoulders folding me up. He held my hands down by my side. I was locked down and at his mercy. His wet tongue twirled around between my lips tasting my juices that he created.

"Mmmmmm," he moaned as he licked and slurped. My moans turned into screams of ecstasy when his tongue slid between my ass cheeks. His head moved up and down as I squirmed trying to relieve myself from the uncontrollable pleasure he was giving me.

"Damn, this pussy sweet," he moaned before sucking on my clit and sliding two fingers inside me.

My mouth watered, and my body shivered. "Oooooohhh, I looovveee yoooouu!" I wailed as I exploded.

"Damn!" He barked as he devoured my creaminess.

His tongue twirled around and around as he slurped and sucked on my drenched pussy. He didn't stop until I was coming inside his mouth again. He looked up at me with my cream covering his mouth. The rest of the ride to the resort was me riding him until he exploded inside me.

Belle

"You can pout the rest of this damn trip. Don't matter to me," Rhino said as we lounged on the beach.

We were all having a great time at the club last night, until he decided to show his ass. He pulled me off the dance floor claiming I was trying to shake my ass for niggas. He insisted I sit next to him like a child for the rest of the evening. I was tired of him treating me like a kid. He gave me orders and expected me to follow them without question. I liked him so much that I did what he said to keep him in my life. I just hated how controlling he was of me. I was relieved when Titan and Miriam came from off the jet skis.

"Y'all nasty asses probably been out there fucking on the skis," Rhino said frowning up at them. I couldn't help but giggle remembering them on the horse. Miriam shot her middle finger at him.

"Freaky ass socialite," he said laughing.

"Will you please shut him up?" Miriam said to Titan.

Titan chuckled and scratched his head. "You did rape me in the woods."

"Ugh!" Miriam stormed away.

She hated that we saw that side of her. I admired her for being so carefree. I didn't know how to be aggressive with Rhino. I felt like if I did, he would respect me more. I know he says he not messing with anybody else, but he still flirts with other girls in my face.

Titan came and sat in the lounger next to me. "When you gone tell him?" He whispered to me.

"I don't know. I don't want to ruin this trip. Why can't I wait until we get home?" I asked.

"The fuck y'all whispering about?" Rhino asked glancing at us.

"Man, chill out. I was just asking about her Granny," Titan lied.

Rhino shook his head. "At least you know her. I'm fucking the hell out her granddaughter and haven't met her yet."

"Stop it Rhino!" I said angrily.

He shrugged his shoulders. "Shit, it's the truth." I got up and went to join Miriam in the water.

"Don't pay Rhino any attention. He just likes getting under your skin," I said to her.

"I don't. I just have a lot on my mind," she said sadly.

"I know we aren't that close but I'm a great listener. I don't judge," I said smiling at her.

She gave me a smile before she spoke. "I just don't want this to end. We are good together. I know it's not going to be this way when we go home. I'm an engaged women. My father is the pastor of an enormous church. They expect me to live a certain way. Trust me, this isn't the way."

"What about what you want? This is your life, Miriam. I understand wanting to make your parents proud, but it's pointless if you aren't happy."

"I just have my life planned. I don't want to invest in a future with a drug dealer. I mean don't get me wrong. Titan is a great guy, but he's not someone I can build a secure future with," she said glancing at him.

"Have you talked to him about it?" I asked. She shook her head. "Maybe if he knew what was holding you back, he can show you more than just him being a drug dealer. Something tells me there's more to him than just that." I knew Titan had many businesses and a college degree. I didn't understand why he hadn't told Miriam.

"I don't want to hurt his feelings," she said.

I hated the secret we were keeping from her and Rhino. This would only be another obstacle for them to bear in their relationship. Sometimes, I wish I had never gone to the club the night Rhino invited me. Then, I think about how happy Hannah was to connect with her father. I might lose Rhino but seeing her happy will be worth it.

"Look at this shit," Miriam said staring at the shore. Two girls were sitting and talking with Titan and Rhino. She hurried out the water and I followed behind her. She stood there staring down at Titan.

"What?" He asked staring up at her.

"Tell them bye," she ordered with her hands on her hips.

He shook his head and laughed, "I told you until you handle yo shit, you don't run shit here."

"Hey everyone," Jetta said walking up.

"Where Shaka?" Rhino asked.

"He was on the phone with Los," Jetta answered him.

"Nigga always working," Rhino said shaking his head.

"So, you coming to our party tonight?" The pretty Jamaican girl asked in her strong accent.

"Shit, why not?" Rhino said shrugging his shoulders.

"No the fuck you are not. You are here with Belle! That's so fucking disrespectful," Miriam said to him.

"Man, shut the hell up. Belle know it ain't shit like that. You need to worry about the nigga you got back home. My business ain't yours," Rhino told her. Miriam looked at Titan waiting for him to defend her, but he sat quietly.

"Bye," Jetta said looking at the two girls. They both giggled before standing up walking away.

Rhino pulled me by the arm, so I could sit in his lap. I jerked away from him and went inside the resort. I started to think maybe it was best we aren't together. I wasn't the type of woman that could handle a man like him. I wasn't strong willed enough to deal with him. I was in the shower when he pushed the sliding door open.

"What the hell you tripping for?" He asked staring at me. He was standing there naked as the day he was born with his rippled abs and dick hanging. I couldn't even get words out of my mouth. He stepped into the shower and pinned me against the wall.

"Them bitches ain't shit to me. I told you. You got me," he said nibbling on my ear as his strong hands caressed my body.

I hated how weak I was for him. My body instantly gave in to him. He kissed his way down to my breasts . I wrapped my arms around his neck as he sucked and nibbled on my hard nipples. I ran my fingers through his dreads as he lapped circles around my nipples before kissing his way down.

"Damn, I love the way you smell," he moaned before dipping his face between my thighs. He was down on his knees licking and sucking my soul out of me. All I could do was take the exhilaration he was giving me. He grunted and moaned as he feasted on me.

"Aaaaaahhhhh Yyyyeesss!" I screamed gripping his dreads tightly as I exploded in his mouth. My legs went limp almost causing me to slip and fall. He picked me up and pinned my legs in the crook of his arms.

"This my pussy?" He asked staring at me with the head of his dick at my opening. Before I could answer he slid inside me. I wrapped my arms around his back while biting his shoulder. He was so huge. It was an enjoyable pain every time he entered me.

"Damn, you feel so damn good," he moaned as he slid in and out of me. I could feel every vein and ridge in his shaft penetrating my walls. I dug my nails into his back when he tried to go too deep. I still wasn't able to take all of him. He pulled back knowing I wasn't ready for all of him.

"Tell me who good ass pussy this is," he said as he started winding his hips. He was hitting every spot inside me and was leaving me speechless. He started fucking me harder and faster. I held on tight to him feeling a mind-blowing orgasm getting ready to rip through my body. I looked down to see his wet dick sliding in and out of me. It had to be at least three inches I still couldn't take inside me.

"Fffffuuuccckkk! You feel good! Who got damn pussy, Belle?" He asked again.

"I'm yours! Oh God! Yes! It's all yyyyooouurrsss!" I screamed as we exploded together.

He pulled my hair from my face and smothered my mouth with his, sucking my tongue into his mouth. I was so caught up in the passionate kiss he was giving me I didn't realize he was growing inside me again. I ended up snuggled in his arms in the bed. I understood how Miriam felt. Everything felt so perfect here. I didn't want to think about the storm we all had to face back home. I kissed him softly on the lips before climbing out of bed. He was knocked out sleeping with a deep snore. I went into the bathroom to call and check on Granny and Hannah. When I called yesterday, Hannah talked my ear off about all the fun she had with her new Grandma. While I was on the phone with Granny, Rhino banged on the door.

"What the fuck you got the door locked for?" He asked.

"Granny, I'll call you tomorrow," I said before hanging up the phone. I rushed to open the door. He stared at me waiting for an answer.

"I was talking to my Granny. I didn't want to wake you," I said before tiptoeing and kissing his lips. I was becoming a professional liar.

"Don't let me find out you on some bullshit, Nerd Girl," he said tapping me on the ass.

I giggled. "I'm not."

"Now, come sit on my face before we get ready for dinner," he said walking back to the bed. His appetite for me was unquenchable and I loved it.

Shaka

It wasn't that I was scared to tell Omega about me and Jetta. I just didn't want to lose his respect. He trusted me to protect her. I didn't know how he would feel about me being in a relationship with her. We all sat around the den having a drink waiting for dinner to be served at his parent's house. I could see the nervousness in Jetta's face. Even though she was ready to tell him, she was nervous about his reaction. I admired her beauty as she sat talking to her great Grandmother. I gave her a wink when she caught me staring at her. She smiled and blushed.

"Let me have a word with you and the fellows," Omega said walking up to me. I gave Titan and Rhino a head nod to follow us. We walked to the huge study where Omega sat behind the tall executive desk.

"I don't know why my old man got this big ass desk. He never comes in here," he said as we all took a seat. Me and Rhino sat in the two chairs in front of the desk. Titan pulled up a chair from the small office table and took a seat.

"I need to know your plans far as the business goes. I'm out. It's all yours. There's no need to inform me of anything. I'm only asking because I can get you a great connect if you plan on staying in."

We looked at each other. "Is there a time limit we have to stay in?"

"He has to make ten million from supplying you," he informed us. I looked at Rhino and Titan for their opinion. I wasn't worried about us making the money. I just didn't want to make a decision without their input. They both nodded their heads letting me know they were in.

"Who's the connect?" I asked.

"He's here in Jamaica. His name is Chiraq. If you are down, I'll set the meeting up for tomorrow," Omega said looking at us.

"We in," I said.

He cleared his throat. "I want you young men to know, I'm proud of you. You came to me young and hungry. You were never careless or untrustworthy. Make what you need to secure your future and get out. Don't let greed take over you. You all have great futures ahead of you. Rhino, open that box you refuse to let anyone enter. Titan, keep investing in your businesses . Be careful with that heart of yours." They both nodded their heads.

He stared at me and chuckled. "I've let you suffer long enough. I'm sick, not blind. I saw what was unfolding between you and my daughter the day you came to my house. Shit, I was the one working behind the scenes to make it happen." He laughed.

"I know you will love and protect her. She loves you. I know you aren't an emotional nigga, but I know you feel the same about her. I can leave this earth knowing she'll be loved by a good man. Whatever you do, stay tough on her. Don't let that love you have for her weaken you. She needs you to stay in her ass." I breathed a huge sigh of relief. I never thought he had an idea about us. I should've known better though. Didn't shit get pass Omega.

"Is there something you aren't telling us?" I asked.

"Always observant," he said smiling at me. "I'm not going back. I want to spend my last days here."

I didn't like what he was saying. Jetta is going to flip out when she finds out he wasn't coming home. "What about Jetta? She still doesn't know you've stopped taking treatments."

"I will sit down and talk with her before you leave," he assured me. I know this wasn't going to go well. She was so happy about seeing how strong her father was. She thought he was beating the cancer.

"How's your health now?" Titan asked.

“Fading,” he stated bluntly.

“Damn,” Rhino said dropping and shaking his head. I didn’t like this emotional feeling I was having. I’ve only cried once in my life. That was when I found Homeless George dead.

“Any questions?” Omega asked.

He had prepared his self for his demise. I’ve had many talks with him walking around his backyard . I knew there was no changing his mind. It was hard, but I finally made peace with his decision. He had already given me all the information I needed to secure Jetta’s future. We all remained quiet . I put my hand on Rhino’s shoulder when I saw him wiping a tear. I knew how hard this was for them. They had hope he would change his mind about the treatments. I knew otherwise.

“Come on, no need to be sad. I’ve lived a good life. Now, all I want to do is celebrate it,” he said standing up.

We followed him out the study. I squinted my eyes to be sure I was seeing who was standing in the foyer with Jetta. She looked nervous and scared as she argued with him. His eyes met mine. I turned my eyes to her. She stared at me with water in her eyes.

"Mr. Murphy, it's an honor to finally meet you," he said walking toward us with his hand extended to shake Omega's hand.

"Who is this?" Omega said looking at Jetta. She dropped her head.

"Jedi is a little scared about us meeting. I'm her fiancé," he said smiling at Omega.

My eyes were glued to Jetta waiting for her to deny what he was saying. She kept her head down. Omega walked over to her and lifted her chin. "Is this true, Boopsy?" She sobbed softly and nodded her head.

I saw nothing but red. I let her play me while she was engaged to another nigga. I fell hard like a damn fool. I wanted to break every bone in the nigga's body as he stood there with a smirk on his face. I had to remind myself I was a guest in Omega's parents' home.

"Thanks for keeping her warm for me," he leaned over and whispered in my ear.

Whatever restraint I was holding on to went out the window. I started raining blows on him as blood spilled over his face. No one was stopping me, and I wasn't thinking of stopping. I could feel myself killing him. I heard all the women screaming for them to stop me.

"Come on fam, that's enough," Titan said as they pulled me off him. He lay with his face covered in his own blood. I kicked him hard in the rib cage as they pulled me off him.

Jetta ran up to me, "I'm so sorry. I can explain."

Before I knew it, my hands were around her neck squeezing the life out of her. "I love you like a son, but this is my baby girl," Omega said standing behind me.

"The only thing saving your life is your father," I said before releasing her. She fell to the floor trying to catch her breath. I left the house knowing if I didn't I could hurt her.

Titan

We didn't know where Shaka went after leaving the house. He took the limo, so Omega gave me the keys to one of his parents' cars to drive back to the hotel. As far as we were concerned, this vacation was over. I can't believe Jetta did some shit like this. I knew she was childish, but I never thought she would play these kinds of games. She got Shaka's heart fucked up right now. He didn't let people in easily. He took a chance on her and got burnt. It made me realize the shit me and Belle was doing needed to come to an end. She has until morning to tell Rhino or I'm telling him. I was going to tell Miriam tonight, but she wanted to stay at the house with Jetta since she was so upset. I didn't understand why she was so upset. She brought all this on herself. Me, Rhino and Belle rode back to the house in silence. Belle wanted to stay, but Rhino wasn't hearing it.

"He still not damn answering," Rhino said as we sat in the lobby at the hotel. Belle had went upstairs to their room.

"Let him cool off. He'll be straight," I advised him.

Rhino shook his head. "Bitches ain't shit. Fuck that love shit. Ain't no female bout to have me out here looking like a fool."

A sickening feeling came over me. I knew Rhino would never forgive us for keeping the secret from him. “Come on, man. You know Belle ain’t like that.”

“I don’t know, fam. She be on some sneaky shit sometimes,” he said glancing at me. I had to tell him. Belle would just have to live with it. Just as I was getting ready to spill my guts, Shaka called Rhino’s phone.

“Damn, where you at?” Rhino asked answering the phone. He put Shaka on speaker.

“I’m straight. I would’ve killed her and that nigga if I stayed there. Omega gave me the code to get in his house. I’m gone chill here for the night. He’s staying at his parent’s. The meeting in the morning at ten o’clock. I’m heading back home after that,” Shaka told us.

“Shit, we all heading back home. This damn vacation is over,” I said.

“Aight, I’ll holla at you in the morning about the spot,” he said ending the call.

“Damn, I never heard that nigga sound so depressed,” Rhino said shaking his head. It was no doubt she broke his heart. I hope she realized what she lost with her lies.

“I’m hungry as shit. We didn’t even get to eat,” Rhino said shaking his head. I didn’t realize I was hungry until he mentioned it. He called Belle to see if she wanted something to eat. She declined the offer. I'm sure she was sick to the stomach, just like me.

"Aight, I'm going to find a spot to get something to eat," he said standing up.

"Here go the keys," I said.

"Nah, it was some spots not too far from here. I need the walk to clear my head," he said before walking off.

I took the elevator up to my room. I decided to stop and talk to Belle while I had the chance. She opened the door with red eyes. She felt the same thing I was feeling. I pulled her into my arms to let her release her sorrow. I walked with her in my arms to the chair and held her until she stopped crying.

"If there's any chance of him accepting this, we gotta tell him. We can't let him, or Miriam find out in a fucked up way," I told her.

She stood up and started pacing the floor. "Did you see how angry Shaka was? Rhino's temper is ten times worse. I don't think I can do it. I'm going to just leave town. I can't do this." She was panicking.

"Belle, you ain't leaving town with my damn daughter. You've kept her from me for too damn long. You either tell him we got a child together tonight or I will in the morning. It's your choice."

"What the fuck you just say?" Rhino stood in the doorway staring at us. Belle stood there unable to move.

"Man, just chill out and hear this shit out," I said walking toward him.

The rage in his eyes told me what was going to happen. He swung and his fist connected to my left jaw. I stumbled but remained standing. I didn't want to fight him, but I didn't have a choice. The blows he was giving me were full of anger. Belle was screaming for us to stop as we tore the room apart. We threw jab for jab. Blood was pouring from both our faces. We knocked over furniture as we wrestled with each other. We didn't stop until security was pulling us apart.

"Leave now or we will call the police," the security guard said holding my arms behind my back.

It was taking two to control Rhino. He was trying to get loose to continue fighting me. I didn't want to fight him anymore. I know his anger was coming from a place of hurt. Belle stood in the corner crying her eyes out.

"Oh my God! What is going on?" Miriam said walking into the room looking around at the destruction we caused. I closed my eyes hating that she walked in to find out this way.

"Ask yo bitch ass side nigga," Rhino said jerking his arms to get out the guard's grip. "Manumit me!"

I knew he was trying to control his anger when I heard the unusual word. He walked over to Belle as she stood in the corner. Her eyes were filled with fear. I knew he would never hit her. That was his reason for using the words to calm his self.

He stared at her, "You parade your oaf girl personality like you so damn seraphic. You ain't nothing but a sneaky ass hoe." Belle slid down to her knees and cried like a baby.

"Stop it!" Miriam screamed pushing him in the back. "Get away from her."

Rhino chuckled. "Your side nigga and Belle been fucking. They have a child together." Miriam's mouth dropped and she stared at me as Rhino walked out the room. She walked over and stood in front of me.

"Is it true?" She asked staring into my eyes.

I didn't have to answer her. She had learned to read my eyes without me speaking a word. She reared her hand back and slapped me as hard as she could before storming out the room. What was supposed to be a vacation to build relationships that started years ago, only destroyed them.

Atlanta

Miriam

After Jetta cried herself to sleep , I wanted to be with Titan. I didn't want to experience what she was going through right now. She was so upset we didn't get a chance to discuss the events that unfolded or who the guy was. I had made up my mind I wasn't marrying Lyle. I had planned to tell him the wedding was off as soon as I returned home. Unfortunately, that wasn't going to happen after what I found out. I booked the first flight back home. I can't believe Titan and Belle would do something so grimy. I was prepared to come home and walk away from everything I invested my life in, for him. He was going to have me call off my engagement, so he could fuck me and Belle behind my back. After finding out the type of person she truly is, I want nothing to do with her. She's no better than him. Now I'm thankful everything was revealed before I made such a huge mistake. All I wanted to do was climb in my bed and forget everything that happened over the last couple days. I took an uber to my job where my car was parked in the garage. I hopped in my car and drove home.

I exhaled heavily when I arrived at my house. I wanted to be alone, but Lyle's car was in my driveway . I grabbed the suitcase that had the clothes I packed for the imaginary trip to Vegas. I left the other suitcase in the trunk. When I entered the house, I heard the television playing loudly . I went straight to the bedroom. I wanted a hot shower and my bed. I removed my clothes and stepped in the shower. The events of Titan and Belle's secret kept replaying in my head. I couldn't understand how he could do this to me. The way he made love to me had me feeling like I was the only woman he wanted. Tears started to fall as I thought about what a big fool I was. I was startled when the shower door open. Lyle was standing there naked. I was in no mood to have sex with him or anyone else. What shocked me was the blunt he was holding in his hand. As far as I knew, Lyle didn't smoke or drink.

"Welcome home," he said before taking a hit of the blunt.

"When did you start smoking?" I asked.

He shrugged his shoulders, "About a week ago." I actually didn't mind him smoking. Maybe that would help him relax and be more fun.

I decided to put more effort into saving our relationship, "Pass it to me. I haven't smoked since my sophomore year in college."

"Nah, you wanna know why I started smoking," he said throwing the blunt in the toilet. I waited for his reply.

"When I found out my hoe ass fiancé was fucking some low life drug dealer!"

Before I could even respond to his comment the back of his hand went across my face. Blood spilled out of my mouth as I fell against the shower wall. He stepped in the shower and slapped me across the face again. I fell to the shower floor. When he jerked me up by my arm, I started swinging and clawing him. He was too strong for me. He turned me around and pinned my hands behind my back.

"You want to act like a hoe. I'll show you how I treat hoes," he whispered in my ear as he rammed his dick inside me. All I could do was cry until he was done.

Once he was done, he left me in the shower on the floor crying. I don't know what has become of my life. I had to get away from him. There was no way I could spend the rest of my life with a man that put his hands on me. I don't give a damn what I did. After pulling myself together, I cleaned up. I slipped on some yoga pants, tee shirt and tennis shoes. I emptied my clothes out of the suitcase and packed some clothes and shoes to take with me. I didn't know where I was going, but I knew I wasn't staying here knowing he had a key.

I walked into the den with my suitcase, "I want you to get everything you have here and be out before I return. This pathetic relationship is over."

He chuckled and stood up to face me, "If I was you, I would put the suitcase down."

"I will not marry you. I don't give a damn how mad my parents are going to be. I'm sure they will understand when they see the bruises on my face."

"Bitch, you will marry me as planned. I have enough information to destroy your father's fake ass ministry," he said throwing a manila envelope at me.

I quickly opened the envelope. My heart dropped. There were disgusting pictures of my father with different women. They were in all kinds of BDSM positions. There was no way this could be my father. He was a good man, a man of Christ. They had to be photoshopped.

"You lying bastard!" I said throwing the pictures at him.

He laughed, "They are real, Honey. You say one word about what happened here, I will expose him. Matter of fact, we aren't waiting to get married in the winter. I say we should get married in a couple of months. That will give you enough time to plan a nice wedding. Oh, and make sure you invite your fuck buddy to the wedding." I could hear him laughing hysterically as I stormed out of the house. I was going straight to my parents' house.

*****

I had a key, so I let myself in. I went straight to my father's study where he spends most of his time. I entered without knocking. He slammed his laptop closed and stared at me with a guilty expression on his face. His eyes told me the pictures were no lie.

"Looking at porn, Father?" I asked angrily.

"Excuse me," he said giving me a puzzled stare.

"Open your computer, Father," I said walking over to his desk. I was furious and didn't care about disrespecting him. I started opening his laptop, but he slammed it closed.

"What is wrong with you? What happened to your face?" He asked.

I started to cry, "Lyle did it!"

He exhaled and shook his head, “I guess his anger got the best of him. You should’ve considered the consequences of your actions.”

I was dumbfounded by his response, “What?”

“He came by today. He told me about you having an affair with one of those gang bangers. I didn’t raise you that way. You are above those kinds of people,” he said.

I laughed uncontrollably, “Are you fucking serious? You are fucking all kinds of women with bondage and whips! You have no room to judge anyone!”

“Watch how you speak to me! I am your father. You will respect me in my house,” he demanded.

“You are defending a man for beating me. How do you expect me to act?” I asked.

“Like the respectful, young lady we raised you to be. Not some hood rat opening her legs to a thug,” he said.

“Well, explain the women you have been fucking,” I stated.

“What is going on here?” Mother asked walking into the den. She looked at me. “Oh my God! What happened to your face?”

“Tell her Father,” I demanded.

She looked at him for an answer, but he didn’t reply. At this point, I didn’t know what to do. If I reveal my father's secret, I would break my mother's heart. If I didn't marry Lyle, her heart would be broken and his career destroyed. If I married Lyle, I would live a miserable life, while they carry on as if nothing happened.

"What is going on?" Mother asked again glancing from me to Father.

"Father is just upset, because I got too drunk while on my trip. I fell and as you can see I fell on my face." There was no doubt, I was a professional liar.

"Jesus child, what is happening to you?" Mother asked shaking her head. "Come upstairs and let me clean you up."

"No, that's okay. I'm going home," I said storming out the den. I didn't want to be near any of them. I left their house and checked in a hotel.

Jamaica

Jetta

All I could do was lay in the bed. I had been in the bed for two days. The only time I got up was to shower and use the bathroom. I didn't want to see or talk to anyone. It feels like my heart had been ripped from my chest. There was so much hate in Shaka's eyes. He didn't want anything to do with me. I can't believe Cassius showed up to my grandparents' house. I had given him the money he asked for to stay away. I pleaded with him to leave but he refused. Everyone else left the house except my grandparents and Cassius. His face was covered in blood, and I didn't give a damn. I wish Shaka had beaten him to death. Granny tended to his wounds. I had to sit and agree to the lies he was telling Daddy.

"Explain to me what is going on here," Daddy glanced at us as we sat in the study. I couldn't stop crying. All I could see was the hate Shaka had in his eyes.

"Jetta, stop the tears. They're not going to work this time," Daddy said sternly. I knew then he was heated. He only called me Jetta when he was furious with me.

"Sir, I can explain," Cassius said in his charming British accent. As swollen as his bottom lip was, I was

surprised he could talk. He wiped the blood that leaked from his nose. Daddy sat quietly waiting for an explanation. I didn't know what to say. If I told the truth, it would cost me my freedom and reputation.

"Jedi and I fell in love in Europe. She accepted my proposal of marriage. I made a huge mistake by being unfaithful. I will never forgive myself for breaking her heart. She finally decided to give me another chance. After finding out about your illness, she rushed home. She didn't want to spring the news on you while you were battling with your treatments. Being a man, I became jealous of the friendship she seems to be developing with Shaka. I came here against her will to let it be known she belongs to me." Damn liar. Everything he said was a complete lie, but very convincing. Cassius had a way of making people believe the unbelievable. He reached over and held my hand making my skin crawl.

"Is this true, Jetta?" Daddy asked staring at me. I wanted to tell Daddy everything he said was lie. The words were stuck in my throat, but wouldn't come out. I reluctantly nodded my head in agreement.

Daddy took a deep breath and exhaled heavily, "What do you do young man?"

Cassius smiled, "I'm a trust fund baby. I used my inheritance to invest."

Cassius' parents were hardworking people that he wanted nothing to do with. He felt his parents were low class because they weren't rich. I realized I thought the same way for the longest. I felt if people didn't have as much money as my father and mother, they were beneath me. Having to fend for myself for a while humbled me.

"When is the wedding?" Daddy asked.

"I'm waiting for my Jedi to set a date. If it was up to me, we will marry as soon as the sun sets ," Cassius said smiling at me.

"Well, she is my only daughter and I want her to have a beautiful wedding," Daddy said. Cassius nodded his head in agreement.

"I don't know what you said to Shaka to piss him off. I would advise you to stay out his way. He's a rational man until he's pushed," Daddy warned him.

"It's obvious he's smitten with my Jedi. I can't blame him. She is beautiful," Cassius said.

"Well, I will leave you two to talk. I'm exhausted. Jetta, I will speak with you in the morning.

As soon as Daddy left the room, I slapped Cassius as hard as I could. "I can't believe you. You said you wouldn't come. I gave you the money to keep you away."

He rubbed his jaw. "I changed my mind. I've been thinking. Maybe a million isn't enough. Your old man is going to die. You are the only child. I'm sure he's leaving you with millions. I think you would make a great wife."

"My father is not dying. Even if he was, I'm not fucking marrying you. You are damn crazy," I stated angrily.

He chuckled, "We will see. I advise you to start planning our wedding. We will be married in a month, or you will be going to prison. I might save you from prison and give the information to his family. You know how ruthless those people are." He leaned forward and kissed me on the cheek. I wiped my cheek hard to get the stench of his breath off me. Now, it was prison or my life.

I pulled the covers over my head and balled up in a fetal position when someone knocked on the door. The only person I wanted to see hated me. The cover was snatched from my body. I opened my eyes to see Daddy staring down at me with a scowl on his face.

"Come downstairs . We're having lunch on the patio. You have fifteen minutes," he demanded before walking out the room. I've seen Daddy mad before but never like this. I hurried out of bed. I washed my face and brushed my teeth. I was surprised to see only Daddy sitting at the patio table.

"Where is Papa and Nana?" I asked looking at the breakfast feast spread on the table. I didn't have an appetite to eat anything.

"Out, I needed some time alone with you," he said. I sat at the table with my head down.

"What are you doing, Jetta?" He asked.

I started to cry. "Stop with the manipulative bullshit!" He roared banging his fist on the table. I was so startled by his anger, I jumped and nearly fell out the chair.

"Who is this man?" He asked angrily.

"Daddy, I just need to talk to Shaka. Can you please get him to come over? I know he will never come if I asked."

"No, I will not. This is one mess you will clean up yourself. I don't know what the hell going on, but you better fix it. My time on this earth is limited. I will not spend my last days thinking you are going to marry that damn clown."

"Daddy, don't say that. You are getting stronger every day," I said sadly.

He stared at me with eyes full of regret, “Boopsie, I’m not getting better. I’m dying. I stopped taking treatments. I wanted to spend my last days enjoying life. The cancer is progressing rapidly. Soon, I will be bedridden . Until then, I want to live a joyous life.”

I stared at him in disbelief. I can’t believe he was giving up on life. He has to fight to stay here with me. “Daddy, no. You can’t do this. I need you. I’m sorry. I promise I’ll fix this.”

“This is not a punishment for you. It’s a decision I wrestled with for months. You are beautiful and smart. It’s time you start pushing yourself. I’m not going to be here to spoil you and make everything okay too much longer. It’s time to start taking responsibility for your actions. This bogus ass engagement will be a start. Shaka has all the information to secure your future. Use it wisely, Boopsie. I love you more than I love my own life. I know there’s greatness inside you. Make it happen. You got this.”

I didn’t hear nothing he said after his statement about Shaka. I can’t believe he knew Daddy was dying and didn’t tell me. He was letting Daddy give up on life. I was outraged. I knew Shaka was at my father’s vacation home. He was going to see me rather he liked it or not. My reasons for wanting to see him are different from when I awakened this morning.

Shaka

"What the fuck you mean y'all back in ATL?" I asked Rhino over the phone.

I called him and Titan nonstop over the phone before our meeting with Chiraq. Neither of them answered. I didn't have time to look for them, so I attended the meeting alone. Everything went smooth, and we were set to secure our future with the money we'll be making.

"Man, shit got crazy when we got back to the resort. I'll have to fill you in when you get back. You should know me and Titan fought last night," he said.

"What the fuck happened?" I asked.

We joked and cussed each other out on a daily basis. We would get mad with each other about some dumb shit, but we never fought. We were brothers. We never allowed things to get to the point where we wanted to fight each other.

"Him and Belle grimy as fuck. I wanted to kill both their asses last night," Rhino said.

"Belle?" I asked.

I know how jealous and possessive Rhino was over Belle. I still didn't see him thinking Titan would go there with Belle. Titan is so hung up on Miriam, he's playing the side nigga. Rhino had to be on some paranoid shit.

"Fam, they been fucking. They've been fucking so much, they got a kid together," Rhino said angrily.

"What?" I asked unable to believe what Rhino was saying.

"I heard the shit with my own ears. I walked in on them having a conversation about their child. Man, you know I fucking lost it. That nigga been in my face every day lying to me. She's a hoe just like the rest of the bitches I fuck with," Rhino explained.

He was angry and hurt. I could hear it in his voice. I felt his emotions right now. As much as I wanted to defend Titan and Belle, I couldn't. I wouldn't voice my opinions to Rhino until I talked to Titan. I know there has to be more to this story. Titan is a loyal nigga with a big heart. I don't think he has it in him to be grimy. As far as Belle goes, after what I experienced last night it ain't shit I won't put passed a female.

"Yo fam, just stay calm until I get home. I'll be there tonight," I said.

I had just left the resort picking up my luggage. I was heading back to Omega's vacation home to wait to discuss the meeting with him. I didn't want to take the chance of running into Jetta at his parents' home. She had my heart in her hands. I was willing to give her the love I've never given to anyone in this world. She helped me discover and hate love at the same time. My only focus now was securing my retirement. Only thing that will ever receive love from me again is money.

"Yo, I'm good fam. Just make sure you keep that nigga out my face," Rhino stated.

"Man, how I'm gone do that when we got money to make?" I asked. I don't give a damn what they going through, it's not going to fuck up our money.

"Los can work with him. I'll take Los' spot," Rhino suggested.

"We'll talk when I return," I told him.

I wasn't splitting them up. Los was making his moves alone the way he preferred. Titan and Rhino made crazy money working as a team. I wasn't changing shit. They were going to work through their problems and make this money.

"Yea," Rhino said ending the call. I hoped they stayed away from each other until I returned.

Omega's father's car was parked in the driveway when I returned. I know he was wanting to discuss last night, but I didn't. It was over for me. It was no point in dwelling over it. I will honor his request and make sure she's financially stable without him. That's all I can offer her. The only thing we needed to discuss was my meeting with Chiraq. The moment I walked through the door, I was knocked across the head. I stumbled forward holding the side of my head. I looked at my hand to see blood. A porcelain vase was shattered on the floor. Jetta was standing there with swollen, bloodshot eyes. Her hair was a mess, and she wore a pair of sweats and a tank top. She charged toward me.

"I hate you! How could you do this to him! He loves you like a son!" She screamed as she kept swinging at me.

"What the hell you talking about?" I asked grabbing hold of her.

She squirmed trying to get out my arms, but I wasn't releasing her until she calmed down. She screamed and cussed for me to let her go until she became exhausted. I finally released her when she started crying uncontrollably . Tears ran down her face, and snot ran from her nose.

"You are letting him die. Why didn't you tell me he wasn't taking treatments?" She asked as she cried and breathed heavily.

“I’m not letting him do shit. This is his choice. He didn’t want you to know,” I explained.

As much as I didn’t want to feel anything for her, I couldn’t stop the ache in my heart. She was hurting, and I didn’t want to ever see her this way. I reminded myself what she did to me to try and stop feeling sorry for her.

“You could’ve made him change his mind. He always listens to you,” she said with a trembling voice.

She took a few steps back and laughed, “I know what this is all about. You want his money and power. I will not let that happen.”

I chuckled, “If you weren’t so wrapped up in your damn self, you would’ve known he wasn’t taking treatments. How many times have you seen him leave the house for chemo? You so fucking selfish, you never took the time to notice. You came back for him, but not once did you ask to attend a doctor’s appointment with him. Not once did you ask him about his chemo treatments.”

“I love my father! How dare you?” She screamed. I never doubted her love for him. As long as; shit was good with her, she never considered how anyone else was feeling.

I shrugged my shoulders, “Never said you didn’t. Only stated facts.”

“You will not get away with this. I will not let you walk away with everything he built,” she said before walking away. I let her go. She was an emotional wreck. I couldn’t allow myself to get sucked back into her world. I went to the bathroom to see how bad the gash was in my head. After tending to my wound, I started picking up pieces of the broken vase.

“What happened in here?” Omega asked walking in the house. He looked around at the shattered pieces of vase on the floor.

“Your daughter,” I said without looking at him.

“Leave it. Come, sit down,” Omega said walking into the den. I sat on the sofa while he sat in the adjacent chair.

“Give her time to calm down. We knew this would be hard for her to accept,” he advised me.

“She blames me. Thinks I’m trying to steal your money,” I told him.

He chuckled, “Why didn’t you tell her you refused to accept one brown penny from me?”

Omega’s worth was over thirty million dollars. He wanted to give me five million in his will. I refused. Jetta was left with twenty million, and the rest will be disbursed to his parents, Ms. Clara and charities.

"She would've never believed me. It doesn't matter. She'll get what's rightfully hers when its time," I said.

"I'll talk with her," he said.

"Nah, let her use me to vent her anger," I said. She was angry, hurt and scared. Her using me as her target would only help me get over her. She would be helping me without knowing it.

He shook his head, "I don't know what's up with that clown, but it ain't real. I know you aren't going to let that happen. You promised to love and protect her. I know you are a man of your word." Jetta's personal life was no concern of mine anymore. My only job was to make sure she gets the money Omega left her.

Titan

"I don't know what you did to her, but if she don't bring my Granddaughter back to see me I'm whooping yo ass," Ma threatened me as I lounged on the couch. Belle caught the first available flight back to Atlanta. She didn't want to be near me or anyone else. Ma said she picked Hannah up and rushed out the house.

"Ma, I ain't do shit to her," I said sitting up on the sofa.

"Well, what happened? That girl's eyes were swollen she had cried so much. She looked scared out of her mind," she stated . I took a deep breath before explaining to her what happened.

She flopped down in the chair and shook her head, "So, now he thinks y'all been fucking?" I nodded my head.

"Well, just explain to him what happened," she said.

"I will when he calm his ass down. You know how crazy that nigga gets when he's mad. I ain't scared of him, but I'm not gone keep fighting him over shit that ain't true. He like a brother to me."

"I know. I've ran him and Shaka away plenty of times. He would look at me with them crazy ass eyes.

That's why I kept my butcher knife by the bed," she said. I laughed. "Give him a couple of days. Then step to him." I nodded my head in agreement.

"Now, what you gone do about my grandchild living conditions?" She asked.

"Ma, I ain't trying to take her child from her. We are going to co-parent," I said.

"Boy, I know that. I'm talking about them living in that little ass two bedroom apartment," she said.

"She won't let me do nothing like that for her. The most she would accept was daycare and medical expenses," I informed her.

"And she need a new car. That damn car on its last leg," she added.

"Fine Ma, I'll make some shit happen," I said wanting her to shut up. "How's Unc doing?"

"He's good. I checked on him yesterday. Now, tell me who you took to Jamaica," she said smiling. I didn't want to think about Miriam. I knew she was done fucking with me after finding out about me and Belle's child.

"You don't know her. It's nothing like that anyway," I said getting off the couch. She followed me in the kitchen.

“You are my son. I know what touches your heart without you speaking. The only time I’ve seen that look on your face is when I wouldn’t let you eat any meatloaf I cooked,” she said taking a seat at the island . I laughed, but she was right. Meatloaf was my weakness just like Miriam.

“Whoever she is, it’s over. She found out about Hannah plus she’s engaged,” I said pouring myself a double shot of Hennessy .

“Boy, I know damn well you ain’t in love and playing a side nigga. I raised you better than that,” she said angrily.

I chuckled and shook my head, “I’m good, Ma.”

She started pulling out pots and pans. She rambled about her and Hannah’s time together while I sat scrolling through my phone. I didn’t stop her when I saw she was preparing meatloaf. I had missed several calls from Shaka. I didn’t feel like explaining the situation again. I decided to call him later.

“So, let me see a picture of her,” she said after cutting up an onion and bell pepper.

I didn’t feel like arguing with her, so I slid my phone to her. “Oh wow, she’s pretty. Don’t get caught up in bullshit. If you aren’t good enough to be the only man in her life, cut her loose. You should get together with Belle. Damn her and crazy ass Rhino."

"Ma, you don't even like Belle," I said laughing.

"Sho don't. Lil four eyed heifer kept my grandbaby from me all these years. At least if y'all together, I'll get to see her whenever I want," she said as she started putting the meatloaf in the oven. All I could do was laugh.

"Well, at least you smiling now," she said looking at me. I was seeing a totally different side to her. It felt good having her to talk to about things that bothered me.

"How's work going?" I asked wanting to change the subject.

"You know it's some hoeing going on in the A. I see so much fucking going on between friends and family. It's like they all choose to use the same hotel, except on different days," she said shaking her head. "I mind my business though."

"Shit, I saw Omega's fine ass come through going to the penthouse . I started to go whoop the bitch's ass he had up there and replace her. That nigga fine with cancer," she said shaking her head.

"Come on Ma, cut that shit out," I said getting up from the stool. The last image I wanted in my head was my mama having sex.

"Boy, I'm still young enough to get it in," she said as she started twerking.

I shook my head and walked out the kitchen. I went into my study to call Shaka, but he didn't answer. I'm sure his head was in a fucked up place, just like mine. I kept calling Miriam only to be sent to voicemail. I knew things were over between me and Miriam, but I felt like I owed her an explanation . I sent her a text and waited to see if she would reply. I fell asleep waiting on a response.

"Titan, I gotta go. I'm going home to get a couple hours of sleep before work. All the food is done," Ma said waking me up.

I thanked her as she left out the den. I checked my phone as I made my way to the kitchen to eat my favorite meal. I knew I would have to work extra hard in the gym tomorrow. I hadn't had any of Ma's meatloaf in a while. I saw the text from Miriam and eagerly opened it.

Please do NOT contact me anymore. I will be getting married to the man that truly loves me in a couple of months. What we had was sex, nothing more. I love my fiancé too much to jeopardize losing him

I didn't believe a word of what she texted me, but I wasn't going to press her. My focus was on building a relationship with my daughter and making my money. If she wanted to spend the rest of her life with a man she doesn't love, that's on her. All I can do is offer the love I had to give.

Rhino

"Shut the fuck up," I barked at Mena as I fucked her in the bathroom at a local pool hall.

She was screaming like I was trying to kill her. Being inside her pussy wasn't fazing me. The only thing running through my mind was the conversation between Belle and Titan. I rammed inside her as hard and deep as I could. She tried running from me, but I held on to her hips. She started flirting with me the moment I entered the pool hall. After too many drinks, here I was fucking the life out of one of my best friend's exes. I know he didn't give a damn about her. I thought he was strung out over Miriam. Belle and him both played me and Miriam for a fool. The more I thought about them the madder I got.

"Fuck Rhino, you too damn big! Take it easy," Mena pleaded as I ignored her.

"Hold the fuck still," I demanded gripping a handful of her hair.

"Ooooohhhh sssshhhit!" She screamed as she came hard on my dick. No matter how hard I fucked her, I couldn't come. I finally gave up and pulled out. I peeled the condom off, and threw it in the trash.

"Damn, I've been fucking the wrong nigga all these years. That dick is a beast," she said pulling up her panties and tights.

"Pussy like duck soup," I said while taking a piss with the stall door open.

"What does that mean?" She asked. I glanced over my shoulder at her. She was smiling.

"A sad, easy fuck," I said staring at her.

"Fuck you nigga. You ain't shit anyway. You so damn disrespectful and crazy," she said angrily. I chuckled as I washed my hands. I walked out the bathroom while she followed and cussed me out. Nothing she was saying was resonating as I made my way out the pool hall.

"I'm telling Titan you fucked me," she yelled as I opened my car door.

I laughed, "Please do."

I hopped in and left her standing in the parking lot. I was too wasted to drive to my house. I decided to crash at their house, since it wasn't too far to drive.

*****

When I arrived, I was able to slip in without waking them since I still had a key. I went straight to my old room.

I hated closing my eyes. All I could see was her face. She always looked so innocent. There was so much I wanted to share with her. She saw something in me that no one else did. Everyone said that my eyes showed craziness. She saw the passion I held inside. I tossed and turned until I fell asleep. When I woke up the next morning, I checked my phone. I had missed calls from Shaka. I was surprised to see a missed call from Belle. I texted Shaka to let him know I'll be at Omega's house in a couple of hours. When I opened my room door, I smelled breakfast. I regretted coming here the moment I stepped into the kitchen.

"This is not a motel," Pops said as he sat to the kitchen table drinking coffee.

"I'm headed out," I said kissing Ma on the cheek.

"Sit down and eat some breakfast before you leave," she said. I loved my mother, but I hated how she always sided with him.

"Nah, I'm good," I said.

"You are a huge disappointment. You could've been playing in the NBA. You chose to waste your time following behind a pussy ass dream and selling drugs," Pops said shaking his head.

"A pussy ass dream?" I asked cocking my head to the side.

"Yea, what six-foot six-inch tall man wants to be an artist?" He asked laughing. "You see where that shit got you when you tried it." I hated to think about those days when I tried sharing my talent with the world. It was the reason I kept it all to myself.

"Wilfred, that is enough," Ma said staring at him.

"No Janice, the boy needs to hear the truth. I'm starting to wonder did I raise one of those down low niggas. Your granddaddy always said you was too damn soft," he said with a smirk.

I knew he wanted to make me angry. He hated I didn't pursue the dream he wanted for me. I had several colleges wanting to give me a full scholarship. Sometimes, I wish I had taken one of them and studied what I loved doing most.

I charged toward him, but Ma jumped in front of me. "Wilfred, stop it. You are only trying to infuriate him."

He chuckled, "I couldn't do that, if it wasn't the truth."

*****

It wasn't his words that angered me. Memories of seeing my older brother laying in a casket is what infuriated me. Without saying another word, I left. Ma was a good mother, but a weak woman. She never voiced her true opinions to Pops. She loved what I did, but not enough to stand by and support me. She would come by the house to admire my work. She was so scared of supporting me she wouldn't take any of the pictures home to hang up. I gave several to Shaka, Titan and Omega. I would tell them I traded them for drugs from some drug addicted artist. I never knew Omega knew of my paintings until he spoke to us in Jamaica. He spoke in words that only I could understand. I'm sure Shaka and Titan thought he was referring only to my anger issues. I went home, showered and headed over to Omega's house. I prayed Titan wasn't there. I couldn't be held accountable for my actions at this time. I knew Jetta had to still be in Jamaica. There was no way her and Shaka was in the same house after what went down. I drove around the circular driveway and parked in front of the house. Ms. Clara opened the door for me.

"He's in the study," she said with her precious smile.

"Damn, what happened to you?" I asked looking at the bandage on his head.

"Fuck that! We need to squash this shit between you and Titan. We got money to make," he stated.

"Nah, ain't no squashing shit. I'll kill the nigga before I work with him," I warned Shaka.

"Ok listen, we got a shipment coming in next week. I need everyone there to make sure this shit goes smooth. We'll discuss how we will team up everyone after we secured the work. I've been calling Titan all morning, he hasn't returned my calls."

I shrugged my shoulders. "I haven't killed him yet."

Shaka shook his head. "I'll stop by on the way to my place. Make sure the team is ready for the drop next week. Get with Los, and fill him in." I nodded my head in agreement.

"Now, you ready to tell me about that bandage on yo head?" I asked. He filled me in on what went down.

"Where her punk ass fiancé?" I asked.

"Don't know and don't care. I've got other shit to focus on. I'm not responsible for the decisions she makes," he said trying to convince himself.

"I take it she's still in Jamaica?" I asked.

"Yea, gives me time to clear my shit out of here. I don't have a reason to be here since Omega's not coming back," he said. I still couldn't stomach the thought of Omega dying.

“Yo, I’m ‘bout to get out of here. You need me I’ll be at the crib,” I said standing up.

“You know you can vent to me about bullshit, right?” He asked with a serious face. We never shared our personal feelings with each other. Then again, we’ve never had our fucking hearts stomped on.

“I’m good, fam,” I said before walking out the den.

It took every ounce of strength inside me not to call her. I sat in my car in my driveway looking at all the pics I had taken of her. I couldn’t pour my heart out to her, so I went inside and poured her on a canvas.

Belle

"Chile, get yo ass up!" Bernadette demanded pulling the covers from me.

I had been locked in my room since I returned from Jamaica. I asked Titan could he keep Hannah for a few days and he rushed over. I didn't have the energy to do anything. I was due to return to work tomorrow, and wasn't sure if I would. I've never felt this lost before. I'm just a body with a ruined heart and mind that won't let me forget the pain I'm in. His eyes were dark and cold. I felt every mean word he said to me. I was nothing to him. It was like the sight of me disgusted him. I only tried calling him once. I had only built up the nerve because I sat in my room alone getting drunk. I tried calling Jetta to see how she was doing, but I was sent straight to voicemail. I guess she hated me as much as Rhino and Miriam.

"What are you doing here? Is Hannah okay?" I asked sitting up in the bed.

"She's fine. Even though, her mother hasn't called to check on her in two days," she replied.

"She's with her father. I know she's in good hands," I snapped back.

"Watch the damn attitude. I will whoop your ass," she said. I rolled my eyes at her, but I didn't doubt her words.

"Granny!" I yelled as I hopped out of bed. I wanted her out of here. I didn't have the energy to deal with her. Granny was sitting in her recliner watching television.

"She's the one that called me. She's tired of your musty ass moping around the house," Bernadette said standing behind me.

"Granny, why would you do that?" I asked staring down at her.

"You gotta pull yourself together. You start school in a month. At the rate you are going, you will fail in the first semester," she said.

I stomped back to my room and started to get dressed. "Fine! I'll go and get my child. I should've just left things like they were."

"You mean keeping a father from his child?" Bernadette said walking back in the room. I didn't reply.

"He loves that little girl, and so do I. I know what happened in Jamaica. You have no one to blame, but yourself."

I was defeated. I didn't have it in me to argue with her. I flopped down on the edge of my bed and dropped my head. I realized what a huge mistake I made not telling Rhino before it all blew up in our faces. I made an even bigger mistake by not telling Titan about Hannah sooner.

"Stop pitying yourself. What's done is done. Now, you have to ask yourself what are you going to do to fix this mess. Do you love the psycho?"

"He's not crazy. He's very smart," I said defending him.

She laughed and sat next to me on the bed. "I don't like you, but you gave me the second greatest gift in this world. I made a lot of mistakes raising Titan. I have a beautiful granddaughter to try it again. So, I'm going to help yo lil' blind ass."

"I'm not blind! I can see!" I stated angrily.

She laughed, "Barely. Now, do you want me to help you?"

"How?" I asked.

"You can't be timid with a man like Rhino. You gotta be forceful. Stand your ground with him. Hiding in this room is not going to bring him back. Trust me, he's not coming back on his own. You gotta make him want to come back. You fucked this up, so you gotta fix it."

"You telling me to chase him?" I asked.

"No, I'm telling you to make him listen. Once you've stated your case, let it be. Never chase a man, child," she said winking at me.

"How's Hannah doing?" I asked glancing at her.

She smiled, "She's spending the day with her daddy and uncle. She's doing great. Well, I have served my purpose. If I have to come back, it won't be pretty," she said standing up.

"Thank you," I said looking up at her.

"Yea, whatever. I don't do the emotional shit," she said waving me off before walking out the room.

I couldn't understand how Titan was her son, they were totally different. I ran a hot bubble bath and soaked in the tub. I thought of ways I could get Rhino to sit and talk to me. I knew it would be hard for him to accept, but I know he would understand. I finally came up with a plan. I just needed someone to help me make it happen. I hurried out the tub and prayed Jetta will answer my calls and texts. I couldn't go to Miriam for help.

*****

After cleaning up the house and cooking for Granny, I decided it was time to go get Hannah. My car wouldn't crank, so I called an uber. It was dusk when I arrived at his house. He opened the door with Hannah on his back.

"Mama!" She screamed with excitement. I laughed at the big smile on her face.

"Hi Mommy's baby girl," I said reaching for her. I gave her a big hug before putting her down.

"Thank you," I said to Titan as he stood there. Hannah ran toward the den. "Stop running in the house, Hannah."

"No problem, come in," he said stepping to the side.

"I just came to pick her up. I gotta go back to work tomorrow, so I need to get her settled in for the night," I said not wanting to stay any longer than necessary.

"I just ordered pizza and she picked out some animated movie on the firestick," he said disappointedly. "Just stay and watch the movie, then you can go." I didn't want to ruin her time with her father, so I decided to stay.

I made myself comfortable in the den while him and Hannah rolled around on the floor playing. He was like a five year old kid with her. I smiled as I watched them enjoy each other's company.

"That must be the pizza," Titan said.

"I'll get it," I said standing up. I regretted my decision to stay the moment I opened the door. Miriam stared me in the face with the same hurt she felt the night she found out about our child together.

"You fuckin' grimy ass bitch," she said staring at me.

If looks could kill, I would be dead. She turned and walked away from the door. All I could do was call Titan's name. It was best he try and stop her from leaving. I knew if I did, we would be rolling around in the grass.

"Yea," he said coming out of the den.

"Hurry, she's getting in the car! That was Miriam!" I yelled. He ran outside, but was too late. She was pulling out of the driveway .

"Fuuucckkk!" He barked swinging in the air.

I know seeing me here only made matters worse for them. He tried to enjoy the movie with Hannah, but I could tell his mind was a million miles away. After the movie was over, he took us home.

"I'm sorry," I said sitting in front of the apartment building.

"It's not your fault, but I know that didn't look good to her," he said shaking his head.

"Listen, I'm getting you a damn car. This shit ain't up for debate," he said. I didn't argue with him. I was tired of dealing with pouring money into my car. I would need a vehicle to get around to carry out my plans of winning Rhino's heart again anyway.

Miriam

I didn't know what to do. It felt like I was losing my sanity. I had returned back to my home only to find Lyle had moved in. He's turned into a complete monster. All he does is drink and smoke. He hardly goes to work. One night I came home he was snorting cocaine on the kitchen table. It's gotten so bad, we fight every night. I fought him back with all the strength I had in me. Sometimes, he would leave me with bruises. Other times, I would leave my mark on him. I couldn't keep living this life. I needed to talk to someone. I was still furious with Titan when I went to his house, but I needed to feel loved. A simple touch from him made me feel all the love I needed. I knew I made a mistake by going there when Belle opened the door. All this time, they played me for a fool. I wanted to snatch her glasses off and beat the hell out of her. I made this bed, now I had to lay in it. Maybe I was the reason Lyle turned into the monster he was now. Titan has been calling my phone nonstop since I showed up at his house. I decided to block his number. It was the end of another work day, and I was dreading going home. I rode around the city until I ended up parked in my parents' driveway. I needed them to understand the predicament I was in. I couldn't go through with marrying

Lyle. Mother was in the kitchen cooking. I hoped she would help me reason with Father.

“Hi Mother,” I said kissing her on the cheek.

“Hi Baby, shouldn’t you be home cooking dinner for your fiancé” She asked as I sat at the kitchen table.

“Mother, I can’t marry him. You don’t know the hell I’ve been going through. He’s not the man everyone thinks he is,” I told her.

“Every relationship has its ups and downs. You have to be willing to work through those times. No relationship is a honeymoon, Miriam.”

“We haven’t even made it to the honeymoon. He hits me, Mother. We fight like two damn men. Yes, I had an affair but that doesn’t give him the right to put his hands on me. He’s drinking and doing drugs,” I explained as I fought back the tears. I wasn’t a crier. I was built to handle my emotions. I wasn’t going to let a weak ass man like Lyle cause me to shed another tear.

“Sometimes, we have to reap what we sow,” she said staring at me. I couldn’t believe she spoke those words to me.

“Are you saying I deserve what he’s doing to me?” I asked with wide eyes.

“All I’m saying is we have to be held accountable for our actions,” she tried explaining. That was when I lost it.

“So, Father should be held accountable for fucking hoes BDSM style?” I asked angrily. Her mouth dropped open. “Yea, he’s fucking all kinds of different women. Lyle is blackmailing me to marry him or he will expose Father.”

She walked over and sat at the kitchen table. “Sit down, Miriam.” I hated the way I was coming at her. Mother was the wife of a minister. She played her role and obeyed his every command. I shouldn’t have taken my frustrations out on her, but I had to vent. I sat across the small kitchen table from her.

“Your father is speaking the word of God. He is a flawed man with a message to God’s people. He repents for his sins every night. He’s battles with his addiction and gives his worries to the Lord. That’s what you have to do,” she said.

All I could do was stare at her for a few seconds. The woman I loved and admired was now a weak and pathetic woman. She knew what he was doing and accepted it. I don’t care what I’ve done wrong with Lyle, I’m not going to allow him to demean me.

“Are you serious, Mother? You know about this?” I asked.

“He goes to counseling. It’s an addiction. I am his wife. I chose for better or worse. I can’t run because he isn’t the perfect man I thought he was,” she explained.

I laughed, “You know what? If you choose to live with him, that’s your choice. But, what am I supposed to do? I’m sacrificing my life to save Father’s ministry.”

“Sometimes, we have to make sacrifices in life. You brought bad energy into your relationship by having an affair. Lyle has absorbed your negativity. You need to cleanse your soul to rectify the relationship. I’m sure Lyle would never do anything to damage your father’s ministry. He just wants the woman he fell in love with to love him back, Miriam.”

I was at a loss of words. She was basically telling me everything was my fault and I should marry Lyle. I stormed out the house as she pleaded with me to stay. I wanted to get as far away from them as possible. I hopped in my car and drove with no destination. Jetta had arrived home yesterday, so I decided maybe I could talk to her about my situation. I only became angrier when I pulled in front of her father’s house. She was coming out the front door with Belle. I can't understand how she could forgive her after what she did. I jumped out my car angrily.

"Really Jetta? You hanging with this grimy ass hoe?" I asked walking toward them. Jetta jumped in front of Belle like her protector.

"Calm down, Mir! You have every right to be mad, but let her explain," she said.

"Fuck that! That bitch has nothing to say to me. You ain't shit either! I've been your best friend for years, and you choosing this bitch," I stated furiously.

"I'm not choosing anyone, Mir," Jetta said walking up to me.

I backed away, "Fuck both of y'all. Shaka and Rhino don't know how lucky they are to be rid of both of you."

"Miriam, please just let me explain. It's not what you think," Belle said with regret in her eyes.

I laughed, "How the fuck can you having a baby with Titan be misunderstood. I trusted your ass. Bitch, you fucked with the wrong one. The difference between me and you is when I'm come for you, you will know."

I rushed back to my car. Jetta stopped me by grabbing my arm. "Mir, we all need to talk. I know you're angry, but don't do anything you'll regret."

"I defended you when everyone talked shit about your spoiled, selfish ass. I should've cut your ass loose a long time ago. Maybe I wouldn't be in the mess I'm in," I said before jerking my arm from her.

I ended up in my driveway. My day only got worse. When I walked in the house, it reeked of weed. I heard noises coming from the bedroom. I ran to my bedroom to see Lyle in the bed naked with two women. One female was sucking his dick while the other one ate her out. I had no emotions. I walked into the bedroom and sat in the chair in the corner of the bedroom.

"Welcome home, baby. Meet Diamond and Princess," he said with a smirk on his face. Both the girls looked at me.

"Don't stop on my behalf, continue. Maybe you can fuck them better than you do me," I said.

Lyle pushed the girl's head down to make her keep sucking him off. The other girl started back eating her friend from behind. I sat unfazed by the disgusting scene in front of me. The only thought running through my mind was the feeling of Titan's hard dick slamming in and out of me. I imagined his wet tongue licking every inch of my body as the girl sucked my fiancé' dick. He grunted as he nutted in her mouth. I nearly vomited when she turned around and kissed her friend with Lyle's semen in her mouth. I didn't give a damn about anyone's feelings from this point on. I walked out the room and locked myself in the spare bedroom. I took a long, hot shower and climbed into bed. The next morning, I waited until Lyle left before packing all my clothes. I checked into a suite until I found a new place to stay.

Shaka

I knew I had fucked up when I rolled over to see Dayzee's naked body laying next to me. I was hanging out with Titan last night and we both got wasted. When Dayzee approached me at the club, all I wanted to do was forget about Jetta. It's been over a week and I still hadn't seen or heard from her. Ms. Clara informed me she was back in the states. I make sure she's not at Omega's house when I go by to check on things. I talk to him everyday to check on him. He says he doing okay, but I could hear in his voice he's getting weaker. I took a shower, before going downstairs to see what there was to eat in the kitchen.

I was cooking some eggs when Dayzee walked in the kitchen wearing one of my tee shirts, "This place is beautiful. I finally got a chance to see where you live." She wrapped her arms around my waist and placed kisses on my back. I was mad as hell at myself for slipping up and bringing her here.

"Yo, don't read too much into last night," I said. I didn't want her to think this was anything more than a fuck.

"I know Zaddy. I know how we roll. I knew that lil stuck up, spoiled bitch couldn't give you what I could," she said walking to the fridge. I didn't like how she was making herself at home in my place. Just the mention of Jetta made my chest hurt and stomach churn.

"Yo, you gotta get up outta here. I got some shit to handle," I said. I wasn't totally lying. I had a business day ahead of me. I was landscaping two yards. I also needed to check up on some spots, meet the team for the drop later tonight.

"Fine Shaka. You gone regret treating me like shit one day," she said slamming the fridge.

She went upstairs. I sat at the kitchen island eating my eggs when she came back down. She rolled her eyes at me and left. I called a locksmith to have my locks changed. I knew how Dayzee rolled. She'll set a nigga up quick for a lick. I dressed and started my day. After finishing my landscaping jobs, I called Ms. Clara to check on the house.

"You need to come over here. I don't know what Jetta is thinking," she said. I knew she was on some childish bullshit. I hurried to the house.

*****

Ms. Clara met me as I was walking in the door. "What's going on?" I asked.

"Some man is moving in here. She knows her father wouldn't stand for this," she said shaking her head.

I felt like I couldn't breathe I was so mad, "Where she at?"

"In the study. He's lounging by the pool like this his house," she said angrily. I walked away and barged in the study .

"You got five mothafuckin' minutes to get that nigga the hell out this house. If not, I'm throwing him out!" I demanded with rage.

She stood up from the desk , "You have no right to tell me who can stay here. This is my father's house."

"Yea, well pick up the damn phone and call him," I demanded walking up to her. I stood there staring at her waiting for her to pick up the phone.

"Why do you care? We aren't together anymore. I can do what I want," she said sadly.

"I don't give a fuck what you do! You just won't do it in this got damn house!" I barked. She started crying. This was typical Jetta. Every time she gets caught in her shit, she turns on the water works.

"Please, just leave me alone. You've hurt me enough," she said as she cried. I could only laugh. It felt like she stuck a fucking sword in my chest, and she's playing the victim. I wasn't going to let her manipulate her way out of this.

"You got three damn minutes," I said staring at her.

She started to cry harder. "I don't know what to do, Shaka. I love you and I just don't know what to do." I knew when Jetta was faking her tears. This was real. Against my better judgement, I pulled her into my arms as she cried like a baby.

"Who this nigga, Jetta?" I asked. I waited until she stopped crying and released her. I waited for her response.

"He's someone from my past. I don't know how I'm supposed to let him go and love you the way I want to," she said.

I cocked my head to the side. "You telling me you love that nigga?" If she said she did, I didn't know how I would react.

"Do you still love me, Shaka?" She asked staring at me.

I hated that I did. She had snatched my soul when I didn't even know I had one. "Right now, I hate you with everything in me, because I still do."

"I don't want to disappoint you," she said softly. Her phone rang as it lay on the desk. "It might be Daddy," she said rushing to answer it. I stood quietly waiting as she stared at her phone. She looked up at me with rage in her eyes. She threw her phone at me.

"You fucked her! I fucking hate you!" She screamed. She flopped down in the chair and cried. I picked up the phone to see a pic of me and Dayzee in my bed. I was going to kill the bitch. She took a selfie with me while I was sleep.

"Yo, you moving a whole nigga in this house and you mad at me?" I asked.

"Man, I ain't got time for this shit. Have the nigga out by the time I come back tomorrow. And stay yo ass home tonight, none of us are going to be at the club." I didn't like her being at the club if me, Titan or Rhino wasn't there.

I left the house. I didn't want to see his face. I would've finished what I started in Jamaica. Titan called my phone as I got back in my work truck.

"Yea," I said answering his call.

"Man, when the last time you talk to Rhino?" He asked.

"Shit, it's been a couple of days. You know how he is when he's mad. Y'all need to squash that shit," I said.

"He's out here acting a damn fool. He done beat the chef bloody at the Waffle House. The shit was live on

Facebook. I had to go down there and pay to keep them from pressing charges," Titan said.

"For what?" I asked.

"Man, because the dude put eggs on his plate," he said. I couldn't help but laugh. Rhino hated eggs.

"Damn, how much you came off?" I asked.

"That's not the issue. He's a loose cannon. He was fighting at some club last night because somebody wasted liquor on his shoes," Titan informed me. I knew it was only a matter of time before he gets locked up again. He still was facing charges for the incident at Walmart.

"Aight, we meeting up at ten o'clock. I'm going to swing by and check on him. I don't need you and him fighting tonight," I said. I didn't know how this was going to go with them in the same place . I needed to make sure Rhino had a level head tonight.

Belle

"How did you learn to pick locks?" I asked Jetta as we broke in Rhino's house.

I couldn't believe I was doing something so careless. After explaining everything to Jetta, I asked her to help me apologize to Rhino. I told her about his artwork, and she came up with a brilliant idea. Jetta called me after finding out Rhino wouldn't be home tonight. It was the perfect chance to get the paintings. She was going to help me set up a private showing to display in artwork at the country club. He had so many paintings in the room. I could take at least fifteen and he would never miss them.

"There's a lot you don't know about me," she said as the door opened. She looked at me and smiled.

We crept our way inside the dark house. She followed me down the hall to the room that held the paintings. Jetta picked the locked, so we could enter the room. I felt against the wall until I found the light switch. Jetta looked around the room in amazement.

"Oh my God, he painted these?" She asked as she admired the paintings.

"Yes, I don't understand why he doesn't share them," I said. We walked around admiring all his beautiful artwork.

"Well, we're going to change that," she said smiling as she started to uncover the one of the easel.

"No, don't touch that one," I said walking up to her.

"Why not? I want to see what he's working on," she said.

I blushed, "It's a painting of me. I want him to show it to me." I remembered walking in on him painting, but he had only started. I asked him about it several times. He said I would see it when it's finished.

She smiled, "You really love him, don't you?" I nodded my head.

"Thank you for helping me. I know this is putting a strain on your friendship with Miriam," I said graciously.

"Me and Mir been friends forever. We'll get through this when she's ready to sit down and listen. At least one of us needs to end up with the man they love," she said sadly.

"If you love Shaka, why are you marrying that man?" I asked.

She looked at me with sad eyes. "I don't have a choice. If I don't, he can destroy me."

"How Jetta?" I asked. I had only known her for a short time, but I know she'd never let anyone make her do something unwillingly.

She took a deep breath, "You have to promise you won't say anything."

I agreed to keep her secret. She told me everything about her past. I was beyond shocked. It was strange, but I admired her resilience to survive on her own . Even though she chose the illegal way, she didn't come running back home like the spoiled girl everyone says she is.

"I hurt some one very special to me. His name was Xavier . At first, he was a target. Then, I found out he was gay. He only wanted me to pretend to be his girlfriend because his family wouldn't accept him being gay. He decided to bring home a black woman," she said laughing.

"How did they accept that?" I asked curiously.

She smiled. "At first, they didn't like it. I won them over. I guess they realized I was a woman with class and her own money. Little did they know, I was broke as hell.

"What happened to him?" I asked.

Her eyes teared up. "He lied to me. He told me we would only take enough jewels to give us a good lick. I begged Cassius to call the hit off, but he refused. I know if I didn't do it with him, he would steal the family jewels. I thought me being there would save them. Xavier held the priceless family jewels in his safe with other jewels. When I drugged Xavier one night, I let Cassius in the house. I opened the safe and got some jewels out. I mistakenly left the safe open, and Cassius stole the family jewels. I didn't know until we left the house. I pleaded with him to put them back, but he didn't."

"What happened next?" I asked intrigued by her story.

"He used me. He had pictures sent to Xavier's father of him with a man. The man was him, but they never showed his face. He was furious with Xavier for breaking things off with him. Xavier realized Cassius was only using him for his money. I had no idea they were ever involved. Xavier's family disowned and cut him off for being gay and losing the family jewels."

Jetta wiped her tears as they fell, "He killed himself, Belle. I'm the reason he's dead. He was so nice to me. We had so much fun together. I told him everything about myself. He never judged me for being spoiled and selfish. He taught me so much about the fashion industry. We wanted to start our own clothing line together. He was so excited about going into business with me."

"I'm so sorry, Jetta," I said wrapping my arm around her.

"He has a video of me going into the safe. If I don't marry him, he will turn it in," she said wiping her tears.

"Tell Shaka, he will help you," I told her.

"No, I can't let him. I've made a mess of my life. It's time I grow up and fix my own mistakes. I don't want him to know what a fuck up I really am," she stated.

"Jetta, he loves you. You were vulnerable. He will understand," I said.

"Forget it, Belle. I swear you better not tell anyone what I just told you," she warned me.

"I won't. I promise," I assured her.

"Come on, let's get these paintings out of here before his crazy ass comes home," she said standing up.

We took fifteen paintings and left out the back door. Jetta was so good at breaking locks, it was as if we were never there.

Rhino

I couldn't get the rage out of me. The harder I tried to get Belle and Titan out of my head the angrier it made me. I had a long talk with Shaka. I hated to tell him it was best I didn't come to the drop. I didn't want my anger to fuck it up. I know seeing Titan would only make my anger worse. I was in a hotel bar trying to get my mind right. I knew I was losing it and needed to get a grip before I end up in prison or dead.

"Rhino?" Miriam asked taking me out my thoughts.

"Nah, I'm his long, lost twin brother," I said sarcastically. I chugged down my fifth shot of double Hennessy .

"Whatever. What are you doing here?" She asked.

"Minding my business as should you," I said signaling the bartender.

"I think you've had enough," she said examining me. It didn't take much to see that I was wasted. Without my permission, she sat at the table with me.

"I guess you're feeling the same way as me," she said.

"What way is that?" I asked.

She shrugged her shoulders. "Betrayed, angry and hurt."

I chuckled. “Nah, I’m good. What you doing here anyway?”

“I’m staying here for a few days. Trying to find a new place,” she informed me.

When the bartender came over, she ordered a double shot of Vodka. She proceeded to tell me about finding Belle at Titan’s house. The information only made me drink more. She joined me in drowning our woes. After my entire body went numb, I knew it was time to go. I stood up nearly falling.

“Woah, you are in no condition to drive. I have a suite. You can crash on the couch,” she said wobbling as she stood up.

I didn’t argue with her. I leaned against the wall in the elevator to hold my balance. Miriam stood in front of me with a pair of tight pants that were hugging her round ass. She didn’t have nearly as much as Belle, but she was blessed. I shook my head trying to stop thinking about Belle as the elevator took us to the top floor. When we got to her room, I flopped down on the sofa. I fell asleep the moment I closed my eyes. I woke up to Miriam’s wet, naked body on top of me.

“Yooo,” I said sitting up with her straddling my lap.

“They did it to us. It’s only right we return the favor,” she said with red eyes. I didn’t know if they were red from her being drunk, or if she had been crying.

“Come on, Miriam. You don’t want to do this. You’ll regret this shit in the morning,” I said.

“I’m fucking numb. I can’t feel anything,” she said as she started licking and kissing on my neck. I was only a man. I couldn’t stop my dick from swelling inside my jeans. She started unbuttoning my jeans. She reached her hand inside my boxers and wrapped her soft hand around my shaft.

“I swear Miriam. You better stop this shit,” I said grabbing her hand.

“I don’t want to stop. Make me feel alive again,” she moaned as she continued to caress my dick. I didn’t stop her when she pulled my dick out. I started licking and sucking on her full breasts .

“Ooohh yes, Titan. I miss you so much. I love you,” she moaned in ecstasy causing my dick to go south. I immediately lifted her and sat her on the couch next to me. I stood up and put my dick back in my boxers.

“You need to sober the fuck up,” I said staring down at her .

She buried her face in her hands, “I’m sorry. My life is just so messed up. He was the only thing right in my life.”

I grabbed her robe that was laying across the bed. I wrapped it around her as she sat on the couch staring at the floor. I didn’t know what to say to her. I didn’t know how to handle my own feelings right now. I know us fucking would only complicate the situation more.

“Why did he make me love him? Why did they do this to us?” She asked glancing at me.

“I don’t have the answers for it, Miriam. I know us fucking ain’t the answer. Shit, you don’t even like me,” I said with a smile.

She giggled a little, “I don’t, but you do smell good.” I laughed. We sat there quiet for a few minutes.

“Time, shit like this takes time,” I told her.

She stared at me. “Do you still love her?”

“If that’s what you call this harrowing pain inside my chest that makes me sick to my stomach, I guess the answer would be yes,” I said.

She smiled. “You think they love each other?”

I shook my head wanting to forget the thought of that possibility. “I don’t wanna think about that. It is what it is.”

"Thank you for stopping me from making a big mistake," she said smiling at me. I nodded my head.

"No problem. You wasn't ready for it anyway. I better get out of here before I inform you of why they call me Rhino," I said standing up.

She laughed. She stood up to walk me to the door. I said good night and hopped on the elevator. When the elevator doors opened to the first floor, I looked in the eyes of the last person on earth I wanted to see. Titan charged toward me, but his mama jumped in front of him.

"No the fuck you don't! This is my job!" She said.

I continued to walk pass them. We stared each other down. I smirked at him and grabbed my dick. I know I was wrong, but I wanted him to feel just a little of what I was feeling. Titan didn't want to fight me again. It wasn't because he was scared. He was my equal when it came to fighting. His jabs were just as hard as mine. I know he was sorry for what went down, but that didn't mean anything to me.

Titan

After we were done unloading the work, I decided to check on the club. I never made it to the club. Ma called and told me something I didn't want to hear or believe. She was at work and saw Miriam and Rhino getting into the elevator. Something told me to just let it be. If she was that grimy to fuck him, I didn't need her. I kept telling myself she wasn't worth it, but it didn't work. I made a U-turn in the road and headed to the hotel. Ma wouldn't give me the room number. She never wanted me to come there. She was trying to prove to me I need to leave Miriam alone. She wanted me to be with Belle because for our child. Belle is a beautiful girl, but she was not the one that has my heart. I wanted to rip Rhino's head off when he stepped off the elevator. After pleading with Ma for a while, she finally gave me Miriam's room number. I knocked on her door and stood waiting for her to answer.

"Decided you couldn't drive?" She asked opening the door. Her eyes opened wide as she stared at me. She immediately tried to slam the door in my face. I blocked the door from closing and stepped inside.

"Leave or I will call the cops!" she demanded angrily.

“Call the mothafuckas then,” I barked so loud she jumped back. My blood was boiling. She only had a towel wrapped around her. All kinds of crazy images of her and Rhino was going through my mind.

“Get out Titan! I don’t want you here!” She demanded.

“You think fucking one of my best friends gone make you feel better? You think that shit gone hurt me?” I asked her.

“I hope it makes you feel exactly how I felt,” she said.

I chuckled, “It don’t. It lets me know you ain’t shit.”

She slapped me hard across the face. “You ain’t shit. All that bullshit you spit to me about choosing and loving you. I was willing to walk away from everything for you. I wish I never met you!”

She started laughing, “Fuck love! I didn’t fuck Rhino tonight, but the next time I see him I will. I’m going to let him fuck me in every hole until I get over you. Then I’m going to fuck him some more, because I’m sure his dick is better than yours.”

Without hesitation, I tore her robe off, “That’s all you want is some dick. I’ll give you that.”

I slung her on the bed. She landed on her stomach. She tried running from me, but I held one of her legs while I pulled my dick out. I didn't realize my dick was brick hard until it sprung out.

"Let me go!" She screamed as I positioned her on all fours . I pinned her hands behind her back with one hand and pushed her head down into the mattress with the other. I slammed my dick inside her with no remorse.

"Aaaaaaahhhhh!" She cried out in ecstasy and pain.

Her pussy was gushing wet. I couldn't contain the roar inside from feeling her tight, slippery walls around my dick. Her juices splattered out of her as I rammed inside her repeatedly. She was gripping my dick as I hammered inside her. I was so caught up in the pleasure of being inside her wet tunnel I let her hands go. I gripped her plump ass cheeks and spread them apart. My throbbing dick fell deeper inside her pressing against her weak spot.

"Oooooohhhhh Ggggooooddd!" She wailed as her creamy essence poured from her. Her body quivered and jerked as I continue to not miss a stroke.

"This what you want? You want me to fuck you like this?" I asked angrily.

I continued to slam inside of her. I was furious that she almost fucked Rhino. I wanted her to feel how mad I was. Her ass bounced and jiggled while I shoved every inch I had inside her pussy. Her walls were gripping my shaft every time she exploded. Her body was pouring out sweat. Her toffee colored skin was glistening making her look magical. The head of my dick was crushing her g-spot.

"I-I can't stop coming!" She screamed as she exploded liquid and cream. Her milky fluids were dripping from my nut sack.

When I pulled out, I flipped her over and pinned her legs on the sides of her head. I slid back inside her allowing the weight of my torso to keep her legs in place. I started driving deeper and harder inside her. If heaven felt like this, I was ready to repent and leave this earth. Her moans and cries mixed with my grunts and growls drowned out the sound of the rocking bed. I was fucking her so hard her head was hanging off the side of the bed. I didn't stop. I wrapped her legs around my waist as she placed the palms of her hands on the floor. My heart was pounding, stomach became so tight it cramped along with my toes. I let out a gut wrenching growl as I nutted deep inside her. I came so hard, I felt dizzy. I fell back on the bed onto my stomach with my eyes closed. I felt her wet mouth on my dick. I looked down and she was staring at me with eyes full of passion. She sucked my dick into her mouth.

"Gggggrrrr!" I growled from the thrill of feeling her wet mouth around my dick.

I was still sensitive from coming so hard. She licked, slurped and sucked me into another world. I felt my damn eyes tearing up she was sucking my dick so good. Saliva poured from her mouth and down to my cum filled nuts. She dipped down and gently sucked them into her mouth. She massaged my shaft as her tongue did gymnastics on my balls. I felt myself getting ready to explode. I tried pulling her head away, but she wasn't having it. She moaned as she sucked my brick hard dick back in her mouth. She bobbed her head allowing me to glide in and out.

"Ffffuuuuccckkk! Ggggooottttt ddddaaammmnnn!" I bellowed as I erupted in her mouth.

She moaned as she slurped and drank every drop. I shook and jerked unable to withstand the sensations flowing through my body. When I looked down at her, she was playing in her creamy pussy. My dick was still hard. I laid her down and slid back inside her. Tears rolled down her face as she cried out how much she loved me. She started coming back to back.

"Sssssshhhhiiittt! I-I-I can't take it no more!" She pleaded.

NATAVIA PRESENTS

Jetta

After dropping Belle off, I headed home. I dreaded going to the house, because I knew Cassius was there. He surprised me by showing up to the house a few days ago saying he was moving in. I couldn't make him leave. He held the blackmail video over my head. I was beyond exhausted trying to get rid of him. He was in the den drinking and watching television when I walked in.

"What do you want from me?" I asked him in frustration. I knew when Shaka came back there was going to be hell.

"I want you to be my wife. You're worth millions," he said smiling at me.

"I don't have any money. All that money is in Shaka's name. I can't touch any of it without his consent," I informed him.

"I'm sure you'll figure something out," he said.

I did figure something out. I would never let him know. I took Daddy's money in Shaka's account, I moved it to a private account Lyle set up for me. I made him promise not to tell Miriam. I know she would scold me for going behind Shaka's back. I can't believe he went and fucked Dayzee without giving us a chance. I know he would never allow me access to Daddy's money. It's going to be hell when he finds out.

"I regret I ever worked with you," I told him.

He chuckled, "You didn't feel that way when you were broke and almost homeless. Get over Xavier's death. He was weak. He killed himself. I couldn't even get rid of those damn jewels. I couldn't find anyone with enough money to buy them."

I was happy to hear that, "Where are they?"

He smiled, "I will give them to you after we are married."

I stomped my feet like a child, "I'm not marrying you. I will give you the one million."

He shook his head. "You are worth so much more than that."

I stormed out the room while concocting a plan to get rid of him. I wanted to know where those jewels were, so I could return them to Xavier's family. I wasn't sure how I was going to do that without incriminating myself. I will worry about that later. My first task is getting them back while getting rid of Cassius. There was only one way I could guarantee Shaka wouldn't come by. If I was at the club, I know he wouldn't come here. I called Miriam to see if she was ready to talk. I called several times before giving up. I called Belle and pleaded with her to go with me. She gave in deciding she owed me for helping her set up Rhino's surprise debut tomorrow afternoon.

I didn't feel like getting all dolled up. I wore a pair of multicolored Versace tights, a Balmain crotchet body suit, and a pair of Louboutin six-inch stilettos. I had cut my long, honey blond weave into a short bob. I grabbed my clutch and headed out the door. Cassius was still in the den enjoying the luxury of living in my daddy's house. I despised everything about him.

*****

I smiled when Belle walked out the house. She had truly blossomed and didn't know it. She was wearing a short, black sequined body dress and a pair of stilettos. He hair was styled with Peruvian body wave with a part on the side.

"You think he will be there?" She asked worriedly as I drove us to the club.

"So, what if he is? He doesn't own the club," I said. She didn't want to run into Rhino before tomorrow.

"I don't think he will, since Titan owns the club," she said. She relaxed as I drove us to the club. As always, the club was packed. We waltzed to the front of the line. Security stopped us from entering the club. I looked at him like he had lost his damn mind.

"The fellas ain't here. Shaka said not to let you in if they're not here," he said smiling at me.

"Ugh!" I said stomping my feet. "Come on Belle, this isn't the only club in town." He laughed as we walked away.

"Maybe this is a sign we should just stay home," Belle said as I drove to a nearby club.

"No, he can't stop me from going out. He's probably laid up with that bitch, Dayzee,"

*****

We entered the next club. I didn't care for the atmosphere, but I was determined to prove a point to Shaka. The club was overcrowded with some of the meanest looking men in the city. The women were no better. They barely had on clothes. Belle looked scared out of her mind. We found a table in the corner and sat down. After a couple of drinks, I started to loosen up. I was talking to Belle, and realized she wasn't paying me any attention. I followed her eyes to see Rhino grinding on some random bitch. He had his hands all over her. She was smiling like she won the lottery. I never saw Belle mad before, but there was rage in her eyes behind her glasses. I joined her in anger when I saw Shaka walk up to Rhino. He whispered something in his ear, and Rhino looked in our direction. I jumped up and went on the dance floor.

"You can't stop me from going out! You are not my father. Stop acting like it," I said staring up into his face. He chuckled.

The next thing I know, Belle was attacking Rhino. Rhino held her hands as she tried swinging at him. Shaka grabbed Rhino while I grabbed Belle. The girl Rhino was dancing with hit Belle knocking her glasses off her face. I let Belle go, and she went crazy on the girl. She had her on the floor beating her head into the floor. Shaka was making his way through the crowd to stop the fight. Before he could break it up, Dayzee started hitting Belle in the back of the head. I jumped on Dayzee's back and started beating her in the head. She was screaming for me to let her go. She tried throwing me off her back, but couldn't. I was finally pulled off her back and hauled out the club with Belle beside me.

"Take yo ass home, Jetta!" Shaka barked as we stood outside of the club.

"Fuck you Micah! You just mad because I found out you here with that bitch," I yelled at him.

"Man, you deal with this shit. I'm out," Rhino said walking away. I laughed when Belle picked up an empty beer bottle and threw it at him. I was glad it didn't hit him in the head. It landed on his back. He didn't even turn around to look at her. He kept walking.

"I'm gone whoop this black bitch's ass!" Dayzee said charging toward me as she walked out the club. I wasn't a fighter. I only jumped on her back to help Belle. I was glad when Shaka stopped her.

"I swear, you fuckin' touch her and you dead," he said staring at her.

"Nigga, you just fucked me the other night and defending this bitch?" she asked angrily. I stood behind him licking my tongue out at her in a childish manner. She charged for me, but Shaka stood in her way.

He ignored her and turned to face me, "Go home." His tone was calm but stern this time. I know I messed up, but I couldn't believe he was choosing her over me.

"You want her?" I asked staring at him. I didn't want to leave him here with her. I wanted him to come with me.

"Man Jetta, this ain't the place," he said.

"I'm sorry. I promise I'll fix everything," I pleaded. I didn't care how pathetic I looked. I love him and wasn't going to lose him.

He reached in his pocket and pulled out his keys, "Here, go to my spot. I'll be there later."

"You fuckin' dog! You gone pay for this shit!" Dayzee screamed as she stormed off.

"My glasses are ruined," Belle said looking at her broken glasses as we walked to my car.

"I'm sorry Belle. I'll buy you some more," I said sincerely.

"He couldn't even stand the sight of me. I've lost him," she said sadly. I hated to see her hurting like this.

"Don't worry. I have everything set up for tomorrow. He won't be able to deny you once he sees what you've done for him," I said trying to reassure him.

Shaka

I didn't understand Jetta. Everything in my body told me she loved me. I just couldn't understand what she was doing with this other nigga. I wasn't going to beg her to choose me. That was her choice. I do know he wasn't going to be living in Omega's house. After a few words with Dayzee, I left the club. I knew she was heated but didn't care. I never led her to believe we were doing anything other than fucking. After leaving the club, I went to Omega's house. I checked every room. I felt a sense of relief when I found him in one of the guest rooms. I knew she wasn't sleeping with him. I crept to the side of the bed and cocked my gun. His eyes popped open.

"I don't want to hear a word come out your mouth. All I want to see is you getting yo shit and getting the fuck outta here," I said staring at him. He opened his mouth to speak and I shoved the gun in his mouth. He jumped out the bed and started packing his stuff. Without saying another word, he hauled ass.

*****

I rode around debating if I wanted to go to my house. I had an ache in my chest that only she could stop, but she was still playing childish games. I finally couldn't fight it anymore as I pulled into my driveway behind her car. She was pacing the floor when I walked in. She ran to me and wrapped her arms around my waist resting her head on my chest.

"I thought you weren't going to come," she said. She was a rotten brat that I didn't want to let go.

I pulled her arms from around my waist. "I thought I told you to get that nigga out the house." She followed me as I walked upstairs to the bedroom.

"I tried. He wouldn't leave. I tried breaking things off with him," she tried explaining.

"How the fuck you try to break up with somebody, Jetta?" I asked angrily turning to face her.

"You don't understand. He's very demanding," she said nervously.

My blood started to boil, "He put his hands on you?"

She shook her head. "No, he just makes me feel guilty about leaving him."

I chuckled and shook my head. She wasn't telling me the truth. Jetta always got what she wanted. If she wanted to get rid of him, he would be gone. I grabbed my boxers and tee shirt out the drawer and walked toward the door.

"Where you going?" She asked grabbing my arm.

"You were worried about me fucking Dayzee. I'm not. I'm here," I said staring at her. "I'm sleeping in one of the spare rooms."

I went down the hall to one of the bedrooms. I took a cold shower and lounged in the bed. When my phone dinged, I knew it was Dayzee cussing me out for the umpteenth time. I regretted opening the picture. Jetta sent me a picture of her laying in my bed playing with her shaved pussy. More photos started to come through of her naked body. My dick was throbbing to feel her insides. The only thing kept me strong were Omega's words. He warned me not to let her break me. I had to prove to her she couldn't get her way all the time. I did something I hadn't did in years. I jacked my dick until I unloaded. It didn't stop my hunger for her, but it relieved some pressure off me. I tossed and turned until I realized sleep wasn't coming. I decided to go downstairs and workout. I stopped by my bedroom to hear sniffling. Her bratty ass was crying. I slowly opened the door to see her sitting up in the bed Indian style. I walked into the room and sat on side of the bed.

“What you crying for, Jetta?” I asked.

She wiped her tears. “I called Daddy. He’s in the hospital. He won’t let us come see him.”

I wasn’t surprised by this news. He told me when he felt his time nearing he didn’t want us to see him that way. I didn’t think it would be this soon. All I could do was pull her into my arms. She cried until she fell asleep. When I woke up, the bed was empty. I rush to the bathroom to pee. After washing my face and brushing my teeth, I went to make sure she was okay. I found her sitting out on the balcony of the bedroom. I was happy to see she wasn’t crying.

“You okay?” I asked.

She looked up at me and smiled. “I called Daddy this morning. He told me he was proud of me. That’s all I ever wanted was to make him proud. I’m going to be successful, Shaka. Not for myself, but for him.”

“Jetta always gets what she wants,” I said smiling at her. She giggled.

She stood up, “Come on, I’m going to cook you breakfast.”

I laughed, “Nah, I’ll pass.”

“It’s not funny. Belle has been teaching me how to cook simple things,” she said pouting.

"Yea, but food ain't what I got a taste for," I said walking up to her. I held the rim of my tee shirt she wore and pulled it over her head.

"Micah, you have neighbors," she said bashfully looking around.

"Shit, they might learn something," I said kneeling in front of her.

I lifted her leg and propped it on the chair. Her chocolate mound was in my face. She quivered when I stroked my tongue over her pussy lips. I pressed my face between her slit inhaling her sweet musk. I sucked her into my mouth. She moaned and held the back of my head. I dipped down lower allowing her pussy to sit directly in my mouth. I licked and slurped her juices as they started to pour from her.

"Mmmmm," I groaned enjoying the taste of her sweetness.

"Yyyyeeesss," she moaned as she started to twirl her hips smearing her fruity sauce over my face.

I used my fingers to open her swollen pussy lips. My tongue twirled around and stroked back and forth until she was crying out my name. I slid two fingers inside her tight, wet tunnel. I finger fucked her while violating her throbbing clit. My fingers teased her g-spot. I spread her tight tunnel and inserted my tongue inside with them. My other hand was massaging her clit. Her sugary juices were spilling over my face and up my nose. I couldn't stop. I wanted to devour every drop of her sweetness. I released her swollen clit and reached behind her. I massaged her plump ass cheek while my tongue and fingers continued to fuck her. I used my one hand to spread her ass cheeks. I fondled around her anus until my finger slowly slid inside. I removed my tongue from her tight tunnel and latched on to her clit. I finger fucked her pussy and ass while sucking her pulsating pearl. Her body was shaking and jerking as she moaned and screamed out in ecstasy. She gripped my head with both hands and started fucking my face.

"Ooohhh Yyyeessss! Mmmiiiccaaahhh! Sssshhhhittt! Aaaaaaahhh! Don't stop! Please don't sssstoooopppp!" She screamed loud enough to wake the neighborhood as her creamy nectar poured over my face nearly drowning me. It flowed down my chin to my chest. I picked her limp body up and carried her to the bed. I fucked her until she vowed to love me forever.

Miriam

He was still asleep when I awakened with a throbbing headache. I stared at him sleeping peacefully. I said a silent thank you to Rhino for not letting me make a huge mistake last night. I didn't know what was going on between him and Belle, but I know he loves me like I love him. I slipped out of bed and took a quick, hot shower. I slipped on a pair of yoga pants, tank top and Puma slides. Today started a new life for me. I was done living a life that was planned for me before I knew what living truly was. I was like a programmed robot. I thought I wanted everything I was told I was supposed to have before Titan. I never felt what it meant to be truly loved by a man. I needed some closures in my life and to mend some broken friendships. I kissed his lips and turned to walk away.

"Titan!" I yelped when he yanked me down on the bed. I laughed hysterically from being surprised that he was awake.

"Where you going Star?" He asked kissing on my neck. I missed hearing that name.

"If you stop, I'll tell you," I said feeling myself getting heated. He stopped and sat up in the bed. I straddled his lap.

"I have some things I need to handle. I'm coming back. I promise," I said staring at him with a serious face.

"What things?" He asked.

"There's so much that has been going on with my life over the past couple of weeks. I need closure. I also need to mend friendships," I said.

He stared at me trying to read my face, "I will explain when I get back."

"I'm not fucking Belle. Our child is almost five years old," he explained.

I put my finger to his lips. "I don't care about that anymore. I know you love me. I said I was going to mend friendships. I owe her and Jetta an apology."

"The closure?" He asked.

"I don't need closure from him. I need it from my parents," I said. He looked at me strangely.

"I might not be here when you get back. Belle putting some surprise shit together for Rhino. I don't think it's a good idea, but Jetta in her ear. We know what Jetta wants, she gets," he said shaking his head. I giggled, because it was the truth.

"I'll see you there," I said smiling down at him.

"So, you forgive me?" He asked.

"Yes, and I love you," I said sincerely.

"Does Rhino know you're coming?" I asked.

"Shit, Rhino doesn't know he's coming," he said laughing. "Los is bringing him there. Jetta got everybody in on this."

"I hope he'll sit down and talk to you," I said.

"He will. I learned years ago how to deal with Rhino's rage. It ain't easy, but that's my brother," he said. I leaned forward and slid my tongue in his mouth.

"You better get the fuck outta here, before I chain you to this bed," he said massaging my thighs.

I laughed. "I think we broke the bed. There's a hole in the wall," I said staring at the hole where the headboard was banging against it.

He looked over his shoulder. "Damn." I laughed as I got off his lap.

*****

My first stop was to my parents. I didn't waste a lot of time telling them what I had to say. I let them know I wasn't marrying Lyle under any circumstances. I apologized for not being the daughter they wanted me to be. My father was furious and swore to never speak to me again. Mother pleaded with me not to destroy the family. I couldn't live for them anymore. I found my life and I wasn't giving it up for anyone.

My next visit was to see Belle. Her grandmother informed me she left early this morning. I guess she was out planning whatever they had going on for Rhino. I decided to wait and speak to her and Jetta at the event for Rhino. I went by my house to get some personal belongings I needed. I didn't care about breaking the lease. It'll be worth it to get away from Lyle. When I walked in the house, there were suitcases everywhere. Lyle was throwing clothes in them like a man in a hurry to get away.

"Bitch, you decided to come home," he said staring at me.

"I just came to get some things. You can have this house," I said walking in the bedroom. He didn't know I had a trick for him. I wasn't going to let him walk away without payback for putting his hands on me. I was going to hit him where it hurts.

"I'm leaving this mothafucka. I don't want your stank ass or this raggedy ass, cheap house," he yelled as I ignored him. I laughed and shook my head.

*****

I gathered my belongings and left without us getting into a fist fight. I didn't even think to ask Lyle where he was going. I didn't care as long as he wasn't in my life. When I returned to the hotel, Titan was gone. I texted him to find out where the event was Jetta and Belle was planning. After receiving his reply. I started getting dressed. I was headed out of the lobby when the lady at the front desk called me over.

"Hey you, come here," she said pointing at me. I looked around to make sure she was talking to me. She was very unprofessional.

"Excuse me," I said walking over to the desk.

"Don't act all high and mighty with me. I know you fucking my son," she said.

"I'm sorry, but who are you?" I asked looking around to see if anyone heard her. She was talking loud enough for the entire lobby to hear.

She propped her hand on her hip and bopped her head. "I'm Titan's mother." My heart dropped as I stared at her with an open mouth.

"Yea, you was a busy girl last night. First, Rhino's retarded ass. Then, my son."

I shook my head. "It wasn't like that. I didn't sleep with Rhino. He,"

She interrupted me before I could finish. “Blah, blah, blah. I don’t wanna hear it.”

She leaned over the desk and stared me in the eyes. Her eyes were cold and serious. “If you break my baby’s heart, I will fuck you all the way up. I will slice and dice yo pretty ass ‘til you would have to be identified by her teeth.”

I gulped out of fear. I believed every word she said. “I-I love him.”

“You better heifer. I’ll be watching you,” she said pointing at me.

“Hi, I hope you guys enjoyed your stay here,” she said turning on her professional voice to the couple that walked up. Her entire demeanor changed. If I didn’t know any better , I would never think she was ghetto as hell. I hurried out of the lobby to get away from her.

Rhino

"Man, why we converging with these fools at a damn country club? You know I don't like going to that place," I asked Los as he drove.

"I don't know, man. This where they wanted to meet. They looking to cop a good lick, so I wasn't arguing about the place," he said.

We rode in silence. I hated the country club, because my old man wanted to be a member but couldn't afford it. That's one of the reasons he wanted me in the NBA. Sometimes, I felt guilty for not going. Then, I would think of the torture he allowed to happen to me by my grandfather. I had been on edge since seeing Belle at the club the other night. I was trying to control my anger, but I was feeling like a caged animal. Instead of the pain in my chest easing up, it was getting worse. Sometimes a slight breeze would come, and I could smell her natural sweet aroma. I imagined laying my head on her thick thighs while she oiled my scalp and played in my dreads.

Los valet parked his car, and we entered the country club. Los said something to the front desk and he lead us to meet our guest. I was surprised we weren't meeting in the bar area. We were lead to a huge room that had the doors closed. I almost pulled out my gun and started shooting when the doors slung open. Everyone yelled surprised. I was dumfounded. It wasn't my birthday. Who the hell were they surprising? I looked around to see what was going on. That's when I noticed my paintings sitting on easels. I started to get furious until I looked and saw Belle nervously standing by one of the paintings. I walked over to her.

"What the fuck, Belle?" I asked in a low voice.

"Please don't be mad. I know you hate me but these paintings deserve to be in an art gallery," she said anxiously.

I grabbed her by the arm and pulled her out of the room. I pulled her into a bathroom and locked the door. I took deep breaths to calm my anger. My paintings were never to be shared with anyone.

"What would make you think I would approbate of this?" I asked angrily.

"I don't know. I-I just wanted to do something to show you how much I care about you," she said.

"How about not fucking my brother? That would've showed me a lot," I barked.

She slapped me so hard, I almost forgot she was a female, "I'm not fucking him!"

"Drop the impeccant role! You ain't Virgin Mary," I said with a smirk.

She stared at me with sadness in her eyes, "I always thought someone like you would never look at someone like me. I had a crush on you ever since the first day I saw you. I thought I never stood a chance with you. Titan was your friend. He was always nice to me. I made myself believe being with him would be like being with you. I know it sounds stupid. He didn't want to do it, but I begged him. It only happened once. That one night created the greatest gift God could give. I wish I could say I regret it, but I don't. I wish I could forget that night, but not my daughter. My daughter is my life. I regret not telling Titan about his daughter when I got pregnant. I was ashamed and scared. I was scared to tell you, because I felt like I finally had a chance to be with the man of my dreams."

I wanted to stay angry. I didn't want to forgive her or him. I didn't know how to forgive them. My brother had what I felt always belonged to me. I punched the wall hard as I could. She ran toward the door to get away from me, but I stopped her by grabbing her from behind around the waist. I hated I still wanted her. I buried my face in her neck to inhale her aroma. My dick grew pressing against her voluptuous ass. I started licking and kissing on her neck. She exhaled and moaned my name. I slid my hand inside her trousers slipping my fingers between her wet folds . She quickly turned around wrapping her arms around my neck. I lifted her up wrapping her legs around my waist. I walked over and sat her on the bathroom counter. She pulled her shirt over her head as I pulled her pants and panties off. Her heels fell to the floor with them. I pulled her succulent breasts from her bra. I pushed them together massaging, licking and sucking them as I entered her velvety tunnel. I groaned as my dick slid deeper inside her. I leaned forward releasing her breasts and cuffed her legs in my arms. I stared at her as I stroked in and out. Her syrupy juices coated my dick. Her eyes were full of passion. She leaned forward and wrapped her arms around my neck. She buried her tongue deep inside my mouth. I lifted her by her ass cheeks off the counter. I wrapped my arms around her waist and started bouncing her up and down on my dick. I could feel her essence gushing out of her and down my thighs. I knew I was going to deep when she dug her nails in my back. I pulled back.

"No, I want all of you. Go deeper," she whispered in my ear. I obeyed like a whipped dog. I pounced her harder and deeper against my aching dick. Her nails dug deeper into my back as she bit and sucked on my neck. All the pain she was inflicting on me made me want to go deep as I could inside her.

"You still wanted it all?" I groaned ready to slide every inch inside her.

"Yyyyeesss!" She moaned loudly.

I sat her on the counter and spread her legs as far apart as they could go. I lost my concentration when I looked down to see her creamy essence spilling off the counter to the floor. I held her legs apart as I dipped down to lick her cream covered pussy. Slurping sounds echoed through the bathroom as I groaned at the enjoyment of feasting on her. Neither one of us cared about the loud sexual noises we were making. My tongue annihilated her drenched pussy until she couldn't take it anymore.

"Aaaaaaahhhh! Ooooohhhh! I'm ccccoommmminnng!" She screamed. Her body froze and jerked. Her gooey, sticky cream poured out of her and into my mouth.

I stood up and slid deep inside her. I didn't think she was ready to take all of me. I didn't want to hurt her. Her eyes read my mind. She pleaded by opening her legs wider. I leaned forward and kissed her to muffle the moans I knew would come from her. She relaxed her walls and I fell inside a euphoria. Not only did I have to muffle her moans, I had to restrain myself from roaring like a beast. She opened up more for me. I knew I was as deep as I could go when I felt my nut sack hitting her ass. The sweat pouring down my back burned from the scratches she was leaving on my back. She surprised me when she started winding her hips and matching my strokes. She was in a world of bliss as she repeatedly came as tears poured down her face. Once I felt the electric shock waves shooting through my body I knew I was done. Her next movement caused shooting stars to flash in my eyes as my soul drifted from my body to hers. She pushed me back, got down on her knees and slid my dick inside her warm, wet mouth. Her mouth had a suction on my dick I couldn't get away from. I exploded causing my body to jerk and toes to curl up. She pulled my dick from her mouth and jacked it allowing my cum to unload in her mouth. I couldn't hold myself up. I stumbled backward almost falling to the floor. I leaned against the counter trying to catch my breath.

"Do I send everyone home?" She asked standing at the door wiping her mouth.

"You think they that good?" I asked.

"People were already asking for prices to buy before you came. I didn't know what the starting price was," she said smiling.

“Give me a couple of minutes,” I told her.

“Rather you choose to forgive and give us another chance or not, I just want you to know I’m thankful for having you in my life. I love you,” she said before walking out the bathroom.

I stood there speechless. We had never said how we felt about each other. To give us another chance, I would have to find a way to forgive them both. I couldn’t stand the thought of him being inside and experiencing what I just did with her.

Jetta

I was calling Shaka's phone repeatedly only to be sent to voicemail. He knew he was supposed to be here for Rhino's event. Now, everyone was waiting for Rhino and Belle to return. . After growing impatient, I went to find them. The noises coming from the bathroom stopped me in my tracks. I smiled knowing they were back together as I returned to the event. I kept the guest entertained until I saw Belle.

"Where's the artist?" I asked. She looked sad.

"He's coming," she said forcing a smile.

"I heard the noises. Why the sad face?" I asked smiling at her.

"Yea, but he can't forgive me," she said sadly.

I was happy when his parents and grandfather walked into the room. I know he had a strained relationship with them. Having their support will mean a lot to him.

"Give him time. He will. Come on, his parents are here," I said taking her by the hand. Rhino looked just like his father and grandfather. They were all handsome men.

"Hi everyone, I'm glad you decided to come," I said smiling at them. His mother forced a smile. His father and grandfather stared at us without saying a word.

"Hi Jetta, it's been a while. How's your mother?" Mrs. Thomas asked.

"She's doing great," I said smiling at her. I hadn't talked to my mother in months. I gave myself a mental note to call her. It was time for me to stop blaming everyone for my mess ups.

"I would like you to meet Maribelle. She's the one responsible for putting this event together," I said smiling at Belle. She stood beside me with rattled nerves.

"And who are you?" His grandfather asked staring at Belle. Belle cleared here throat to speak, but was interrupted by Rhino walking up to us.

"Well look, the artist himself," Mr. Thomas said looking his son up and down. I didn't like the vibes I was getting from them.

"What you doing here?" Rhino asked them.

"We were invited to this embarrassment," his grandfather said shaking his head.

"Excuse me," Belle said staring at him.

His father laughed, "A drug dealing black man painting tulips and shit. Who's going to take him serious? He wasted a chance for the NBA for this."

"He's very talented," Belle said. I glanced at Rhino, and I didn't like the look in his eyes. I could see the crazy getting ready to come out.

"Come on, Rhino. There's some people wanting to meet you," I said trying to pull him away.

"Get the fuck out," He said in a calm voice staring at them

His grandfather walked over and stood in his face, "You always been a pussy ass boy. Out here painting and shit like some faggot."

Rhino stared him down. I saw his fist balled up. I knew he was getting ready to hit him. I jumped in front of him. He walked away with rage running through his veins. He started knocking all the paintings off the easels. Titan stopped him, but he jerked away from him. He stood in the middle of the room.

"Hello everyone. I'm the black artist that embarrasses his family. Seems like I can't be a black man that loves to paint unless I'm gay. Ain't that right, family?" He shouted staring at his parents. Everyone's eyes landed on his family. His parents walked out the room with their heads down.

Belle walked up to him, "I told you this shit was personal," he said staring down at her.

"I know I ain't the nigga you fucking with right now, but this ain't the place. You know these white folks will call Twelve. Just walk out of here and calm down," Titan said staring at him.

He stood there breathing heavily. He stared at Belle before walking out the room. Titan followed behind him. All the guest started leaving. I was relieved when I saw Shaka walk into the room. My feelings changed the moment our eyes met. He was staring at me with the same look in his eyes that Rhino had. I had no idea why he was so furious.

"Where fuck is the money, Jetta?" He asked gritting his teeth.

"I'm sorry. I did it when I was mad at you. I'll transfer it back," I explained.

"Do it now!" He roared.

I jumped, "I can't. I have to wait until I get home. It's in a private account."

"Well, why the fuck you still standing here?" He asked staring at me.

"I said I was going to do it. It's no big deal, Micah," I said with an attitude. I hated when he treated me like a child.

“You so fucking childish and irresponsible. That’s the reason your father ain’t leave you over shit,” I said.

“Forget you! I’m not doing anything. It’s my money anyway!” I said stomping my feet. I tried to walk away from him, but he yoked me around the neck with one hand.

“Don’t fucking play with me, Jetta. Put it back,” he said.

“Micah, you’re hurting her,” Belle said trying to pry his hand from around my neck. He stared at me with disgust before releasing me. He left me standing there trying to catch my breath. Belle gave me a bottle of water to quench my dry throat.

“What is going on?” Miriam said walking into the room. I had never been so happy to see my best friend. The entire event was a disaster.

“He’s just being dramatic,” I said waving him off. I was going to transfer the money at my convenience. “I’m happy to see you.”

“I’m so sorry for the things I said to you,” she said. I smiled and hugged her accepting her apology. She looked at Belle. I didn’t want anymore drama. Today has been bad enough.

“Can we talk?” She asked Belle. Belle nodded her head.

"I'll leave you to talk. Let me go home and handle this before Shaka shits bricks," I said hugging them before leaving.

Titan

We rode in silence until we made it to his house. "You good?" I asked as he opened the door. He didn't reply. He went inside his house. I got out the truck and followed him inside. He was chugging a bottle of white Hennessy as he sat on the couch.

"You can go nigga. We ain't got shit to talk about," he said looking up at me.

I chuckled and shook my head. "So, you Michael Angelo?"

"Fuck you," he said before turning the bottle up again.

"Seriously though, you got mad ass talent. Why you ain't tell us that?" I asked sitting in a chair.

He laughed. "So y'all can clown me like my own family?"

"Man, come on. That shit they saying don't make sense. Even if you were gay, so what?" I said shrugging my shoulders.

"Mothafucka, I ain't gay," he said. I laughed knowing I was only making him angrier.

"I'm just messing with you. People were trying to cop yo work. I'm talking five figures. You can let your parents hold you back or you can share your gift with the world," I advised him.

I laughed. "All those paintings in our houses is your work. You got some serious skills."

"Do you want something else?" Rhino asked ignoring my comment.

"We was wrong for lying to you. It ain't what you think. Our child is almost five years old. It," I said before being interrupted by banging on Rhino's door.

"Fuck!" Rhino barked getting up from the sofa. We knew it was the police or FEDs by the knock. It was no point in trying to run. We looked at each other and walked toward the door. Sure enough, twelve was standing on the other side of the door.

"Yea," Rhino said looking him up and down.

"Yes, are you Brutus Thomas?" The officer asked. I guess the country club called about his outburst.

"Yea," he said.

"Do you know Micah Taylor?" He asked.

"Man, what the fuck you want?" Rhino asked getting frustrated with the questions.

"We're here to inform you he's been shot. He's currently in the Piedmont Hospital getting ready to undergo surgery." We never replied to the officer's comment. We rushed to the hospital.

*****

When we got to the hospital, Shaka was already in surgery. We sat in the waiting room waiting to be informed of his condition. We knew niggas were going to start coming for us. We were taking over the city. The more money we started making, the more enemies we made. Rhino kept ignoring his phone as it rang. I knew it was Belle calling him.

"Don't let your pride cost you," I said without looking at him.

"Man, I swear I ain't ready to talk about it with you," he said never looking at me.

"I feel ya. Just to let you know. It was the worst experience of our lives. Shit, she was saying your name," I said. He looked at me. I shrugged my shoulders.

"If I ever catch you looking at her funny, I'll kill ya," He warned me.

I chuckled, "Don't act like you wasn't almost foul."

I laughed with him and shook my head. He reached his hand out, "We good."

I shook his hand. I guess with Shaka laying in surgery he realized how short life can be. You can lose someone without having a chance to resolve issues or tell them how you feel. They always considered me the soft one. Often told me I was too emotional. I had to be the balance between the two of them. Shaka didn't have enough emotions, and Rhino had too much anger. I felt like I was the balanced one.

A couple of hours later, the doctor came to inform us Shaka was out of surgery. We waited until they moved him to a room before seeing him. He was hit twice. Once in the arm and chest. He was knocked out cold. I called Los to put ears and eyes on the streets to find info about the hit. I texted Miriam to tell her to get Jetta to the hospital.

Belle

"Miriam, you have every reason to be angry with me. I just didn't know how to tell anyone. I was so scared of being judged, and losing Rhino," I said as we sat at a table in the country club.

She took a deep breath. "I was angry because I thought you wanted him. I thought you were still sleeping with him. I can't fault you for what happened in the past. I see how much you love Rhino and I know how much Titan loves me. We all have faults."

I breathed a sigh of relief. "Thank you for understanding. I hope you and Titan can work things out."

She smiled, "We have."

I smiled at her, "I'm happy for you. Fair warning, his mother is crazy."

She laughed, "I know. I had the pleasure of meeting her. She threatened to slice and dice my pretty ass if I hurt her son."

I laughed and nodded my head, "Sounds like her."

Miriam stayed and help me clean up the mess. We talked about Hannah. She was excited to meet her. I'd been calling Rhino ever since we left the country club. I finally gave up. I went home to Granny and Hannah. Those were the only two people that I knew would always love and forgive me for my mistakes. Granny was watching television. I went next door to get Hannah from Pam. She was taking a nap on the couch. Pam insisted I let her finish her nap. I decided to come back later to get her. I was getting ready to walk back inside our apartment when Jetta called my phone hysterical.

"Jetta, you gotta calm down. I can't understand anything you're saying," I told her.

She cried more. "It's gone. All of it is gone!" I had no idea what she was talking about.

"Jetta, what's gone?" I asked.

"The money!" She screamed. I almost dropped my phone. Shaka was going to kill her if she didn't find that money.

"I'm on my way," I said ending the call.

*****

I went back and asked Pam to watch Hannah and check on Granny. I didn't know what I could do for Jetta, but I had to try and help her find that money. I hurried to her father's house. When I arrived at the house, Jetta was in the study frantically typing on the keyboard.

She looked up at me with fearful eyes. “It’s not here, Belle.”

“Let me see,” I said. She started going through her accounts. I stood behind her to see if she was overlooking the transaction. Nothing was there.

“I can’t even find the account the money was transferred into,” she said steadily clicking buttons.

I know Jetta couldn’t have taken the money from Shaka’s account on her own. “Who helped you do this Jetta?”

“Lyle, I’ve been trying to call him. He’s not answering,” she said.

“Maybe Miriam knows where he’s at,” I said as I dialed her number. Miriam never answered her phone.

“What am I going to do?” Jetta asked with tearful eyes.

Shaka was really going to shit bricks. I didn’t know how to help her. I prayed Miriam would be able to find Lyle. I thought God was answering my prayers when Miriam rushed into the den .

“Jetta, we have to go the hospital. Shaka has been shot. He was just getting out of surgery when Titan texted me,” Miriam said . Jetta jetted out the chair.

*****

Within no time, we were breaking speed limits on our way to the hospital. We were given Shaka's room number at the front desk. Jetta was an emotional wreck. Jetta ignored the nurse at the front desk when she told us only two visitors at a time. She chased Jetta to the room trying to stop her.

"You can't go in there. He already has two visitors," the nurse said.

"I wouldn't give a damn if Trump's ignorant ass was in there. I'm going," she said mean mugging the nurse.

"Yo, she can go in," Titan said stepping out. Rhino followed behind him.

"He's okay?" Jetta asked staring at Titan.

"He will be. He's resting now," Rhino answered.

He walked past them and grabbed me by the hand. I followed behind him to the waiting room. I know he was going to give me hell for the way things turned out with his parents. If I had known they felt that way about his talent, I would've never invited them. He has a gift that he deserves to be proud of. They made his talent feel like a curse or something. I sat beside him in the waiting area.

"I'm sorry. I didn't know they felt that way," I said before he spoke.

"I started painting in third grade. All the teachers complimented me on my pictures. They tried to get my parents to put me in art classes, but they didn't. My father and grandfather told me no one would take a black man seriously as an artist. They said it was for gay men. I had an older brother. He killed himself when he was fourteen. I was in the fourth grade when it happened. He was gay. He lived a life of hell when he admitted it to our parents. He couldn't take the verbal and physical abuse from our old man and Granddaddy. He tried to beat him into being a straight man . When I was in the seventh grade, I had a crush on this girl. I painted a picture for her. I took it to school to give to her. At first, she liked it. Once all the kids started laughing and calling me gay, she gave it back. I couldn't stop though. I loved painting. I would paint and hide them. I could never hide them good enough. My parents would always find them. My Granddaddy would beat me like a damn slave. He said he was going to make me a man. He said only soft as boys would want to be an artist. I'm not talking about regular ass whoopings. He would beat me until I promised never to paint again. I would stop for a while but start back. I pour my emotions into my artwork."

"I'm so sorry. There are plenty of black painters, but I'm sure you already know that. They just don't get the recognition like most white artist. Never let anyone make you feel ashamed of your gift."

"I appreciate what you did," he said staring at me. I smiled. "I'm fucking yo ass up for breaking in my shit."

I giggled, "I'm sorry."

"I know that was some shit Jetta had her hand in," he said shaking his head. I didn't reply.

"And us?" I asked hoping he was ready to forgive me.

"I don't know," he said staring at me. I felt it in my heart, I had lost him.

Jetta

I sat beside Shaka's bed thankful that he was going to be okay. I know he is furious with me. I would rather have him mad at me than dead. I had to fix all the messes I had made. I left the room to find Miriam. She was standing in the hall talking to Titan.

"I need to talk to you," I said to her. Titan went back in the room with Shaka.

"Where's Lyle?" I asked.

"I don't know. I left him. What's going on?" She asked curiously. My stomach started to do flips.

"Miriam, I think I've made a huge mistake," I said as tears filled my eyes.

"What's wrong?" She asked.

"I was furious with Shaka for not telling me Daddy had stopped treatments. Lyle hacked the computer in the study and found Daddy's money in an account. I asked Lyle to move the money into another account. He said he set up an account for me, but I can't find it."

Miriam's mouth dropped open. I knew then what happened. Lyle has stolen all the money in the account. She told me the last time she saw Lyle he was packing to leave town. Everything in my stomach felt as if it was going to come up. I fell against the wall, weak from being overwhelmed.

"What am I going to do?" I asked Miriam.

"Don't worry. I might be able to find it. I burned everything from his laptop to mine. I took all his money from his accounts. Maybe we can find the one your money is in. I'll explain why on the way to the hotel," she said.

*****

We left the hospital and headed to the hotel where she was staying. I couldn't believe everything she was telling me about Lyle. She had been trying to find the videos of her father to destroy them. She found out his business was in the red. He was broke. I felt bad for not being there for her when she was going through hell with him. I'm glad she found the strength to leave him. I paced the floor while she searched for the account. We spent hours unable to find the account.

"Hold on!" Miriam said just as I was about to give up hope on finding the money. She rapidly started punching the keyboard .

"Damn it! I can't figure out the password ," she said angrily.

"What is it?" I asked rushing to her side.

"There's some secret folders, but I need the password to get in them," she said. After numerous attempts, she was still unsuccessful. I had given up hope. Everything Daddy worked for was gone.

"I'm such a fuck up," I said flopping down on the sofa in the sitting area.

"We'll figure this out," she said sitting next to me.

"You don't understand, Mir. This isn't the only bad decision I made," I said.

I went on to tell her about my involvement with Cassius. I hadn't heard from him since Shaka made him leave the house. I knew it was only a matter of time before he showed up again. I decided not to sit and wait for him to destroy my life. I left Miriam at the hotel trying to break into Lyle's secret files.

*****

I went back to the hospital to check on Shaka. He was still asleep. I sat quietly orchestrating a plan to get Cassius out of my life. I had to get that video from him. I wanted to get Xavier's family jewels, also. I knew the only way I could do that was to give him the money he wanted. I was flat broke. I gave every damn dime of Daddy's money to Lyle. I knew Shaka would hate me forever once he wakes up and finds out what I've done. I breathed a sigh of relief when he started to wake up.

"Hi," I said smiling at him .

He stared at me for a few minutes before trying to sit up. I called for a nurse to come check him out. I stood by his bed quietly as the nurse checked all his vitals. He never said a word to me or her. I couldn't read his facial expression. He reminded me of the Shaka I first met. It was like he had no emotions. He only nodded his head when the nurse asked was he thirsty. She left and returned with something to drink for him. He finally spoke when she left the room.

"Where's my phone?" He asked.

"I-I don't know. I haven't thought about your belongings. My only concern was you," I said softly.

He pushed the button for the nurse. When she came back in the room, he asked for his phone. A different nurse returned with his belongings. She was a young, pretty, chocolate girl. She smiled at him as she placed his belongings on the bed beside him.

"We were so worried about you. I'm glad to see you awake," she said still smiling.

"As you can see, he's fine. You can leave now," I said staring at her.

"I'm his nurse. It's my job to be here," she stated with an attitude.

"It's going to be my job to whoop yo ass if you don't leave out this room," I warned her.

I couldn't fight at all, but I'll take an ass whooping to stake my claim. It didn't take a genius to see she wanted him. She rolled her eyes and walked out the room. He looked at me and shook his head. He declined my offer to go get him something to eat.

"You put the money back in the account?" He asked.

I had no choice but to lie. I couldn't tell him. I still had hope Miriam could get into files. I had to get the money before he was released from the hospital. I figured I had a few of days before he was released. That should give me enough time to fix the mess I made. He typed away on his phone ignoring me like I wasn't there.

"I'm sorry. How long are you going to stay mad at me?" I asked.

"Go home, Jetta," he said never looking at me.

"No," I said adamantly.

He pushed the button for the nurse to come dismiss me from the room. I was furious at this point. I stood up and walked toward the door but turned around. I walked over to his bed and punched him in his wounded arm. He bellowed in pain as I ran out the door. I ran into Belle almost knocking her down.

"What's wrong?" She asked worriedly.

"Nothing, he threw me out the room. He's still furious about the money," I said.

"I was just getting off from work. I wanted to stop by and check on you and him. I guess this isn't the time," she said.

"No, it isn't. I lied and told him I returned the money. I only pray Mir can get into those files she found. Listen, I'm planning a meeting with Cassius. I need to get that video from him. Will you come with me?" I asked. I had no plan.

I would brainstorm tonight and decide how to proceed. Belle didn't want to come with me. She pleaded with me to let Shaka handle it. I didn't want him to know anything about my past with Cassius. I pleaded with her to come with me until I was in tears. She finally agreed to come. I told her I would call her with more details tomorrow. I told her to go in the room and make sure Shaka was okay. I didn't punch him hard, but enough to cause some pain for making me leave.

Shaka

I woke up pouring in sweat trying to catch my breath. My night was filled with nightmares of getting shot. I could feel the hot lead piercing my chest in each nightmare. I know the niggas that tried to kill me and I was going to handle them when they least expected it. They fucked up the job. They thought I was dead. They left me in my doorway leaking blood. I could hear them tearing up my spot looking for more money. I had just did a few pickups, so they had approximately fifty thousand. They left after not being able to find anymore money. There was plenty of money in the house, but I knew they would never find it. After they left, I called 911 before passing out. I looked at my phone to check the time. It was almost three o'clock in the morning. Rhino and Titan was supposed to have been here a couple of hours ago. I was dialing Titan's phone number when they walked through the door.

"What the fuck took y'all so long?" I asked sitting up in the bed.

"We were putting eyes on Fiasco and his boys," Rhino said handing me the duffle bag.

Fiasco was Dayzee's older brother. He never liked me. He tried working for me but I didn't like the way he moved. I heard them mentioning Dayzee's name as they ransacked my spot. I knew I fucked up when I brought her to my spot.

"Man, you ain't well enough to be leaving the hospital," Titan advised me.

He was right, but I didn't give a damn. I ignored him and snatched all the tubes from my body. I forced myself to sit up and started getting dressed. The pain in my shoulder and chest was almost unbearable. It was hard to breathe . I wasn't going to let it stop me from handling my business. There was no way I was staying in this hospital. I had too much shit going on. Niggas wasn't going to walk on the same earth as me after coming for my head. Plus, Jetta was on some sneaky shit. I could feel it in my bones. I was still mad as hell at her. I can't believe she moved the money from the account. I know she didn't do it on her own. All I could think was she had Cassius help her move it. She better pray that isn't the case. I needed to get back to Omega's house to make sure the money was there. Right now, I didn't trust a word coming from Jetta's mouth.

"Y'all good?" I asked Titan and Rhino. With being shot, I forgot they were beefing. They glanced at each other and nodded their heads.

"I mean are y'all truly straight? I can't be having y'all giving each other side eyes when we out here trying to make moves," I asked.

"Man, we copacetic," Rhino said impatiently. I chuckled and shook my head.

"What are you doing?" the pretty nurse asked walking in the room.

"Getting the hell out of here," I said continuing to dress.

"You can't leave. You aren't well enough. The doctor is coming in today to check up on you," she said.

"Yo man, we can handle it. You need to rest," Titan said.

"It's mine to handle. Y'all can step out while I slip on my jeans," I said staring at him.

"I'll help you," the nurse said.

Rhino laughed, "Shit, you seem a little too eager to help."

I declined her offer and dismissed her out the room. She told me to stop by the nursing station to get some pills for the pain before I left. I didn't even take time to wash my ass. I wanted to get out of there before the doctor made his rounds. I was weak as hell and feeling pain like I never felt before. After declining her offer to take her phone number,

I grabbed the pills and left the hospital with Titan and Rhino.

*****

"Los has some boys sitting on them," Titan said as we entered Rhino's car. I popped the top off the pill bottle and took two of them. I had to ease the pain.

"Man, you look bad as fuck. You need to take yo ass back in the hospital," Rhino said glancing at me.

"I'm good. Just take me where they at," I ordered.

I sat in the back seat resting as they drove. They woke me up when we reached our destination. I looked around to see if I knew where we were. I chuckled when I realized we were in Dayzee's neighborhood. I never thought I would have to kill a female, but she good as dead. One of Los' workers jogged down the street to the car. He informed us it was three guys and Dayzee in the house. It had to be the three that robbed me. I told them to watch our backs as we made our way inside the house.

"Save Dayzee and her bitch ass brother for me," I told Titan and Rhino.

Rhino went around the back while me and Titan went to the front door. We could hear loud music and talking from outside. I nodded my head telling Titan to knock on the door. The pills I took had me groggy. I tried to keep my blurry eyes focused. Titan knocked on the door as hard as he could. He had to bang hard to be heard over the loud music.

"Who the fuck is it?" Fiasco asked.

We both remained quiet. We stood on each side of the door with our backs against the wall waiting for it to open. He asked again who was at the door. We remained quiet. He started unlocking the latches on the door. As soon as the door opened , we both rushed in.

"Oh shit!" Fiasco roared running through the house. The other two guys jumped up form a card table and started firing shots trying to take cover. Titan covered me as I ran through the house at Fiasco.

"Caught this mothafucka trying to run out the back door," Rhino said with a big smile. He was holding a gun to the back of Fiasco's head.

"I got him. It's quiet as fuck in there. Check on Titan and find Dayzee. She probably upstairs hiding," I told him.

I held my gun to Fiasco's forehead, "Where my money?"

"Man, I got it. Just don't fucking kill me. I got a baby on the way," he pleaded. Too bad he didn't consider my life's worth when he tried to kill me.

"Get my money and I'll think about it," I demanded.

"I-It's in the den," he said.

I nodded my head for him to walk. I followed behind him with the gun to the back of his head. He wasted no time getting the money out of a small safe. I could tell they had spent some. I wasn't concerned about the money. I could make it up in a day. He had to die off GP. You can't steal from a nigga, try to kill him and expect to live. It doesn't play out that way in the hood. I ordered him to follow me to the kitchen. I put on the latex gloves I took from the hospital.

"Man, what," was all he said before a gunshot went off.

I prayed Titan and Rhino were okay. I kept my eye on him as I backed out of the kitchen. The other two guys were on the floor dead. Rhino and Titan came down the stairs arguing.

"What was that shot?" I asked looking at them.

"Man, he killed her," Titan said in a low voice. I still had Fiasco in my eye sight.

“What?” I asked in disbelief.

“Man, that bitch jumped out the closet trying to tase us. That’s why he got white shit on the side of his mouth,” Rhino said looking at Titan. I had to laugh, because Titan did have spit coming out his mouth. He wiped his mouth with the back of his hand.

“You could’ve just wounded her,” I said.

“Fuck that, she was gone die anyway. You look like you only good for one kill anyway ,” he said looking at me. I felt like I could pass out at any time.

“Yo, guess who else was upstairs?” Rhino asked with a big smile. I asked who, to appease him. “Bri’s bitch ass baby daddy. The nigga was under the bed naked.”

I squinted my eyes. “I only heard one shot.”

“Because I broke his damn neck,” Rhino said.

Titan laughed, “This fool apologized to him for beating him with a can of baked beans, and asked for a hug.” I laughed and shook my head.

Titan shook his head, “Man, we gotta get out of here. We don’t have time for landscaping this nigga.”

Rhino looked at my latex gloves and smiled, “Let’s take him to one of the traps. You know I like seeing you work.”

*****

We put him in the trunk and drove to a safe house we used. Rhino laid the plastic over the floor while Fiasco cried and pleaded for his life. I started with his fingers as I told him a story about the first time I got caught stealing food to survive. Every time I cut a finger off, Rhino would pick it up and throw it at Titan. He loved seeing shit like this. He was barely conscious when I started on his toes. By the time I was done with his fingers and toes, he had went into shock from the pain. I slit his throat from ear to ear to take him out his misery. Titan called Los to come in and clean up the mess. I was too exhausted to deal with Jetta tonight. I needed to go home and get some sleep. I was weak and sweating profusely. I had them drop me off. I soaked in the tub before crashing in my bed.

Belle

"What exactly is the plan?" I asked Jetta over the phone.

"You will be hiding in one of the bedrooms with a gun. Once he shows me the tape, you will come out with the gun. I'll tie him up and take the tape. Once I have everything I want, we will let him go. No one will be hurt," she exclaimed.

I've never held a gun, much less shot one. I was horrified at the thought of pointing a gun at someone. I know this was a bad idea, but I couldn't deny her help. I tried convincing her to ask Rhino and Titan for help, but she declined. She was determined that Shaka could not find out what she was doing.

"What time are we supposed to be doing this?" I asked.

"I'll pick you up about eight o'clock tonight," she informed me.

"Ok, I'll be ready," I said nervously. I prayed everything went as planned.

"Have you been to see Shaka this morning?" I asked.

"No, and I'm not going or calling. He threw me out because he's still mad. If he wants to see me, he'll call. I just pray I get this money before he gets out. It's going to be hell if I don't," she said.

"If this goes bad, he's really going to be pissed. Maybe you should just tell him," I advised her.

"It's not going to go wrong. Cass doesn't think I'm smart enough to outsmart him. He'll never expect me to double cross him," she explained.

I had a call coming through. My heart pounded as I smiled when I saw Rhino's picture on the screen. He usually called me every night before I go to bed and every morning. He didn't call me last night or this morning, so I was worried. I hurried and answered the phone.

"Hi," I said softly.

"Where you at?" He asked.

"I'm at work. Why? Do you want to see me?" I asked. I held my breath hoping he say yes.

"Nah, I was just calling. I don't want shit. Get back to work," he said nonchalantly.

"Rhino, I'm sorry. How long are you going to stay mad at me?" I asked.

"I'll holla at you later. I got some shit to do," he said ending the call.

I was furious. I didn't feel like he was being fair. He had forgiven Titan, but not me. I finished the rest of my shift thinking about all the things I wanted to say to him. My problem was I forget everything I want to say when I'm with him. I'm so happy when I'm with him, I forget everything he said or did to make me mad.

"What's the matter with you?" Quita asked.

"I'm okay. Me and Rhino just going through a rough patch," I said.

"Girl, forget that nigga. He a dog anyway. He fucked me and never called me again," she said.

"What?" I asked angrily.

She laughed, "You said you didn't like him. So, we fucked." I wanted to whoop her ass, but I held my composure.

"You knew I liked him," I stated.

She shrugged her shoulders, "But you said you didn't."

I was furious. Before she knew it, my fist was ramming into her jaw. She pushed me and charged into me. We started swinging at each other. We were knocking over equipment behind the counter until two employees pulled us apart. I knew I had lost my job, so I jumped in my car and left. I can't believe Rhino. Here I was feeling guilty about something I did years ago, and he been fucking my coworker. I wanted to confront Rhino about his cheating ass but decided to let it go. I should've known he was cheating anyway. I decided to spend the rest of my day with my daughter until it was time to meet Jetta.

*****

Later that evening

"Hey Daddy's girl," Titan said when he opened the door. They had developed a bond in such a short time. Her face gleamed with joy when he picked her up. He picked her up and smothered her face with kisses.

"Thanks for watching her. I shouldn't be long," I said.

"You don't have to thank me for watching my Princess," he said smiling down at her.

"Daddy can I watch your big TV?" She asked excited.

"Yea, go ahead," he said. She took off running down the hall.

"Stop running, Hannah," I demanded.

"You can just let her stay the night. I'm in for the night. Miriam coming over to meet her. I hope that's okay," he said.

"It's fine. I'm glad you are working things out with her," I said.

Titan started asking questions about my plans for the night. He wanted to know why Miriam wasn't hanging out with me and Jetta, tonight. I always get nervous when I lie. I knew he could tell I was hiding something. I decided to change the subject before I spilled my guts.

"How's Shaka doing?" I asked.

He laughed, "That fool discharged his self from the hospital last night." My heart dropped. It was only a matter of time before he found out about the money. I hurried out the house and called Jetta.

"Shaka is out of the hospital," I said when she answered.

"What?" She screamed.

"Titan just told me. He's probably going to be coming there soon. I'm sure he knows the money isn't there," I warned her.

"Oh God, he's going to kill me," she said with fear.

"Go to him. Don't wait until he finds out. We both know how things turn out when we do that," I told her.

She sighed heavily, "Ok, forget the plan. We'll do it later tonight. I'll call you."

“Ok, I’m free for the night. Just call me anytime,” I said.

“Thanks Belle. I really appreciate you being a good friend. I would ask Mir, but she’s trying to crack that file for me,” she said.

“No problem,” I said ending the call.

I hoped Jetta would tell Shaka about the money and Cassius. Rhino was calling my phone nonstop. I didn’t have anything to say to him at this point. He was such a hypocrite. Since we weren’t meeting Cassius as planned, I decided to enjoy some me time. I hadn’t been to the movies in a while. I decided to catch a movie before returning home. I went to pull out of Titan’s yard, but was stopped by Rhino pulling in the driveway.

“Get out the got damn car!” he said trying to open my door.

“No, fuck you! Go fuck Quita!” I yelled. I made sure my doors were locked and windows were up .

“You got five seconds to fissure this door,” he said staring through the window at me.

I stuck my middle finger in the air and ignored him. I watched him as he walked to the opposite side of my car pulling his tee shirt over his head. I had no idea what he was going to do. He wrapped the tee shirt around his hand

and punched the window hard enough to shatter it. I screamed in disbelief at what he had done. I tried jumping out the car and running in Titan's house, but I wasn't quick enough. He picked me up and threw me over his shoulder.

"Yo, y'all gotta get out of my neighborhood with that hood shit!" Titan yelled as he stood on the porch.

"Fuck you, Titan! Tell him to put me down!" I screamed. He laughed and walked back in the house.

*****

I didn't realize how crazy he was until he tossed me in the trunk of his car. All kinds of crazy thoughts started going through my mind. I knew he was going to kill me. I decided Titan wanted him to kill me, so he could raise Hannah. I wondered who would be there for my Granny. I cried, prayed and repented until I felt the car stop. It felt like we had drove forever. When he popped the trunk open, I started pleading for my life. He threw me over his shoulder and I kicked and screamed for my life. He didn't put me down until we were upstairs in his bedroom.

"Man, shut the hell up! Ain't nobody gone kill yo nerdy ass!" He demanded.

I exhaled relieved to know my life would be spared. After realizing he was sparing my life, I became furious. I started crying and throwing punches at his chest. He wrapped his arms around me pulling me in a bear hug. I pulled away from him and slapped him.

"You are fucking Quita!" I yelled.

"I fucked the bitch before we hooked up," he said.

"I don't care! You judge me, but you are no better," I told him.

"I didn't fucking lie to you. You have a whole child by one of my best friends. You kept that secret from me while I fell in love with your nerdy ass," he stated furiously.

I stood there in shock. Never has he used that word with me. "You love me?"

"If I didn't, you would be dead right now. Don't ever fucking lie to me again, Belle," he said with a stern face.

My eyes shifted from his knowing I was still keeping Jetta's secret from him. I didn't consider it a lie since it wasn't my business. The painting hanging over the fireplace in the sitting area of the bedroom caught my eye. My mouth dropped open as I walked toward it. It was a painting of me. I was wearing my favorite light blue shirt.

My hair was pulled back in a ponytail with a swoop bang. It was a painting of my high school years.

"I always liked when you wore this shirt and your hair like that in school," he said standing behind me.

My eyes became teary. I never knew he saw me. I turned to face him. I tiptoed and pulled his face down to mine. I slid my tongue into his mouth while sucking his into mine. He groaned and wrapped his arms around my waist. After becoming dizzy from our kiss, I kissed my way down to his chest and ripped abdomen. I stared at the huge bulge in his grey sweats before pulling them down. His thick, curved dick sprung out nearly hitting me in the face. He chuckled. I looked up at him and smiled.

I wrapped both hands around his shaft as I licked his mushroom shaped dome. I began stroking and licking up and down his dick getting it super wet. Saliva started to spill from my mouth as I licked and sucked him in and out of my mouth. The low groans and grunts coming from him made me take him farther into my mouth. I started moaning and flicking my tongue up and down his throbbing dick.

"Fuuucckkk!" He barked grabbing a hand full of my hair. He stepped back pulling his dick out of my mouth. I looked up at him to see a disgusted scowl on his face.

"How the fuck you know how to suck dick like that?" He asked angrily.

I giggled and stood up, "I watch a lot of porn. I'm that good?"

"You never sucked dick?" He asked.

"No, I have a vibrator I practice on," I said smiling.

He laughed, "Take off those clothes. I want some of the juice you make."

I giggled and did what he said. Sex between us was different this time. I was in control. I rode him until he was groaning and confessing his love for me. I didn't stop until we exploded together. I fell asleep on top of him wrapped in his arms.

Jetta

I texted Cassius to postpone our meet. I didn't have a plan. I just wanted to see if I could get the tape from him. If everything went well, I could walk away with the tape and Xavier's family jewels. I had to make this happen before Shaka checked the accounts. I pulled into his driveway and took a deep breath before I exited my vehicle. I rang his doorbell several times. After he didn't answer the door, I started to get nervous. I called his phone several times, but he didn't answer. I decided to jimmy the lock.

After breaking in, I found him in his bedroom. He was sleeping soundly in his birthday suit. I stared down at his perfectly sculpted, tattooed, dark chocolate body. Every inch of my body was screaming for him. I never took my eyes off him as I removed my clothes. I straddled his lap, but he never moved. I leaned forward and started placing soft kisses on his lips. He stirred in his sleep, but didn't wake up. I kissed and licked my way down until his rod was inside my mouth. He woke up, but I didn't stop. I looked up into his eyes.

"Damn Jetta," he groaned staring back at me .

My hand glided up and down his rock hard shaft along with my wet mouth. I could feel juices flowing down my thighs from the excitement of having him inside my mouth. I moaned in pleasure sending vibrations through his shaft. He gripped my weave and started pumping in and out of my mouth. The head of his dick was ramming against my throat.

"Play with that pussy for me," he moaned as he fucked my mouth.

I did as he commanded. I massaged my throbbing, wet clit as he drove his dick inside my mouth. I licked, slurped and sucked while pleasuring myself at the same time. His groans became uncontrollable. I slid two fingers inside myself pressing against my soft spot. I moaned loudly with his dick deep inside my mouth as I exploded on my hand. I felt my essence running down on my hand.

I sat up and straddled his lap. I slowly slid down on him. My head fell back as I cried out in ecstasy as his shaft grew inside me. He grabbed my hand and licked my cream from my fingers. I rocked back and forth allowing his dome to hit my walls. I felt myself getting ready to come again. I started bouncing up and down slamming my ass cheeks on his muscular thighs. He sat up and pushed my breasts together. He sucked and bit my hard nipples sending unimaginable sensations through my body.

"Mmmmmm," he groaned as he massaged, licked and sucked my breasts .

He released my breasts and gripped my ass cheeks. He started slamming me down on his dick. I screamed out my love for him.

"Oh God! I love you so much Micah! Yes baby, fuck me hard!" I screamed before exploding like a broken damn during Hurricane Katrina.

"Got damn, this pussy feels good!" He roared.

He flipped me over on my back, and pushed my legs up to my head. He pressed the palms of his hands on the back of my thighs. He started long stroking inside me. His long, slow, deep strokes had tears falling down the side of my face . I could feel every inch of him drilling in and out of my soaked pussy. He drove deep inside me and pressed against my g-spot. My back arched, mouth watered , and body trembled as I came again. Gushy, sloppy sounds echoed throughout the room.

"I fuckin' love you, Jetta! Got damn, I can't get enough of you. Shit, you coming all over my dick," he bellowed.

He pulled out and dipped down. He ate my pussy like a man that's been starving for years. I screamed and cried for mercy only to go unheard. I tried pushing his head away and scooted away. He wasn't having any of it. I felt as if I was going into cardiac arrest. My body couldn't handle the pleasure he was giving me.

"Bring me my got damn pussy!" He barked pulling me back toward him by my thighs.

I don't know what position he put me in. My body was like a pretzel. I couldn't move as he licked and slurped on me. I couldn't stop the tears from falling. He had drained me. All I could do was take the orgasms he was causing to rip through my body. Once he was done, he started licking my salty sweat from my body. He licked and sucked from my toes to my neck before sliding back inside me.

"Ooooohhh Miccccaaahhh!" I wailed. I could feel his heartbeat in his shaft.

"Aaaaarrrrggghhhh! Ffffuuccckkk!" He roared digging deep inside me until his body convulsed and trembled. We exploded at the same time and collapsed in each other's arms

I woke up a few hours later to a snoring Shaka. I noticed his bandage was bleeding through. I realized he had no business having sex the way we just did. I slipped out of bed to find something to change his bandage. I spotted plenty of bandages on his dresser. I grabbed a pill from his medicine bottle and a bottle of water from the small fridge. I woke him up to take the pill, but he wouldn't take it. He did allow me to change his bandages. He fell back to sleep as I changed him. I guess he didn't like the pills, because they made him sleep too much. I took a quick shower and went downstairs. I needed to hear my Daddy's voice. He didn't answer his phone, so I called Papa. He told me Daddy wasn't doing very well. I don't care what he says I'm taking a trip in the morning to see him. I called Cassius for us to meet in the next hour. He agreed. I couldn't reach Belle. I tried calling Miriam, but she wasn't answering her phone. Lucky for me, Shaka left his gun laying on the kitchen counter. I grabbed it and headed out the door. I would have to handle this on my own.

Miriam

I was so nervous about meeting Titan's daughter. I wanted to make a good impression on her. I could tell how much he loved her. His face would brighten up whenever he talked about her. I decided to swing by Walmart to pick her up a couple of gifts before heading to his house. I gave myself a once over in the mirror before heading out of my room. I needed to start looking for a new place to move. I couldn't live out of a hotel too much longer. Especially one that Titan's mother works at. She always rolled her eyes at me when I walked through the lobby. I tried to hurry out of the lobby while she was with a customer.

"Hey," she called out to me before I made it out the door. I walked over to the front desk.

"Hi Ms. Travis, how are you doing this lovely evening?" I asked with a smile. She rolled her eyes at me.

"Don't get smart with me girl," she said.

"I-I wasn't," I said nervously.

"Uhm mm, so you going to meet my granddaughter?" She asked.

I smiled. "Yes ma'am. I'm so excited. I hope she likes me. What kind of things she like. I wanted to go by Walmart and buy her a couple of gifts."

"Are you ready to be a stepmother?" She asked.

I hadn't really thought about the responsibilities of being a stepmother. I just knew I wanted to be a part of Titan's life. I wanted his daughter to love me as much as he loves her. I think I would make a good parent. I knew not to make the same mistakes my parents made with me.

"I don't know if I'm ready, but I know I want to try. I know you don't like me, but I love your son. I promise I will love his daughter just as much. If you give me a chance, you might like me," I said.

"I never said I didn't like yo uppity ass. I can tell you one of those privileged chil'ren. I just want to make sure you are ready for the responsibility before you meet her. You can't walk in and out of her life. So, you need to make sure you can handle it," she advised.

"I'm ready," I said with uncertainty.

"My son loves you," she said.

"I love him too. I've never had anyone treat me like him. He's sweet when I need it and hard when he needs to be with me," I told her.

"Well, I'm gone give you a chance. If you fuck it up, I'm coming for you," she warned me. I knew she was serious.

"Thank you," I said smiling at her.

“She likes to play with makeup,” she informed me. I reached over the counter and hugged her.

“Girl, get yo ass out of here before I hurt you,” she said pulling away from me.

I left out the hotel with a smile on my face. I felt like I was finally living the life I wanted. I wasn’t worried about what my parents thought of my choices. I was living for me now. Just as I was opening my car door, someone snuck up behind me. A wet cloth covered my mouth and everything went black.

Few hours later

“Wake up, bitch!” I heard Lyle’s voice say.

He slapped me across my face nearly knocking me out the chair. My cheek burned from the sting of the slap. It was hard getting my eyelids to open, but they finally did. I looked around and realized I was at my old house. He looked a mess. His eyes were blood red. He needed a haircut. His beard and mustache had grew out. His clothes were wrinkled and hanging on his body. I could smell the alcohol coming from his pores.

“Bitch, where is it?” He asked slapping me again. I had no idea what he was talking about.

"I don't know what you are talking about?" I said as my eyes filled with water.

He wrapped his hands around my neck. "I will kill yo ass. I have nothing to lose. I owe big money to some ugly people. If I don't get that money, I'm dead. If I die, I'm taking yo hoe ass with me."

"I don't have it. I promise," I said as tears started to fall from my eyes. He hit me so hard this time, blood spewed from my mouth.

"I guess that bitch got it back. You better find a way to get the money back to me," he said.

"I don't know what you are talking about?' I lied. I knew he was talking about Jetta's money.

"Call her," he said shoving my phone in my hand.

I dialed Jetta's number, I was relieved when she didn't answer the phone. He was so intoxicated he had forgotten to take the phone from me. I noticed several missed calls from Titan. I pushed the button to dial his number. I held the phone praying he answered. Lyle paced the floor.

"Lyle, she's not answering. Please let me go. I'll help you get the money," I pleaded.

"Bitch, shut up! Let me think!" He barked pointing the gun at me.

"Someone is going to come looking for me at my house. I know someone is looking for me by now," I warned him.

He back handed me, "That fucking drug dealer you fucking? Is that who's looking for you?"

I sobbed silently. I know my face was badly bruised, but I didn't care. I only wanted to get out of here with my life. Lyle pulled out a small vile and started snorting cocaine. I looked at the phone screen and realized Titan was listening to our conversation. He demanded I keep trying to call Jetta, but I didn't. I didn't want to lose the connection I had with Titan.

"Lyle, how long are you going to keep me at my house?" I asked hoping Titan heard my location. Lyle snatched the phone from me. I was relieved when he never looked at the screen. He started pushing numbers on his phone as he paced the floor. I sat quietly waiting for Titan to come save me.

Titan

I was in panic mode. No one was answering their phones. I could hear the distress in Miriam's voice. I was wondering why she didn't show up and I hadn't heard from her. I kept calling her phone. I was relieved when she finally answered only to get upset again. I was going to kill that nigga if he put a hand on her. I jumped out of bed and threw on some clothes. After waking Hannah up and getting her dressed, I hurried out of the house. I kept calling Belle, but she never answered. I decided to call Ma. I needed her to watch Hannah. I dropped her off and headed to Omega's house. After discovering Jetta wasn't there, I went to Shaka's house. I banged on the door for the longest before he answered.

"Where's Jetta?" I asked barging inside the house.

"I don't know. I just woke up," he said running his hand over his face.

"Fuck!" I barked. I prayed Belle knew where Miriam stayed. I was headed back out the door before Shaka stopped me.

"What the fuck going on?" He asked.

"Man, Miriam's ex got her," I told him.

"What you mean?" He asked puzzled.

“I don’t have time to explain. I have to find her,” I said. I headed out the door.

“Let me grab a shirt, and I’ll go with you,” he said as I walked to my car.

A couple of minutes later, we were headed to Rhino’s spot. I explained to Shaka what happened as I drove. He kept trying to call Jetta but was sent to voicemail every time. He started to wonder did Lyle have Jetta also.

“Why would he have Jetta?” I asked.

He told me about Jetta taking her inheritance from an account and putting it into another one. Jetta didn’t know as soon as Shaka found out, he had Genius track Lyle down. He thought it was Cassius, but Genius discovered it was Lyle. He found him in Vegas gambling. Genius slipped into his hotel room and hacked his computer. The money was back in its rightful place.

*****

“Yo, why the hell you banging on the door like the police?” Rhino asked when he opened the door.

“Belle here?” I asked ignoring his question.

"Yea, she upstairs about to have a fucking heart attack. What's going on?" He asked looking at me and Shaka. Shaka ran down everything to him.

"Belle!" He yelled. Belle came down the stairs fully dressed.

"What's wrong?" She asked with fear in her eyes.

Before she could answer, my phone rang. I answered immediately when I saw Miriam's phone number.

"I want two million dollars by midnight tomorrow or the bitch is dead. I'll call back with instructions on the drop," Lyle warned me before hanging up the phone.

"What she say?" Shaka asked.

"That mothafucka wants two mil or he killing her," I told him .

"Damn, is she worth that much?" Rhino asked. I gave him the look of death while Belle hit him in the arm.

"Man, I'm just fucking with you. What's the plan?" He asked.

"Let me think," I said pacing the floor.

"Where's Jetta?" Rhino asked looking at Shaka.

"He's probably got her too. I took the money from his account that she had him help steal from my account," Shaka told him.

"What? Jetta stealing damn money?" Rhino asked surprisingly.

"Jetta was with me tonight. When I woke up, she was gone. She gotta be with Miriam," Shaka said.

"Sh-She's not with Miriam," Belle said in a low, scared voice.

"How you know?" Rhino asked her.

"I didn't hear my phone ringing. I missed several calls from her. I was supposed to go with her tonight," Belle said.

"Go fuckin' where, Belle?" Rhino asked angrily.

She looked at Shaka with tears in her eyes, "She was going to set Cassius up to get the video and jewels from him." We all gave her a confused look.

"Nerd Girl, what the hell you talking about?" Rhino asked her.

"I have to find her," Shaka said storming out the door.

"Yo fam, you don't even know where to look," I said following him outside.

"We were going to meet him at her grandparents' old house," Belle said standing on the front porch.

"Stay yo ass here! I'm fuckin' you up when I get back!" Rhino barked at Belle as he walked out the door pulling a shirt over his head.

"Fuck you Rhino! I'm tired of you talking to me like I'm a child! I don't have to take this shit! Titan, where is Hannah?" Belle asked.

"Chill out, she's with Ma," I said.

Belle stormed toward her car only to be thrown over Rhino's shoulder. She kicked and screamed for him to put her down. Rhino started hollering out in pain.

"Fuck! She got damn biting me!" Rhino barked. He let her go but Belle was latched on to him. She was biting his back and pulling his dreads. We ran over and tried pulling her off of him. She had a death grip on his dreads. Rhino brought a side out in Belle we never knew she had. After tussling with her a few minutes, she released him.

"You fuckin' crazy! I'm gone kill yo ass!" Rhino threatened her as we held her.

"Nigga, you ain't gone do shit. What you gone do is start treating me with some got damn respect or this shit is over! You want crazy, I'll give you crazy. Keep trying me, Brutus!" Belle yelled at him. No one ever called Rhino by his name. He hated it. Me and Shaka dropped our heads. We knew he was going to lose it. He surprised us.

"How I disrespect you, Belle?" He asked calmly. Me and Shaka looked at each other in disbelief.

"Listen, y'all stay and hash this shit out. I gotta go get Jetta," Shaka said walking off.

"Yo, y'all stay here and settle this," I said letting Belle go. I glanced over my shoulder as I walked away. They stood their staring at each other.

"You think she safe with him?" Shaka asked when I hopped in the car.

I chuckled. "That nigga is officially pussy whipped." We pulled out of the driveway while Belle stood in the yard giving Rhino every thought on her mind. He stood there like a scolded child listening.

Jetta

I kept sending Shaka to voice mail. I know he was wondering where I disappeared to in the middle of the night. I had to come and get this over with. I was about to do something I never imagined I would do. I had to kill Cassius. It was the only way out of this mess. I would do anything to protect my relationship with Shaka. I know he would never forgive me if he knew my past. I was going to make sure it was buried with Cassius. I was growing impatient waiting on him. My palms were sweaty and my heart was pounding. My stomach started churning when I saw head lights shining through the window. Cassius had arrived. I was going to make sure he had the video and jewels before I killed him. I had taken all the money from Daddy's safes. It was over two hundred thousand dollars. I stacked the real money over fake money in a briefcase . I paced the floor until I heard the door open. Cassius walked in with a small duffel bag. The sight of him made my skin crawl. I never thought I would want to end someone's life, but he made the thought possible.

"Jedi," he said giving me his charismatic smile. I rolled my eyes at him.

"Let's make this quick. Let me see the tape and jewels," I demanded. He walked closer to me.

"Not until I see the money," he said staring at me.

I walked over to the desk and popped open the briefcase . He stared at the money with wide eyes. I held my breath as he flipped through the money. I stared at him. I thought I was busted until the huge grin appeared on his face. I snatched the duffle bag from his hand and poured everything on the table. Memories of Xavier flooded my mind as I looked at his family jewels. I didn't know how I was going to get them back to his family, but I was going to make it happen.

"How do I know you don't have the video still in your phone?" I asked.

"You don't. You will just have to take my word for it," he said smiling. It didn't matter, because I was going to kill him.

"There's one more thing that will make this transaction complete," he said before licking his lips. I knew exactly what he was suggesting, but he had to be out of his mind.

"You are gay," I said stepping backward.

"No, I'm sexually free. I fuck whoever I want. Right now, it's you," he said walking up to me.

I slapped him across the face and pushed him in the chest. He wrapped his arms around my waist. I struggled to get out his grip causing the gun I had behind my back to fall to the floor. We both stopped and looked down on the floor at the gun. I tried to react fast enough to pick it up, but he kicked it away from me. He rushed over and picked it up off the floor.

"Oh sweet Jedi, what are you doing with a gun?" He asked with a smile. I didn't reply as he walked toward me holding the gun. He ran the gun along the side of my face.

"I always wanted to know was your pussy as sweet as you smelled," he said as his other hand roamed between my inner thighs .

I couldn't stop the tears from building up in my eyes. I know he's going to rape me and there wasn't anything I could do about it. I finally realized how stupid I was for coming here alone. I wanted to fix this mess on my own, but I failed. Now, I'm going to have to pay the price. Shaka wasn't here to save me this time. Tears started to fall down my face when he demanded I remove my clothes. I thought of fighting him, but I know I would lose. If I do what he says, I could at least walk away with my life. I sobbed softly as he watched me remove my clothes. I felt as if I was going to vomit as his hands caressed my flesh. He gazed over my body as he held the gun.

"Lay on the couch and spread those thick, chocolate thighs. I'm going to taste you first. When I'm done, you're going to suck my dick. Then, I will fuck you in both holes, since I'm gay," he said winking at me.

He grabbed me around the waist and pushed me down on the sofa in the living room. I tried not to cry, but I couldn't help it. This was my punishment for all the wrong I did with him. I stole from men that cared about me. I was responsible for Xavier taking his life. No one can ever run from their past. This moment proves it.

"Shut the fuck up!" He demanded angrily as he positioned his body on top of mine.

He was still holding on to the gun. All I could do was close my eyes and pray for it to be over. He started licking on my neck as his free hand massaged my breasts . His tongue started lapping circles around my nipples and his finger slid between my slit . My sobs were loud to the point I couldn't stop crying. *POW!* It felt as if my heart stopped . The gun went off, but I wasn't in pain. I felt wetness on my face. I felt the weight of his body on me then it wasn't. I slowly opened my eyes to see the most beautiful, black man I've ever known. Shaka was standing over Cassius's lifeless body. Cassius's brains and blood was spilling out the side of his head. The wetness on my face was his blood splattered on me. I jumped up off the sofa and wrapped my arms around his neck and cried my eyes out.

"I'm sorry," I said holding him as tight as I could.

Without saying a word, he unwrapped my hands from around his neck. I noticed Titan standing in the corner with his back turned. I realized I was still naked. At this moment, I didn't have any shame. I was too grateful for them coming here to save me.

"Get dressed and take yo ass home," Shaka demanded with cold eyes. I opened my mouth to say something, but kept quiet. The look in his eyes told me this wasn't the time.

"Yo, call Los in to clean this shit up," he said to Titan.

Titan stepped outside to make his call never turning around. Shaka grabbed the briefcase and duffle bag. He walked out the door never saying another word to me. I did all this to save my relationship with him, but it seems like it did just the opposite.

Shaka

I don't know if I was angrier with myself or her. That nigga was going to rape her and possibly kill her. I failed at protecting her. I became so wrapped up in loving her, I forgot to protect her first before anything. I don't know what she was thinking meeting him alone. I knew it was something up with the nigga being here. I still don't know what the situation is she got herself into with him. I know it's some shady shit. I had a background check ran on him. He was a con artist. I wanted to bring him back from death and kill him again for putting his hands on her. Every time I think there is growth in her, she does some dumb shit to remind me how childish she is. I needed to stay as far away from her as possible. I placed her money in her account. I know Omega didn't want her to have it until she matured, but I couldn't deal with her anymore. I was too emotionally attached to her. I wasn't thinking like the protector I was once was with her. I was letting her get away with shit I normally didn't condone. She was steady blowing my phone up, but I kept sending her to voice mail. By the time me and Titan made it to my house, the sun was coming up.

"I know you mad at Jetta, but we need Miriam's address," Titan said as we sat in my den.

We were both trying to figure out how to get Miriam out safely. He was right. As much as I hated to do it, I texted Jetta asking for Miriam's address. Just like I expected , she called my phone without replying to the text.

"Yo, I don't have time to discuss shit with you. All I need is Miriam's address," I stated when I answered.

"Why?" She asked.

"Jetta, just give me the fucking address please," I pleaded impatiently.

She ran the address down to me with sadness in her voice. Just the sound of her broken voice did something to me, but I couldn't let that distract me right now. I had to help get Miriam back to Titan. I hung up the phone, before I fell into her spell.

"We'll make our move as soon as the sun sets ," I said looking at Titan. He nodded his head.

"We gone get her out. He ain't built for this shit," I said trying to lift the worry off Titan's face.

"Yea, I gotta go check on Hannah. I don't know whether Belle and Rhino decided to reenact *War of the Roses* or make up," he said.

I had no idea what *War of the Roses* was. I'm sure it was some romantic type of movie. That's the type of man Titan was. I took a long shower after Titan left. I changed the bandages on my wounds. The pain was severe, but I couldn't take a pill to ease it. I had work to do.

*****

I hopped in my very first car I purchased. It was an old model mustang. I only bought it because it was cheap and I needed a ride. I kept it for sentimental reasons. I put a lot of work into it over the years. Now, it runs like a brand new car. I headed to my destination. I parked several houses from the location. I pulled my cap down and observed my surroundings before getting out the truck. It was still early in the morning, so mostly everyone was at work in this neighborhood. I was dressed in a business suit and carrying a briefcase . In case anyone was home peeping out their windows I would look like an insurance salesman or something. I walked around to the back of the house. All the blinds were pulled down, so I couldn't see inside the house. I carefully started picking the back door lock. I was skilled at breaking into houses, so the door opened easily. The moment the door open I heard Lyle's voice. He was on the phone.

"Man, just give me until morning. I'll have all your money. I got some shit put together," he said into phone. While he kept talking, I eased farther inside the house.

"I swear Dolla. The money is coming," Lyle assured him.

Dolla was a loan shark. He would kill you if you came up a dollar short of what you owe him. I remember hiding in an abandoned house when I watched him slaughter a man for not paying him back. He did some of the most fowl things to the man with a knife. I would love to see him do them to Lyle. If Lyle thought he was going to pay Dolla back with our money, he was mistaken. I followed his voice. He was pacing the floor in the den. Anger and hurt took over me when I saw Miriam tied to a chair. Her face was badly bruised and mouth was gagged. Lyle turned his back from the den's entrance. I showed enough of myself to get Miriam's attention. Her eyes were big when she saw me. I put my finger to my lips for her to remain quiet. Tears started to fall from her eyes. I knew they were tears of joy that someone was coming to save her. Lyle sat behind a small desk and started snorting lines of coke. His gun was laying on the table next to him. I walked a few feet down the hall into the kitchen. I rattled a few dishes loud enough for him to hear. I stood against the kitchen wall waiting for him to come in. Just like I suspected, he came running into the kitchen with his gun. I hit him with the butt of my gun and he went crashing to the floor. His gun flew from his hand and across the floor. I kicked and stomped him until he was unconscious. I rushed back into the room to untie Miriam. She cried and collapsed in my arms. I laid her on the couch. I went back in the kitchen to make sure Lyle was out.

I called Rhino's phone, "Yo, get in touch with Dolla. Tell him I got a package for him."

I picked Lyle up off the floor and carried him into the den. I gagged him and tied him to the chair Miriam was in. She started to wake up. She sat up and looked around. She went fucking crazy. She started cussing at Lyle as she attacked him. I didn't stop her. I let her unleash the anger she had on him. His groans were muffled from the gag. She clawed into his flesh with her nails, and punched him in the face. I had to grab my own dick when she kicked him between the legs. The chair fell over with him in it. She didn't stop until she heard my phone ring . It was Dolla.

"What you got for me?" He asked.

"That payment you supposed to be receiving in the morning. It's not going to happen. I'm sitting here with the lying nigga now," I said.

"Bring the bitch ass nigga to me," he said.

I called Los and told him where to pick Lyle up. I knew Dolla was going to pay for delivering Lyle. I told him to keep whatever it was. I stayed there with Miriam until Los showed up. Once he came, it was time to get her to Titan.

*****

She fell asleep time we got in my car. She was still asleep when I pulled into Titan's driveway. I gently shook her to wake her up. I wanted to go back and stomp him some more for the bruises on her face. After realizing where we were, she jumped out the car. She banged on the door until he flung it open. The expression on Titan's face was priceless. He pulled Miriam into his arms and held her tight as she cried. I walked up to the door. I looked at him as he held her.

"If I hadn't taken the money out his account, this wouldn't have happened. I owed you this. Lil Mama here fucked him up really good, before delivering him to Dolla. He owes him some money," I said. He nodded his head.

"I'm gone let you take care of her. I'll holla at you later," I said before walking away.

My phone rang the moment I sat in my car. It was Jetta again. As much as I wanted to ignore the call, something told me to answer it.

"Yea," I answered.

She was crying softly, "He's gone." *Damn!*

A Week Later

Jamaica

Jetta

Anyone who meant anything to Daddy had taken the trip to Jamaica for his burial. He wanted to be buried near his parents. He said he didn't want fake people attending his funeral. He knew there would be many if it was Atlanta. I pleaded with him so many times to let me come visit him, but he wouldn't allow it. When we viewed his body, I collapsed in Shaka's arms. The man laying in the casket wasn't my daddy. His skin was dark and face sunken in. He had loss tremendous weight. The embalming added weight to his skeletal frame. I said my final goodbyes to him at the graveyard. I promised to make him proud. He felt like he failed me by spoiling me. I prayed he died knowing how much his love meant to me. When we got back to my Grandparents' house for the Repass , I went upstairs to the bedroom. I didn't have an appetite and wasn't in the mood to converse with anyone. I just wanted to turn back the hands of time to the day I made the mistake of walking out of Daddy's life. I sat up in the bed and wiped my tears when someone knocked on the door.

"Come in," I said.

Shaka opened the door holding a plate of food. He sat it on the nightstand . He looked so handsome in his Kiton's black suit. We hadn't talked much since he killed Cassius. He came over the day I called him about Daddy's death. He held me in his arms the entire night. We talked about Daddy until I drifted off to sleep. He had never worn a suit, so I accompanied him to purchase one. He flipped out when he saw the price of the suit I picked out for him. That was the first day I laughed since Daddy's death. Shaka wasn't frugal, but he didn't like to splurge unnecessarily. He decided attending Daddy's funeral in class and style was worth the money. He's been by my side every day, but I can feel him trying to keep his distance from me. I don't even know if he still loves me. He never truly looks at me anymore. He hasn't mentioned Cassius and neither have I. I just wanted to forget it all happened.

"Thank you, but I'm not hungry," I said softly.

"You need to eat something. You haven't eaten a full meal in a week, Jetta," he said. I would only nibble on whatever food he tried to give me.

"What are we going to do with everything he owns?" I asked before he walked out the room. I didn't want to be the one responsible for handling his estate. Shaka was the one who was always there for him.

"Everything is yours, Jetta. It's all in his will," he said turning to face me.

"What about you?" I asked.

"He gave me everything I needed while he was alive. He built everything for you," he said. I didn't want to cry anymore, I couldn't help it. Shaka walked over and sat on the edge of the bed. He pulled me into his arms and allowed me to cry on his shoulder, again.

"I don't want any of it. I don't deserve it," I said.

"Jetta, stop being fuckin' dramatic," he said standing up.

"I'm not! It's just me. What am I going to do with a mansion and all those expensive cars? Hell, I can't even cook to use the big ass kitchen in the house," I said seriously.

For the first time, I saw him smile. He chuckled. "Well, I guess you better add cooking classes to your list of things to accomplish. Listen Jetta, I don't know the pain you feeling. I only know my pain. I'm sure yours is ten times worse. I do know you will push through this. You can't sit around regretting choices you made. All you can do now is start living the life he wanted for you. If I don't know anything, I know he loved you until his last breath."

I smiled, "Thank you for being the son he never had. I was jealous of your relationship with him. He bragged about you all the time. I hated that. That's why I tried to make your life a living hell." He laughed, and so did I.

It was silent for a moment until I spoke, "My mother and stepdad got tired of me sponging off of them. All I did was party and spend their money. It was funny, I didn't get mad at them for cutting me off the way I did with Daddy. Daddy never told me no. I didn't know how to deal with rejection from him. Now I know he was trying to make me grow up. I refused to come back to him begging for help. When I met Cassius, I was almost broke. I had to make some money. He propositioned me about setting up rich men for him to rob. I was desperate, so I eventually agreed to do it. I wasn't a whore, Shaka. I only slept with two of the men. That was because I really liked them. The others were easy to manipulate and finesse. Everything changed when I met this guy named Xavier ."

I went on to explain to him what happened with Xavier . I looked up into his eyes to see him staring at me. I knew he would think the worst of me, but I didn't see that in his eyes. He wasn't judging me. He wasn't looking at like me like I was the lowest type of woman.

"We'll get the jewels back to his family without revealing where they came from," he assured me. I smiled graciously.

"I wanna go downstairs ," I said getting off the bed. He nodded his head. I slipped on my heels and he grabbed my plate of food. I have a lot of wrongs to correct and I'm starting with him.

We parted ways when we made it downstairs. Belle and Miriam walked up to me hugging my neck. Shaka had filled me in on everything that happened to Miriam. I felt bad not being there for her. She's always been there for me. The one time she needed me, I wasn't there. I promised myself to be a better friend to them.

*****

Two days later

Atlanta

The lawyer had just left the house. It wasn't much to discuss. Everything Daddy owned was left to me. I remember the thought of having millions of dollars felt like having an orgasm. It didn't feel the same anymore. I was grateful for Daddy's gift to me, but I would rather have him here with me. I felt so empty inside. Shaka walked the lawyer to the front door while I sat in the study.

"Yo, I'm bout to get up outta here," he said walking back in the study .

"Wait," I said jumping up from the desk. I walked over to him and grabbed his hand. I pulled him out of the study and toward the garage.

"What up, Jetta? I got a couple of yards to do," he said as we walked.

I stepped into the garage with him behind me. I took the keys to the Maybach off the wall and placed them in his hands. I loved the car, but it was too big for me. It fit Shaka perfectly. Of course, I was keeping the Spyder. I just didn't feel the same enjoyment of driving it anymore though.

"You can't have the Spyder though," I said smiling at him .

He chuckled, "Jetta, I can't take this. This what your father left you."

"I know, but I want you to have it. I'm sure he would be happier knowing you are taking care of it," I said.

He smiled, "What if I wanted the Spyder?"

"I'm willing to exchange it for something," I said nervously.

He looked at me curiously, "Like what?"

I stared at him, “Another chance with you.”

“I’ll take the Maybach,” he said without smiling. My heart shattered, but I fought back the tears. I nodded my head.

“I’ll be back to pick you up for work in the morning,” he said.

“Work?” I asked puzzled.

“Yea, you took twenty thousand dollars from the safe. That was my money. You’ll work with me landscaping yards to pay it off,” he said. I stood there waiting for him to laugh. This had to be a joke. He never laughed. If it meant spending time with him, I was going to be the best worker he ever had.

“I’ll be ready, Boss,” I said smiling. He laughed.

Miriam

"I don't know why you so nervous. She's going to love you," Titan said as we sat in his den.

I was a nervous wreck about meeting Hannah. I wanted to make a good impression on the little girl that stole Titan's heart. He was so proud about being a father. For the first time, my life felt complete. I didn't feel the need to over accomplish things that I didn't need to make me happy. I loved my job and wanted to be successful, but I wanted a life of love and happiness. I had that with Titan. I was still getting his Mom to warm up to me. That was a work in progress. The doorbell rang and I jumped up. Titan laughed as he stood up. He grabbed my hand and walked me toward his front door. I held my breath waiting for him to open the door.

"It's me Daddy!" The little voice shouted on the other side of the door.

I giggled at her cheerful voice. My heart melted when he opened the door. I looked down at his twin. She was absolutely adorable. She stood there looking up at him with a big smile. Her hair was up in a big bushy ponytail on top of her head. She wore a pair of colorful tights and a pink top. A pair of nude sandals were on her little feet. She walked in and wrapped her arms around his legs. He picked her up and smothered her with a hug and kisses.

"Come on in, Belle," he said moving to the side.

"Mama can't stay long. She going to see her friend," Hannah said with a big smile. Belle giggled and shook her head.

"How do you know what I'm going to do little girl?" Belle asked her.

"I heard you on the phone," she said.

"It's rude to eavesdrop," Titan said.

"I'm sorry," she said sadly. She was too cute to be mad at.

"Well, Daddy wants you to meet his friend," Titan said turning to face me.

"Hi," I said smiling at her.

"Hi, my name is Hannah. What's your name?" She asked.

"My name is Miriam. It's nice to meet you," I said. She giggled.

"I have to go. I'm already late. Hannah, you be good and I'll see you in the morning," Belle said to her.

"Make it tomorrow evening. We going to the Aquarium and a few other places," Titan said.

"Yayyyy!" Hannah screamed with excitement.

"Ms. Miriam, you going with us?" She asked.

"If that's okay with you," I said.

"You can come with us. We are going to have a lot of fun," she said smiling with me.

After Belle left, we made our way to the den. Hannah talked nonstop. I wasn't complaining. I enjoyed her energetic personality. We watched Frozen, ordered pizza and wings. After watching her movies, she opened the gifts I bought her. We went to her room and played dress up while Titan worked in his study. After letting her do my makeup, we went downstairs to show Titan. He laughed when we walked into the den.

"Don't laugh, you're next," I said smiling at him.

He shook his head, "Nope, we got a long day tomorrow. It's time for bedtime for the little one."

"Can Ms. Miriam read to me?" Hannah asked holding my hand. She filled my heart with joy. Being here with him and her made my life better than I ever imagined it.

Belle

"Ooohhhh yyyyeessss!" I screamed as Rhino drilled deep inside me causing me to explode again.

"Yea, that's it Baby. Come on this dick," he moaned in my ear.

He had my legs cuffed in his elbow and pushed up over my head. His balls were slapping against my ass cheeks as he started pounding inside me. He licked and sucked his way down to my breasts . He released one of my legs and massaged my breasts with his free hand. The soft bites to my hard nipples and the constant pressure on my g-spot was causing another orgasm. He released my legs and I wrapped them around his waist and I pulled his long dreads.

"Goootttt ddaamnnn! This pussy so good! This my damn pussy! You hear me, Belle?" He asked sucking and biting on my neck.

"Yes Baby! I'm yours forever," I moaned as I winded my hips. His massive dick was sliding in and out of my dripping wet center. I couldn't stop my juices from flowing out of me. He pulled my hands from his hair. I felt something in his hand.

"You love me enough to wear this for the rest of your life?" He whispered in my ear.

I stopped moving and looked as he slid this enormous diamond ring on my finger. Only Rhino would ask me to marry him this way. It was no doubt in my mind, I wanted to spend the rest of my life with him. I had more than me to consider. I had a daughter he hadn't met and a Granny that I care for. He stopped and stared at me waiting for my reply.

"What's it going to be Nerd Girl?" He asked. He was still deep inside me. I could feel his dick throbbing inside me.

"Really Rhino, you are going to ask me at a time like this?" I asked.

"Perfect timing," he said smiling.

"I never imagined in my wildest dreams I would be here with you like this. I never forgot you. I want an eternity with you, but it's not just me. I have a daughter and my Granny to consider," I told him.

"I know that shit, Belle. We ain't getting married tomorrow. I'm just putting this on your finger to let you know I'll kill you about my pussy," he said with a stern face. I could only laugh and shake my head.

"You ready to be a family man?" I asked.

"The minute you let me slide all the way in, it was over," he said with a smile.

I slapped him on the shoulder, "I'm serious Rhino. Being a parent isn't an easy job. Where ever I go, my daughter and Granny comes with me."

"As far as your little Shawty, I'll be a damn good parent. I can teach her how to paint. I'm starting construction on a house to build a wing for your Granny. She'll have all the care she needs while you are in school," he said. I can't believe how serious he was. He truly wanted a life with me.

I smiled at him , "Yes, I'll marry you. Now, will you please let me come again." We ended the night making nasty, sweet love to each other.

*****

The next morning we woke up and got dressed. He was adamant about meeting Granny. I called her and told her to get dressed. We were taking her out for breakfast. I giggled as he drove. He didn't realize he was singing along to my favorite song . He knew every single word.

"Don't turn crazy on me. What you laughing at" He asked glancing at me.

"You, singing my favorite song," I said smiling at him .

"That's a damn lie. I don't know that shit," he said. I laughed.

Granny was standing outside the apartment waiting on us. This was definitely one of her good days. She looked strong and beautiful. Rhino jumped out the car and opened the door for her.

"I don't get in the car with strangers. Who you?" She asked looking him up and down.

"I understand. My name is Brutus Thomas. Most people call me Rhino. I went to school with Maribelle," he said nervously. This was the first time I ever saw him intimidated by anyone.

"Well, I'm not calling you a damn animal. Belle said you don't like to be called by your name. So, what do you prefer I call you?" She asked him.

"I'll make an exception for the woman that cared for Belle. You can call me Brutus," he said.

I never knew Rhino could be charismatic. Granny got in the car. She asked numerous questions, and he didn't hesitate to answer. I thought he would get agitated with her questions about his family. He didn't hide anything. She encouraged him to pursue his passion. We were immediately seated when we made it to the restaurant. He got pleasure out of the childhood stories she told him about me as we ate breakfast. I sat and watched as they got to know each other.

"So, you engaged?" She asked looking at my finger. I was so nervous about them meeting I forgot to take the ring off. I nodded my head, but never looked her in the eyes.

"What you acting scared for? Is he making you marry him?" She asked me.

"No ma'am. I love him. I want to marry him," I explained.

"Well, act like it," she said. He sat there with a smirk on his face. I thought she would be upset about me considering getting married before becoming a doctor.

"You're not mad?" I asked.

"As long as there is an MD after your last name, I have no problem with it," she said.

"You don't have to worry. She will finish med school. That's a promise," Rhino assured her. She smiled and nodded her head at me. I breathed a sigh of relief.

"You ready to be a father?" She asked. I held my breath.

Rhino took a deep breath, “To be honest, I have no idea what it takes to be a parent. I know what it takes to be a bad parent. I’ve lived that life. I promise to love and protect Hannah the way you did Maribelle. I’ll do anything to make Nerd Girl happy.” He smiled and winked at me.

Granny giggled, “She is nerdy, ain’t she?” He laughed.

“So, how much longer are you going to sell drugs?” She asked.

Rhino’s eyes grew just as big as mine. Granny didn’t care what came from her mouth. I knew this would be a problem for her. She hated what the drugs did to our communities. I waited to hear Rhino’s reply.

“I can’t tell you when. I can only promise to protect them with my life. I plan to walk away from this life. If I don’t walk away with my life, none of you will ever have to worry about being provided for,” he said.

She sat quietly for a few seconds, “Get out and do what you love to do. Don’t wait until it’s too late.” He nodded his head. All I could think about was how I was going to suck his soul from him tonight. Hannah would be staying another night with her father.

Six months later

Shaka

Money was coming in nonstop. If things keep going this smoothly, Chiraq would make his requested amount for being our supplier. Today we were attending Rhino's art showing. Belle, Jetta and Miriam worked hard putting it together. He tried to act calm, but I could see the nervousness in his demeanor. He finally relaxed when guests started complimenting him on his work. It took no time before all the paintings were sold. I don't know what Belle did to him, but she had my boy locked down. They were good for each other. He brought her out of her shyness. She didn't mind speaking her mind now. If he tried to act up, she would give him a simple look and he would fall in line. His parents didn't attend his showing. It was a shame they didn't support the talent he had. It was their loss. I watched him interact with Hannah. She had stolen his heart. She has become a big part of all of our lives. Rhino walked over to me .

"Congratulations Picasso," I said.

He laughed, "Thanks fam. Never thought I would be doing some shit like this. Didn't think it was possible."

"It's only the beginning," I told him.

“We hitting the club to celebrate tonight,” he said.

“Belle said you can go?” I asked.

He laughed, “Belle runs shit in public. I run shit behind closed doors.” I laughed, but I know he was telling the truth.

“Yo, Miriam damn feet swelling. I’m going take her home. Told her not to wear those damn heels anyway,” Titan said walking up to us.

Miriam was three months pregnant. Once Titan found out, he wasting no time marrying her. They had a small wedding with close friends and family. Her father didn’t attend the wedding. Miriam was grateful to have the rest of her family there. I stood as his best man while Jetta stood as her maid of honor.

“Man, we hitting the club tonight,” Rhino told him.

“I’m going. I’m just making sure she gets home. I’ll be there. This your night,” Titan told him. He dapped us up and left with Miriam on his arm.

My eyes roamed over the room until they landed on Jetta. She was in the corner talking to some nigga in a suit. Our relationship has changed over the past six months. We’ve become best friends. She’s grown a lot. She’s in school to become a stylist. She’s working with me to build a homeless shelter and rec center for young kids living on the streets. It won't be long before the foundation will be laid. I was shocked when she offered to donate two million dollars of her own money. I graciously accepted only if she agreed to be my partner. I finally relieved her of her duties of working for me after three months. I hated to let her go, but she was starting school. I enjoyed working side by side with her. I made sure her friend's jewels were returned to his family without tracking them back to her. I had fallen more in love with her than I ever thought was possible. I just didn't know how to tell her I wanted that life with her. She seemed to be so comfortable with our friendship.

"Yo, I'll holla at you later tonight," I said to Rhino before walking away. I walked over to Jetta and her new friend.

"You ready to go?" I asked.

"You can go ahead. Morris agreed to give me a ride home," she said glancing at her friend with a smile.

"Morris won't be giving you shit. You don't know him. Bring yo ass on," I said angrily before walking away.

"Micah!" She called my name. I ignored her and kept walking.

I sat outside in my car waiting for her to come. I was getting ready to get out and drag her to the car, but she came storming toward the car. She hopped in the car and slammed my door. I reached over and grabbed a handful of her hair.

“Slam my damn door again and that’s yo ass, Jetta,” I said before releasing her hair. This was the first argument we had in months.

“You can’t tell me what to do Micah,” she said straightening her hair. She crossed her arms and pouted. Even though her growth was amazing, she still was a spoiled brat. She hated not getting her way.

*****

She hopped out the car without saying a word when we arrived at her house. I followed her inside the house. I could hear her bedroom door slam from down stairs. I decided to give her a few minutes to calm down. About thirty minutes later, she was coming down the stairs as I was walking out the den. She looked more beautiful than she did getting out my car. She wore a silver sparkling loose fitting dress. The spaghetti strapped dress showed too much cleavage and barely covered her ass.

“Why are you still here? Don’t you have a house?” She asked with an attitude.

"Where the hell you going with that lil ass dress on?" I asked.

"Out," she replied rolling her eyes at me before walking off. A loud rumble of thunder came through and caused her to jump, but she kept walking. There was no way I was letting her go out with bad weather. I took a deep breath preparing to deal with her attitude.

"Yo, it's getting ready to rain. You need to stay yo ass home," I said following her out the door.

"I know how to drive in the rain," she said without turning around.

I reached out and grabbed her arm as she approached the back of her car. She still wasn't driving the Spyder yet. She was still driving the Mercedes her father purchased for her graduation gift.

"Belle is home with Hannah, and Miriam is home with swollen feet. Who the hell you going out with?" I asked.

She scoffed, "I have a date."

I chuckled, "With the corny ass nigga from earlier today?"

"That's none of your business," she said. The rain started to come down.

"Take yo ass in the house. You ain't going nowhere," I demanded.

She pushed me in the chest, "No! I'm tired of trying to prove myself to you. I'm done trying to love someone who doesn't love me anymore. I'm going to start dating."

Her words stung me. I didn't know she thought I didn't love her anymore. I thought my feelings for her were obvious. She was the reason I woke up every morning. The joy of being in her presence made every day worth living. I just didn't know if she was ready for me to love her. The rain started pouring down on us. Her dress and hair were ruined.

"Jetta, come in the house. You getting soaked. You gone get sick," I told her.

"I don't care. I'm not staying here. I'll find somewhere to go," she said turning away from me. I pulled her by the arm to face me. She stared up at me. I used my hand to move her wet hair from her face.

"What you want from me, Jetta?" I asked.

"I want you to love me again. I want you to trust me with your heart. I know I messed up, and I'm sorry. I've learned from my mistakes. I want the Micah back that shared himself with me. I love our friendship, but I miss us.

I miss your eyes staring at me with so much love. I want you to stop being afraid to love me again," she said.

I leaned down and sucked her bottom lip into my mouth. Our kiss turned into a dance battle with our tongues in each other's mouth. Neither of us were concerned about the rain pouring down on us. My dick was throbbing so hard inside my pants. I lifted her up and sat her on the trunk of her car. I licked , sucked and nibbled on her neck as she wrestled with unfastening my pants. My dick sprung from my boxers in full attention. I pushed her panties to the side, I drove my aching dick inside her wet, tight tunnel. She cried out in ecstasy as she wrapped her arms around my back. I started giving her slow, deep thrusts .

"Oooh yesss! I miss you so much!" She moaned.

I bit on my bottom lip to keep from groaning out loud. I felt like I could explode in any moment. The harder the rain came down on us, the deeper I drilled inside her. She dug her nails into my back and screamed out releasing her sweet cream. Her walls were gripping my shaft so tight I couldn't hold it.

"Fuuucckk! I can't hold this!" I roared before unloading inside her.

She started winding her hips sucking my semi-hard dick inside her. I lifted her off the car by her ass cheeks and spread them. My dick slid all the way inside her. I could feel it growing inside her. I started bouncing her on my dick. She moaned and screamed just as loud as the thunder that kept coming. Our wet bodies flapped against each other as we fucked each other standing in the front of her house in the broad daylight. We were so caught up we didn't care who pulled up and saw us.

"Oooohhh Mmmiiicccaaahh! Yyyyeesss!" She screamed gripping my dick and squirting her juices out of her.

"I fuckin' love you, Jetta! I always will!" I groaned in her ear.

I felt the tingling sensation flowing through my body as my toes cramped up inside my shoes. She started doing that little trick where she clinched and released her walls around my dick as it slid in and out of her. My legs started to become numb. I couldn't hold it any longer.

"Aaaaarrrrrggghhh!" I roared unloading another load of cum inside her. I was so weak I almost dropped her. I sat her back on the trunk and leaned on her trying to catch my breath and regain my strength.

After gaining enough strength, we made our way back inside the house. We took a shower and I feasted on her sweet pussy until she pleaded for mercy. We lay in the bed looking out at the rain from her window.

"I swear we moving to another room. I'm not spending every night in a pink ass room, Jetta," I said. She sat up and stared down at me.

"You're moving in with me?" She asked happily.

"Yea, before you make me have to kill a nigga outchea," I said.

She giggled. "The guy at Rhino's showing, his name is Phillip. We've been friends for years. We were just going out for drinks. He's gay."

I chuckled. "Still manipulative as hell." She played me. She knew I would get mad about seeing her with another man.

"I promise, I won't do it again. I just had to do something to get your attention," she said sincerely.

"You never lost my attention," I said smacking her on her thick thigh.

She laid on my chest. "I love you Micah."

She is a spoiled, little rich girl that turned my disdain for her into love.

The End

NATAVIA PRESENTS

NATAVIA PRESENTS

CPSIA information can be obtained
at www.ICGtesting.com
Printed in the USA
LVOW13s0753140718
583547LV00023BA/375/P

9 781721 781997